Sandra Heath is the ever-popular author of numerous Regencies, historicals, novellas, and short stories. She has won Readers' Choice awards for Best Regency Author and Best Regency Romance, among others. You can contact her at sandraheath@blueyonder.co.uk.

Carla Kelly, one of the most beloved Regency authors, has written more than a dozen novels and won several awards, including two RITAs for Best Regency. She lives in Valley City, North Dakota.

Edith Layton, critically acclaimed for her short stories, also writes historicals for Avon and has won numerous awards. She loves to hear from readers and can be reached at www.edithlayton.com.

Amanda McCabe is a talented new Regency author who is quickly becoming a favorite. She lives in Oklahoma and loves to hear from readers via e-mail at Amccabe7551@yahoo.com.

Barbara Metzger, one of the stars of the genre, has written more than two dozen Regencies and won numerous awards, including two *Romantic Times* Career Achievement Awards. Contact her through her Web site at www.barbarametzger.com.

A
Regency Christmas

Five Stories by

Sandra Heath

Carla Kelly

Edith Layton

Amanda McCabe

Barbara Metzger

A SIGNET BOOK

SIGNET
Published by New American Library, a division of
Penguin Putnam Inc., 375 Hudson Street,
New York, New York 10014, U.S.A.
Penguin Books Ltd, 80 Strand,
London WC2R 0RL, England
Penguin Books Australia Ltd, Ringwood,
Victoria, Australia
Penguin Books Canada Ltd, 10 Alcorn Avenue,
Toronto, Ontario, Canada M4V 3B2
Penguin Books (N.Z.) Ltd, 182–190 Wairau Road,
Auckland 10, New Zealand

Penguin Books Ltd, Registered Offices:
Harmondsworth, Middlesex, England

First published by Signet, an imprint of New American Library,
a division of Penguin Putnam Inc.

First Printing, October 2002
10 9 8 7 6 5 4 3 2 1

 REGISTERED TRADEMARK—MARCA REGISTRADA

Printed in the United States of America

CONTENTS

The Amiable Miser
by Edith Layton

Alfred Minch was an amiable miser. He didn't kick beggars out of his way when they pleaded for alms in the street. He actually smiled at them. He just never gave them anything. Nor did he dine on gruel and water. He enjoyed a gourmet meal—if someone else bought it, because if it was his own coin being spent, it was on victuals marked down at the last hour of the last day of sale, because one more hour and they would be rubbish. When he did let go of that coin, it was after much thought and with great sorrow. His clothing was neat, but secondhand, his style of life entirely meager. But his pleasures were very expensive, because his only pleasure was making and saving money. Since he did that very well, he was jolly, he was amusing, he had a grand sense of humor and was charming, as long as it didn't cost him anything.

His cousin wished he was a monster.

It would be so much easier, Joy thought sadly as she watched her cousin Alfred readying his shop for business. Then she could despise him. But she couldn't because although he was definitely *mean*, he wasn't mean to her. Smiles and compliments cost nothing, and he was free with them, and good at them, too. That didn't change the fact that he was a clutch-fist and a pinchpenny. He was a handsome old fellow, tall with white hair and a wide smiling face, with cheeks

that turned ruddy with the cold, which they were all
winter, since he didn't like to waste coal.

Alfred Minch is an old purse pinch, Joy thought
with rare ingratitude as she busied herself dusting
shelves in the cold little shop. But Christmas was coming, and all the other shops on the street were brim-
ming with luxuries, chocked full of delicacies she could
only watch being carried off by other people as they
hurried past Cousin Minch's bookshop windows. No
matter what preachers said about rewards of the flesh
being suspect, she suspected a little luxury would go
a long way to warm her heart at Christmastime. And
little was exactly what she'd get.

But how could she complain? She flicked her
feather duster across the gilded spines of *Literary Crit-
icism,* and tried to brush unkind thoughts away, too.
Cousin Minch had given her a roof over her head
when her parents died. Feeding an extra mouth and
heating an extra room cost a man money. And he was
a man who hated to part with money. It was true she
had to work to earn the protection of that roof as well
as clothes, soap, and such "fribbles," as he called
them. Also true, her parents would rather have died
than to see her working. . . .

But they *had* died, and if it weren't for Cousin
Minch, Joy would have gone to Aunt Augusta, and
that would be worse, because her aunt would have
married her off to her hideous stepson, and then
merely breathing would have been work. An only
child with no one to look after her, Joy *knew* she
should be thankful to Cousin Minch. Her parents had
left her banks of fond memories and a fine education,
and not much else. Both youngest children of younger
sons, her parents had good names and slender fortunes. Father had been profligate with money. Mama

had thought the good times would never end. But they had ended when they met their untimely deaths in a coaching accident.

Joy sighed as she moved on to attack *History*. It was past time she accepted her life's lacks and learned to live with them. But even after seven years it was difficult.

She'd come to London at seventeen, a frightened girl who'd never ventured far from the village where she'd been raised. She'd come to London filled with apprehension. She needn't have worried. Nothing much had happened since then. She was twenty-four now, and looking down the aisles of years could see that nothing much would change as she trudged on toward sixty-four. Nothing really changed here in Cousin Minch's bookshop. Volumes came in, volumes went out, spaces on the shelves emptied and filled, but the years only placed her more firmly on the shelf.

There were worse fates than working in a bookshop, she thought as she climbed higher up the ladder to give *Geography* a dusting. So what if it was small, cramped, and dim, the air old and stale as the contents of the ancient tomes? So what if the crowded shelves made the place even smaller than it was? It was a lot better than Cousin Frederick's damp clutches, or the workhouse, or some unimaginable other place homeless females wound up in.

It was also preferable to working as a servant, a governess, or companion to strangers. Because if she had little, Joy still had her dignity. That was priceless. Just as well, she thought, if it cost anything, Uncle Minch would have said he couldn't afford it.

But her lot was harder for her to bear than it had been when she'd first come to Cousin Minch. Because now spinsterhood no longer loomed. It had arrived. It didn't help that the year was ending and the growing bleakness of the days matched the growing gloom in her spirit.

Christmas was around the corner, but she couldn't look forward to holiday pleasures. It would dawn sensible and frugal as it always was under her cousin's roof. She'd wake to find Father Christmas had consulted with Cousin Minch, and then brought her a handkerchief, a boiled sweet, and best wishes of the season. Later, after helping put together a Christmas dinner, she'd get a tot of rum to usher in the glad season, a charming compliment on her looks, and a caution to go to bed so she could retain those looks and still be up early for work the next day.

At least she didn't have to do all the work; she wasn't Alfred Minch's only pensioner. He had three unfortunate females under his wing. One to run his shop. One to order his house. And one to keep it free of mice. Clara, his widowed sister, acted as his housekeeper to earn her way. She'd give Joy something pretty for Christmas, something she couldn't afford, to make Joy merry. As ever, it would make Joy feel guilty. The other female under Cousin Minch's wing was Boots, a battle-scarred old tabby who slept in the shop. She'd let Joy scratch behind her torn ears, and maybe, in the spirit of Christmas, she might not, for once, scratch back.

In truth, even a lavish Christmas couldn't hide the fact that another year was lurking behind Yuletide, ready to pounce on Joy. Marriage was not. How could she meet eligible men? The thought of Cousin Minch offering her a Season was ludicrous. The idea of him offering a dowry would be amusing, if it weren't so sad.

Four-and-twenty and unwed was unfortunate, Joy

thought as she brushed by *Philosophy*. Five-and-twenty and unwed would be tragic. She was lonely and lovelorn; the worst part was that there was no one to be lovesick for.

Not that she didn't have any suitors. Only impossible ones. Tom Ford always had his eye on Joy. That was all he'd ever put on her, and not because she was as much of a snob as Cousin Minch. But Tom was a butcher who thought a firm red liver was a perfect offering to the object of his affections, and whose conversation ran from meat to sporting matches, stumbling when it ran across anything else.

Plump George Potts's jokes weren't as fresh or sweet as the milk he delivered. Mr. C. B. Hatch, the myopic actuary, was dry as the tables he calculated for the firm of Strothers and Blink. Mr. Blink himself, a humorless fifty-ish widower with five hopeful children, pretended to buy books as he tried to muster a rakish smile for Miss Joy Ayres. She felt sorry for his motherless children, but not enough to give their father more than a smile back.

Other admirers included every single man who lived or worked anywhere near Alfred Minch, bookseller, and not a few married ones, too. Because Joy was as beautiful as she was educated.

Her father used to call her his "Saxon princess" because of her blond good looks. But Joy didn't think much of that compliment since most of the girls in her village were fair. What she didn't see was that few had such intelligence sparkling in clear blue eyes, nor were their eyes framed by such long dark lashes, nor did they have mouths as full and quirked with good humor. Her sheaf of straight flaxen hair was always shining clean, her profile faultless from nose to toes. She was slender yet full bosomed, with a curving waist that current fashions ignored, even if the men didn't.

But even if by some stroke of fortune she finally did meet someone whose face and form pleased her and whose mind marched with hers, Joy knew she didn't have money and that was what made for a proper match. As for an improper one—the sort of thing that existed between the pages of the books she sold? Such goings on were not for an *Ayres*. She mightn't be as class conscious as her cousin, but she had standards. They were one of the few things she could afford, after all.

"Well, well, well," Alfred finally said, rubbing his hands together. "Are we ready? Shall I ring up the curtain, my dear?"

Joy managed a smile as she always did. Because he said the same thing every morning.

"Ready, cousin," she replied. Useless to say it would be nice to bring up the fire, too, she thought as she stepped down from the ladder. It had been warmer up on the ladder, the scant heat in the room rising to the ceiling. She rubbed her hands together, too, to get the circulation going.

Cousin Minch unlocked the door. A swarm of customers did not charge in. His business come slow, stayed long, and sometimes left him a profit. A large profit. He knew how to buy cheap and sell high, and make the most of every asset, using his expertise to stock the shop, and Joy as window dressing. As the morning sun rose higher, his customers filtered in.

"Anything new from old Horace?" ancient Mr. Throckmorton joked to Joy as he came in to browse through recent acquisitions.

"P-perhaps you could show me some volumes of

p-poetry?" Lord Tully's new schoolmaster stammered to Joy, his spotted face growing fiery red. "I wish to send Mama a present."

"Why, I can help you there," Alfred said heartily. He moved between the fellow and Joy, knowing a young man thwarted was one who'd come back to buy another volume for another excuse to talk.

A timid clerk came in to stare at Joy and leave with an almanac. Mr. Blink stopped by on his way to lunch.

"How are you, my dear?" he asked Joy. "Has my book come in yet?" he asked when all questions about health and weather had been fully explored.

"It has not, I'm afraid," Alfred put in, frowning. Not because the book hadn't arrived, but because he'd realized Blink had been clever enough to order a book that would take weeks to locate, weeks during which he had an excuse to look in on Joy every day.

"Colder than a witch's ti—watchman's teakettle out there!" Tom Ford laughed, ducking his head in the doorway. "Could you do with a string of fine sausage links, eh?" he asked Joy, his round brown eyes growing soulful. "Got some in that are beaut, fat and juicy as stuffed leeches, hand on my heart. Half price because of your lovely blue eyes, Miss Ayres. Quarter price if you come to tea with me," he added with a wink.

"I think you'd better stop discounting before you get into trouble," Joy warned him. "Half is generous enough, thank you. And sorry, tea is not possible today." Nor tomorrow and tomorrow and tomorrow, she thought.

"Bring them round back to my sister, Tom, and thank you," Alfred said with a smile of content. Half was better than nothing off, and Joy's continuing refusals ensured tomorrow's discount, too.

The store was quiet for a spell, the only sounds that of Alfred humming as he tallied receipts, and the hushed flutter of a customer leafing through a volume. Joy stood looking out the window, watching the day going on out there.

Alfred Minch didn't fret. More business of a different sort was coming. Joy would bring it in as surely as she'd drawn in the gentlemen.

The idea had struck the week she'd come to him.

Minch's Books was located not far from the best residential neighborhoods, if nearer to those that had once been best. Alfred had learned that faded gentry had few coins to part with, and those still in the money didn't like to part with pennies any more than he did. Still, he'd done well enough. Until Joy came along. Then he'd done better.

She'd stood in his shop that first day, brightening his dim shop just by her presence, glowing like the gold leaf on the margins of pages in his most expensive volumes.

"Do you like to read, child?" he'd asked.

"Oh, yes, sir . . . cousin. I do."

"What sort of books?"

"Histories, and plays, and poetry and . . ." she'd hesitated.

"And?"

Her face went rosy. "Mama enjoyed novels from the Minerva Press. I do, too. I doubt you'd think of them as *literature,*" she added quickly, seeing his dumbstruck expression, "which is why I don't see them here, I suppose."

She hadn't known his expression was that of awestruck inspiration. "You ladies do like them, don't you?" he asked slowly, as a brilliant idea spun round in his head.

"Oh, yes! Mama lent hers out to friends when she

was done, because some of them couldn't afford to buy them as she did." Joy hung her head, realizing Mama couldn't have afforded them, either.

Alfred's eyes widened. Charity was its own reward, sometimes it paid better than that. The girl was already showing him the way to a profit! Scholars bought weighty tomes, collectors searched for bargains. The ladies read popular fiction. If it was popular, it was lucrative, and as such, definitely his business.

And so since that inspirational day, ladies books were the backbone of his establishment. Joy oversaw them, females being more comfortable with another female in matters romantical, at least in books. Let the gents seek out ancient Greek poets, literary arguments, natural history, and tomes that refought old wars. The ladies came for the wicked dukes, erotic earls, and vicious viscounts that constantly threatened virtuous girls.

Alfred was soon in as much ecstasy as a Minerva Press heroine on the last page of her story. If an esteemed bookshop like Hatchard's could do it, so could he. Because of Joy's random comment, he'd discovered the best business invented since prostitution: a lending library. He could sell what he had and still keep it.

When the sun was at its zenith and the time for morning calls was over, the ladies arrived at the shop. Joy saw the door open, heard various exclamations of mock surprise, and took a deep breath. They were a little overwhelming when they came en masse. They liked to do that, each pretending to have met the others unaware. Their various social stations precluded them actually *arranging* a meeting to discuss books together, though that was what they'd come to do. They crowded into the lending library alcove of the shop and delivered reviews of recent reads.

"I was *appalled* at how Rudolpho tried to trick sweet Eugenie," Lady Turnbull said, handing a volume to Joy. "No one *warned* me!" she said, shaking her head so the plumes on her bonnet waved wildly. "I vow my cook was almost in *tears* at having to put back dinner, wasn't she Ella?" she asked her maid, standing behind her. Without waiting for an answer she went on, "But *how* could one eat when Eugenie's honor was in such jeopardy?"

Little Mrs. Crab, a chandler's widow, nodded so hard her gray ringlets quavered. "Oh, yes! That was dreadful," she said sympathetically, though she'd no one to put back her dinner but herself. "Almost made me miss my supper, too!"

"And wasn't our Horatio heroic when he sent that bounder about his business!" the Honorable Miss Cummings trumpeted, her long, unfashionably tanned face growing ruddy with pleasure at the memory. "It is quite my favorite book this month, I believe."

"I don't know," young Mrs. Holcombe said, tilting her pretty head to one side. "How can we forget Lord Wright, when he routed that dreadful Egyptian and saved young Arabella?"

The other ladies agreed.

"I'm so glad you like that author," Joy said. "I thought you would and specifically asked my cousin to order *two* of her new book. We might have them by next week," she added happily, "so best put your bid in now. We'll draw lots for who gets first look."

"Oh," Mrs. Holcombe said, "I'll have to leave the honors to the others, as our entire family's descending on us for Christmas. I won't have a spare moment. I'll read it after the new year."

"Count me out, too," Miss Cummings said. "Off to

the family seat for Christmas, don't you know. Tradition."

"My boy and his wife and his family will be visiting," Mrs. Crab put in. "They'll take up all of my time during Christmas."

"We go home for the holiday," Lady Turnbull announced. "It is expected. I doubt I'll have a moment to read. My brother makes quite a to-do for the holiday. Dinners and dancing, pantomimes, carols, wassail, and the lighting of the Yule log, of course."

"Of course," Joy said sadly, as she realized the only lighting she could look forward to was if Cousin Alfred threw an extra coal on the kitchen fire. "But they'll be here when you get back."

"Fine," Miss Cummings said, "because I must say I didn't care for Mrs. Edgeworth's latest, you know."

"Nor I!" Mrs. Crab agreed.

The ladies began discussing their favorites again, trading opinions as they swapped volumes, one woman handing a book back to Joy only to have another lady snap it up again. Joy made careful notations of each transaction in the book provided for them. After a half hour, the women regretfully took their leave, going toward the door together, still chatting.

"I say," the Honorable Miss Cummings called to Joy, as she paused in the doorway. "Have you seen Lady Gray? I quite expected to see her here."

Lady Gray's absence had been silently noted by all. There were other members of their reading circle who weren't there this morning, but Lady Gray was a constant, showing up each week at the same time. It was a breach of conduct to ask about her, the glue that held these meetings together was the fiction that they happened by accident. But Miss Cummings was an

Original, and rich enough to be one. The others paused to hear what Joy answered.

"I don't know," Joy confessed. "I thought to see her, too."

"Well, I might drop 'round her house to inquire if she don't show up next time," Miss Cummings said. "No cause for alarm yet. Good day, and Happy Christmas if I don't see you before then."

The others all chorused glad holiday wishes and left.

Joy sighed when they'd gone. The only interesting part of her day had effectively ended. Well, she thought, if that new book titled *Clara's Bad Bargain* was as good as she hoped, she might yet have some pleasure at the end of the day.

And then the door flew open, and her world tilted and spun, and changed her viewpoint forever.

They came in on a gust of wintry air, bringing with them the scent of the damp day: coal fires and wood smoke, horses and good shaving soap, and a faint fragrant hint of spice and fresh-cut fir.

They were both men of a sort that Joy had never seen in the shop, indeed, had only ever seen passing by. She'd watched them driving by her window in open carriages or strolling along the street with exquisitely dressed ladies on their arms, riding in the mornings on their way to the equestrian paths in the park and back again at dusk with their horses blowing, though they still sat high and straight in their saddles. They were unmistakably gentlemen.

Not gentlemen of the old school, who lived for their books, the kind that frequented the shop. Nor were they even like Lord Shawn, celebrity of her home district. He and his kind were rough-and-ready horsemen and hunters, dressed for sport and careless in their clothes and habits. No. These men were true bucks, blades, men of fashion, tulips of the *ton*. Joy blinked. They were even more impressive up close.

Her eyes went to the first gentleman at once. What breathing female's eyes wouldn't? He was youthful, of middle height, slender, and had the face of a poet. For a moment Joy caught her breath, thinking she beheld the notorious Lord Byron himself. Then she remembered that the errant poet had left England for Italy months ago. And though this gentleman's dark tousled curls fell over his alabaster brow, his light eyes held sheer merriment, not brooding majesty. His open greatcoat showed glimpses of a jay's-wing blue waistcoat and canary inexpressibles, and his elaborate, snowy neck cloth held his head high as a visiting prince's.

Aware she'd been staring, Joy darted a glance at his companion. There was nothing to hold her attention long. The other gentleman was taller, more mature, dressed elegantly but soberly, and had a distinctly bored look on his lean face. Dark gold hair showed beneath his high beaver hat, his face was unfashionably tanned, his eyes gray and remote as the winter day. He tapped a walking stick impatiently against a long booted leg as his companion paused to examine Joy with obvious appreciation.

"May I help you?" Joy said coolly, recovering herself. She knew that look. They might be gentry, but a man was a man, and she didn't encourage familiarities from strangers. This fellow obviously had money and position, but she had a serious position here, and her tone of voice let them know it.

"You certainly may help me," the handsome young man said. "I've come on a commission from my aunt, Lady Gray. She's a bit under the weather and sent us

down to return a book to you and pick up another
for her."

Joy nodded. His easy smile was so charming, she
felt small for having been curt with him. Seeing her
reaction, the young man smiled more widely and
looked at her with even more interest.

The other man spoke, his deep mellow voice
amused, "She'd usually send a servant. But since she
regards her nephews as such, here we are." He handed
Joy a slim volume, and said, "She specifically asked
that you recommend a book to her." He glanced at
the books on top of the little table Joy kept her accounts on, books she hadn't had a chance to return
to the shelves yet. "Is *Escape from the Harem* or *Emily's Evil Suitor* better reading?"

There was more than amusement in his voice now.
Joy distinctly heard condescension.

"I'd opt for reading about the doings of a lecherous
sultan, myself," the younger man said merrily. "But
perhaps she wants the seducer, that seems to be what
you ladies prefer. What do you say?"

Joy's head went up, her shoulders rose, and her
spine stiffened. Handsome gents or toads, it made no
difference now. She knew how to deal with these two.

"I'd say you take both and let her decide," Joy
said abruptly. "Though from your inference, I suspect
you'd rather bring her a book of sermons or a treatise
on mathematics. We have them, of course. I'd be
pleased to help with your selection. Or perhaps you'd
prefer to deal with my cousin Alfred? He is after all,
another male."

The older man laughed. "Peace," he said, flinging
up one hand. "Forgive us. Popular men's literature
generally runs to sporting magazines, and we well
know it. We didn't mean to mock. It's just that Aunt

can be a terror if she's thwarted, and we don't have a clue as to her reading habits. So could you please forgive us and recommend a book? She ordered something with romance and adventure. We daren't bring her the wrong book, or she'll send us straight back again. She terrifies us, actually," he confessed, with a smile that gentled his face so much that Joy was astonished at the transformation.

The younger man was so appealing, she'd been afraid of making a fool of herself by goggling at him, but this was the more dangerous man, Joy decided. His smile warmed and encompassed her, she was nearly overwhelmed by its power. But not quite. She knew her place, after all. He was probably as charming to anyone he wanted help from.

"Oh, well, yes, certainly," she said, looking away from those bright and knowing eyes. She fumbled *Emily's Evil Suitor* from the tabletop where Miss Cummings had left it. "Tell Lady Gray that this comes highly recommended."

"Thank you," the older gentleman said, pocketing the book. He touched a finger to his hat. "Give you good day, ma'am. Come along, Arthur. If we keep Aunt waiting, we get no pudding for dessert." He flashed another tilted smile at Joy, and taking his reluctant cousin by the elbow, shepherded him out the door.

Joy stood still, watching their retreating backs as they sauntered out into the gray day.

"A pair of aces, eh?" Cousin Minch remarked from her side. Joy startled, he'd come up that quietly. He wore soft shoes and moved around his shop as silently as dust.

She could only nod.

"Top of the trees, the pair of them," Alfred said.

"Visiting their aunt for the holidays, no doubt. Too bad they didn't opt for buying her any books for Christmas. You might mention that if they come back, my dear," he reminded her gently. "They don't need to lend books, they could buy her a library if they chose." His sigh was as good as a reprimand.

Joy gave herself a mental shake. "Of course, I'm sorry I didn't think of it. They just took me off guard, be sure it won't happen again." Because they'll never come in here again, she thought with chagrin and sorrow. Their appearance was as rare and unexpected as seeing a pair of exotic parrots suddenly fly in and out the window. At the very least, it had been a brief visitation from another world. It would make it impossible to look at city sparrows the same way again. But she too was a sparrow, she thought, turning to her notebook to mark the transaction.

Her hand shook. Suddenly *Clara's Bad Bargain* didn't look like such a good way to pass a long dark evening, after all. She'd had a glimpse into another world, just for a moment that would never return. And it made all her wildest dreams seem meager by comparison.

That night Joy had trouble sleeping. It wasn't because of the thin winter wind that found all the chinks in her window and pinched at her nose where it poked up from her bedcovers as the fire in her hearth died. That only added to her discontent. She was trying to stop thinking about the two gentlemen that had blown into the shop on a similarly chill wind. Men as free and vital and of the world as she was not. She mostly tried to banish the image of the gentleman with the surprising, disturbing smile. The one she'd likely never see again, or if she happened to, only as he passed by her window, along with the rest of the world. She turned her face into her pillow and wept a few silent tears because of that and because of the cold that never seemed to leave her now, and likely never would.

But the next morning, moments after the shop was open, against all Joy's expectations, he came into the shop again.

Today he wore a greatcoat with many capes. It made him seem taller and more important. Joy stopped what she was doing, including breathing.

He looked at her, eyes alight.

"We meet again," he said.

She bit her lip. They'd never really met. She throttled an urge to tell him so. But she saw Cousin Minch from the corner of her eye, and knew his ears, if not eyes, were also upon her, and she worked for her living. "Good morning," she said civilly. "How may I help you?"

He handed *Emily's Evil Suitor* back to her. "Aunt said that she read it last week, and asks that you please pick another."

Joy looked down at the notebook on the counter and flipped open to the book's title. Every book and each lender's name was there. Of course. Lady Gray had been the first to read it.

"How remiss of me," Joy murmured, her face growing hot. "Please extend my apologies to her, I ought to have remembered. Well, then," she said briskly, "I'll be happy to pick another."

She marched over to the shelf, plucked out a book, and keeping her eyes firmly on the cover, said, "This just arrived, no one's read it yet, she ought to enjoy it, she's liked the other books this author has written."

A large hand in tan kid glove plucked the volume from her. "Mmm," the deep voice rumbled, "*The Disappointed Damsel.* Interesting."

That did it. Her eyes snapped up, blue fire in them. "I daresay you wouldn't think so. But it *is* well written. The author is literate, the prose lyrical, and best of all, it ends happily as life does not."

His smile slipped. "I never said otherwise. Nor was I mocking you or the book."

"Forgive me," she said, "I presumed."

"With cause, I suspect," he murmured, watching her closely. "At any rate, I'll take this, and thank you. Aunt doesn't get out as much as she used to, your books are a great comfort to her."

Joy couldn't think of a word to say.

Cousin Minch could. "My dear sir," he said, easing between Joy and this prosperous-looking customer, who was gazing down at her with such intensity. "Perhaps, then, you'd care to purchase some books for your aunt? Perhaps as a gift for Christmas? Then she wouldn't have to return them, or go out when the weather's foul. Nor would she have to commission you to, either."

"Yes," the gentleman said ruefully. "An excellent idea. I already suggested it. But she won't hear of it. She says returning books is the only way she gets her exercise. She didn't even want to send me this time, and was, in fact, trying to get up and dressed to come here herself this morning. But the doctor insists she stay in until all signs of illness are gone, and then for another week after that. She is sulking mightily about it, I can tell you. I think the truth is she enjoys discussing the books when she does come here. She finds it enlivening, and says your other patrons have some

splendid ideas. She also says you're a 'clever puss,' "
he told Joy.

She glanced up at that, and their eyes met.

There was a moment's silence.

Well," he said finally, as they stared at each other
and Alfred looked back and forth at the pair of them,
"thank you for the book. I suppose I'll go, then.
Thank you again."

His gray eyes were brilliant with light, with interest,
with curiosity and more that Joy could no longer bear
to see, because there was nothing she could say to
express her own interest and curiosity.

"You're welcome," she said softly.

He frowned, inclined his head in a semblance of a
bow, turned, and began to leave.

He turned round again quickly. "But wait," he said.
"Don't you need my name? You can't just send me
out with your merchandise. I'm Paget. Niall, Lord
Paget. And you . . . ? Miss . . . ?"

"I am Alfred Minch," Cousin Minch said smoothly.
"This is my niece, Miss Joy Ayres. Do come again."

Joy murmured, "Yes, do."

Lord Paget started to speak again, then with a last
reluctant look at Joy, he left. The door closed, the
little bell on top of it jingling. It was the only sound
in the sudden silence of the shop.

"Well," Alfred said, rubbing his hands together.
"Well, well. Paget, is it? Of the Somerset Pagets. He
is the baron no doubt. I shall have to look him up,
but I believe I know the family. A very good family,"
he muttered, "lots of money, extensive lands . . . You
liked him, my dear?"

She laughed. It wasn't her usual pleasant laughter.
"How could I? I don't know him. He might be a cruel

man, a callous one, a drunkard—a who knows what? *And* a married who knows what at that. But what difference does it make? I'm only a clerk in a book-shop, cousin, and he is a nobleman."

" 'Only a clerk?' " Alfred echoed in shock. "You are an *Ayres*!"

"Yes, of course, and much good it does me," she said bitterly, before she could stop herself, because the injustice of the world seemed very hard this morning.

She bit her lip and swallowed all the other words that came to her. They were too traitorous, ungrateful, self-pitying to utter aloud. How could she tell him she wasn't the kind of woman a baron—much less one that looked, spoke, an acted like Lord Paget—might ask out for a carriage ride, could ask for a dance at a ball, or would one day ask for more. *If* he were free and unwed—and maybe even if he weren't. But she said nothing more, because none of it was Alfred's fault, and even if it were, nothing she could say would change it.

"Yes, my name is important," she said instead, her voice unsteady. "I mean, anyone would want to buy a book from an *Ayres,* I suppose." She turned her head sharply as an unstoppable tear coursed down her cheek. It wouldn't do to get the merchandise wet.

There was another moment of silence.

"Yes. Well," Alfred said in an altered voice, "best make a note of the transaction, my dear. We don't want to make any more mistakes, do we?"

It was as good as a lecture. Joy blinked the tears from her lashes, and quickly bent to make a mark in her notebook.

It was cold enough for snow outside, but the parlor the two men were in was snug, the fire in the hearth casting a ruddy glow that matched the wine in the glasses the two gentlemen were holding. The younger gentleman stopped drinking and stared at his companion, his lips opened in a gasp of dismay.

"*You* returned the book?" he asked in horror. "Before I could go with you? Oho! So you *did* notice her. I thought so. Damn you for a cool customer, with that care-for-nothing expression of yours. You're cool, but not dead. Who but a dead man could resist such a honey? Hair like sunshine, eyes like forget-me-nots, and a form not even that ghastly frock could hide. But now I have to nip round to the shop and make a better impression on her, and quick!" He swallowed the last of his wine as if he meant to set out that instant.

"No, Arthur," his cousin said quietly. "You will not. She's not a game we're playing, nor am I considering trifling with her. Nor will you."

Arthur sat down abruptly, his wineglass dangling from his fingertips. He stared. "You're serious. Damn me for a blind man! Well, it's about time. Turned thirty, with nothing to show but a flirtation with wedlock. We all thought you'd ask for the Edgerton chit last Season, but you took off and left the field clear for Hamilton. Wise move, that. Who'd have known? Once she got a ring on her finger, it loosed her tongue; she hasn't stopped gabbling since she said, 'I do.' Hamilton's got a bride and a headache, and so say all. But how did you know?"

"I never said I did."

"Always the gentleman, ain't you? And usually right. But this bookshop charmer, pretty as she is, ain't got a cent, that's clear. I know you've got enough blunt to ask a beggar to marry you, but it ain't done, Niall, damn me but it's not."

"I'm not doing it," Niall said mildly.

"But you're thinking about it."

"Am I?" He stared into his glass, as though seeing the future in its claret depths before he drained it. "At any rate, thinking is not doing. And money is the least of the attributes I look for in a wife. *And,* before you start tossing wedding bouquets my way, I remind you that pretty is not necessarily virtuous, kind, or considerate. I don't know her and am not likely to. After all, I'll be leaving Town as soon as I can. I only came to collect you and Aunt, and bring you both home for the holidays, which I'll do as soon as the doctor gives her leave to go."

"Do you good to get out of the country," his cousin protested. "You've been gone from London too long."

"Did me better to get the estate back into good heart," Niall said, holding up a long hand and turning it so his cousin could see the ridge of newly won calluses on his palm. "Hard work shook the nonsense out of me," he mused, flexing his hand. "Uncle George neglected the place shamefully. It is our family seat and deserves some respect. I inherited a wreck and tried to put it right for the family, and found something very right about it for myself. The longer I worked with my hands and not just my mind, the more I came to enjoy myself."

He wore a bemused smile as he went on. "Believe it or not, I find I like the countryside, raising cattle instead of Cain, worrying about sheep and not faro tables, draining ditches instead of wine bottles, spending the night with a good book instead of just another bad woman."

"Putting up fences instead of merely fencing?" Arthur said with a grin.

His cousin laughed. "Yes, I suppose I do wax lyrical,

and thank you for stopping me before I started composing sonnets to the chickens." Then he grew serious. "Who'd have guessed? I enjoy the quiet life, Arthur. But I'm no hermit, nor monkish in the least. I haven't changed that much. I also find I'd like to share the quiet."

He shrugged. "So yes, I confess, I'm thinking of taking a wife and settling down at last. I'll be back in the spring to make the rounds and find out what the possibilities are. Don't worry, I'll canvas Almack's, *ton* parties, all the tedious rest, to see what acceptable young females are available.

"In the meanwhile, my interest in Miss Ayres is only human. She *is* a pretty creature and an appealing one. But we don't have to collect every pretty female we see. There are other ways to prove we're men, and leaving her alone is an excellent way to prove we're actually gentlemen."

"Who'd have imagined you'd turn so sober and sensible?" his cousin lamented, rising to pour himself another glass. "I hope it's not catching. I always followed your lead, Niall. I patterned myself after a Corinthian, a top of the trees fellow, a man about town. But I tell you right now, it ain't for me—I don't fancy myself knee-deep in mud and pulling radishes! I'll follow my own way now, thank you. But what are you going to do if that fair-haired angel of the bookshop turns out to be afraid of cows and allergic to turnips?"

"My wife, when I take one, will not exactly be living in a cow byre," Niall said patiently. "The Hall has more than thirty rooms, all have ceilings, and most of those were painted by Adams. It is just barely possible to remain civilized outside of London, you know. And as for Miss Ayres and her possible dislike of cows or turnips, I won't have a chance to find out."

"Well, then. Why be a dog in the manger?"

His cousin's eyes turned the color of steel in ice. "I said she's not to be trifled with, Arthur."

His cousin gave him a bright look, and bowed from the waist from his chair. "Done! So be it. I'll leave her alone . . . this year."

Not all the work of the bookshop ended with the day. Alfred never left the shop before he tallied his numbers, making a neat record of what had been sold and what had to be ordered. Then there was the ritual of locking his money away in the safe that he kept in an alcove in the back room, behind a stack of volumes on a shelf that swung out from the wall if the hidden button was pressed, and which then opened to the right combination of numbers that only he knew. Joy believed that was the best part of his day, because he lingered there so long each evening. Tonight, he seemed to be taking even longer.

She could hear him humming from where she sat at her desk. She sometimes fancied that he wished his coins and bills a tender good night each evening, telling them to be fruitful and multiply before he forced himself to leave them. She bent to her own work. Before she left the shop, she also had to balance the tally of books borrowed with the names of those who had taken them.

She sat back, rubbing her neck, stretching it to get the kinks out. Done. She glanced out the window and saw nothing but black. It was the beginning of another long winter's night, and she was at last free. Now to dinner, a chat with her cousins, a scratch exchanged with the cat, and her cold, cold bed.

"Woolgathering, my dear?" Cousin Minch asked, suddenly appearing at her side.

"Yes," she said absently. "I suppose I am. but I'm done for the night." She rose. "Shall we go?" They always left together so he could lock up.

"*All* done?" he asked.

"Why, yes," she said, wondering if she'd forgotten anything.

"Are you sure?" he persisted. "Are you feeling quite all right?"

The tabulations were done, her shelves neat, all papers put away. Was he actually worried about her? She felt a little rush of warmth. "I suppose I'm a little distracted. Christmas is coming, it makes me sentimental, nostalgic," she invented, never mentioning "defeated" and "despairing," which was what she truly felt. It had only a little to do with Christmas and a lot to do with attractive, well-mannered men of polish and sophistication. They ought not to wander into dim bookstores to give drab little women ideas they could do nothing about, whatever season they appeared.

"Yes, so I thought," Alfred said gently, holding out a book. "Because you never put this away, did you, my dear?"

Emily's Evil Suitor was in his hand. Lady Gray's reject.

"So I didn't," Joy said in vexation. Lord! She was sure she'd put it back in the lending library after Lord Paget had returned it to her. The man really had addled her wits. Joy took the book, automatically riffling through it. "I'll just put it away now. . . . Oh!"

She always searched a book before she returned it to the shelf. It was one of the first lessons Cousin Alfred had taught her. One never knew what the previous owner had used for a bookmark. He looked for old letters that might have antiquarian value. She ran the lending library and looked for things a reader might have forgotten, too, but that could be returned. In her time she'd found lottery tickets, stubs and receipts for everything from laundry to greengrocers, personal correspondence, pressed flowers, and even now and again a pressed spider, caught by accident. This was different. Very different.

" 'Oh!' Indeed," Alfred said in a slow thoughtful voice, looking over her shoulder. "Oh, my, my, my."

Joy took the banknotes from between the pages, riffled more pages, and took out some more. She shook the book over the desk and watched another two slide out. "Oh, my!" she said, when shaking the book only made the pages tremble. "Oh, dear," she said, taking all the notes in her hands and rapidly estimating the small fortune she held. "What are we to do?"

Cousin Minch's smile curled at the edges.

"Lady Gray cannot be disturbed," the butler said, and then relenting because of the obvious dismay in the young woman's eyes, added, "She is doing well, but is resting on her doctor's orders."

Joy nodded. "I understand. But it *is* important that I ask her a question."

"If it is important, her man at law is Mr. Farrow, in Simpson Street. Or you might ask her nephew, Lord Paget, or his cousin, Mr. Dane. They both visit here daily."

"At what time?" Joy asked humbly.

"I cannot say. If it is imperative you ask at once, Mr. Dane has rooms at the Albany and Lord Paget is staying at the Pulteney."

Joy bit her lip. He'd just named the most exclusive apartments for gentlemen in London, and the best hotel in the city. It *was* important. But she didn't know if it was imperative enough for her to dare beard either gentleman in his den. Especially when she had no other female with her to observe the rules of propriety if she did dare. But since cousin Clara was filling in for her at the shop, there was no one to go with her but the cleaning woman, and she only came on Tuesdays.

She could, of course, go see Miss Cummings, Lady Turnbull, Mrs. Holcombe, Mrs. Crab, or some other client instead. All who had borrowed *Emily's Evil Suitor*—it was a popular book. But Lady Gray had it last, and so the notes must be hers. They had to be returned at once. It was more than a matter of honesty. That was what had concerned her—until cousin Minch had weighed in.

"Lady Gray might have misplaced them," he'd said. "She is, after all, getting older, and older people tend to forget. Then they go to all lengths to cover their lapses. Reasonable enough. But will her nephews see it that away if we delay? One doesn't want to be accused of theft!"

"But we can simply ask the ladies when they come back," Joy protested, envisioning herself on Lady Gray's doorstep, perhaps facing her unnerving nephew again.

"That we cannot," Alfred said sternly. "Then the matter will become a guessing game, and who knows whose wild guess will win the prize? A claim to have left some banknotes must be a sufficient claim to ownership, because perhaps the poor creature forgot how many she'd left! So I strongly suggest you do *not* mention it to the ladies ensemble, but rather broach it to them singly, and *not* in the shop. No, there's nothing for it, my dear. You must travel to their homes to ask such a personal question, and you must begin with Lady Gray."

Joy hesitated. It would be lovely to get out of the shop, to actually visit, like real company, with the ladies who so enlivened her days. Because she suddenly realized that due to her situation and long working hours, they were actually her only friends. Then again, it might be embarrassing or disheartening—since she wasn't sure she'd be considered a friend outside the shop.

"Don't you think it mightn't be a better idea if you went?" she asked Alfred.

He looked appalled. "Me? A man calling on a gently bred female and asking about her *money*?" He gave the word an inflection suggesting it was something intimate, almost carnal. But, Joy supposed, money was that to him.

So here she was let out of the shop on a glorious bright winter's morning, but not enjoying it at all. She had to find the rightful owner of the notes and return them as soon as possible. Cousin Minch hadn't even put them in the safe in the meantime, lest he be accused of trying to hide them. Instead, expecting Joy to solve the mystery at once, he wore them tucked in an inner waistcoat pocket, next to his heart.

Joy pondered her next move. A sudden cold breeze on her neck made her turn, look up, and then up some more, into a pair of widening, interested gray eyes.

"Good morning, Miss Ayres!" Lord Paget said with surprised pleasure. "What have we done to deserve your company?" He answered himself in chagrin. "Never say Aunt sent for you to deliver another book! I told her I'd be her errand boy, there was no need for her to bother you—unless, of course, she wanted to discuss the book with you, but even so, I'd have been happy to come collect you and bring you here. There was no need for you to inconvenience yourself."

"No, no," she said nervously, because he was so close, looming over her. "That's not it at all. You see, my cousin Alfred sent me because . . ." She hesitated. Alfred had said she mustn't name the treasure, because then anyone could claim it. She plunged on, ". . . because someone left something of importance between the pages of the book you returned yesterday. Since your aunt was the last to have it, I'm here to find out if it's hers. If not, I've promised my cousin to visit each and every patron who ever rented the book. After all, your aunt said she'd already read it, so she mightn't have looked in it at all, and so it might belong to one of the previous borrowers."

"Ah," Niall said thoughtfully, "I see. And since what was in the book was valuable, and I assume there's no name on it, you dare not identify it. That's up to the owner to do, isn't it?"

"A game!" a voice said from behind him. Joy saw Lady Gray's other nephew standing on his boot toes behind Paget's broad shoulders, bobbing about, trying to get a look at her. "Oh, capital!" he crowed. "Any clues? No, of course not, where's the fun in that? You think it could be Aunt's? I doubt it. She doesn't forget anything. And something of value? Then, never. Never known anyone to value so much, have you, Niall?"

"Agreed," Niall said, watching Joy so steadily her cheeks grew pink. "But I'll ask her at once. Hampton," he told the fascinated butler, "I'm going up to my aunt to make inquiries. See that Miss Ayres is made comfortable in the salon while I do. Arthur!" he said sharply, "where are you going?"

"To help make her comfortable," Arthur said.

"That would be done by coming with me," his cousin said firmly, taking his cousin by the arm and leading him away.

Lady Gray was having her morning chocolate. Once she heard her nephews' request, it took only moments to have her maid make her presentable. Then, dressed in her best morning attire, propped on pillows in her bed, eyes alight, she admitted them both.

"Interesting!" she said when Niall was done explaining. She looked pleased and excited. "Buried treasure, in a book. Not mine, of course!" she announced with a great show of shock. "I'm not such a cloth-head as to leave *my* valuables about. But it's no case for Bow Street. Depend on it, it's probably a deed or a will or some such that someone was reading—or money someone was counting, stowed in the book when whomever it was, was distracted. Then it was forgotten. Daresay Joy will have to hunt round among all the ladies to find the owner." She paused. "I call her 'Joy,'" she explained, "though I in no way think of her as a servant. Though she's far younger than I, I have come to think of her as a friend, and she's certainly an equal by birth no matter her present condition.

"Now. A lost treasure, is it? Whose could it be?" she mused aloud. "You'd think if someone left something, she'd remember. Or the next reader would have found it. But you know? I've often suspected not everyone reads everything they borrow, the books are traded back and forth too quickly. When a book's not given a good critique, I think it discourages some people. They don't read the book at all, just hand it back straightaway the next day, and pretend they have. Because who'd want the others to know she doesn't make up her mind for herself? Not me, of course," she added quickly. She frowned. "Such lively discussions go on there, I don't know how Joy keeps track. Sometimes we hand a book around three times or more before someone takes it away.

"Let me think," she said, wrinkling her forehead. "Mrs. Crab? No, she's often harried, but no scatterbrain, none of 'em are. But Christmas is coming, and they're all in a tizzy because families are visiting, or they're going out to them. It would be interesting to know who it was and what it was. Wish I could go along with Joy on her inquiries." She stole at look at Niall from under her lashes. "And so I would, if only I still weren't too fragile."

She was a stout woman with masses of curly silver hair, and looked, as her nephews privately thought, about as fragile as a fishmonger on a Friday morning at Billingsgate. But she cherished her occasional maladies because she believed they reminded her relatives of the impermanence of life, as well as the worth of her stocks, properties, and investments. They liked her for herself, but owing to her late unlamented, inattentive husband, she never quite believed it.

"Joy's still downstairs, is she?" she asked. "Good, very good. I'm feeling a bit better this morning; perhaps she'd like to come up and visit with me a while. The child has a head on her shoulders, as I told you when I first sent you there." She fixed Niall with an accusing stare. "Though you're probably too busy looking at that fair head to wonder what's in it. Quite a bit, I assure you. No money there, but a good name, an old solid family. But I suppose you don't count her eligible unless she's presented to you on a plate at Almack's."

"Then," Niall said gently, "it's as well that you're not with Bow Street, Aunt."

"What a fine idea," Arthur said. "Do ask her up for a visit."

"A fine idea—under different circumstances," Niall

said quellingly. "As for today, she said her cousin Minch wants her to find the owner of the object of value as soon as possible."

"Probably hoping for a reward," his aunt observed. "A clutch-fist of the worst degree. She'd overlook a book brought back a day late if she could. But if you return one an hour late, he's there rubbing his hands together, ready to grind the extra penny out of you. I'll wager he sent her by herself, didn't he?"

"She had no one with her," Niall agreed.

"Mmm," his aunt said thoughtfully. She looked at him. "You're right. She can visit me another day. She has to search out the proper owner at once. But it's not done. Coming to me is one thing, there's no way that poor girl should go coursing through London on her own. Send one of the downstairs maids along for propriety, and call a hackney for her, will you, Niall?"

"I'll do better," he said on a sudden smile, "I came by my carriage, I'll take her. Since it's an open carriage, there's no need for a chaperon."

"Oh, good," Arthur said, "I'll just get my hat."

"There's only room for two," Niall said quickly, just as his aunt rapped out, "Arthur, you stay with me!"

Niall and his aunt looked at each other. Then smiled at each other as broadly as Arthur began to scowl.

"And, Niall?" his aunt called as he strode out the door. "Don't exhaust the poor child. In fact, make it worth her while. Invite her to dinner, too! It will do wonders for me, I'm sure I'll be able to join you by then. At least I shall make the effort."

"A monumental one, no doubt," Arthur muttered jealously, as his cousin grinned, saluted his aunt with a finger to his brow, then strode out the door.

* * *

Joy took Lord Paget's proffered hand and stepped up onto the high seat of his curricle. She'd never been in such a magnificent equipage before. Tall and intricate, with high delicate-looking yellow wheels, a gold chassis, and red cushions on the seat to spare her bottom from the pounding she was sure it would get as she rode over London's cobbles. The baron settled in his seat beside her, close as her elbow. She could almost feel the heat emanating from his tall strong form. He picked up the whip to start his team of matched cream horses. Joy held her breath. She was nervous, exhilarated, and excited all at once. Driving in such a carriage would be breathtaking, too.

"Miss Cummings first, you say?" he asked, turning to her.

"Seven Eden Street," she repeated, consulting the notebook she held on her lap. "She had the book just before your aunt did."

He flicked the whip and the horses set out. Joy's hand clutched the rail at her side as the curricle picked up speed. It was so well sprung she didn't jounce, it was so high up she wondered how hard she would fall. It was so thrilling she didn't care anymore.

Especially when he spoke to her again.

"It's good you keep such records," he said, glancing at her notebook. "Have you always worked in your cousin's shop?"

"Oh, no. I never expected to. I was born and raised in Tidwell, and never thought to come to London. But after my parents died, Cousin Minch was the only relative to offer me house room. It's only fair then that I work for my board."

"Tidwell? But I know the place. I had a schoolmate from Holt, and once visited there. As I recall, it's a very pretty region. A tiny village, isn't it? I suppose you were delighted that your cousin lived in London instead of another country village."

"Actually, no," she confessed. "I was terrified. I've come to love the things about London, since—the shops, the variety of people, the excitement. The air's charged with it. Even the most tedious things seem more important here than they did at home. It's difficult to get up much tension about a new crop of peaches coming in, after all. The only real excitement we had at home was when a storm was brewing." She turned a radiant smile to him. "That's just it. There always seems to be some sort of change due any minute here. I like it. But I confess I loved Tidwell. I guess I'm just a country girl, after all."

He wished someone else was driving so he could bask in that smile. She wore a dusty pink pelisse and a pretty little rose-colored bonnet. Nothing modish, not out of style but certainly not the last word in fashion. But she didn't need fashion or its accoutrements. The girl was as pink and ripe and tempting as Botticelli's Venus, she didn't need any heavenly clamshell or London modiste to frame her. The wind whisked wisps of flaxen hair from under her bonnet, dashing them across her cheek. Fine as silver floss, bright as sunlight, scattered against that fair cheek . . . her eyes so blue, lips so inviting, so pink in contrast to those straight white little teeth . . . and she'd just said she was just a country girl.

His horses knew when he stopped paying attention. Niall was suddenly jolted by more than Joy's smile. He had to rein in his team along with his desires and regretfully turn his attention back to driving. But his thoughts stayed with Joy.

"Homesick?" he asked.

"When I talk about it," she said with a shrug. "And when I go to sleep sometimes, you know, those moments just before you drift away?" She fell still, wondering if a well-brought-up young woman ought to talk about sleeping with a gentleman. She hadn't spoken to many gentlemen in a long time, at least since she'd become a woman.

"Those are the times when childhood is closest," he agreed, "when you give up the present, stop worrying about the future, and find yourself sliding to sleep in the past."

She relaxed, even though he was so close, and so very dashing. He wore a dun-colored driving coat and a high beaver hat that sat at a rakish angle on that thick dark gold hair. She didn't mean to stare, but when she looked down at her own lap, she couldn't help seeing that the muscular thighs so close to her own were covered by finely knit inexpressibles, and that he wore high shining brown boots with gold tassels on his long legs. He exuded an aura of confident masculinity, wealth, and good breeding. And still, he smiled at her as though he genuinely liked her. It was easy to pretend she was a friend, possible even to imagine she was a lady he'd asked out because he wanted her for more than a friend. Possible, if foolish. But she enjoyed the pretense, if only just for a minute.

"I live in the countryside," he said suddenly. "To the west, on the Severne. I inherited a neglected estate there and discovered I enjoyed setting it to rights more than all the tension you so admire here in London. You have to admit a roof about to cave in on your head is definitely exciting, and stairs that threaten to give way when you're at the top of them add more drama than even London can."

"But when it's all repaired, what will you do?"

"Grow apples," he said readily. "Raise horses. Discover which hens lay the biggest, brownest eggs. And sit by my fireside of an evening, congratulating myself on my timber. I don't blame you for laughing, no one in my family can believe the transformation restoring a couple of hundred acres and a decrepit estate have wrought in me. But I mean to show them. In fact, I plan to hold Christmas there this year to prove it."

"Is it a big family?" she asked wistfully.

"No. And when I returned from the wars, it had shrunk further. My father and mother were gone long before, when I was a lad, but we lost two cousins and an uncle to the Little Emperor. That's why we, by which I mean Aunt, Cousin Arthur, and a few others, are so important to each other."

"Were you in the army?"

They were still talking about his regiment when he slowed the team. "Speaking of horses!" he said with a laugh. "We have to turn round! Went right past the address, three streets back."

Joy wondered if she'd been chattering too much, so was glad to be reminded of her mission. She quieted as they neared Miss Cummings's town house, eyeing it with interest, because she'd never thought to visit any of her customers and found herself curious about them now. She was pleased for Miss Cummings. Hers was a neat house set in a semicircular ring of similar ones: good gray houses in a district that spoke of old money. There was no excitement here, and none was expected.

"I don't think Miss Cummings is the sort of person to leave anything in a book," Joy said. "She's very precise."

"And very much away at the moment, unless I miss

my guess," he said, noting that the doorknocker was off the front door. "Let me make some inquiries."

He found a boy to hold his horses, then roused a footman next door. After a few minutes and a coin given and taken, he returned to the driver's seat.

"Gone," he reported, "and not expected back until the New Year. Who's next on the list?"

Joy consulted her notebook. She sighed with relief and barely restrained a smile. "Mrs. Crab in James Street." James Street was far from where they were.

He smiled, too. "Good. Now, what were you saying?"

She stiffened, thinking his smile might be a touch too knowing, maybe holding a shade too much knowledge of her own feelings. She ducked her head and consulted her notebook. "I was reading my alphabetized list. But Lady Turnbull lives in Red Lion Square, which is much closer to us."

"But as she is a lady, she might be paying a morning call," he said imperturbably. "Let's leave her for after Mrs. Crab, when we'll be more likely to find her at home."

She looked up, as startled as amused by his flimsy reasoning. She saw his smile, still knowing, but rueful and hopeful, too. They both laughed merrily, as children skipping school to go fishing.

"Yes," she said, "then all right, Mrs. Crab it is."

"Now," he repeated. "As you were saying?"

She was saying things about the war that was over. Then he did; then they said things about the season that was coming. They agreed about politics and had an amusing mock quarrel about a poet. After they consulted with Mrs. Crab, who was elbow-deep in cookie dough, and had tea with her until they were stuffed with fresh gingerbread, they set out again.

Mrs. Crab said she hadn't lost anything. Joy was again relieved but feeling guilty about taking up the baron's time, wondering if she should go on the rest of her errand alone. But her escort seemed unsurprised and wouldn't hear of her continuing the search on her own.

"Things are seldom found where you first look," he said. "Why else would people always say they find things in the last place they looked? Fine fellow I'd be to let you wander London by foot when I have a carriage!" he added as she laughed and he took up the reins again. "Besides, the horses need exercise."

Joy decided she wasn't really imposing too much, and because they found so many new things to talk about as they traveled back across town to Lady Turnbull's house, the trip seemed to take only minutes.

Lady Turnbull was delighted to see them, and took their arrival as a cause to start her holiday, or so she said.

"It's about time you visited, my dear," she told Joy. "And it's a delight to entertain a handsome gentleman anytime," she added to Niall.

Her house was opulent, her servants gliding silently throughout, bringing them a lavish luncheon, because the lady refused to let them leave until they'd dined with her.

She hadn't misplaced a thing, but had her doubts about Mrs. Holcombe, who she said would forget her head if it wasn't attached to her shoulders. "Not that it's not a good head," she added quickly. "A clever party, is our Mrs. H. But forgetful, you see. She'll read a book almost all the way through before she realizes she's read it before. A common failing in many of us, but less uncommon with her, if you get my inference. Am I right, Joy?"

"Is she right, Joy?" Niall asked when they were back in his curricle.

Joy almost protested the familiarity, then bit back the words. Why bother? She couldn't have a better example of how he regarded her. His aunt called her that, but they had a long acquaintance, and they were both females. He wouldn't have called a lady by her first name without permission. But she was a bookseller, no matter her birth, and it was time she remembered it.

He saw her suddenly bent head, the way her lashes shaded the dying of the light in her eyes as she pretended to scan her notebook. Because he called her by her given name?

"Have I offended you?" he asked. "Aunt calls you 'Joy,' as did the other ladies, I just slipped into the habit. Forgive me."

She raised her head and treated him to a brilliant smile. "I'm not offended. Well, maybe I was, but now I understand."

He was relieved. She was well-bred and circumspect. Poor girl, she'd had to be. But he'd swear there wasn't a priggish bone in that entire lovely body. Thinking of that entire lovely body made him look at her again, and damn the horses. If they bolted it would be worth it. He studied her profile in the last of the afternoon light, watching as she looked at her notebook again. She seemed to shiver. At least, her finger shook as she traced the next address.

"What a fool I am, forgive me!" he exclaimed. "I've been so busy talking, I forgot how long we've been out. On such a chilly day, and in an open carriage!

We're going back, Miss Ayres, before my aunt slays me. She expressly told me not to keep you out too long. And asked that I invite you to dinner."

Joy looked up, amazed. "Me? But . . ." she hesitated, thinking of how much she wanted to accept and all the reasons why she couldn't: from not having the proper clothes to wear, to fear of who else might be there, to worry about overstepping her bounds, and about accepting too eagerly and easily because she really was so eager to continue this singularly wonderful day.

"It would make Aunt feel better, and we all want that, don't we?" he asked before she could protest. "It would be just Aunt and me. And Arthur, and he's harmless. There'd be good food, I promise. Please say yes, or Aunt will be bitterly disappointed. Which means *I'll* have a headache for the next week. We'll send a note round to your cousin; I'm sure he'll understand."

Understand? Joy thought, he'd be delighted, considering the deference he always paid to the aristocracy—and the possibilities of her friendliness to them providing more customers for his shop. "Well, if you really think . . ."

"I do!" he said, and snapped the whip, hurrying the horses to his aunt's home.

Joy didn't notice what she ate. She knew it was good, but it couldn't be half as good as the time she was having.

They dined in a snug parlor because Lady Gray announced they were too few and too cozy a crew to dine in state. They dined in laughter instead.

Lady Gray had a lively wit, Arthur was wonderful at mimicry and making funny faces, and Niall was cleverer than any man Joy ever spent time with. He made her say funnier things than she'd ever thought of, too.

Joy came to see they all enjoyed each other's company. Lord Paget really liked his aunt, though she loved to tease him. He was fond of Arthur, less so when Arthur grew too gallant toward herself. Odd, she thought now and again when she saw the spaniel eyes Arthur made at her, that she'd first thought him the more handsome. Now she saw he was just a boy, a frivolous one at that. Not half as good-looking as Niall. How could she have thought tousled black curls and great brown eyes more compelling than a strong lean face with bright watchful eyes? Madness. She looked at the baron whenever she could, which was whenever he wasn't watching her.

Lady Gray watched the pair of them with satisfaction. It was very like watching a badminton match, she later observed, with one of them returning a glance whenever the other left off glancing their way. Let Arthur sulk. He was young, he'd have his turn with other females. Niall had never before shown any respectable woman preference, and Joy Ayres was more than respectable. She was charming, intelligent, and obviously fascinated by Niall.

But when the desserts were finally served, it wasn't a very sweet time for Joy. "It's very late," she said regretfully, "or at least, so it is in our house. I must be at work tomorrow," she added. She raised her chin because she was cringing inwardly at having to use the word *work*. It reminded her of the gulf between herself and these privileged people she was dining with.

It reminded Niall, too. "Yes, too bad. Because I can't forget my obligations, either. I have to see a man

about a horse tomorrow at first light. I've plans to
bring a handsome bay stud home with me when I
return for Christmas."

"Ah, Christmas at the old Hall," his aunt sighed. "I
can't wait. It's been so long since we gathered there
together at Christmastime. Are you going to keep to
all the old traditions, Niall? The ones I remember
from my childhood? The Yule log, the carolers, dressing the house with rowan and evergreen?"

"The crab apple punch?" Arthur asked eagerly.
"The hot buttered punch, the gin and ale punch?"

"The fruitcake," Lady Gray added wistfully, "the
plum pudding, the roast goose?"

"All of it. From the kissing bough to the mistletoe,"
Niall said with a smile. "I'm bringing back the old
place with everyone old and good restored to it as
well."

Joy's happiness slowly ebbed completely away. She
looked down at her plate. It wasn't their fault. Why
shouldn't they rejoice? They'd just forgotten she was
there. She'd been in this position before. It would be
better if she were a servant and not expected to partake in such pleasures, then it wouldn't have mattered
what she overheard or how she was excluded from the
conversation. But now she felt as she had so many
times when the ladies in the bookshop spoke of their
teas and balls and parties. She had to remain silent,
hoping they wouldn't notice. Because if they did,
they'd remember that she wasn't one of their kind, no
matter how much she might seem to be. In such situa-
tions she wasn't.

She was only like a fly on the wall. An underprivi-
leged fly who dared not raise a wing or make a buzz
lest she be discovered observing those who were expe-
riencing so much more of life than she ever could.

Niall looked at his suddenly silent guest and throttled a groan. He'd erred, and badly. He started to speak, then held his tongue. There was nothing he could say. This wasn't the time or place to discuss his plans or hopes for Christmas with Joy.

But his aunt didn't know that.

"And what shall you do for Christmas, my dear?" Lady Gray asked Joy, making Niall wince.

"Oh, we make merry, too," she answered, avoiding their eyes.

It wasn't altogether a lie, she thought. She'd have the day off, and that toast with a jot of rum, and by nightfall, she'd probably be the proud owner of a brand-new handkerchief. She resisted the urge to bawl. "Oh, my, look at the time," she said instead, rising from her chair. "If I sit any longer it *will* be Christmas day! Thank you so much, my lady, but I must go home now."

"Niall will take you," Lady Gray said. "I hope you enjoyed your dinner, child. And be sure, I'd love to have you visit again."

So should I, but I'm not sure my heart can take it, Joy thought, but said, "Thank you."

Niall took her home in his aunt's carriage because now it was too cold to ride outside. Arthur sat with them, as merry a chaperon as any girl ever had—until he was firmly told that he wasn't coming along on their adventure the next day.

"Aunt needs you home with her," Niall said to stop his cousin's outraged protests, having arranged that before he'd even left her house.

Arthur put his chin on his fist and brooded massively and poetically, a trick he'd perfected before the mirror in the last days.

Joy didn't notice, she was too busy looking at Niall.

"I'll come for you at ten," Niall told her, "so we can track down the owner of your mysterious treasure."

"But you have a horse to buy," she said. "I can see the others on my own."

"The horse is bought. All I have to do is deliver the money, and that I can do at any time before I leave London."

"Still, I can't ask you to give up so much time for my quest," she protested.

"You can't ask me to stop. I love a mystery, and I'm as eager as you to solve it now. And who knows?" he added as he thought it. "It may be that the mystery was solved while we were gone. Maybe whoever lost whatever it was has already come back to the shop to claim it."

They both fell still at that. Then they all sat quietly, Niall pondering recent events, Joy feeling as depressed as Arthur obviously was, all the way back to the bookshop.

The next day dawned iron hard and flint cold. But Joy woke early, threw back the covers, and rushed from her snug bed, never feeling the chill of the floor beneath her bare toes, because of the warmth in her heart. She'd asked Cousin Minch when she came in last night: No one had claimed the banknotes! And Niall would be coming to get her at ten. He'd be here, and he'd take her away with him, even if just for another day. But she was grateful for it. It wasn't just that he was handsome and clever. Or maybe it was. Nor because looking at him set her blood bubbling and her pulses racing. Or was it? Who cared? Whatever it was, it was more than she'd ever known, and she would experience it again today. All day!

"I won't take her out past teatime today," Niall told Cousin Minch when he came to collect Joy at ten.

Joy, standing ready with her notebook in her hand and her bonnet already on her head, felt her spirits plummet.

"We can't jeopardize her health," he told Alfred, as naturally as if he was part owner of the shop. "It's too cold for searching farther today. One ride, one visit, a fortifying cup of tea or two, and then home. Tomorrow is another day."

"Indeed," Alfred said smoothly, his hands rubbing together. "Too kind of you to involve yourself in this, my lord. But if the owner doesn't show up at once we must keep searching, and there are many subscribers to our little library who would have to be consulted. We cannot inconvenience you for so long."

Joy's spirits sank further.

"You aren't inconveniencing me," Niall said. "I find the chase invigorating. I'll be home in the country soon enough, where hunting only involves the body. It isn't half as stimulating as the brain work before us here."

"You'll be leaving us soon, then?" Alfred asked silkily.

"In a few weeks," Niall said. "It should do. I looked at your lending library list. I'll have enough time to reach them all."

A few weeks! Joy thought, her heart leaping up.

"Some of your patrons will doubtless come in the meanwhile, too," Niall was saying. "Who knows? The case might solve itself before then. In any event, there's no need to send Miss Ayres out by herself. We'll have your answer before Christmas. If the weather turns bad, I can take her in a closed carriage—

with a housemaid from my hotel, hired for the sake of appearances, of course."

"Of course," Alfred said. "Well, carry on."

Niall's lips quirked.

"Now, you know he only meant 'proceed,' " Joy told Niall as they walked to his curricle.

"Oh, bother. Does that mean we have to change all our nefarious plans?" he asked.

They laughed as they drove off. In fact, they enjoyed themselves even more than the day before, though neither of them thought that possible. They enjoyed every minute of their visit with the two Miss Ives sisters, too. Although not frequent visitors to Minch's compared to the other women, the elderly twins had borrowed the book as well.

Both ladies were delighted with their unexpected visitors, but were unable to help with the mystery.

"Not I," the elder Miss Ives announced at once. "Gemma, did you leave anything in the book?"

Her sister denied it. "Our father was a schoolmaster," she told Joy and Niall, "he'd slay us for wrinkling a page, much less leaving anything in a book! Remember how he carried on when Mama tore a recipe out of a magazine?" she asked her sister. "Or when you put a rose to dry inside of Dryden? Oh, no, old habits die hard, we'd never deface anything in print or put anything into a volume."

"But books do make good hiding places," her sister said slowly, "and so occasionally rules must be broken."

Her twin nodded. They exchanged knowing smiles.

Joy held her breath, Niall went on the alert. In spite of the sisters' denials, it might be that they had an answer. And an end to their adventure. Because the

women wore matching grins, looking less like elderly
ladies than mischievous children.

"Gemma was being courted by a young man Father
thought unsuitable," her sister explained. "So she hid
all his forbidden letters in a book."

"And Father never found them!" Gemma laughed.

"Because you hid them in *Female Complaints and
Their Practical Cures*," her sister cried. Both ladies
giggled and stole glances at Niall. "Excuse our crude-
ness," Gemma said, "but it was so droll."

"And the young man?" Niall asked. "What happened to him?"

"Oh," Gemma said with a shrug, "he *was* unsuitable."

Niall and Joy laughed over that later, when they were
alone again, sharing tea at one of London's most elegant tearooms. They felt like criminals who had gotten
an unexpected reprieve. The game would go on!

They talked about books, they chatted about politics
and the weather, and discussed favorite colors and
foods. But with all the topics they covered, they conveniently avoided any mention of the thing most people were thinking about these days: Christmas. Neither
wanted to bring up the subject. One because he
deemed it still too early, the other because the thought
of it pained her. It hardly mattered. They found a
dozen other things to discuss, and stayed at tea until
the afternoon grew too dark for them to pretend it
wasn't over.

Cousin Minch was still wearing the banknotes like
a secret boutonniere when Niall came to get Joy the
next day.

"Visiting Mrs. Holcombe today?" Alfred said.
"Good, good. The lady has not come here of late, but

then many of our customers are already off for the holidays. I hope you find her home. Off you go then, and good luck with ending this mystery!"

Joy didn't wish for that. She tried not to even think of it. Instead, she told Niall about the lady they were going to visit as they drove to her house.

"Mrs. Holcombe is charming," Joy said. "She may seem fluttery, maybe even scatter-witted, but that's just her way. I assure you, she's no fool. She reads voluminously. Unfortunately, she speaks the same way. In fact," she sighed, "she chatters on like a magpie. But she has a very good heart."

Niall grinned. "Ah, a good heart. That's what you females say about really unfortunate-looking women you want to introduce us single gentlemen to, isn't it? No matter, it's what men say about other men we make excuses for, too. Did I ever tell you about my uncle—by marriage, I assure you—Richard, the fellow with a heart of gold and face of brass?"

He proceeded to, and they were laughing when they arrived at Mrs. Holcombe's house. She was at home. The moment they announced their names to her maid, they heard a glad cry from inside. Mrs. Holcombe rushed out to the hall to warmly welcome them, ushering them in before they could even state their mission.

"Oh, I adore company!" Mrs. Holcombe said. She was a tall, thin woman who waved her arms constantly as she spoke, and she spoke all the time. "What a good idea that you came to visit. Why didn't you think of it before? Or rather, why didn't I? Oh, I ought to have thought of it, though I didn't know you, Lord Paget, of course, but I'm so pleased you've come along with our Joy. Oh, why didn't I think of this before?"

She gave them no time to answer. She kept talking

as they stared with wonder and tried to edge inside her crowded parlor.

The house was filled to the brim with curios, cats, and oddments. The walls were so completely papered with pictures that it was hard to tell what color they were, if indeed they were walls at all and not just an amalgam of framed prints. It seemed as if every souvenir ever made in England along with every seashell that ever washed up on its shores was displayed on one of the many tables that filled the room. Joy had never heard Mrs. Holcombe speak of her husband. It was possible, she thought, looking around in awe, that the poor fellow simply couldn't fit in the house anymore, or else he'd been papered over.

She and Niall caught each other's eye as they sat down on the edge of their chairs, not moving their feet lest they kick a cat or upset a table. But their smiles vanished when they heard what Mrs. Holcombe had to say as soon as she heard the reason for their visit.

"Oh, something lost in a book?" she asked. "I'm *so* glad you let me know. It's mine!"

Niall and Joy sat dumbstruck. He took in a sharp breath; her fair complexion turned to whey.

"So sorry to have sent you running all around London," Mrs. Holcome went on. "I should have sent a note round, but I planned on coming to the shop today. I couldn't, at the last moment, but I'm sure I would have got there tomorrow."

"Indeed?" Niall said, recovering himself. "So, if you please, ma'am, what exactly was in the book? I'd certainly like to know what the item of value was."

"Well," Mrs. Holcombe said, putting a finger to her chin, "I'm not completely sure. I'm missing a statement from my bank. And a letter from my cousin in

America. And an invitation to the Swanson's Christmas ball. Oh! And two pounds ten that I got in change from the greengrocer last week. No, I lie. I found the ten in my pocket, so that's only the two coins, then."

Joy let out her pent-up breath, feeling dizzy with relief. She shook her head. "It isn't any of those things."

"An emerald ring," Mrs. Holcombe went on pensively. "Though I suspect my poor Midge et it by mistake," she added, dimpling at a large gray cat that lay draped over a sofa. "And my opera glasses. Oh. And a program from the Opera, and . . ."

Joy and Niall looked at each other as Mrs. Holcombe rattled off a list of missing objects, most of them impossible to fit between the pages of a book, others not valuable by anyone's definition but hers.

"Well, I declare!" she finally said when she ran out of missing items that Joy denied were the ones she'd found. "Whatever it is can't be mine. Wait! I'll have a look round and see if I can come up with more things that should be here but aren't."

Niall rose. "Yes, do that. But we must be off now. If you find more that's missing, I suggest presenting a list to Miss Ayres or her cousin. Thank you for your time."

"Oh, it's nothing, and I shall," Mrs. Holcombe said. "But that won't be until after Christmas, because I forgot, Mr. Holcombe's family will be here for the holiday and I simply won't have time to search until they leave. Be sure I will then."

She followed them out, stood in the doorway, and called after them as they went back to his curricle. "Miss Ayres, you simply must come again, and bring your young man again, too!"

Niall darted a swift glance at Joy. Her face went ruddy as her cousin Minch's. "You aren't going to correct her?'' he asked in a low voice as he took her hand. He was supposed to help her up to her seat, but he just stood, looking down at her, holding her hand.

Joy shrugged. "It isn't necessary," she whispered back. "She'll forget what she said in an hour. She'd be horrified if she was told her mistake."

He grew solemn. "Is it a mistake, then?"

Her gaze shot to his, it was blue fire. She put up her chin. "Baron," she said stiffly, "I'm a bookseller. You're one of the most eligible gentlemen in London. We have had a fascinating time together these past days, or, at least, I have. But I don't deceive myself. I can't. I may deal in fiction, but I know fairy tale from fact."

"And what are those facts?"

She huffed a little sigh, as exasperated as she was saddened by his joking about something so important to her. "Please," she said, "embrace reality."

"I'd rather embrace you," he said. She gasped. He ducked his head and brushed a kiss across her opened lips.

He moved back immediately, though only fractionally, his eyes searching hers. She stood staring at him, her lips still apart in shock.

Their mouths tingled with electricity, as though they'd touched after crossing a rug on a dry day, instead of standing stock-still on the cold cobbles of a London street. Her hand flew to her lips. His eyes followed. They stared at each other. He put a hand on her waist, slowly drew her closer, watching for the least sign of objection from her. There was none. She was as lost in the moment as he was. He lowered his head and kissed her again, this time slowly, searchingly and thoroughly. With her full cooperation.

Because after a second's hesitation, she wound her

arms around his neck and kissed him back. Her experience in such matters was limited, but her reactions were all he could have wanted and left them both wanting more. She hadn't known that tongues were involved in kissing; he hadn't fully realized how much hearts were. Both were wild to discover more. They'd found the warmest place on a cold day in a cold world, and stayed locked together seeking even greater heat and pleasure. They did.

It was a horse that reminded them of where they were, what they were doing, and what they couldn't do.

" 'Nay,' is right," Niall murmured in frustration, mimicking the horse. He looked into Joy's dazed and delighted eyes and saw slow dawning dismay. He stepped back.

"Not here, not now," he muttered, gathering his wits. "But understand that I'm not sorry for what just happened. I acted on impulse, and that's not like me. But it's very good that I did, now the matter is out in the open . . . if too literally," he added, glancing back at Mrs. Holcombe, standing in her doorway, gaping at them.

He looked down at Joy. "What I have to say to you will be no impulse. But later. Not now, not with Mrs. Holcombe watching, not with half of London able to spy on us." His expression grew grave. Their embrace had set her bonnet slightly askew. He stroked some stray strands of flaxen hair back from her wide blue, somber eyes.

His own eyes were sober, gray as sleet, his voice was deep and sad. He looked cool and unapproachable now, making her feel even more wanton and wrong.

"Joy," he said, "please understand that though my impulse was spur of the moment, my intentions were not. I'll speak of it later. That, I promise you. But for now, please forgive me and don't fear me or my intentions, or regret what just happened."

She read his face, scarcely listening to his words, because she was ashamed and upset with herself, not him. She ought never have thrown herself at him, but the taste of him, the closeness of him, intoxicated her. Holding his broad shoulders, having him hold her, feeling his warm mouth on hers had been wondrous. She'd thought it might be. But she could never have guessed how such closeness could fill her lonely heart. She felt empty now, as well as embarrassed. "It's not necessary to apologize," she said over the lump in her throat.

"Of course it is!" he said, looking as shocked as Mrs. Holcombe did.

"Nor will I hold you to it," Joy said, fumbling in her recticule for something to do, to avoid his eyes.

"You had better!" he said. "You can't pretend it didn't happen. Joy," he said in gentler tones. "I'm not trifling with you, I never meant to. I'm sorry for making such a spectacle. I meant to declare myself in a more approved fashion, at a more appropriate time."

She found a handkerchief. "Ha!" she said on a mournful sniff.

"You doubt me?"

"But we've only known each other a matter of days," she said, daring to look up at him again.

"*That*, I can do something about. I'll see you tomorrow, the next day and the next. But, Joy," he said as he paused in the street with her, one hand still on her waist, the other on his heart, "even if we'd met in a more conventional sense, we couldn't keep seeing each other so steadily for much longer without causing gossip and giving rise to expectations. A fellow's only permitted two dances with a woman at a ball, only a few meetings wherever they go, and those measured out like gold dust. Or else he must declare himself. And so I am. I mean that. I'm absolutely serious," he said as her eyes widened. "I know what I've found. You do, too. You feel as I do, don't you?"

She shook her head, in denial or wonder at what was happening, he couldn't say. He couldn't tell if the tears standing in her eyes were those of sorrow or gladness, either.

"Listen, my Joy," he said urgently, "there's every chance the absence of the damned thing in the book you lent will be discovered by its owner any hour now. That would end this. I don't want that to happen. I don't want *anything* to ever end this. I was going to ask you to come home with me at Christmas, then and there was where I planned to ask you never to leave me again. But I ruined that," he said ruefully. "It's not just me. Didn't you notice my aunt's machinations? She's been praising you day and night, throwing us together so blatantly it's embarrassing. Or would be, if it weren't just what I wanted. Oh, Lord, I thought I was glib, but this . . . Listen. I don't read the books you lend, I don't know exactly how to say this . . ."

So he didn't. He pulled her to him and kissed her again.

"Now," he said, breathing hard, "you will marry me, won't you? Come home for Christmas with me, bring your cousin, your whole household, including the cat if you want. But I won't be alone this Christmas, and I want you to be my wife in the new year. Come to my house, at least. You can always change your mind," he added a little desperately.

He saw the beginnings of her smile. "But later," he said with more confidence. "Much later. Give me— give this, a try. Marry me, Joy. I'll be the best husband you could ever want, because you're the only woman for me. I don't need time to know my heart. It's yours. Joy, my Joy, say yes, please."

So she did.

There was a celebration at Minch's bookshop that day. A toast from a bottle of fine champagne that the baron brought, drunk to the health of the young couple. Then another celebration at Lady Gray's house later. The excitement was enough to get her up out of her bed to receive guests and make plans.

"So all ends well for you," Arthur told his cousin Niall enviously. "Someone lost a treasure, and you end up with one."

"I don't know what was lost, but I know what I found," Niall said softly, watching his fiancée.

"I promised not to say what was lost until someone claims it," Joy said, smiling up at him, "but I, too, know what I found, and believe me, it's worth so very much more."

Late that night, when both households were asleep—Joy in her bed dreaming of when she would no longer sleep alone, and Niall tossing and turning as he burned for his chosen bride—Alfred Minch moved through his bookshop like a wraith. Silent as dust, swift as night falling, he stole downstairs to his shop and went soft-footed to his safe, where he knelt in the dark like a man at an altar.

There, by the light of a single candle, he withdrew the notes from his waistcoat and laid them tenderly with their brothers and sisters, alongside their cousin coins, amid the gold and with the silver. He blinked back happy tears.

"So. There, you are, my fine fellows," he crooned, patting them into place. "Home again. Such a wise

investment I made with you," he whispered. "The best
kind. For I didn't have to part with one of you, and
look at the return I got! They were made for each
other, but how else could I throw them together? And
they say money can't buy happiness," he scoffed.

"Sleep well, my pretties."

He started to rise, stopped, and stiffened. "Yes,
well," he murmured to himself, "there is the question
of a dowry, isn't there? Of a settlement, for a cer-
tainty." He crouched, lost in thought.

Then Alfred Minch smiled. "But he's rich and I'm
just a poor bookseller, and everyone knows it. He'll
waive the settlement, and she'll be so delighted to go
with him that she won't care. Oh, well," he said in a
voice full of surrender, as though he heard argument.
"Yes. Very well, then. It's a once-in-a-lifetime event,
is it not? I won't be mean. I'll give them a handsome
present. A volume on home management *and* a family
Bible, and they'll be very grateful, I'm sure. Why not?
Used volumes hold the same wisdom as new ones.
And, after all, I've already given them the best gifts:
each other."

His voice gentled. "Rest well, my honeys," he
breathed as he slowly rose to his feet. "And have a
happy Christmas. Be sure, I will. For it's more blessed
to give than to receive, and I gave you back, didn't I?
Nor did I make one penny on the arrangement . . .
yet. But with a cousin wed to a top-of-the-trees gent,
and a nobleman at that, who knows what else will
result, eh? Perhaps you, my dearlings, will have more
company, and soon!" He closed the safe on a happy
sigh, and locked it tight.

Then he crept up the stairs to sleep, and dream of
a happy Christmas, the best kind of Christmas, one
he didn't have to pay for.

A Home for Hannah
by Barbara Metzger

1

Hannah was in trouble. This was not the "stand in the corner until you learn your place" kind of trouble, nor the "going without supper" kind of trouble. This was worse even than the birching Hannah would get if she were caught listening outside Matron's office door at the Chiswell London Academy for Girls. Miss Eudora Chiswell was speaking to her brother, Mr. Malcolm Chiswell, about Hannah. How could Hannah not listen, especially when the door was open a crack? Hannah clutched her doll closer to her chest.

"So what are you going to do now that the payments for the chit's upkeep have stopped?" Mr. Chiswell was asking. He was the mathematics instructor at the school and kept the ledgers. He also kept track of every piece of paper, every slice of bread, and every torn stocking. Outside the door, Hannah rubbed one foot against the other, feeling the stitches of her unskilled darning against her toes.

"What do you think I am going to do with the brat?" Miss Chiswell asked with a raspy cackle, almost as untried as Hannah's sewing. "Keep her on for free? This is no charity home, you know."

The school was maintained by donations and tu-

itions. The girls were mostly orphans or simply unwanted, with the occasional boarder whose parents
were traveling. Most often, like Hannah, they were
unwelcome encumbrances of one sort or another, with
families willing to pay to see them schooled and fed,
without actually seeing them. Hannah's mother, a
woman of great beauty and little virtue, according to
the Chiswells, had run off to Russia with her latest
foreign lover last year. The money for Hannah's keep
had run out last month.

Hannah did not miss the mother she'd never met.
In fact, the first she'd heard of the woman was when
a farewell note was delivered, saying "Always in my
heart," along with the doll Hannah held so close. She
did miss the dream of being claimed by a loving family
of her own, though. Now she was going to miss the
only home she had ever known, cold and uncaring as
the Chiswell London Academy was.

"So what will you do with the girl?" Mr. Chiswell
asked again, and Hannah held her breath waiting for
the answer.

"Well, she's too young to go into service, and too
old for adopting out, even if folks were willing to overlook the bad blood in her, from that mother. Couples
with money want a sweet little infant. Them without
blunt want a strong gal to help with the housework
or the farm."

"That Hannah's a scrawny thing," Mr. Chiswell
agreed, as if the girls were ever fed enough to grow
plump and sturdy. "She would not last a week in
the mills."

"Or the mines. The foremen will never pay us for
a puny runt like her."

"What about the bawdy houses? I hear Sukey Johnson is always looking for young girls."

"Hannah is six years old, you old lecher. Besides, she is too homely with that impossible hair."

Hannah's hair was, as usual, out of its ribbon, out of its braid, and in her eyes. She pushed a long, thick, straight lock aside so she could peek through the opening of the door. Mr. Chiswell was licking his thin lips, about to disagree with his sister, it seemed to Hannah.

Before he could say anything, however, Miss Chiswell added, "And how will it look for our reputation if one of our girls lands in a brothel? No, it will have to be one of the city orphanages."

Hannah had to stuff her hand in her mouth to keep from crying out. Everyone knew the foundling homes were filled with disease, crime, and vermin—and hopelessness. Wasn't Miss Chiswell always telling the girls how terrible the institutions were, to make her charges behave?

"That or the streets," Mr. Chiswell suggested, "so no one has to know where she came from."

The streets were worse than the orphanages, worse than anything Hannah could think of, in fact. Boys out on their own became beggars or thieves, or got stolen to be chimney sweeps. Girls— Well, all Hannah knew was that girls suffered Dyer Fates, worse than having to clean the chamber pots. She might not understand what Dyer Fates entailed, unless they were like the time she tried to color her pale hair with ink, but they played a major part in Matron's lectures, so they had to be bad. Hannah did understand cold and hunger, and being all alone in the dark. Her thin shoulders began to shake in fear and in sorrow, but she could not cry. Not yet. She had to keep listening.

"When?" Mr. Chiswell wanted to know, running his fingers over the columns he was adding, estimating, perhaps, how much they could save in Hannah's half-full bowls of gruel. It was all Hannah could do not to shout out a promise to eat less, or to work harder at her lessons, so someone might hire her when she learned to sew or read better.

Miss Chiswell was thinking. Hannah could tell by the way her nostrils twitched. "At the new year, I think. After all, Christmas is not quite a month away. The season of good-will, and all that fustian. We have to show what devout souls we are, to set a proper example for the girls, you know."

And to impress the wealthy patrons, Hannah knew. She wondered how impressed they'd be to see Mr. Malcolm Chiswell use his penknife to clean under his fingernails. He put the knife down and smiled, sending shivers down Hannah's back. "Right," he said. "Then come January, we can toss the brat out in the snow?"

"Exactly."

Gregory Bellington, Viscount Bryson, was wishing he had his own cattle in front of him instead of these hired horses. How could he hope to impress his passenger with such slugs? His own highbred pair were long gone, though, to pay his family's debts, his deceased father and older brother having been singularly unlucky gamblers. He also wished he was in the country instead of Hyde Park, where everyone kept an eye on everyone else, and made note of such financial embarrassments. While he was wishing, Lord Bryson would have chosen weather that was not so cold and raw. If the dull-coated nags from the livery stable did not give Gregory's companion a disgust of him, the annoying drip of moisture he could feel forming at the end of his nose surely would. He pretended to brush back the lock of straight hair that kept falling across his brow while he surreptitiously swiped at his nose with his glove. He knew his blasted hair was too long, dash it, but the services of a valet had gone the way of his prime cattle.

The horses, the weather, the crowds, and his pecuniary problems all might have combined to give Lord Bryson the blue devils, except for the angel sitting beside him in her ermine-lined blue cape. With the fur-lined hood up, and her dainty hands in a white muff, Lady Susannah Fitzjohn was the picture of a Frost Princess. The cold brought roses to her porcelain skin, instead of a revolting runny nose, and perfectly placed golden curls framed her beautiful face. Lady Susannah was a Diamond, a Toast, the Incomparable of the Season. She was wellborn, well educated and, most importantly, well dowered. But what a fortunate fortune hunter Gregory was—he actually liked the young woman. They had shared only a handful of dances, true, and the occasional conversation during morning calls or intermission at the opera, but she seemed everything a fellow could want in a wife. Better yet, she seemed to favor him among her hordes of suitors, and her father had not frowned too severely when the viscount asked permission to pay his addresses. Gregory might not precisely wish to marry any female at all right now, but proposing to the earl's daughter would be no hardship. Nor would kissing her to seal their engagement—once he'd wiped his nose.

Lord Bryson thought to get the deed done today, possibly his last chance to be private with the closely guarded heiress, or as private as one could be in the park, with a hired groom riding behind them.

Otherwise, if he missed today's opportunity, both he and Lady Susannah would soon be off to the Duke of Ravencroft's house party. The annual Christmas affair was a huge gathering, where Lady Susannah would be surrounded by her bosom bows and busy-body chaperons—and every eligible bachelor who could scrape up an invite the way Viscount Bryson had, by listening to the duke's tales of his days in India.

Gregory might be able to steal a few mistletoe kisses at Ravencroft, but he would have a deuced difficult time getting the young woman alone long enough for a proposal. A gentleman could not put his luck to the test amid the inevitable dances and carol singing and greens gathering, not without a herd of old tabbies hanging on his every word. Besides, if he could claim her as his own before leaving London, an announcement in the newspapers would keep the other chaps—and Lord Bryson's creditors—at bay.

The viscount had planned on inviting his would-be wife to step down for a short stroll along a less popular pathway, leaving the groom with the horses, except then he would have to get down on one knee on the cold, muddy ground. A fellow without a valet had to consider such matters. No, Gregory decided, he'd do better to stay in the curricle and send the groom off. He started to look for a likely side path to turn the horses.

He dabbed once more at his nose with his whip hand while Lady Susannah turned to wave to an acquaintance on horseback. When he glanced ahead, Gregory noticed a little girl on the edge of the riding track. He'd seen her before, he thought, a tiny scrap of a moppet in a red cloak and a plain straw bonnet, clutching a doll. He remembered thinking, the first time he'd seen her, that the chit was far too young to be out and about on her own. Her governess or nanny or whatever must be having a tryst, he'd decided, for

the child was too clean and too well dressed to be a
street urchin or a flower seller, despite the cloak being
too big for her, and the bonnet almost hiding her face
entirely. All the viscount could see were big eyes in a
pale, solemn face, staring at the passing carriages. The
poor little puss must be cold and bored, waiting while
her nursemaid had a cuddle in some secluded corner
of the park. He wondered where and how far away
that corner might be, and if he could find it before he
had to return Lady Susannah to her home.

Feeling sorry for the child, Gregory raised his hat
in greeting, the same as he did when he passed Lady
Cowper or Princess Lieven, or any of the other Almack's lady patronesses. That lock of hair fell in his
eyes again, pale blond hair almost as colorless as the
weak winter sun. He tossed his head back and replaced his high-crowned beaver hat, then started to
look again for a more secluded path.

To Lord Bryson's disbelief, dismay, and downright
horror, the little girl stepped dangerously close to the
carriageway. She raised her head and called out in a
high, clear voice that could be heard by everyone
around. "Papa," she cried, looking straight at Gregory. "Papa."

2

"What is the meaning of this, Bryson?" The rose-
bud at Gregory's side was sprouting thorns. Lady Susannah did not appear half as lovely with her eyes
narrowed and her mouth pursed. She looked like a
dried currant, in fact.

"I have no idea," the viscount said in absolute honesty. "Someone's idea of a prank, perhaps."

"Then move on, do," she told him, as one might address a hackney driver. "I am not amused. People are staring."

She was no more eager to get out of the public eye than Gregory, so he flicked his whip over the horses' ears. Then all hell broke loose.

Actually, the viscount thought with the one tiny corner of his mind that remained coherent, that was an exaggeration. There were no floods or famines, frogs or flying locusts. He could only pray for a plague to strike him dead. No such luck, only another knife through his heart, another plaintive "Papa."

"I swear I never saw her be—" He was liable to be struck by lightning after all, for that bouncer. "That is, I do not know the child."

The little girl chose that moment to step closer yet to the horses and remove her bonnet. Lady Susannah gasped, or was that Gregory's sharp intake of air? It sure as Hades was Viscount Bryson's perfectly straight hair on that child's head—a perfect match to his pale, almost white, blond hair, hanging down past her shoulders.

Lady Susannah caught her breath first. Then she caught the viscount on the cheek with her swinging reticule. Jupiter, Gregory thought, reeling, she must carry a cannonball in the thing.

"How dare you subject me to such an indignity?" she shrilled. "My father will hear of this."

If Earl Blakenthorpe was anywhere in London that afternoon, he'd already heard, the woman was that loud. Struck, stunned, and almost stupefied, Gregory jerked on the ribbons. The job horses broke stride. One gelding tried to rear in the traces; the other tried to go back to its stall. While Lord Bryson struggled to regain control, Lady Susannah berated his driving, his ethics, and his ancestors, it seemed. The child jumped back, but the breeze caught the bonnet she held in one hand and carried it aloft—right in front of the already unsettled horses. It was all Gregory could do to keep them from bolting, straining at the reins for all he was worth. The curricle swayed and swerved, and a wheel brushed the red-cloaked child.

A woman screamed. Men shouted. The groom behind him cursed. My Lord, Gregory thought as he fought to halt the horses, he'd struck an infant! Here he'd been worrying over a dripping nose! He leaped out of the curricle as soon as it stopped moving. The groom ran to the horses' heads, and Lady Susannah clambered down without waiting to be assisted. Instead of joining the viscount on his race back to the crumpled heap in the grass, Lady Susannah hurried to join a knot of friends gathered around a barouche and a phaeton some distance away.

Without a second glace toward his disappearing companion—and disappearing hopes of settling his debts—Gregory fell to his knees beside the still figure. The moppet was breathing, thank heaven! But her eyes were closed, and she was deathly pale. He smoothed back a lock of her damnable—and damning—hair, and started to feel the girl's head for bumps and bruises. "Come on, sweetheart," he begged. "Wake up and tell me you are all right."

"I do not think she is unconscious," a calm voice spoke from beside him. "I saw the entire incident and do not believe the wheel actually touched her. She is merely frightened, I would guess. See? She has not lost her grip on the doll."

The porcelain doll seemed to have taken the worst of the fall, suffering a chipped nose, a shattered arm, and a thoroughly muddied dress. If those were the extent of the damages, Gregory would consider himself blessed. He stopped feeling the infant's birdlike bones for breaks and looked up to see a pretty young woman of about five-and-twenty bending over the child. She wore a soft gray cape and a plain black bonnet, with her brown hair in a neat coiled braid at her neck. Two little boys hovered nearby. The errant governess, Lord Bryson assumed.

"How the devil could you—" he began only to be interrupted with her, "How could you let your daughter—"

"She is not my daughter," he said through gritted teeth. She was obviously not this competent-seeming governess's charge, either, then. "I have no idea who she is."

The cursed female raised one dubious eyebrow as she silently studied the admittedly astounding resemblance. The brat even had a tear running down her cheek to land at the tip of her nose.

Gregory cursed under his breath, easily reading the woman's thoughts, that he had the morals of a maggot. "Not acknowledged, not unacknowledged. Not from the wrong side of the blanket, not mine, period, Miss . . ."

"Haney. Claire Haney." She glanced back to make sure the little boys had not strayed away.

Gregory nodded. "I am Bryson, and I do not go around littering the countryside with my by-blows," he said, bringing a blush to Miss Haney's smooth cheeks. He could not tell if she believed him, and he could not understand why it seemed to matter to him. "But if I did, I would not let any offspring of mine wander the city unattended."

"That is all well and good, my lord, but what do you intend to do with her now?"

"What do I . . . ?" He intended to go home and have a brandy. Or two.

"You cannot simply leave her lying there."

"Surely someone will be looking for her. We have only to wait a moment or two before they realize she is gone missing."

Miss Haney did not seem convinced. "I have been in the park with the boys most of the afternoon and noticed her earlier, because she was all by herself."

"Then she had to have come from some nearby house," Gregory said with more confidence than he felt. He'd never seen the little girl with any nursemaid, either, but had always assumed the child was with someone. Now he realized she'd been alone, studying the riders to find a likely target: a clunch who looked enough like her to be mortified by her blackmail scheme. He angrily turned back to the child, who had not moved. "Come now, missy. Open your eyes and tell us where you live so I can see you home."

Her eyes stayed tightly shut, suspiciously so. Gregory frowned. "Well, then I suppose I can deliver her to the magistrate's office, or the nearest Charley. They'll know what to do with a lost child."

The youngster's eyes opened. They were blue, of course, with a darker blue rim. Just like his.

"Hell and damnation!" Gregory swore.

Miss Haney drew in a breath at his language, and the child cringed. "Please, Papa," she said.

"I am not your father, deuce take it! Now, tell us where you live so we can be on our way."

The girl's lower lip started quivering.

"Dash it, you are not going to cry, are you?"

She shook her head and whimpered, "No, Papa."

"I am not—" he started to shout, when Miss Haney laid a small, neatly gloved hand on his arm.

"Let me, my lord," she said. She knelt nearer the child, without worrying over her gown or her cloak, and spoke in a gentle voice. "Will you tell us your name, dearest? We only wish to help, you know. No one will turn you over to the Watch, I promise." She glared at the viscount when he would have protested.

"Hannah."

"That's a lovely name. Does your head hurt, Hannah?"

"No."

"Does anything else hurt? Are you dizzy, and that is why you cannot remember your address?"

Hannah started to say no, but then thought better of it, and changed her head shake to a nod.

"Gammon. Anyone can see the brat is lying. She has a vivid imagination, is all. I shall simply take her to the nearest foundling home if she will not divulge an address," Gregory threatened.

"An orphanage? You could not be so cruel," Miss Haney protested.

What other choices did he have? The viscount barely had enough blunt to buy the chit a new doll. His best chance of satisfying his creditors and saving his estate was driving off with Sir Nigel Naperson in his high-perch phaeton. Lady Susannah was laughing gaily at something the chinless clunch was saying, as if a child's life and near death was of no account. He stared after the disappearing equipage, frowning.

Misinterpreting his lingering glance, Miss Haney clucked her tongue like the schoolmistress Gregory took her to be. He turned back to the brown-haired young woman and asked, "Can you not take her in until her people come for her?"

She glanced toward the two boys who were now

talking to his groom, petting the horses, and then looked back at Hannah. "I am afraid that Lady Handbury, the boys' mother . . ." Her voice faded off.

If Diana, Lady Handbury, was the lads' mother and Miss Claire Haney's employer, Gregory pitied them all, including Handbury. Lady Handbury was a stiff-rumped, prune-faced shrew who fancied herself an arbiter of social behavior. Her long nose was so often in the air, she looked like a jackass reaching for an apple. No, she would never take a waif into her home, which meant he was stuck finding a place for Hannah. The devil take it, the chit had to belong *somewhere*! He asked her again, none too gently, earning him a scowl from Miss Haney. Hannah raised a stubborn chin, enough for him to see she had a tiny cleft there. He quickly lowered his own clefted chin into his neck-cloth. Thunderation.

The terror Lord Bryson had suffered earlier was receding, to be replaced by anger. The whole situation was nonsensical, to say nothing of nightmarish. "How could you have done such a damn fool thing, anyway?" he practically yelled at the child, forgetting the governess's presence. "You could have been killed."

"I only wanted to go home with you, Papa."

"I am not your papa, and you cannot go home with me. Now, get up off the cold ground before you take a chill and lay that in my dish, too." He did not wait for Hannah to stand, but scooped her up. He was astonished at how light she felt. Why, his greatcoat weighed more. She put one arm around his neck and softly patted his cheek where the bruise from Lady Susannah's reticule was still bright red. To Gregory, her touch felt like a butterfly's wing on his skin, and he decided it was simpler to hold Hannah at eye level

than to keep bending down to talk to the plaguey chit.
He turned to Miss Haney, hoping she might have a
suggestion to offer.

Claire looked from one to the other, not knowing
what to believe. Here was a remarkably attractive gentleman behaving like a bee-stung badger, while tenderly cradling a remarkably similar child. Everyone
knew Viscount Bryson's pockets were to let, and he
was dangling after Lady Susannah Fitzjohn and her
dowry. A love child could not further his cause in that
quarter. Yet he had sworn Hannah was not his, and
he was reputed to be an honorable man. Poor, yes,
and seeking to make an advantageous marriage, but
honorable. She shook her head.

Gregory could see the indecision in Miss Haney's
pretty green eyes. She was a respectable female, past
dewy-eyed innocence, but no woman of the world who
would be unfazed by licentious behavior. If she did
not believe him, no one would. He looked down at
the tiny mirror image in his arms. "Hannah, have you
a last name?"

Hannah nodded. "Marvell."

"Marvell . . . Marvell. Lud, your mother isn't Ann
Marvell, is she?"

Hannah nodded again.

"Marvelous Marvell? Why, she used to be the high-
est paid"—he recalled the proper governess—"ah, en-
tertainer in London."

"Then you did know Hannah's mother, my lord?"
Ice dripped from Miss Haney's voice.

"Gads, no. I could never have afforded— That is,
before my time. I would have been at university during the Marvell's reign. But my brother, my deceased
brother, just might have known her." And it would
have been just like feckless Gordon to keep an expen-

sive mistress while the roof of their house rotted. Which made Hannah Gregory's niece, and his responsibility for sure.

"Where is your mother now, Hannah?" he asked, relieved that all he had to do was restore the moppet to the demi-mondaine. "I am sure she must be frantic with worrying over you."

"Oh, no. She has gone to Russia. To the court."

Oh, Lord. "Your mother is visiting the tsar?"

Hannah did not know about any tsar. "She is gone to Russia to be the court's Ann."

Miss Haney coughed.

"I, ah, see. Then who is caring for you until your mother returns?"

Obviously, if anyone cared about her, ever, Hannah would not be in the park on her own, but Gregory had to ask, praying for an aunt or a cousin or a former colleague. Lud, his niece being raised by a retired bird of paradise? The viscount's blood ran cold at the thought. No, he was simply cold. Hannah must be, too, in her lighter cape. He opened his greatcoat and wrapped it around her, still in his arms.

Hannah snuggled closer, making sure the doll was well covered, too. "She is not coming back. Miss Chiswell said so."

Oh.

3

While Viscount Bryson waited outside the door of the Chiswell London Academy for Girls, he was wishing he'd brought an extra handkerchief. Hannah had cried and begged the whole way here from the park, weeping onto his collar and down his shirtfront, turning him and his only handkerchief into a dirty, sodden mass. To think that he'd been worrying over staining his breeches, kneeling on the damp ground to propose to Lady Susannah. Instead his name was being dragged through the mud. His neckcloth was ruined, along with his reputation. Worst of all, his heart was close to breaking.

What else could he do but return the runaway to her school? Lud knew he could not afford to hire her governesses and nursery maids. A hair ribbon and a clean handkerchief were the best he could manage with his current situation. In another month he would lose the family estate unless he could find the wherewithal to pay the creditors he'd inherited along with the title and property. Gregory's father had gambled on 'Change and ended with nothing but worthless stocks. His older brother had wagered on fast horses, and ended with a broken neck. Gregory had just gambled on marrying an earl's daughter—and lost. Now he was in worse straits than before, with the bank sure to discover that his golden goose had flown the coop. Word of the debacle in the park would already be flying from club to coffeehouse to servants' quarters. The bankers would not wait much longer before installing their own manager at Belle Towers, a land agent who would squeeze every last shilling from the already impoverished tenants. Viscount Bryson would have to seek employment—though Zeus knew he was unskilled for any position—or join the army.

If he could not care for his own dependents, Viscount Bryson could certainly not support an unknown infant. Besides, Hannah needed a woman's care, a female's education. She needed a home with people who knew how to raise a child, who could give her respectability along with affection.

The archwife at the academy would not have known affection if it bit her on the arse. Miss Chiswell was a dry old stick, who kept a stick near to hand. Gregory did not wish to think about the uses for such an implement. This was an establishment for little ladies, by Jupiter, not hell-born boys.

He put Hannah down once they were shown into Miss Chiswell's office, but the girl clung to his leg. The headmistress came around from behind her desk when they entered, but all she said was "Well, well, well."

"Not well at all," Gregory replied. "I found one of your charges playing truant."

Miss Chiswell ignored his words, studying the unkempt gentleman and his butter stamp instead. She quickly noted the lack of shine to his boots, the slightly ragged edge of his coat sleeve, the length of his untrimmed hair. There was no money to be had here, so she did not bother with polite insincerity. "I see the brat landed on her feet after all."

"No, she landed in the dirt." Gregory handed Hannah the doll she'd insisted be carried, too, hoping she'd then release his leg. "Why was she not under your supervision? How could you permit a mere babe to be out on her own?"

Miss Chiswell's nostrils flared so, she looked like a hound on the scent of a fox. "You are a fine one to ask, sirrah. Why was she not under your protection all these years?"

Because her mother had never been under his protection, Gregory wanted to shout, but he knew this tight-lipped matron would never believe anything but the evidence of her own eyes. "I never knew of her existence until this afternoon. My deceased brother might have. I have no way of knowing. She is a sweet little thing but she is not mine, so I am returning Hannah to you." He started to pry Hannah's fingers off his legs. A barnacle would have been easier to dislodge.

"Not so fast. Her tuition has not been paid."

What was left of Gregory's poor heart sank, and his light purse grew poorer. He'd have to pay the witch's fees, of course, which meant he was that much further behind on the mortgage payments. What was the difference? He had no chance of meeting the new year's deadline. He nodded.

"No, Papa," Hannah cried. "Do not leave me here!"

"For the last time, poppet, I am not your father, and you have to—"

"No! They take the money and never use it on us. Miss Chiswell buys herself jewelry that she puts on when no one is looking and—"

"That will be enough, Hannah," the headmistress said, reaching for Hannah's arm and dragging her away from Lord Bryson.

"—and Mr. Chiswell visits Sukey Johnson every week, and everyone knows she is a—"

Miss Chiswell slapped Hannah so hard the child would have fallen, except that Gregory caught her, and folded her back against his chest, doll and all.

"I have reconsidered," he told the woman on his way out. "Hannah will not be staying here after all. I would not leave my dog in this place, under your care."

"Do you have a dog, Papa? Can I play with him? What's his name?"

Gregory was so angry that he walked seven blocks with Hannah in his arms jabbering away before he recalled the curricle and groom he'd left waiting. "We can send him back for your belongings."

Hannah tried to brush the dirt off her doll's skirt so the embroidered hearts showed. "I already have Valentina, and that's all I own."

Gregory cursed under his breath. The chit did not have a change of clothes? A nightgown? A hairbrush of her own? He could not decide whom he wished to strangle most: Miss Chiswell, Ann Marvell, or his own dearly—but less dear by the moment—departed brother.

As he lifted Hannah into the curricle, he noticed the scarlet mark of the Chiswell bitch's hand on the child's cheek. "Does that hurt, sweetheart? We'll put a cold cloth on it as soon as we reach my flat."

"Oh, no, Papa," she said, reaching out to touch his own cheek where he'd have a black-and-blue bruise by morning. "Now we just match better."

When they reached the building on the fringes of Mayfair where he rented rooms, Hannah looked up at the soot-darkened town house and said, "It is very small."

"Yes, but it is all I can afford. Bellington House in Berkeley Square is let to mushrooms this year, to help pay expenses." And the bedroom and sitting room on the third floor here were all he needed, actually. They had never looked quite so small, or messy, though. His landlady came once a week to tidy up—when he could pay her extra. Gregory could not quite recall when the last time had been.

No matter, he told himself. This was a temporary arrangement only. Tomorrow he would think of another solution to the problem of Hannah. If he thought his aunt was in Bath, he could ship the tot off to her there—but Aunt Elvira might already be on her way to the Ravencroft Christmas party. Surely he knew some other woman who would take in a pretty little girl who was brave and bright and helpful. Why, Hannah was already pouring hot water into his washbasin.

"There, now Valentina is not so dirty," she announced when he turned back from hanging their wraps on the pegs by the door.

The floor was wet. His bed was wet. The landlady was madder than a wet hen.

"You never said nothin' 'bout no young 'un," Mrs. Cauffin said, breathing hard and wiping at beads of perspiration on her florid face after the climb up the stairs. "That'll be extra on the rent. And more iffen you expect me to feed her. Or make up a cot. Or do her linens. Or—"

"Yes, yes, Mrs. Cauffin. We'll figure it all out in the morning," Gregory said, shooing the fat old woman out the door before she could think of more ways to charge for her slovenly services. "With any luck, I will have made other arrangements by then."

Why Lord Bryson thought he might get lucky now, he could not begin to imagine. Luck had not been on his side for years. Still, one of his friends must know a nice childless couple, or a family kind enough to take in one more little mouth to feed. How much could such a wisp of a thing like Hannah eat, anyway?

Enough for a regiment, it seemed. Mrs. Cauffin's tally was growing faster than she could count on her sausage-shaped fingers. The viscount could not begrudge the child the extra helpings, though, not when she told him of the usual fare at Miss Chiswell's. Hannah had never even seen a trifle before.

"I will be going out later, Mrs. Cauffin," Gregory had to say. "Will you watch Hannah for me? This being a new place, and all, I do not like to leave her alone."

"It'll cost extra."

Everything did.

Gregory waited for Hannah to fall asleep before he left. She was snuggled on the worn sofa, since he was not giving up his own bed, and there was no room in the narrow apartment for a cot. She was wearing one of his best shirts, with the sleeves rolled up, and her silver-blond hair was in the messiest braid he'd ever seen. He'd have to get better at that task, Gregory told himself, for his own mane would need plaiting soon.

He had not known any bedtime stories, so the viscount had read an article on agriculture from the latest farming journal—as if he could ever implement the latest advances at Belle Towers. His choice of reading material did not matter. Hannah fell asleep with a smile on her face and the broken-nosed doll in her arms.

Lud, she looked like an angel. How could anyone not want this little darling? This expensive, scandal-ridden responsibility, Gregory reminded himself with a wrench to his heartstrings, on the way to his club.

Everyone had heard of Hannah already, of course. Being accosted by one's bastard in the park was many a gentleman's worst nightmare, and the best joke, since Bryson was the one singled out as sire, not any of them. He tried to pass Hannah off as his dead brother's, without much success, without mentioning the Marvelous Ann Marvell. Finding Hannah a home would be difficult enough, without adding the onus of a notorious high flyer for a mother.

No one knew of possible foster parents.

"What, for your bastard, cousin? Why should anyone take in your dirty linen?"

Floyd Bellington was the last person Lord Bryson wished to see. Hell, the overdressed Captain Sharp was the last person Gregory would want to have as a relation. The dirty dish was a first cousin, unfortunately, and next in line to the viscountcy at that. If not for Floyd, Gregory could have broken the entailment on the property he'd inherited. He could have sold the London town house to pay the mortgage on Belle Towers, or sold off some of the outlying acres to finance necessary improvements to bring in higher profits. Floyd, however, would not agree. He wished to inherit the trappings of a peer, the London mansion, the country estate, not just an empty title.

No matter that Gregory was not yet thirty, with his whole life ahead, and no plans to cock up his toes in the foreseeable future. As Floyd was wont to remind him, Gregory's brother Gordon had not been intending to break his neck in that horse race, either.

Now Floyd smoothed down his fair hair, which was not as pale as Gregory's, but was fashioned into a stylish Brutus cut. "You might try to claim the brat was Gordon's, but no one will believe you, not after that contretemps in the park. The chit must know her own father, wouldn't you say? And there's no hiding she's your spit and image, I hear. What decent family will take in a soiled piece of goods like that?"

"I am sure there must be one somewhere, Floyd," Gregory replied. "After all, your mother kept you."

After that, the viscount's appetite for cards, brandy, and male company was gone. The stakes were too high, the cigar smoke was too thick, the ribald jokes too much at his expense. Besides, he could not stop thinking about Hannah left in his rooms with no one but the landlady. What if Hannah awoke, frightened? Worse, what if she did not awake, and a candle tipped over? Or she could fall off the sofa. He should have drawn the chair next to her makeshift bed, but what did he know of children? Why, she could have strangled on the cord he used to tie her braid, or been sick from all the unaccustomed food he let her eat. Thunderation, the mercenary Mrs. Cauffin might have sold Hannah to white slavers.

He went home.

Hannah was sleeping peacefully, and so was Mrs. Cauffin, his last bottle of cognac half empty at her side. Well, at least he could make the old besom deduct that from his bill. He shook the landlady awake and sent her off, and then he stood over the sofa, shielding the candle with his hand so it didn't shine in Hannah's eyes. Before taking it to his own bedroom, to finish reading the farm journal, he gently brushed Hannah's hair off her face and retucked the blankets around her. This time he placed the doll on the top of the covers. He'd wanted to toss the ruined thing out, but Hannah had protested that Valentina was the only gift she had ever received from her mother, along with a note that said "Always in my heart."

Always in Ann Marvell's heart? Hah. The woman had no heart, to abandon her infant to Miss Chiswell, and then to leave the country without making provisions for the child. Lud, the little sprite deserved so much more out of life then she'd received, and more than Gregory could give her.

4

Morning brought no answers, just a squawking bird chirping too loudly for Lord Bryson's sore head. No, that was no bird, it was Hannah singing. His brother had never been able to carry a tune, either. The off-key lilt was too cheery, too loud, and too early. Dawn was barely breaking over the rooftops, and Gregory had stayed up half the night thinking, finishing that bottle of cognac. Now he had a headache on top of his other woes, and a barefoot urchin was sitting on top of his bed.

Lud, he'd have to start wearing a nightshirt. He pulled the covers higher.

"Good morning, Papa," Hannah trilled. She grinned, and now he could see that her bottom front tooth was missing. If that Chiswell crone had knocked it out beforetimes he'd . . .

"I am not your papa," he said with a growl. "You may call me uncle, I suppose. Uncle Gregory, or Uncle Bryson. Not Papa. Do you understand?"

Her smile fading, Hannah nodded. She understood tempers, all right, after living with Miss Chiswell for six years. She slipped off the bed and edged toward the door. "Mrs. Cauffin told me all gentlemen were like bloody bears in the morning. Shall I fetch your chocolate?"

Now Gregory had to feel guilty at her wary look, besides feeling like he'd wrestled with that same bear, and lost. He managed a "Please, thank you" before noticing that Hannah's sleeves—the sleeves of his best dress shirt—were no longer rolled up. They were cut off, and raggedly at that, at her wrists.

When Hannah noticed where he was staring, speechless, she held up her doll, and a scissors. "See?

I made a bandage for Valentina's broken arm, and a sling. Now she does not look so sad, except for her nose. Do you not think so?"

He thought he could cheerfully have tossed her and her blasted doll out the window. How could he have thought this imp of Satan an angel?

"Go away, brat, and let me get dressed." When she was almost at his bedroom door, he added, "And do not go outside, do not play with scissors or water or my wardrobe. Do not enter this room without knocking, and do not repeat anything Mrs. Cauffin says. If I hear you say 'bloody' once more, I will wash your mouth out with soap. Unless, of course, you cut yourself with that scissors I wish you would put down. Is that clear?"

"Yes, Papa."

Gregory groaned. What the deuce was he going to do with Hannah? Neither sleep nor spirits had brought him an answer. Now his rooms seemed smaller and dingier, his landlady coarser and less accommodating. This was no place for a child, not for so much as another day.

The viscount was nearly resigned by now to losing Belle Towers. Neither his father nor his brother had shown much interest in keeping the old place going, except for promising to redeem the debts with the next financial coup, the next winning racer. Neither had done more than sink them further in debt, and Gregory was faring no better. His total worldly assets, all he'd managed to scrimp and save from the meager farm rents, the paltry bank interest, a few clever wagers, would still fall far short of the next payment on Belle Towers that was due to his creditors right after Christmas. If he took out a sum for Hannah's care . . .

He had no choices left, after all. What he could do

now was go to Berkshire, to see if there was anything remaining in the Towers to sell. Surely there was something that was not listed in the entailment, some bit of his mother's jewelry, some silver candlestick that could go toward purchasing his passage to America and a tiny plot of land there, after he saw Hannah established in a proper school, with a proper trust fund set up for her future. Perhaps he could send for her in time, if the former colonies proved welcoming, and if he proved a capable farmer. Birth did not matter as much in the New World, he understood, so Hannah would not face as much censure. Hell, away from England and Debrett's, he might even be able to call himself a widower with a little girl, a legitimate little girl.

He could not drag the infant off to Berkshire with him, though, not in this cold weather, not when he meant to ride cross-country and sleep in barns to save money. So what was he to do with Hannah in the meantime? Certainly he could not leave her here with his bloody landlady, Mrs. Cauffin.

The only solution that had come to his admittedly wine-soaked mind, however, was a soft voice, a gentle touch, and intelligent green eyes. Miss Claire Haney would know what to do. He could not afford her services, of course, even if he had a place to lodge her and Hannah, but she might know of another governess with as sympathetic a manner, one who was between positions and might be willing to take Hannah into her own home. It would be a temporary solution, until he could find a decent school. Miss Haney might be of assistance there, too, he thought. She seemed knowledgeable, capable, and caring. Ladylike, she would be a good influence on Hannah, not enriching the chit's vocabulary with gutter language. She was pretty, too.

It was too bad, Gregory thought as he dressed, that he could not winkle Miss Haney away from that harridan, Lady Handbury, for soon enough the governess would lose her sweet, fresh look to become another overworked, underappreciated, downtrodden upper servant.

Then again, at least Miss Haney had a paying position, which was more than Gregory had.

The butler at Handbury House advised the viscount—with a superior sniff toward his tiny companion—that Lord Handbury was not at home. Gregory had decided that he could not simply call on the man's sons' governess, not without seeking Handbury's permission first. Handbury's wife was certain to make Miss Haney's life miserable if she thought the governess was entertaining gentlemen on the sly. With Handbury from home, though, Gregory had no alternative. He was not about to beard Lady Handbury in her den, or in her parlor, as the case might be. So he asked for a few moments of Miss Haney's time. "The governess, you know, about, ah, about a place for my ward."

The butler curled his lip. "Miss Haney is his lordship's sister, my lord, not an employee. Should you wish to confer with the young gentlemen's tutor?"

Gregory felt the tips of his ears turning red. From the cold, he told himself, although the room where he and Hannah were shown was quite warm. "No, I believe Miss Haney would be better informed about girls' schools and such."

"Quite," the butler said, bowing himself out of the room with the viscount's hat and gloves.

Hannah was staring around at the extravagantly decorated parlor. "It is a very fancy house, isn't it?"

Gregory also noticed the profusion of china shepherdesses, jade figurines, and other expensive, breakable items on every surface, so he told her to sit still in a gilt chair. Then he saw a dish of comfits and popped one in her mouth, to keep her happy and quiet.

In a short time—too short for the viscount to reorder his thinking to fit the new circumstances—Miss Haney entered the room. She was prettier than he remembered, with a warm, welcoming smile. She still wore gray, but now he could see that the gown was finely made of softest merino wool, with fancy lace trim, and graced a pleasingly curved figure. Her hair was pinned looser today, too, with soft curls framing smooth cheeks. Her green eyes were sparkling with tiny gold flecks. All in all, Handbury's sister looked as delectable as one of the bonbons Hannah was eating.

"Thank you for seeing us," he began, after making his bow and nudging Hannah into a curtsy. "We met yesterday in the park, although I fear there was no formal introduction that would have made this visit proper."

"He thought you were the governess," Hannah piped up.

Gregory clamped his hand over her mouth, leaving his palm with the sticky residue of the sugared sweet she'd eaten.

Claire looked down at her gray dress. "I am in mourning, my lord. But it is a natural mistake."

"I am sorry for your loss, ma'am," Gregory said, wondering how he was to wipe his hand before taking his leave, and taking hers in his. She solved that problem by ringing for tea, and the cook's special gingerbread biscuits for Hannah. Napkins appeared along with the welcome refreshments.

After she had poured, letting Hannah help add milk and sugar—far more sugar than Gregory liked—she smiled at him and asked how she could be of service to him and his . . . ?

"Ward, Miss Haney. I found that the school where Hannah was residing was unsuitable, and I have no knowledge of any others. I was hoping you might know a woman interested in keeping Hannah for a bit, while I make other arrangements."

Claire was admiring Hannah's doll, thinking what a handsome pair these two callers were, with their matching blue eyes and long, straight, silvery-blond hair. She was pleased, somehow, that the viscount was finally meeting his responsibilities toward the child, for handsome was as handsome did, and his lordship was handsome indeed.

She wished she could help him, and the adorable little miniature version sitting beside her. She could not take in the child, of course, although if she were still in the country, running her father's house, she would not have hesitated an instant. Miss Haney of Handbury Hall could be as generous as she pleased. Her father was gone, though, and Claire was mistress of nothing. She had never felt her helplessness so strongly, nor the loss of her parents. "I am sorry, but I have not been in London long enough to know many people, and those friends I have made are gone away for the Christmas holidays. My old nurse would be perfect, for she adores children, although Diana, Lady Handbury, that is, feels Nanny is too ancient to have charge of her sons. But Nanny is in Wales visiting her own family while I am away from home."

Claire was in London against her will, but she saw

no reason to mention that to this town-bronzed gentleman. Diana had insisted on Claire's presence so a husband could be found for her, now that Claire's mourning period was almost over. Lady Handbury knew she could never be true mistress of Handbury Hall, not while the beloved daughter of the house remained there.

Gregory stood to leave, having stayed longer than the proper time for a morning call, but with no further excuse to remain except the warmth of Miss Haney's smile. He had no business being here in the first place, with no chaperon but Hannah. If he could not afford to hire Miss Haney as governess, he could definitely not afford to call on Miss Haney, Lord Handbury's sister.

Lady Handbury agreed with him. Having berated the butler for not informing her of the callers at once, Diana bustled into the room, all fluttering flounces and flapping strings of beads. She did not pause for polite greetings, but rapped Miss Haney's wrist with her closed fan. "What is the meaning of this, Claire? Entertaining a gentleman on your own? You ought to know better by now, at your advanced age. How many times have I told you, country manners will not do in town? You will have the entire *ton* gossiping about us, especially after that scandal in the park yesterday. I told your brother we will never be able to find a gentleman willing to wed the gauche female you have become."

She paused for breath and turned to Gregory, fixing him in her beady-eyed stare. "As for you, Bryson, how dare you bring your rubbish here to further besmirch my sister-in-law's good name? Heaven knows you ought to know better than to parade your bastard around the city. Feckless, you are, just like your brother and your father before him."

Gregory clamped his hands over Hannah's ears this time. "My apologies, madam, for mistaking this for a house of good will. My ward and I will not be troubling you further. Good day."

"And good riddance, I say. No doubt you thought to foist your by-blow off on my tenderhearted sister-in-law, who is known to be forever taking in wounded birds and feeding toothless old dogs. Well, that won't wash, sirrah. The very idea of bringing that creature into my home makes me shudder."

"Me, too, Lady Handbury, me, too," Gregory told her as he lifted Hannah into his arms. "And you are perfectly correct. Such a precious little girl does not belong here." He walked out of the room without a backward look, not even making his bow to Miss Haney, he was that furious.

So was Claire. She had been rapped with that fan once too often, and been subjected to her sister-in-law's harangues twice too often. She might be no more than Lord Handbury's beloved younger sister, but she was a woman grown, and not beholden to her brother—or his wife—for her sustenance. She reached for the fan when Diana raised it once more to emphasize her last point. Claire made a point of her own, several, actually, in small broken pieces of the dratted thing that fell one by one to the floor.

"Never again," she said, snapping the last stick. "You will never raise your hand to me again. Nor will you insult a guest of mine again."

Then she flew down the hall, past the butler, out the door, and onto the walkway. "My lord," she called, not caring that she was, indeed, creating grist for the rumor mills. She was not even wearing a bonnet or gloves, although hailing a chance-met gentleman in the street had to be a far greater crime against society's strictures. To the devil with society, the city, and her sister-in-law, she decided. Claire Haney could not turn aside a fellow man—not this one, at any rate—in need.

5

"Lord Bryson, wait!"

That got his attention, and that of a passing jarvey, Lady Harkness who lived next door, and a maid and a footman sneaking a kiss behind the garden gate.

Gregory turned with Hannah still in his arms where he thought he could protect her from everything but insult. "Miss Haney, you have no coat on. Go back inside."

"No, not until I apologize for my sister-in-law and invite you and Hannah to return."

"I doubt Lady Handbury sent you out in the cold to request our company. She is correct, however. I do not belong there, yet I was indeed hoping to appeal to your gentle nature. Now I could not feel welcome inside, nor would I subject you or Hannah to any more of Lady Handbury's vituperation. You have nothing for which you need apologize, for you have been nothing but kindness itself. Thank you and good day."

She had been dismissed. Claire nodded. "It is quite cold." And she had cold feet about offering her aid to a top of the trees gentleman. Her idea was so presumptuous, he was liable to think her some poor country spinster tossing her handkerchief at his feet, which she was not, of course. What, consider Lord Bryson an eligible *parti*? Never. His lordship was known to be pockets-to-let, seeking to repair his tattered fortune with a dowry darning needle. After yesterday's events, rumor had him the worst kind of rakehell, seducing a young woman and then abandoning her and the resultant infant. Diana had been pleased to announce at the breakfast table that all doors were likely closed to Gregory, Viscount Bryson, from that day hence.

The butler coughed, reminding her that the door to Handbury House stood ajar. Well, Claire had no intentions of sending out lures to a gazetted fortune hunter and libertine. It was nearly Christmas, though, and he did seem concerned about finding loving care for the love child, whosesoever Hannah might be. Claire liked him, and she liked Hannah. It would never do to say so, naturally, but perhaps she could convince her brother to lend assistance to the gentleman. Right after she convinced Handbury to let her set up her own establishment.

Claire retraced her steps, thinking of what she could do when she had the ordering of her own household, but she halted when Lord Bryson called out, asking her to wait. She could feel her heart lift, foolish thing that it was, as she turned back.

Gregory strode up to her, holding Hannah as effortlessly as if she were an umbrella or a cane. "We were about to sample the wares of a nearby sweetshop, to relieve a somewhat bitter taste. Would you care to accompany us? With your outer garments, of course, and a maid, to play propriety."

She would, more than she should. Claire ran off to fetch her cloak and bonnet.

While they waited, Gregory made sure that his hair was neat, that his cravat was unrumpled by Hannah's grasp around his neck, and that his nose was not going to disgrace him. He retied the bow on Hannah's bonnet and tried to gather her loose hair back with another ribbon. "We have to make a good impression on the lady, poppet," he told the little girl.

"Why, Papa? She already likes us."

Gregory remembered Miss Haney's smile when he extended his impromptu invitation. He smiled himself. "She does, doesn't she?"

While Hannah tried to decide whether cream-filled pastries or raspberry tarts were her favorites, Claire and the viscount discussed his predicament. Gregory made no secret of his financial straits, for the so-called polite world would learn of Belle Towers's loss within days of the new year.

"If I had enough time, I might be able to turn things around. But now with needing to make provision for Hannah, I fear I am out of options."

Claire feared he would never accept assistance from her brother, if she could urge Handbury into offering any, which was dubious, considering Diana's attitude. Handbury and the viscount were acquaintances, merely, not close friends. Neither would Lord Bryson accept a loan from her, she knew, for gentlemen had their odd notions of honor. She could offer an interim proposal, however.

"My lord, do you have plans for the Christmas holidays?"

Gregory's eyes clouded. He'd forgotten all about Christmas, thinking of New Year's and the mortgage payments. "I had intended to go to Ravencroft for the gala, along with half the *ton,* I suppose. Now . . ." He shrugged, not wanting to say that, with the heiress turning her back on him, he had no reason to go and would be uncertain of his welcome. He also had Hannah to worry about, but did not want to ruin the imp's enjoyment of her first lemon ice by saying so.

Claire nodded. "I thought you would be invited. I will be going, and I think you ought to come, you and Hannah."

Hannah put down her spoon, her eyes wide. "To a duchess's house?"

Gregory could have echoed her sentiment. "I do not think Her Grace . . ."

"The Duchess of Ravencroft is my godmother, you know. Any guest of mine will be welcome," she stated with conviction. "The nursery will be filled, with scores of maids and nurses, so one more child will not matter. And I will have time to spend with Hannah, for I do not intend to partake of many of the entertainments, since I am in mourning."

"That is a generous offer, indeed, Miss Haney. Ravencroft is near Belle Towers, where I was thinking of going anyway. And my aunt will be at Ravencroft," Gregory mused out loud, "since she and the duchess are bosom bows. My cousin Floyd is also attending, unfortunately, but I could then ask Aunt Elvira if she would care for Hannah in Bath until I come about. If you are sure the duchess will not mind?"

"Her Grace is everything generous. In fact, I am intending to ask her if I cannot stay on after the holidays. She is always urging me to consider a long visit, and this shall be it. I doubt she thought I meant to stay until I reach my majority, but Ravencroft can house any number of guests, and we go on well together." Much better than Claire rubbed along with her sister-in-law Diana, but that, too, was left unsaid. "If your aunt cannot look after a young child, perhaps you would consider leaving Hannah with me, if you need to."

Gregory was almost speechless with the offer, but he had to ask, "And after you attain your majority, what then?"

"Why, then I shall have a home of my own, and may invite whomever I wish."

Gregory assumed she meant with a husband of her choice. Perhaps she was merely waiting until she was out of mourning, or came into an inheritance at that date. Her eagerness to leave the London Marriage Mart meant she had the lucky gentleman already selected. Of course she did, such a charming female. Otherwise, eligible gentlemen would be swarming Handbury House. The chap must be a paragon indeed, if she was so sure he would accept Hannah into his home.

"I will think about attending," he said, half decided that he should have one happy Christmas among family and friends, with good food and good cheer, before the vicissitudes of life intruded again. His raspberry ice went untasted as he considered that this might even be his last Christmas in England. Hannah should enjoy herself, too, for he doubted there had been much celebrating at Chiswell Academy. He doubted the sprout had ever played snapdragon, or tasted wassail. Likely she had not ridden on the Yule log as it was dragged back to the house, helped decorate kissing boughs, nor made pudding wishes, all the things he recalled from his own youth. He wondered if she had ever received a Christmas gift—and doubted it.

Hannah deserved this holiday for, despite Miss Haney's kindly meant offer, who knew what the new year would bring to any of them? The duchess could decline to house a baseborn child, or she could decide to go traveling with Miss Haney as companion. His aunt's rheumatics might make her refuse to take Hannah. A hundred things could happen, all of them dreary and depressing. The mention of dreary reminded Gregory of his shabby flat. The thought of spending Christmas there, with the greasy goose Mrs. Cauffin was bound to cook, was appalling. So was the cold lonely trek to Belle Towers to sell off the silverware, leaving Hannah with who knew what strangers.

"You might also consider the visit a chance to mend your fences with Lady Susannah," Claire forced herself to say.

He laughed. "I doubt there is any hope in that quarter. Nor do I wish to try. I find that I cannot be comfortable with the notion of courting a woman who thinks the worst of me, without waiting to hear my side of the story."

"But she is so beautiful."

"Yet I would have to converse with the woman, spend years in her company, not just look at her."

"What of her dowry?" Not that money would solve all of the viscount's problems, Claire knew, but it would make the others easier to swallow.

"No, not even for her father's blunt. I am not that much of a fortune hunter that I would live my life with a shrew, no matter how pretty or wealthy." He looked over at Hannah, and tucked the serviette more securely under her chin. "Nor ask Hannah to live with one." They both knew that Lady Susannah would never accept Hannah into her family, no more than Lady Handbury would. Gregory realized he wanted a different type of woman to be mother to his children, a woman who was kind and loving, not merely a beautiful ornament of the beau monde.

Claire silently agreed that he was well out of that match. She was also much relieved that he was not pining after a lost love, or a lost opportunity. "Then

you will come? I was going to offer to take Hannah
with me, if you would not. I am leaving within days,
and have already bespoken a carriage and outriders,
and rooms reserved along the way. I am sure my
brother would welcome my having a gentleman
escort."

So he would not have to hire a coach or horses? So
Hannah would be warm and watched at night? Gregory suddenly felt years younger, pounds lighter, and
he owed it all to this darling young lady. He could
have kissed her, if they were not in public. Instead he
dabbed at a bit of strawberry jam that had landed on
the corner of her mouth.

Blushing, Claire looked down at her plate. "My elderly cousin goes, too, of course, so there is no need
to worry about our reputations."

It was hers that was going to be affected by their
proximity. "Are you sure? You could wait and go with
Lord Handbury's party."

Claire looked up and met his concern with a smile.
"Positive. This way Diana will have to cope with her
own children by herself, for a change. The nursemaid's
mother died, which is why I was in the park with
my nephews."

So they made plans, and set times. Claire had much
to do, with packing and sending messages and appeas-
ing her brother.

Gregory and Hannah had to go shopping. His ward
could not appear at the ducal residence with one faded
dress and one yellowed pinafore, to say nothing of her
one pair of badly darned stockings. She had no hope
of being treated like a gentleman's ward if she looked
like a debtor's daughter. Gregory decided that his own
honor would be at stake if his niece, which was what
he was calling Hannah in his own mind, were not

treated with respect. He could not go around calling out children in the Ravencroft nursery, but he could deuced well make sure his charge looked as prosperous as they did.

The hackney driver knew of a shop on the fringes of Mayfair that sold made-up goods for children. Some had been worn only once, when the rich swells' youngsters outgrew their party clothes. The castoffs were often given to the maids, who in turn sold them to a used clothing merchant. That would have to do, since they had no time to buy fabrics and hire seamstresses—and Gregory had as much understanding of little girls' wardrobes as he had of a Hottentot's.

The proprietress of the store knew exactly what was required, thank goodness. She had two sprigged frocks and a crisp pinafore with eyelet trim, in just the right size. She also carried flannel petticoats, flannel nightwear, white stockings, and an assortment of ribbons. Gregory added them all to their growing pile, while Hannah stood with her eyes wide and round.

She tugged on the viscount's arm until he bent down, then whispered in his ear, "I thought we were poor, Papa."

"Next month we will be poor, poppet. Today we are merely in straitened circumstances, not so far below hatches we cannot afford a special dress for Christmas." He knew the children would be brought down to join the company for the holiday, and wanted Hannah to look her best. Her birth might be questionable, but she would not be ashamed of her appearance, not if Gregory had anything to say about it. "Something in velvet," he told the shopkeeper.

The woman brought out a pretty red velvet dress, perfect for the festive season, she cooed, ideal for

Hannah's pale hair. It was too red for Gregory's taste, too suggestive of scarlet women. "Blue, I think. To match her eyes."

The woman did have one small blue gown, but it was new, exquisitely embroidered with tiny flowers, and dear. The child's wealthy mother had decided she wanted her daughter dressed in green satin to match her own gown, instead of the ruffled blue velvet. "We will take it," Gregory said the instant he saw the thing. Hannah would look as pretty as a princess.

"You mean no one has ever worn it before?" she whispered again, this time in awe, cautiously touching the soft fabric. "I am to be the very first?"

"And the most beautiful."

"But will our 'stances get straighter?"

"We will stand tall and proud, looking our finest."

6

They were not poor yet, but they would be soon. Gregory figured he could save the month's rent, at least, by deciding not to go back to Mrs. Cauffin's hovel after the holidays. Lud knew he had few enough possessions, so what he was not taking with him to Ravencroft could be put in storage at Bellington House. The place might be rented, but the attics were still his.

They still needed to bring gifts for the duke and duchess, however.

The used apparel storekeeper directed them to a curio shop nearby, where they could find trinkets and treasures at far better prices than on Bond Street. Gregory was not familiar with the establishment, but he was all too conversant with its three-balled brethren.

He instantly spotted an intricately carved briar for the pipe-smoking duke, an ivory needle case for the duchess, and a silk scarf with a gold fringe for his aunt Elvira. In a tray of combs and brushes, he found a set with the initial *A* carved into the backs, but with so many loops and flourishes, it might have been an *H,* for Hannah.

She was staring at a row of dolls on a shelf, so Gregory put back the fob watch he fancied, having pawned his own ages ago. "Which one do you fancy, poppet?"

None, it seemed, were as perfect as Valentina, despite her chipped nose and bandaged arm. Hannah did want a tiny sewing kit, though, so she could make pen wipes out of the remnants of Lord Bryson's butchered shirtsleeves for Gregory and Mrs. Cauffin and Miss Haney.

Gregory wanted to get something for that young lady, too, but nothing seemed appropriate. Jewelry was too personal—and too expensive. He did not know her taste in books, doubted she'd want a fan or a knickknack after living with Lady Handbury, and hated the idea of giving her something as commonplace as a pair of gloves or an embroidered handkerchief. There was nothing commonplace about the lady who was rescuing Hannah and him from the doldrums.

Miss Haney deserved something special, something magical—something so far beyond his finances that Gregory lost the delight he'd been enjoying at shopping for Hannah and picking gifts, after years of counting his pennies. Claire had offered him a reprise, if not a permanent solution to his problems, and who

knew what might happen in the ensuing days before
the new year? Miss Haney had given him hope; Gregory had to find something better for her than a filigree
flower holder.

Hannah wanted him to buy their friend a porcelain
box for storing her hairpins, because it was heart-
shaped, like the embroidery on her doll's skirt. "And
we can say she will always be in our hearts, like
Valentina."

Too intimate? Too encroaching? Too absurd, with
her already promised to another man. Besides, the
clerk recalled that the box used to belong to a wine-
merchant's widow, for her false teeth.

They looked at perfume bottles and hair combs and
cameos and card cases. Hannah thought Miss Haney
might enjoy a pin cushion in the shape of a horse and
carriage. The clerk felt every lady ought to have a pair
of opera glasses. Gregory was undecided between a
velvet-covered journal with silver corners and a
mother-of-pearl inlaid music box. Then he saw the
telescope.

He'd spent hours in one of Belle Towers's towers
as a boy, memorizing the planets and constellations,
forgetting his mother's final illness, his father's reck-
less investments, his brother's restless spirit. He could
not give Miss Haney diamonds and pearls, but he
could give her the moon and stars, in gratitude.

The journey to Ravencroft would have been a nightmare on Gregory's budget, with bad horses, bad food,
and bedbugs, to say nothing of a bored child. Instead,
the trip was a pleasure. And why not, with Lord
Handbury footing the bill? Miss Haney told Gregory
he could settle with her brother later, but that everything for her and her cousin's comfort was arranged

and paid for in advance. They had a modern, well-sprung carriage that easily seated the two Haney ladies, their maid, Hannah, and him, though the maid chose to ride up with the coachman, her beau, when the weather was nice. Lord Handbury's own horses were waiting at the stages, and the finest accommodations were reserved when they stopped for the nights.

Hannah was a good traveler, despite never having been out of London before. She liked to watch the passing scenery, but liked to hear Miss Haney's cousin's stories more. Cousin Maudine knew every Minerva Press novel by heart, it seemed to Lord Bryson, who took his own turns sitting up with the driver, instead of listening to the overly dramatic tales. Luckily Cousin Maudine napped a lot. Then Hannah was happy to sit with the picture books or the pencils and drawing paper that Miss Haney had been wise enough to bring, experienced as she was with traveling with her nephews. Other times Hannah stitched together her pen wipes, with Claire's help, or she slept, usually in Gregory's arms, where she could be protected from the jouncing of the carriage.

During those quiet intervals, Claire did her needlework while Gregory read aloud from the book of poetry she'd brought, or they played backgammon, or simply talked. Or even more simply, did not, comfortable enough with each other now that silences were not awkward.

The viscount could not help comparing his current companion to his previous one. Lud, a mere jaunt through Hyde Park with Lady Susannah had been more of an ordeal than days spent in a coach with Miss Haney. The heiress had constantly whined about the cold and the wind, fussing with her furs, the hot bricks, and the lap robe. Miss Haney, comfortable, competent female that she was, never complained. And when she slept, he could watch her for hours.

For her part, Claire was satisfied that she'd done the right thing, taking Lord Bryson to her godmother. Despite her sister-in-law's ravings, the viscount was no rakeshame, not with a little girl asleep in his lap. He was courteous and caring, intelligent and good-humored. He'd even charmed Cousin Maudine, who was a confirmed romantic until it came to actually speaking with a gentleman. Surely, Claire prayed, the duke and duchess would find some way to help the viscount and the precious child sleeping so trustingly next to his broad chest. She told herself the twinge of jealousy she felt was over Hannah's adoration of her new papa, not the child's secure place against his heart—and *in* his heart.

When they reached Ravencroft, Hannah took one look at the huge, sprawling edifice that encompassed acres and centuries, and refused to get out of the carriage. "It is so big, Papa."

"Do not worry, puss, I will not let you get lost," Gregory told her, lifting Hannah out of the coach despite his own apprehensions. He had only Miss Haney's word that they would be welcome here.

The duchess dispelled his misgivings as soon as he'd made his bows, as best he could with Hannah clinging to his legs. Her Grace accepted Hannah's uncanny resemblance to him without a blink, then nodded. "Your brother Gordon was a gudgeon. Your father was a flea-wit. You, on the other hand, appear to be making something decent of yourself, my boy. You are already a better man—and a worthier peer—than either of them. Welcome to my home."

The duke was too eager to have his old friend's son listen to him recount the Indian wars to cavil about yet another infant in the nursery. Gregory could have brought Miss Chiswell's entire academy, and His Grace would have deployed them as Maratha soldiers to illustrate his maneuvers. He'd never had much to do with his own offspring. What did he care what Viscount Bryson did with his, as long as they left his maps and his books and his stuffed tiger alone?

Only three other children were yet in residence in the third-story nursery wing: two infants Hannah was better at soothing than their nursemaids, and an older boy with spectacles, who was happy enough with a little girl who admired his butterfly collection, instead of his soon-to-arrive, bullying older cousins. Lester shared his books and toys and puzzles and secret paths to Cook's pantry with Hannah, who shared her versions of Cousin Maudine's stories.

Hannah still carried her doll everywhere, even when Gregory and Claire took her outside the sprawling mansion. The viscount stopped protesting, to no avail anyway, when Claire reminded him of how much upheaval Hannah had known in such a short life, away from everyone and everything familiar. The doll was an old friend.

Claire and Gregory were like old friends by now, too, calling each other by first names when in private. For the next several days, there were many such times.

With the houseguests due to start arriving shortly, the duchess had much to accomplish, so Claire helped wherever she could. In the afternoons, Her Grace rested, to face the evening's entertainments. So did Cousin Maudine.

The Duke of Ravencroft invited Lord Bryson to follow along with him and his steward in the mornings, seeing how a great estate was run and how the home farms prospered, in case Gregory had a chance to restore Belle Towers to a profitable venture. After luncheon, the duke also rested, possibly with his duchess, which made Gregory envious of their long, happy marriage.

While their hosts were so occupied, Claire and Gregory collected Hannah, and often Lester, too, and went riding or driving or walking or exploring the ancient castle. The arrangement might not have been perfectly proper, but the two children made adequate chaperons, and who was to see or tell, anyway, when they kept to the vast Ravencroft grounds?

Gregory could not remember when he had last been so carefree, certainly not since before his father's death, when he realized the precarious state of the Bellington holdings, and also realized he was the only one of the family to care. For this interval, he vowed, he would not think of those responsibilities. He swore to enjoy himself for a change, without fretting over the future. He had the Ravencroft stables at his disposal, one of the duke's footmen to act as valet, and every comfort imaginable. The countryside was lovely and the company was . . . more so.

He found joy in giving Hannah new experiences: her first pony ride, her first try at milking a cow, her first glimpse of the nearly tame deer in the duke's home wood. Sharing the sprite's excitement with Claire only added to his own pleasure. She seemed to revel in the simple country pastimes, the companionship of children, the camaraderie of slipping away from duty and decorum for an enchanted holiday. She did not care that Hannah's birth was irregular, nor that his nose regularly ran in the cold. She never even held it against Gregory that he was a former fortune hunter or a down-at-heels debtor. No, she was having fun. In London the young ladies had pleasant times, being seen at the correct balls and banquets. They enjoyed themselves at the theater and the opera, or broadened their minds at artistic pursuits. They did not have fun. They did not laugh out loud, grin at silly jokes, run, or sit on the floor playing jackstraws. Claire did.

The sound of Claire's sweet laughter mingling with Hannah's little girl giggles as they played hide-and-seek among the ancient sets of armor in the castle's old wing was a memory Gregory would cherish forever, when this idyll ended.

End it must, although not because Miss Haney was promised to some rustic suitor or such, as Gregory had supposed. According to the duke's dinnertime teasing about her unwed state, Claire was simply fussy, not fixed on any particular gentleman. To Gregory's amazement, Claire was available then, which should have gladdened his heart even more than the sight of her sewing a cape for Hannah's doll. Miss Haney was available, however, to a gentleman of means with a secure future and untarnished reputation, one who could support her in comfort. Gregory could not keep a six-year-old child in comfits, much less afford a wife. No matter how Gregory tried to act the gentleman of leisure, his Bellington forebears had borne that fatal gambling flaw. If only—

Ifs were only for fools. If Gregory were not at point-non-plus, he would be at Belle Towers, not Ravencroft, engaged in agricultural pursuits, not play. He would never have gone to London searching for a wealthy wife to pull him out of River Tick, and so he would never have found Hannah or Miss Haney. He would have been poorer by half.

Instead of mooning over the past, or mourning for a future that could never occur, Gregory forced himself to wish for snow, so he and Claire could take Hannah sledding and building snowmen, or ice, so he and Claire could teach her to skate. He and Claire— Perhaps this holiday was not such an idyll after all.

And then the other guests arrived.

7

Claire was worried. With the advent of Advent, her holiday from her sister-in-law's harangues was over. She'd be tossed, willy-nilly, back into the matrimonial pond, with all the eligible young chubs and older lampreys come to ride the duke's horses and drink the duke's wine. She would rather stay out of those waters altogether.

She was also concerned for Lord Bryson. What if, contrary to his words, his feelings were still drawn to Lady Susannah? He might just take Claire's previous advice and renew his suit of the heiress. Worse, what if he pursued the beauty anyway, without affection for the female, or dangled after another well-dowered if not so comely daughter of the nobility? Claire could not bear to see her friend—for that was what they were, was it not?—either disappointed again, or proven a cad. If he did form a sincere attachment, not solely with the lady's purse, then he'd be leaving to restore his estates, taking Hannah away, and a part of Claire's heart, too, she feared. So she spent more time in the nursery with Hannah and the other children, away from Lady Handbury and away from the company, and away from Lord Bryson and his pursuit of heavy-pocket happiness.

Hannah was worried. She did not fear the boy bullies nor the silly befrilled girls now sharing the nursery wing. She had heard taunts all her life, and knew how to retreat to her own world, with her own doll for company. Besides, Miss Claire, called "Aunt" by half the children present, spent hours there, showing the others that Hannah was her particular friend. If they wanted to hear stories and play games with Aunt Claire, they had to be nice to Hannah. If that was not enough, bespectacled Lester seemed to have grown taller and stronger when one of the Handbury brats threatened to use Valentina as a croquet ball. No, Hannah was not afraid for herself during the house party; she was worried that her new papa might leave her here. Ravencroft was not her home, and never could be. She was sure that every young lady at the party was trying to trap him into marriage, for that was what Lester said his older stepsisters were always attempting to do to eligible gentlemen. Then Lord Bryson would go off with someone, like that tight-lipped lady in the park, and forget all about Hannah. She hugged the doll close and wished Miss Haney would return to the party, to watch out for Papa.

Gregory was worried, too, that Miss Haney's reputation had been blackened by association with him, that Hannah would be slighted, that Lady Susannah might expect him to renew his courtship.

No one needed to lose a moment's sleep over the situation. The earl's daughter gave Gregory the cut direct, at which he laughed out loud and continued down the steps to greet his aunt Elvira. Before dinner, when the children were brought down, the duchess herself declared Hannah the prettiest chit she'd seen in years, and the best behaved. No one dared whisper about her parentage after that, not to her face or Gregory's, at any rate.

They all had a good laugh at his expense the next

evening, though, when Hannah ran into the drawing room in tears, begging the viscount to tell that nasty Master Harold that they did have a house of their own, only they were raising toadstools there.

"No, poppet, I am letting Bellington House to mushrooms, the Murchesons, not letting them grow there."

"What about Belle Towers, cousin?" Floyd asked loudly enough for most of the company to hear. "What are you growing there, except deeper in debt?"

Gregory did not answer, escorting Hannah back to the nursery instead. Let them have their smirks and snide remarks. He was not finding any pleasure in the duke's guests anyway. The young men were idlers, the young ladies insipid. The older men were hardened gamesters like his cousin Floyd, drunks, debauchees, or dodderers. The older women were hard of hearing like his aunt Elvira, or hardened flirts, pea-hens, or harridans. Lord Bryson would much rather spend his time with Claire in the nursery, or with the duke and his steward.

He was not given the choice, however, as he could not offend his hosts by playing least in sight. No, he had to play at charades, and at whist, and at doing the pretty among the unattached females, the ones whose parents had not warned them away from a penniless viscount.

There were enough young ladies, or their mamas, willing to overlook his debts and his supposed daughter in favor of his title and his looks. Now that the duke's own valet had cut Lord Bryson's hair, Gregory was more in demand as a dinner companion or a dance partner, with a few invitations to dalliance thrown his way from older women. He could have picked the wealthiest one and secured his future, but he had lost interest in a marriage of convenience. Creatures like Lady Susannah were raised to expect an arranged match, and he would not have felt guilty offering one. The wife he wanted, the only woman he could envision spending his life with, was neither cold-blooded nor calculating—and he had nothing to offer her.

There were enough other females at the gathering, the ones like Lady Susannah who turned their backs on his attempts at conversation, or who drew their skirts aside when he stepped close, that Gregory became uncomfortable, as well as bored. The duchess's party seemed to be dividing into enemy camps, with the high sticklers on one side, the hopefuls on the other, with hecklers like Cousin Floyd in the middle.

It was time to leave. Gregory was not enjoying himself, never got to see Claire or spend time with Hannah, and was causing dissension at the duchess's do. His holiday was almost over, anyway, and he should see what funds he could squeeze out of Belle Towers before the bank took over. He'd thought to spend this season in luxurious surroundings, amid gay companions, drowning his despair in wassail and covering his cries with carol singing. Now he only wanted to go home, to spend this last Christmas under his own roof, leaky as it might be.

He could not take Hannah. She was happy here, well looked after, with friends of her own. Claire would see to her, he knew, but that was an imposition. The child's welfare was a matter of family, so he asked his aunt Elvira.

"What's that you say, Gregory? You want me to climb those stairs twice a day to look in on an orphan we have no proof is our relation? Oh, my joints ache at the very notion. I could send my maid, I suppose, but the lazy creature complains if I so much as send her to the kitchens here for a tisane, they are so far away."

As for taking Hannah home with her to Bath after the house party ended, Aunt Elvira was even more adamant. "What, keep a child? I am barely keeping household as it is. Besides, the house is hardly large enough for me and my maid and Floyd when he comes to call, which is seldom enough, I admit, yet I do need to have a bed for my dear boy, do I not?"

Gregory knew his cousin only visited Bath on repairing leases, hoping to winkle a few guineas from his mother until the dibs were in tune. Aunt Elvira could not afford a larger house, much less a little girl, but Floyd could afford rooms at the Albany and an expensive way of life. Not even the freshly cut evergreens could remove the stench of that.

Already feeling at fault that he could not lessen his aunt's burdens, Gregory had to humble himself further by begging his host's indulgence, leaving a child in his care while Gregory went off to conduct his business.

Surprisingly, Ravencroft made the viscount an offer of a loan. "No blame on you for the situation, I say," the duke declared, proposing to pay off the Belle Towers mortgage. "Asides, she's a sweet little thing, one of my favorites. I'd like to see the chit happy."

Gregory hoped His Grace was talking about Hannah, and not Ravencroft's goddaughter Claire, or else the feelings he'd been at such pains to conceal were obvious to everyone. Lud, that did not bear thinking on. Nor did accepting a loan he had no hopes of repaying.

"Well, think about it, my lad. Consider the offer for a few days more, just till Christmas, else the ladies will be upset if you leave. It never pays to disarrange a duchess's seating arrangement, you know. Now, did I ever tell you about the time that Punjab native went—"

Floyd had another offer, another loan in mind. Bellington's mother might be boiling her tea twice, but Floyd had enough blunt to pay Gregory a handsome sum—to leave the country. "You will never get to keep Belle Towers anyway, you know, cousin. The bank will have it before you can say jackrabbit. I am sure you would rather see the old pile stay in the family."

And Floyd would rather see himself there, as viscount. He'd pay Gregory to emigrate and renounce the title.

Gregory was astonished that his cousin had enough bold-faced brass to offer money in exchange for Bryson's heritage, and that he had enough of the ready to redeem the vouchers on Belle Towers, once it left Gregory's possession.

Floyd shrugged his padded shoulders. "The cards have been lucky. Too bad you did not have my talent for the baize tables, or good fortune at snabbling heiresses. I have half a mind to try for Lady Susannah myself, once I have a title to offer the Incomparable and her incredibly wealthy father."

"You have half a mind, period," Gregory said, "if you think I will accept your offer. Once I am quit of the succession, you will sever the entailment and sell the place off anyway, leaving the tenants and the retainers to starve while you seek your pleasures in London. You are no farmer, and you will not be master of Belle Towers. You will not be viscount while I have a breath in my body, no matter what I have in my bank account. I never wished to succeed my brother, but I did, so I will be Bryson until the day I die, and my sons after me."

Floyd straightened his expensive lace cuffs. "And what of your, ah, daughter? Will she like living out on the streets? Rest assured, I shall not support another man's bastard. Or did you think to offer for Miss Haney, inviting her to take up residence in that sty you call home?"

"Leave Miss Haney's name out of this, damn it, and climb back under your rock, Floyd. Or else accept *my* offer to name your seconds, if you have any acquaintances you call friend."

Floyd merely chuckled and strolled off, making Gregory rue the hasty words that were all too revealing about his feelings. Floyd was sure to make Claire the subject of more gossip now, damn him. And damn his fancified lace-edged shirtsleeves, too.

With dragging feet, Gregory climbed to the nursery wing, to explain to Hannah why he was leaving. She seemed to understand about debts and honor and obligations and selling one's prized possessions. She could not understand why she must stay behind.

"Because Belle Towers is a hard ride away and half shut up, with leaking roofs and smoking fireplaces. You will be much happier here with Miss Haney and the duchess and the other children. There will be a lot of wonderful surprises, too."

"But I have a surprise for you."

A pen wipe, he'd wager. "And I shall look forward to having it, on my return." They both knew he might not return at all.

"But, Papa," she said, "it is Christmas."

The tears in those blue eyes—eyes the same color as his—were like a knife to Gregory's innards, twisting. "Don't you cry," he ordered, to cover his own misery. "You always knew our holiday could not last. It was make-believe, a pretty story like the ones Miss Maudine told. I never was your father, and never can be. If I were going to have a little girl, I would wish for an angel just like you. But I cannot take care of you now, poppet. Miss Haney can, for the time being. Maybe someday . . ." He offered false hope, and they both knew it.

Hannah offered him her doll.

Gregory could feel his nose growing stuffy, and it wasn't even cold in the nursery. Valentina was Hannah's inseparable treasure, her beloved, the only reminder of the mother she never had, yet she would part with the doll, for him.

"I cannot take your Valentina," he said, embracing them both, being careful not to crush either of them. "She will be happier here, too. But know that I am not abandoning you, Hannah, either of you. I will always make sure you are safe, and that you will never have to go back to a place like Miss Chiswell's, no matter what I have to sell or do. You will always be in my heart, just as your mother wrote, as I hope to be in yours."

8

What a day for offers.

Claire heard that the viscount was leaving for his own derelict property the next morning, fully expecting to lose what was left of his patrimony. He had not yet lost his pride, according to her godfather, who admired Lord Bryson for turning down his loan and for not pursuing another heiress. "The chap is a fool," Ravencroft told her, "but a noble fool for all that.

He'd make some female a deuced fine husband," the duke hinted, "except that his honor will not let him ask a gentlewoman to share his penury, of course."

Of course.

Claire had pride, too. She knew her worth, knew her value in the Marriage Mart, knew she could have half a dozen marriage proposals before Christmas Eve. None would be the one she wanted, however. None would be the only offer she would accept, the only one, she feared, that she could ever accept. Claire vowed to remain a spinster, despite her sister-in-law's machinations, rather than wed where her heart could not follow. She'd have Hannah, at least, if not a child of her own.

Was pride going to brighten her days or warm her nights, though? Was pride going to be her closest companion for the rest of her days? Heavens, was she going to let Viscount Bryson walk out of her life without so much as trying for one of Cousin Maudine's happy endings?

On the other hand, did she dare? Claire's mouth went dry and her skin felt clammy at the thought of what she had to do. Her sister-in-law would have palpitations if she knew. Handbury would lock Claire in her room, no matter how much he loved her. No decent woman was so forward, no lady so demeaned herself. Why, it was practically begging to importune a man who showed no interest.

Gregory did show interest, Claire reminded herself, so she was not a total ninnyhammer hanging a welcome sign on her air castles. He sought her out and stayed by her side whenever he could. He laughed with her and shared his thoughts. He knew where every sprig of mistletoe was hung and made use of each, but only with Claire—and the duchess once. He never went beyond the bounds of polite conventions, but even those company kisses hinted at deeper passions, Claire knew. He felt the same spark she did when their lips met, no matter how briefly. He was interested, all right, but was that enough to counter the man's wretched sense of honor?

Most of all, Claire did not know if she could stand the mortification if Gregory laughed at her proposition or made light of it—or if she could stand watching him leave without her. She practiced her words all afternoon, knowing he would come to her sooner or later.

Gregory had one more farewell to make, one more leave to take, one more soul-rending, gut-wrenching good-bye. He'd sooner cut off his arm. That might be less painful than parting from Claire.

"I suppose you have heard by now that I am leaving in the morning."

Claire had brought her courage to the sticking point. Unfortunately, it was sticking her tongue to the top of her mouth. She could only nod.

"I spoke to the duke. His Grace has, ah, graciously agreed to stand as guardian to Hannah until I, that is, if I . . ." Gregory was having trouble of his own, trying to form the right words.

"My lord, Gregory, I—"

"I know you offered to keep her, but as soon as you are out of mourning, you will take up the social rounds once more, eventually forming a family of your own. You will make a wonderful mother, but I think Hannah will do better without being uprooted again and again. If you could look in on her when you can, while you are here, I would be more than grateful."

"I would like to do more than that. I—"

Gregory had to interrupt again. If he did not say the words now, he might never get another chance. "She adores you, you know. Thinks you are top of the trees, in fact. We both do. You are the finest young lady of my experience. Because of that, I cannot, must not, let you sacrifice your future for us."

"But that is what I have been trying to say. I wish to share my future with—"

"Claire! There you are, impossible girl." Lady Handbury rushed into the room, nearly shoving the viscount aside as she stepped between him and her sister-in-law. Or between Claire and social ruin, as she saw it. Warned by her maid, she had hurried through her toilette, leaving one curl paper still tucked in her hair. Now she wrapped her fingers around Claire's wrist like an owl clutching its supper mouse, and started tugging her toward the stairs. "The dressing bell rang long ago, and your maid is frantic. I want you to look particularly fetching tonight, for the Ravencrofts' neighbor joins us for dinner and cards. Lord Amblemere is a baron, as rich as Croesus"—she raised her voice lest Gregory missed a syllable or the warning—"who needs a mother for his three adorable children. Or is it four? No matter. Come along, do. I had your maid lay out that lavender silk with the ecru lace. With your mother's pearls"—which Lady Handbury felt ought to have come to her, as the heir's bride—"you are sure to catch his eye, even if you do insist on holding to half mourning. What with the holidays, I truly believe you could go to colors, but I will say no more on that head. Oh, and good day to you, Lord Bryson."

Looking over her shoulder as she was chivied from the room, Claire did manage to say that she would speak to his lordship again after dinner.

Not if Lady Handbury could help it, she would not.

Before the gentlemen could join the ladies, Claire's sister-in-law volunteered her to play the pianoforte for the company, and made sure Lord Amblemere reached her first, to turn the pages. When they divided up for cards, Claire found herself partnered by the same worthy but dull gentleman, or the very young Sir Nigel, or the married Mr. Macomber. All too soon the tea tray was brought in, after which the duchess decided to retire for the night, forcing the other ladies to seek their chambers also. Claire could not remain with the gentlemen, nor lurk in the corridors waiting for the viscount to go to bed, so she asked to be awakened at dawn, to make certain she saw him at breakfast. She doubted she would fall asleep, anyway.

Once the ladies had departed, the stakes at the card tables were raised. Gregory found himself playing in elevated company, too: Ravencroft, Lord Handbury, Lady Susannah's father Earl Blakenthorpe, that neighboring baron Amble-something, and, unfortunately, his cousin Floyd, who was winning, as usual. They all had deeper pockets than Gregory—hell, the butler had deeper pockets—and were more frequent players. The company and the stakes were too rich for Gregory's taste or purse, but at the duke's urging, he stayed on until the end of another hand, which he won. And the next. He had the suspicion, after the ordinarily canny Ravencroft made a blunder, and Lord Handbury misplayed his hand on the following deal, that the two gentlemen were letting him win. He appreciated their kindness, but could not accept charity. He tossed down his cards and collected his winnings. Floyd had a bigger pile of coins and pound notes in front of him, but the other players claimed they wanted a chance to recoup their losses.

"I am sorry, gentlemen, but I am not a dedicated gambler, and I need to make an early start in the morning." He started to tuck his winnings into his pockets. "But your coins will go to good use." They were not enough, he estimated, even with his bank savings, to make the January payment for Belle Towers, unless he found a Rembrandt in the attics or a Shakespeare folio in the library.

"One more hand ought to go further," the duke urged.

"Unless you have not got the stomach to try," Floyd taunted. He tossed back the lace at his cuffs to bring a glass of brandy to his smirking lips.

"I have the stomach, but not when my tenants' children's are empty. When a gambler cannot afford to lose, he should not play."

"Hear, hear," Blakenthorpe commended, raising his own glass. "Fellow's got a good head on his shoulders. Too bad about m'daughter. Still, are we here to play or to spout philosophy? Whose deal is it?"

It was Lord Handbury's, who passed the cards after exchanging a look of chagrin with Ravencroft. They'd tried to help Claire's beau.

Gregory sat, watching the play while he finished his drink, for he did not have much to pack, after all. The stakes went higher yet, and so did Floyd's pile of winnings. The viscount could not stand to see his cousin victorious, so he stood to leave. When he did, a few coins slipped from his pocket to the floor. If they were at White's or one of the other gentlemen's clubs in London, tradition would have left the money on the floor, for the major domo and his staff. Gregory was certain the duke's butler was amply paid, though, and those were sovereigns shining on the carpet, not shillings. He bent to pick up the fallen coins while Floyd dealt the next hand.

Under the table, something else shone besides the coins, a flash of white amid the sea of dark-colored pant legs. It seemed that Gregory was not the only member of the Bellington clan who was not a gambler, because Floyd was not taking chances on this night's card game, either, not with three white cards in his lap. The dirty-dish cousin was cheating, and likely had been all night, if not forever. With a roar of outrage, Gregory tipped the whole table away, sending cards and coins and drinks and the duke flying to the floor.

"What the devil?"

The others shouted, then they looked where Gregory was pointing.

"They fell when the madman overturned the table," Floyd cried, leaping to his feet. Unfortunately for his alibi, another ace fell out of the lace at his wrists.

At first the other gentlemen were dumbfounded, then they were furious. Floyd Bellington would never turn another female's head when they were finished with him. Her stomach, perhaps, but no father would let the cad get that close. Floyd was finished. He would not be allowed into the clubs or welcomed in polite society—if the duke and his friends did not see him clapped in prison. Instead, they dragged him into the estate office at the back of the house.

To save Gregory the ignominy of having a swindler for a relative, they gave Floyd the gentleman's option: a closed door and a loaded pistol. Why anyone would think that a confirmed cardsharp would take the honorable course was a mystery. Floyd took the pistol, along with two silver candlesticks and the duke's petty cash. Then he took to his heels, out the window.

"It is better this way," the baron said when they realized what had happened. Amblemere was the local magistrate and ought to know. "No gunshots to explain, no dead bodies in the middle of the night. No inquiries."

"And no stains on my carpet," the duke agreed. "We've seen the last of the dastard, anyway, without the public scandal. He'll never show his face in England again."

They all drank to that happy outcome, from the tray Ravencroft's butler brought. The man also carried in a Sevres bowl filled with money, collected from the card room floor.

"Duece take it, we'll never straighten out the accounting," Lady Susannah's father grumbled.

The duke had the perfect solution. "I say we give the pot to young Bryson."

"Me?" Gregory protested. "But I had already taken my own winnings."

"Nonsense, we'd have lost the blunt anyway, if not for you," Lord Handbury was quick to say.

His Grace added: "Think of it as a reward for ridding Ravencroft of vermin. I'm sure half the gentlemen in London will second my gratitude. Asides, you'll need it to take care of the mawworm's mother. She won't be able to hold her head up in Bath, you know. Too many servants know what happened here tonight, too many other guests will hear about it with their morning chocolate. My duchess will never let me hear the end of it if I leave her friend Elvira without support. No, you'll need the blunt for that Belle Towers of yours, to make it comfortable for the old dear." He lowered his voice and said, "Else I'll be stuck with her here."

"And you saved me from considering that felon as

a future son-in-law," the earl said. "It's worth the cost, to have one less fortune hunter on Susannah's trail."

"And we can give out that Bellington lost his fortune to you, so left the country. It won't be believed in every quarter, but enough." Lord Handbury raised his glass in salute to the duke. "It will serve, Bryson. So swallow your brandy, and swallow your damned pride."

9

"My aunt wishes to leave Ravencroft," Gregory told Claire the following morning. "I suppose you heard why?" At Claire's nod he continued: "So I have decided to delay my departure by a day, and to take Hannah along. My circumstances have changed, for the better, thank goodness, except for the new blot on the family escutcheon. I was wondering if there was any chance, that is, if you would not mind, although Christmas is nearly here and you would most likely rather be with your own family— Dash it, Claire, will you come along with us? The place is a mess, and I do not know if I can keep it longer than the next quarter day, but I would value your opinion, your woman's touch. That is, to see if it might be made respectable, someday, if you think it might be suitable. Someday." He pulled at the knot of his too-tight neckcloth. "Unless you think you could not, or worry that people might see your visit as something you do not wish them to see, which it is not, until you see the place for yourself. Thunderation, I am saying it all wrong."

"Yes."

"Deuce take it, I know I sound like a blithering

idiot, and I have been practicing all morning." He took a deep breath and started over. "What I wish to say is—"

"Yes."

"—that I would be honored if you joined my family at Belle Towers because it is Christmas, and I would like to share it with you. Share them. Hannah and Aunt Elvira and Belle Towers and Christmas."

"Yes, dear sir. I have said it three times. Shall I say it again? I would be pleased to accept your invitation. And I am half packed, because Hannah invited me this morning as soon as she heard she was to go along."

"Yes?"

"Yes."

Luckily there was a sprig of mistletoe hanging in the doorway, so Gregory had an excuse to kiss Claire. He had an excuse for the first kiss, anyway.

The Bellington family seat was in worse condition than when Gregory had left it after the summer. Houses and gardens and driveways all deteriorated without attention or money for repairs, and Belle Towers had had little of either in decades. Now the place seemed abandoned, with vines covering boarded windows and goats doing the only grass cutting. Still, when Hannah got down from the carriage, she declared it just right. Not too big, so a person did not have to worry about getting lost, like at Ravencroft. Not too small, like the rooms in London, which could have fit in the entry hall here. Not too fussy, with the valuable pieces sold long ago. Not too plain, especially with the tall rounded towers at each corner that made the place appear enchanted.

"It is perfect, just like home," she said.

Gregory was watching for Claire's reaction as she took in the dilapidated structure, half afraid she would refuse to step inside. "I know it needs work," he started to say. Lud, anyone could see that. And if the house was bad, the barns and stables, the outbuildings and the tenants' cottages were ten times worse. He would not have lied to Claire, even if her own eyes were not telling her the truth. She was used to Handbury House and Ravencroft, not a ramshackle residence for rats and bats and down-at-heels aristocrats.

She smiled. "It will be perfect. Just like home."

Three days later, Gregory was not so sure. He'd hired servants from the village to assist the Hapgoods, the old couple he'd left as caretakers, so more of the rooms were livable every day. Deliveries kept arriving of the coal and candles he'd ordered there, too. The kitchen was well stocked, and Mrs. Hapgood proved a good cook who specialized in pastries, it seemed, to Hannah's delight. Now they were comfortable, if exhausted. Claire had taken over the female staff, directing the maids and working right alongside them with the soap and beeswax. Aunt Elvira mended sheets and curtains and chair cushions. Gregory toiled with the men, clearing vines, repairing the roof, shoring up the old stable's walls so the pair of workhorses were sheltered from the cold. And he visited his tenants and rode the farms and studied the ledgers.

"I just do not know if it is all worth it," he said on the afternoon of Christmas Eve.

Aunt Elvira looked up from the orange she'd been sticking with cloves. "What is that, dear?"

Gregory lowered his scissors and raised his voice. "We are bailing a sinking boat with a teacup, Aunt, and I do not know but that we should abandon ship." He'd been cutting out paper snowflakes to help decorate the parlor, but set the paper and scissors on the table beside him now, brushing the scraps into a pile.

Claire was folding paper into swan shapes, because she had read they were good luck. They were pretty and cost nothing, at any rate, made with the useless old parchment pages Gregory had unearthed. Hannah was hanging them, along with the viscount's snow-flakes, on the pine boughs they'd hung earlier, on the mantel and the windows and off the wall sconces, until the room was looking like a sorcerer's snowstorm. With the fire burning and the candles gleaming, the scent of evergreens and spices in the air, Christmas had found a home here at Belle Towers, too.

Unless Gregory had decided to give up on the old place. Claire came to sit beside him on the couch, with Hannah on the floor at their feet.

"What do you mean, Papa?"

"I mean that perhaps we should reconsider staying here. Belle Towers needs far more money than I have, even with the windfall. I can pay off this quarter's mortgage, and next's, too, but then I will have no funds to reinvest in the farms and fields. Without new equipment and new livestock, the place can never support itself, so we will never be ahead of the bank."

"Oh, but I do not want to return to Bath, Gregory." Aunt Elvira's voice had a tremor in it.

"Or to London, Papa." So did Hannah's.

The viscount looked toward Claire.

"Do you have other ideas?" she asked.

"With my cousin gone, I could break the entail. The bank would get most of the money if I sold Belle Towers, but the London town house might bring in enough to keep us in modest circumstances some-where else, America, perhaps."

"No, Papa! I do not want to leave here. Please?"

Gregory reached out and touched her silky hair. "I am sorry, poppet, but we might not have a choice."

"Yes, we do. You can have Valentina." She thrust the doll into his hands.

He smiled. "I appreciate the thought, Hannah, but I don't see how—"

"The note said it, Papa, the note that came with Valentina. 'Always in my heart.' I told you."

"Always . . . ?" Claire asked, but Gregory was already pulling the cape and the bandage and the faded gown from the doll. Under the layers, the china-headed toy had a cloth body, with big loops and inexpert stitches holding closed a crude tear, right where the doll's heart would have been.

"I sewed it back up myself," Hannah proudly announced, "after I opened the seam I found in her."

"And an excellent job you did of it, sweetheart," Gregory said, even as he reached for his scissors and cut the threads, then reached inside. Twelve diamonds fell out into his hand, one for each of the hearts embroidered on Valentina's dress.

If Ann Marvell had been half as marvelous as rumor had it, these gems were of the first water, and worth a fortune—Hannah's fortune.

Gregory took a deep breath, then said, "I cannot take these, sweetheart. Your mother put them there for you as your dowry, so you can make a splendid match." With such a sparkling portion, Hannah's muddied birth would not matter as much.

Hannah was about to protest, for what good was a future husband without a house, now, but Claire spoke first.

"I have a dowry, too, you know," she said. Although the invitation to Belle Towers had been as good as a declaration, the formal words had not been spoken. Claire supposed Gregory, with all his scruples, was waiting to make certain he could keep a wife in style, the clunch.

"Do you, my love?" Gregory squeezed her hand and placed a chaste kiss on her cheek, a promise to formalize their betrothal in private now that she had not run away from the shipwreck that was Belle Towers. "Then our daughters will be provided for."

"But our sons deserve their patrimony, too, and it is a very large dowry, Gregory. My godparents added to the sum in my father's bequest, and my mother left me a goodly amount for when I reach my majority. My brother never wanted the sum made public lest I be deluged with fortune hunters, but he invested the monies wisely. I might not be as well dowered as Lady Susannah, but I do believe we can pay off the mortgages on Belle Towers and still improve the farms."

Diamonds, dowries—Gregory's mind was in a dither. The mention of fortune hunters, though, disturbed him. "I cannot like living off my wife. It just isn't right, dash it. A man should be able to support his own family." He reached over to the end table and picked up a sheet of paper from the stack he'd been cutting for snowflakes, the worthless stock certificates from his father's failed ventures, shares in empty mines, unused canals, tunnels that were never built. There were enough valueless stocks left for a flock of folded swans, a blizzard of snowflakes.

"Deuce take it," he said, "why could my father not have invested half as wisely as your brother, instead of gambling everything we owned on these harebrained schemes? We'd be solvent now, if he'd had a particle of common sense."

"I do not know, dear," his aunt said. "But not all of your father's investments were unsound. Why, one of those speculations was such a sure thing that I let him invest my savings. The sale of half my fifty shares in the Steiner Rouse Spice Syndication was enough to finance my house in Bath, with the remaining shares still paying dividends for its upkeep. I suppose your father lost his profits in some other scheme, but if I sell my twenty-five shares, we can use that money to purchase more cows. Or was it sheep you wanted to raise, dear?"

Gregory was not paying attention. He was reading the name engraved across the top of the page he now held. The Steiner Rouse Spice Syndicate. "Good Lord."

Hannah was spelling out the words. "Does that mean we are solved?"

"Solvent? No, poppet." He pulled her onto his lap, after carefully setting aside the stock certificate—for twenty-five *hundred* shares—then put his other arm around Claire, pulling both of them closer. "It means I am the now the richest, luckiest man on earth."

"And we can stay here?"

"As long as we want."

"I can stay, too?"

"Forever. I would not be half as wealthy without you, poppet, diamonds or not."

That night, Christmas Eve, Gregory took Claire to the north tower, and gave her the telescope, which never got focused on a single star. "I wanted to give you the sun and the moon. Instead I am offering you a derelict estate in return for your dowry, a half-deaf auntie, a daughter whose birth does not bear inspection, a disgraced cousin, and debts."

"And yourself?"

"And myself, with all my heart." After sharing a

kiss that would have set the stars spinning, whether the telescope could see it or not, Gregory asked, "Will you accept such a bad bargain, my beloved?"

Claire stepped out of the circle of his arms to dab at the tears of joy in her eyes. "Oh, I don't think it such a poor trade. All I have for you for Christmas is a monogrammed handkerchief, the one I just used."

Gregory kissed away the moisture she missed. "And your love?" he whispered as the church bells from the village rang out.

"And my love," she told him as they sealed their promise with another kiss, "for Christmas, and for always."

A Partridge in a Pear Tree
by *Amanda McCabe*

Prologue

"Vultures! They are all vultures." Harriet, Lady Kirkwood, flung the letter she was reading to the floor. Her lace cap quivered on her white curls, while her wrinkled face creased even further in a fierce frown.

Rose, Lady Kirkwood's faithful maid, looked up in alarm. "My lady! Please do not upset yourself. You will have a spell." She quickly poured out a glass of wine and pressed it into Lady Kirkwood's shaking hand.

"A spell is just what my husband's *dear* nephew is counting on," Lady Kirkwood said bitterly, but she took the wine and sipped at it. Slowly, color came back to her cheeks. "Sir Reginald Kirkwood writes to tell me that his son Edward is getting married soon, to a Miss Bates from Bath, and that they would make me—" Lady Kirkwood paused to pick up the letter from the floor and look at it. "—'most suitable heirs.' And they wish to visit me for Christmas, so I may meet this Miss Bates. They say they will 'condole with me in the waning light of my life.'"

Rose laughed. "Waning light of your life, my lady?"

"Exactly. Well, I am not dead, nor dying, just yet."

"A betrothal is good news, though, is it not, my lady?" Rose asked cautiously.

"Of course. Except when it is dim-witted young Eddie's. He is just as snobbish and grasping as his parents." Lady Kirkwood balled the letter up and tossed it into the fireplace. "They are vultures, just waiting to pounce on my money." She tapped her cane thoughtfully on the floor. "We shall just see about that."

"My lady?"

"They will get this house, of course, when I am gone. That was in my husband's will, and there is nothing I can do about that. But they will not get my own money. Do you remember the house party we had about four years ago, Rose, right before my husband died?"

Rose blinked at this abrupt change of topic. "Oh. Of course, my lady."

"My own nephew's widow was here, with her three little daughters. I am sure they are not little anymore—the eldest will be of an age to marry. And my husband's sister's son, young William, was here. How handsome he was! They have all written to me, of course, but I have not seen them since that party."

"Are you thinking to make one of them your heir, my lady?" Rose asked, getting caught up in the intrigue.

"Oh, Rose, you have been with me for twelve years—you should know me better than that! I cannot make things so easy. I must set up a challenge."

"A challenge?"

"Yes. A scavenger hunt, perhaps, like the ones I remember from my youth. Do you recall the song about the twelve days of Christmas, Rose?"

"The one with all the birds, and the dancing ladies, and the gold rings, my lady?"

"The very one. It was my husband's favorite Christmas song. I will have everyone come here for Christmas, and whoever can bring me each of those twelve objects will be heir to my personal fortune." Lady Kirkwood laughed in delight at the prospect. "It will be vastly amusing!"

Rose looked a bit doubtful. "Are there not a great many objects in that song, my lady? Won't it be hard for them to find them all?"

"Hm. You may be correct, Rose. And we would not want lords a-leaping and ladies dancing all over the place! Perhaps we will only go up to, oh, seven swans a-swimming. Yes, that should do it."

"But, my lady, what if Sir Reginald and his family wins?"

"I am sure they shan't. Completely bacon-brained, the lot of them. Besides, the object is not *really* to win. It is only to have an amusing holiday. So bring me my lap desk, Rose. We have invitations to write."

"This is a godsend, Allison dear! An absolute godsend." Mrs. Josephine Gordon clutched Lady Kirkwood's newly arrived letter in her thin hands. A rare smile lit her pale, care- and illness-worn face.

Allison also smiled to see her mother smile, and went back to stirring the pot of soup. "It *is* most agreeable to be invited to Kirkwood Manor for Christmas. We have not left the cottage for an age. But a godsend, Mama?" She pushed some stray red curls back under her cap. "I don't really see that."

"Of course it is! This is obviously not just an invitation for Christmas, my dear. Lady Kirkwood is getting on in years. She will be choosing her heir." Josephine looked back down at the letter. "She wants to see us again to be sure *we* are worthy to be her heirs!"

"I thought her husband's nephew, Sir Reginald Kirkwood, was the heir."

"Only to the Manor. But Lady Kirkwood has her own fortune, and who better to benefit from it than her nephew's children? I am not well enough to travel there, of course, but you and the twins must go. As soon as she meets you again, she will see how wonderful my girls are. And all our troubles will be at an end."

Allison glanced at her mother thoughtfully. There was no way to know if Lady Kirkwood was indeed looking for an heir, or if she would even consider the daughters of her late nephew. But a Christmas in the comfort of Kirkwood Manor would indeed be a treat, especially for the twins, who had scarcely traveled anywhere in all their twelve years.

Yet how could she leave her mother all alone at Christmas? She added an onion to the soup, and said, "I could not leave you, Mama."

"Of course you can!" Josephine looked around the shabby kitchen, the only room of the cottage that was ever truly warm. "This is our only chance, Allison. Your father, though certainly charming, was no manager of money. You know that when he lost our funds in that silly shipping scheme, your dowry and those of the twins went, too."

Allison nodded. She knew *that* very well.

"So you must go see Lady Kirkwood," Josephine continued. "She is the only one who could help us. And it will be such a treat for the twins."

As if summoned by the mention of them, Kitty and Jane came bursting through the back door, cloaks flying, wild red hair escaping their ribbons. Snow flurries and the Gordons' two old spaniels came with them.

"Are we to have a treat?" Kitty cried.

"A treat? Oh, what is it?" Jane threw her arms around Allison in an exuberant hug.

Allison hugged her back, breathing in the fresh scent of cold air and the rose soap they all used. She loved her sisters dearly, and if it meant securing their future, she would definitely go to Kirkwood Manor for Christmas.

Even if she was sure to see William Bradford there.

The last time, the only time, she had seen Lady Kirkwood's husband's sister's son was four years ago, at another house party at Kirkwood Manor. He had been seven years older than her own fifteen, and had obviously regarded her as a child to be teased. But she had thought him so handsome and dashing. The most handsome young man she had ever seen.

Four years of isolation in their country cottage had not dimmed her memory.

Oh, what *would* she do if she saw him again? Surely he would never remember her . . .

William Bradford tapped Lady Kirkwood's letter against his palm as he watched his thirteen-year-old sister Gertrude out the window. She wandered about the garden like a little ghost, her blue cloak a dark spot against the snow. She looked quiet and withdrawn, as she had been ever since their father lost all their money and then shot himself in the library over a year ago.

Was Lady Kirkwood's letter the answer to his prayers?

He looked back down at the neatly penned words, inviting him and Gertrude to Kirkwood Manor for a

Christmas house party. He had not been invited there since the last house party four years ago; indeed he had heard that Lady Kirkwood ceased entertaining after her husband died.

This new sociability seemed to signal only one thing; Lady Kirkwood was feeling her age, and perhaps looking about for a suitable heir.

William glanced up at the drawing room he stood in. There was very little furniture in it, and no paintings or ornaments at all. Only a very small fire burned in the vast marble grate, hardly warming the room.

It was not a place where a quiet, shy young girl could learn to laugh again.

William had thought to go to London in the spring, to find an heiress who could restore their home and help Gertrude. But to be the heirs to the Kirkwood money would be even better in the long run.

He felt a sharp stab of guilt at the idea of taking advantage of an elderly lady. But for his sister, he would do it. For his sister he would do anything.

As he refolded the letter, he wondered idly if he would see that pretty girl, Miss Allison Gordon, again.

1

"Oh, Allie, it's *huge!*" Kitty pressed her nose against the window of the luxurious carriage Lady Kirkwood had sent for them, gawking unashamedly as they rolled up the muddy drive to Kirkwood Manor.

"It is a castle," Jane added, crowding in next to her sister. "Just like in a book."

Kitty giggled. "Then that would make Lady Kirkwood a *queen!*"

Allison peered out at the looming-closer house with

more trepidation than the twins were obviously feeling. It was indeed very grand, a concoction of weather-beaten gray stone crowned with leering gargoyles. There was no softening shrubbery or greenery in winter's depths, so the house seemed even more austere and majestic. She did not remember it being so intimidating four years ago.

Allison bit her lip. Her green pelisse, with its black velvet collar and cuffs and matching black hat, had seemed so nice before they left home. Here it felt shabby and unfashionable; *she* felt shabby, like the poor country cousin she was.

Well, there was nothing for it. The pelisse was the best she owned, and Lady Kirkwood knew they lived quietly in the country. Surely she was not expecting London fashions.

And your family is as good as any, she reminded herself sternly. *Never forget that.*

Allison sat up straighter, and smoothed her hair back up beneath her hat. The wild red curls, the bane of her life, always escaped from their pins so!

"Girls, sit down, please," she said, tugging Kitty and Jane back into their seats. "What if someone saw you there, pressing your faces to the glass like two little monkeys?"

"There's nobody to see us, Allie," Kitty protested. "The place looks almost deserted."

"Yes," Jane said. "Are you sure they're expecting us?"

"Lady Kirkwood sent this carriage for us, didn't she?" Allison said briskly, retying the girls' hair ribbons and straightening their matching red cloaks.

She just finished wiping a smudge from Kitty's nose when the carriage rolled to a stop, and the front doors opened to reveal a stern-looking man.

"The Misses Gordons, I presume?" he said.

"Yes," Allison answered slowly, allowing the man to take her arm and help her alight from the carriage.

"I am Matthews, butler here at Kirkwood Manor."

Kitty ignored his outstretched hand and jumped down herself, closely followed by Jane. "How do you do, Matthews," she said genially. "I am Miss Katherine Gordon, and this is Miss Jane Gordon."

Matthews blinked at her, nonplussed. "Er—yes. Indeed." His lips pursed disapprovingly.

Oh, dear, Allison thought, hurrying her sisters up the front steps into the house. Only at Kirkwood Manor five minutes, and already they had committed a *faux pas*!

But she was glad to see that the interior of the house was not as forbidding as the exterior. Lamps were lit against the encroaching twilight, casting a warm golden glow over the marble foyer. Fresh greenery, pine boughs, and holly tied together with red velvet bows twined up the length of the staircase banisters, a cheerful nod to the holiday season.

"Lady Kirkwood and the others are in the drawing room, Miss Gordon," Matthews said as footmen carried the twins' cloaks. "I know her ladyship is eager to greet you."

Already? Allison glanced at the girls, who were gazing about wide-eyed, silent for once in their lives. Then she nodded, and said, "Yes. As we are eager to greet her."

The drawing room, a vast expanse of cream-colored satin and gilt trim, was also decorated for the season. Greenery festooned the two marble fireplace mantels and curved around every picture frame. A pile of gaily wrapped parcels was stacked in the corner.

And gathered about the largest fireplace was—
everyone.

Lady Kirkwood, white-haired but tall and erect, and
very elegant in a gray satin gown and lace cap, sat on
a thronelike red velvet chair. A silver-headed cane
rested in her hand like a scepter. The others gathered
about her, a cluster of humble subjects.

As they moved closer, Allison recognized their sort-
of cousin, Sir Reginald Kirkwood, as silly as ever in a
bright purple coat and yellow waistcoat, his shirt
points so high he could hardly turn his head. He
watched their approach through an emerald-trimmed
quizzing glass, one brow raised.

Next to him stood his wife Letitia, clad in an elaborate gown of gold-and-black-striped velvet and a
matching turban. She was studying a figurine on the
mantel, obviously pretending that no one else was in
the room.

On a settee sat their son Edward with a rather
plump young blond lady in blue silk. They shared a
large plate of pastries, giggling and whispering together. Allison remembered how Edward had tried to
kiss her four years ago, catching her behind a door
and pressing his clammy hands on her. She shuddered
at the memory, and resolved to stay far away from
him this time.

Then she turned her attention to the other settee,
the one pulled up next to Lady Kirkwood. There sat—
William Bradford.

Allison's steps faltered a bit, and for one long second she forgot to breathe.

She had told herself that her memories of him, the
schoolgirl crush she had had on him four years ago,
had become distorted and elaborated. But now she

saw that he was every bit as handsome as he was then. More so, for then he had been a boy. Now he was a man.

The firelight cast his lean face into dancing shadows, lining his sharp, straight nose, strong jaw, and narrow mouth into an artist's chiaroscuro. His waving, dark gold hair was cut short and brushed straight back. Unlike the other men, he still wore his traveling clothes, buckskins, a blue wool coat, and simply tied cravat, as if he had been rather late, like Allison and her sisters.

He made the others look a bit like yapping, fat spaniels next to a lean panther.

Then he leaned over to speak to the girl sitting beside him. She could only be his younger sister, who had not been at the last house party. She had the same golden hair, the same lean features. She looked to be about the age of the twins, but where their eyes flashed and danced with mischief, hers were solemn. She was very thin in her blue dress and fur-trimmed spencer, and she nodded at her brother's words, but did not smile.

"Is that the Gordon girls?" Lady Kirkwood suddenly called, banging her cane on the floor. "Come closer!" Allison was snapped out of her musings on the Bradfords, and quickened her steps.

She took the girls by the hands and drew them next to her, but for once they needed no urging to stay close. They crowded against her of their own volition.

Allison stopped in front of Lady Kirkwood's chair and dropped a small curtsy, trying not to look at William. She did not need the distraction just then. "How do you do, Lady Kirkwood. I am Allison Gordon, and this is Jane and Kitty."

Lady Kirkwood studied them carefully through her still-bright green eyes. "How much you have all grown since last I saw you! I am very glad you could come to my home for Christmas."

Allison relaxed just a bit. So Lady Kirkwood was *not* going to eat them, after all! In fact, she seemed almost—genial.

"It was very kind of you to invite us, Lady Kirkwood," she answered.

"You must be tired after your journey," Lady Kirkwood said. "Have some tea, and a pastry, too, if Edward will surrender them. Then I will tell you all what I have planned for our holiday."

Lady Kirkwood gave a sly little smile when she said the word "planned," but Allison was too relieved to see it. The royal introduction was over. She sat down on the last remaining settee, and drew the girls down beside her.

Only then did she allow herself to look at William Bradford. He was watching her, his handsome golden head cocked to one side.

Then he gave her a wide smile. And she promptly choked.

William's grin widened. So *this* was his little cousin Allison. He remembered her, of course; remembered how much fun she had been to tease, what a good rider she had been, and that she had freckles across her nose. He had even remembered that she was rather pretty, but not *this* pretty.

Curls the color of a sunset sprang from beneath her hat, surrounding her heart-shaped face in a fiery halo. She still had freckles, but they were much lighter, sprinkled across a little, upturned nose and creamy cheeks. She choked when he first caught her eye and smiled at her, and thereafter threw him little, surreptitious glances from her hazel eyes.

How interesting this Christmas was turning out to be already!

He watched as she situated the fidgeting, redheaded twins, giving them tea and sweets that had been practically wrestled away from Edward and Miss Bates. "Those girls look to be about your age," he whispered to Gertrude.

She gave the twins a wary glance. "I don't think they would like me," she whispered back.

"Why ever not, sparrow? You are a perfectly charming girl."

Gertrude just shook her head.

Then Lady Kirkwood banged her cane on the floor again, obviously the signal for everyone to look at her. Gertrude slid her trembling little hand into his, and he squeezed it reassuringly.

"Now that we are all here," Lady Kirkwood announced, "I can tell you of the game I have planned."

"Game?" Reginald said sharply. "Whatever do you mean, Aunt Harriet?"

"Isn't Christmas a time for games?" Lady Kirkwood said unconcernedly. "This is one of my own devising. It is a scavenger hunt."

A murmur arose from Reginald and Edward. Even Letitia looked vaguely discomposed, as if this was not what she had been expecting.

"What is a scavenger hunt?" Jane asked Allison quietly.

"It is a search, where you must find certain items on a list," Allison answered her. "The person who finds the most objects wins. At least I think that is what it is."

Allison tried to keep her voice low, but Lady Kirkwood heard her. "You are exactly right, Miss Gordon," she cried. "It is a search for certain items."

"What would these items be, Aunt Harriet?" Reginald asked.

Lady Kirkwood made a gesture with her cane, and a maid came forward to hand each of them a sheet of paper. Allison looked down to see that it was a copy of the song, "The Twelve Days of Christmas."

"You must find some of these twelve items by Christmas Day. Up to the seven swans a-swimming," Lady Kirkwood said.

"A partridge in a pear tree?" Letitia said sharply. "However are we supposed to find *that*?"

"Letitia," Lady Kirkwood replied impatiently. "You may bring me whatever *you* think a partridge in a pear tree would be."

Letitia shot her husband a bitter, reproachful glance.

He shrugged helplessly, as if to say, "We must humor the old lady."

Edward and his fiancée just looked at each other vacantly.

"How exciting!" Kitty whispered.

"Yes, Miss Kitty, it *is* exciting," Lady Kirkwood answered, giving the girl a little smile. "You will all be divided into two teams. You, Reginald, will be with your *dear* wife and son, and Miss Bates. Miss Gordon, you will be with Mr. Bradford. Your sisters may all help you, if you wish."

Allison choked again, on the sip of tea she had just taken.

William grinned at her.

The twins giggled in delight.

And Lady Kirkwood, obviously pleased by the reaction to her challenge, rose to her feet and said, "Well, then. Shall we all go change for supper?"

2

A Partridge in a Pear Tree

Despite the fact that supper, a parade of several
courses, had run quite late, Allison was up early the
next morning. She wanted to have breakfast alone,
before the exuberant twins were up and about, so that
she could think in peace.

And she had a great deal to think about. The past
few years of her life had been very quiet; she spent
her days keeping the cottage in order, looking after
her frail mother, and trying to give the girls their lessons and keep them from running completely wild.
Aside from an occasional assembly or card party,
there was very little society. There were certainly no
attractive young gentlemen!

Now, in only a day, her life was turned tip over tail.
There were so many people about, family and servants, that she hadn't a moment alone, and she needed
to think about this scavenger hunt challenge. She had
never been particularly good at puzzles and games,
but her family was counting on her to do well at this
one and impress Lady Kirkwood.

The hunt *was* worrisome, of course, but it did not
occupy her thoughts as much as her assigned team-
mate did.

William Bradford was a handsome devil, and a bold
one to grin at her as he had last night! She felt terribly
flustered and nervous around him. Men like him,
good-looking, sophisticated, and flirtatious, were completely out of her limited realm of experience. She
hardly knew how to behave around him.

She had managed to avoid speaking to him very

much last night, but that could not go on much longer. They were meant to be finding the items of the "Twelve Days of Christmas" together, after all.

"You are being an absolute widgeon," Allison muttered to herself as she hurried down the corridor toward the breakfast room. "He is a person, just like everyone else. A person—not a god."

A very handsome person, though.

Then, as she rounded the doorway into the room, she saw that she was not the first person to breakfast after all, despite the early hour.

William was already seated at the round table, a heaping plate of eggs, kippers, and sausages in front of him.

He jumped up when he saw her, that same wide smile on his face. "Good morning, Miss Gordon!"

"G-good morning, Mr. Bradford." It was too late to run away now. Perhaps if she said very little, she would not embarrass herself. She slowly sat down in the chair next to his, and asked the footman for just some tea and toast.

"I am very glad to see you are an early riser," William said.

"Oh, yes?"

"Yes. It means we will have a head start on the others. I would wager that Sir Reginald and his family never rise before noon!"

Allison had to laugh at the image of Sir Reginald and his perfectly coifed wife, not to mention their pastry-snatching son, getting up at dawn to do all the things she did at the cottage. Start the porridge, feed the chickens, get the twins up . . . "I would wager not! But do *you* always rise so early in Town, Mr. Bradford?"

William's smile faded a bit, and he looked away from her. "I no longer live in London, Miss Gordon. I am a country man now."

Allison felt herself blushing, and quickly turned her own attention to her tea. She remembered now her mother saying that the Bradfords had suffered some reversal in their fortunes, that the elder Mr. Bradford had died scandalously, but they had not heard the details. It was obviously a subject William did not care to discuss.

Allison had thought him a London gentleman, with his fashionable haircut and well-tailored clothes. But perhaps he needed to win the scavenger hunt just as much as she did.

Somehow that thought lessened her nervousness. She smiled at him, and said, "Then we must plan our strategy! Today is the first day, so we have to find a partridge in a pear tree. I must confess I am at a complete loss as to where we might find something like that."

William ate the last of his eggs, and pushed the plate away. "I had thought we might go hunting, Miss Gordon."

Allison blinked at him in surprise. "Hunting? You mean for a *literal* partridge?"

He shrugged. "Perhaps. Or for whatever else we might come across. Unless you have a better idea?"

"No ideas at all, I fear. I shall just go get the twins ready, then, and we can be off. I am sure they will want to go with us; they are so excited!" Allison looked at him over the edge of her teacup. "Perhaps your sister would care to join us? Jane and Kitty would love to get to know her better."

The veiled look came back into William's lovely blue eyes, and he shook his head. "Gertrude is—shy of strangers. It would be better if she stayed here with her governess."

"Oh." Allison remembered how quiet and withdrawn the girl had been the night before, and how little she had eaten at supper. Her heart twisted in sympathy. Something bad indeed *must* have happened to the Bradfords, then.

She wished Gertrude would come with them. Kitty and Jane could cheer anyone up. But it was none of her business really, so she just said, "Perhaps some other time, then."

William smiled at her again, but a bit sadly. "Yes. Some other time."

"Allie, look at this!" Jane cried, climbing up on a fence post to look out over a field.

They were standing about on the road into the village, waiting for William, who had gone into the woods with his gun. It felt as if they had been waiting for a long while, and Allison's feet were getting chilled in their half boots.

She stamped them a bit, and crossed the frosty road to where Jane was perched. "What is it? Do you see Mr. Bradford coming back?"

"Not yet. It's a pond! See? And people are skating on it."

Jane pointed, and Allison saw that there was indeed a pond in the distance, with colorful figures gliding back and forth. The faint sounds of laughter and "Wassail Song" floated to them on the clear, cold breeze.

Allison smiled at the sight. She had not gone skating in longer than she could remember, but she recalled the delicious sensation of it, floating free, flying. . . .

She closed her eyes and imagined being among the

happy skating party, zipping about the ice on the arm of a strong, handsome gentleman. A gentleman like William Bradford.

The misty daydream was dissipated when Jane said, "Can *we* go skating with them, Allie?"

Allison's eyes opened, and, despite the chill in the air, her cheeks felt uncomfortably warm. No doubt they were now as unattractively red as her hair!

She pulled the black velvet collar of her pelisse closer about her throat, and said, "We don't even know whose pond that is, Jane, and we don't have time to skate today."

Kitty, who had rejoined them with her arms full of sweet-scented pine boughs, said, "Can we skate some time before we leave?"

Allison nodded. "Perhaps."

"Wonderful!" Jane sighed. "But we won't be leaving for a long time, will we? There must be time for lots more fun."

"Oh, no!" said Kitty. "We still have all the twelve days of Christmas."

All the twelve days of Christmas. It sounded so short when at the end of it they would have to go back to their lonely life at the cottage.

But they *did* still have twelve days, and Allison wanted them to be wonderful for the girls. Maybe even for herself.

"Speaking of the twelve days of Christmas," she said, "we have heard nothing from Mr. Bradford for quite a while. Do you suppose he has found our partridge?"

"Maybe we should go look for him?" Kitty suggested.

"He said to wait here," Jane said.

"Pooh! And miss all the fun? I think we should go find him."

"*I* think we should wait!" Jane insisted.

Their argument was cut short when William emerged from the woods alongside the road. The game bag he held looked suspiciously flat.

"Mr. Bradford!" the twins called, running toward him.

Allison followed them at a more sedate pace. "I take it there were no partridges to be had?"

William grimaced. "Not a bird of any sort, I'm afraid. They must have all heard of the scavenger hunt. I don't know what else to do for our partridge."

Allison gave him a commiserating smile. "Me, either. I fear I have little imagination for things like this."

"Let's go into the village," Jane suggested. "They are sure to have some kind of bird there."

"And hair ribbons!" Kitty added, tugging at her own, which were, as usual, untied.

Allison thought of the pitifully few coins in her reticule. "I don't think we really need new ribbons today, girls."

"Don't worry, Allie!" Kitty called as the two of them skipped ahead. "Lady Kirkwood gave us each half a crown."

"She said we were to spend it on something pretty and useless," added Jane. "Like ribbons, and sweets!"

It was Jane who saw the pears first, glistening golden in the shop window.

"Look at this, Allie, Mr. Bradford!" she called.

"What is it, Jane?" Allison said, crossing the street with Kitty in tow and William trailing behind. "More skaters?"

"Of course not! It is pears."

"Pears?" Allison and William echoed. They looked at each other.

"Do you think this is a sign of some sort?" William asked.

Allison slowly shook her head. "Where would they get pears in December?"

"They aren't *real* pears, silly," Kitty said, examining the window display. "They are sugar pears."

"You want what?" the woman in the confectioner's shop said, in a most disbelieving manner.

"A sugar partridge," Allison said. "Just like this lovely fruit."

William held up the pears they had collected from the window in illustration.

"We need a sugar tree, too," Kitty piped up.

"A sugar pear tree," Jane clarified.

"I only have this." The woman ducked behind the counter, and came up with a bluebird, fashioned of marzipan and sprinkled with sparkling sugar.

"Partridges aren't blue," Kitty said doubtfully.

"Well, this is all I have. We sold everything else for Christmas," the woman said, obviously growing irritable at having to deal with such choosy customers. "You can take it or leave it."

Allison looked at William. "What do you think?" she whispered.

"I think we had better take it," he whispered back, leaning so close to her that his warm, mint-scented breath stirred her loose curls.

"A bluebird in a pear tree?" Allison said, trying to ignore the delicious sensations this invoked.

"At least we have the pears. And my sister has a

paint box. Perhaps she could make the bird less— blue."

"I suppose you are right. I don't have any better ideas, and at least then we will be done with the first day of Christmas."

"And on to the second! I don't suppose this shop would have turtledoves?"

"I'm not even entirely sure what a turtledove is," Allison answered with a sigh.

3

Two Turtledoves

The walk back to Kirkwood Manor was much more lighthearted than the walk away had been. William had been saved from hunting, which he secretly loathed doing, and now he could just enjoy Allison's companionship.

The two girls hurried ahead of them, munching on the sugared almonds they had bought as a treat. Their red cloaks darted in and out of the frozen greenery, bright flashes against the snow. Their laughter echoed and resounded.

How different they were from Gertrude, William reflected sadly. If she were walking with them, she would stay close by his side, quiet and always watching.

"Your sisters are very—energetic," he said.

Allison laughed. "Oh, yes! And you should see them at home. Here they are on their company manners." She looked up at him with sparkling hazel eyes. "Your own sister is very pretty. I'm sorry she could not join us today."

"As I said, she is rather shy."

"Oh. I see." They fell silent, the only sound the crunch of their shoes on the frosty road. After a long moment, she said, "We did hear of the death of your father last year. I am very sorry."

William nodded shortly. He did not like to think of his father, or the terrible thing that had happened. He hated the pitying way people would look at him, and Allison's clear gaze obviously saw far too much. She seemed to be looking at his deepest soul, where all that shame was hidden.

At least she did not look pitying.

"Thank you for your condolences," he said.

"It must be very hard on your sister," she answered. "Kitty and Jane were so confused and lost when our own father died. . . ."

"Gertrude was the one who found our father's body," William blurted, without thinking.

Allison stopped walking, and stood perfectly still there in the road. "I—beg your pardon?" Her cheeks were pale under the cold pink.

"Forgive me," William said, not meeting her gaze. "I should not have mentioned anything of the sort. It was most indelicate."

She shook her head. "I live in the country, Mr. Bradford; delicacy has little place in my life. But do you mean to say that after your father—did away with himself, it was your sister who discovered him?"

"I fear so."

"Oh, that poor, poor girl!" Allison cried. "No wonder she is so quiet."

"She scarcely speaks unless spoken to, and sometimes not even then. I was hoping it would help her to be here, away from our home." It was such a profound relief to speak of it with someone, instead of keeping it pressed down inside. And Allison did not look appalled or shocked; she looked very, very concerned, and sensible. She took his arm and continued walking beside him.

"Do you think it would help for the twins to socialize with her? They can be very cheering, but I would not like for her to be frightened by their exuberance," she said.

"It would be worth a try," William said. "Perhaps we could set them all to constructing our partridge in a pear tree?"

Allison laughed. "*That* sounds like an excuse to get out of doing it yourself!"

Kitty and Jane came running back to them then, their freckled cheeks flushed with excitement. "We have found our turtledoves!" Kitty cried.

"On the road, just up ahead," Jane added.

"How do you know they are *turtle*doves, and not just ordinary doves?" William asked them.

The twins looked at each other, and giggled. "Oh, we just know!" said Kitty. "Come and see."

Kitty and Jane's "turtledoves" proved not to be doves, or indeed any kind of birds, at all. They were people, a prosperous-looking young farmer and his golden-haired sweetheart, sitting on a log by the side of the road holding hands. They gazed up at each other in a distinctly rapturous manner, and didn't even seem to notice the four people staring at them.

"Don't they look like two turtledoves?" Jane whispered.

"Indeed they do," Allison answered. "But who are they?"

Kitty gave a very loud cough, making the two turtledoves start and look up at them, confused. Then they smiled when they saw the twins.

"So you're back, Miss Kitty!" the man said.

"Of course we are back! This is Mr. Albert Potter, Allie, and his betrothed, Miss Susan," said Kitty. "I have told them that if they help us win the scavenger hunt, we will help them organize their wedding. Miss Susan has her heart set on a very large wedding, you see."

Allison looked at her sister sternly. "Oh, you did, did you?"

"Oh, miss, it would be so wonderful!" Miss Susan burst out. "Then me and my Bertie could get married ever so much sooner."

"Of course we would be happy to help you," William said. "But what if we lose the hunt? We won't be able to—help you then."

Bertie shrugged. "We would still have had a lark, wouldn't we?"

"And I've always wanted to see inside Kirkwood Manor," sighed Susan.

"Done, then!" William said, reaching out to shake Bertie's hand. "You may be our turtledoves."

The twins laughed, and danced around merrily.

"Two done," Allison said, pulling her list out of her reticule and checking *Partridge* and *Turtledoves* off. "Five left."

That night, a supper was planned at Kirkwood Manor, to be followed by the presentation of the first day's objects. It was to begin at seven o'clock sharp, but the setting sun found the Gordons and Bradfords still hard at work.

They turned the small sitting room adjoining Allison's chamber into a workshop, with a large table set up down the center and covered with an oilcloth. Allison and William were using bits of wood and colored paper to fashion a little tree, while Bertie pasted the whole thing together and Susan tried to dry it by the fire. It had not helped at all that she set the first tree on fire, but the second one looked to be a great success.

Gertrude had been assigned to turn the bluebird into a partridge, using her paint pots. At first she had been highly doubtful, shrinking back against her brother and looking at the bird as if it would come alive and bite her. But she had quickly become engrossed in her task, her pretty face scrunched as she plied her brush over the delicate marzipan body. She did not even notice the twins any longer, as they sat on either side of her, closely watching her work.

She was very talented, Allison noted, watching as Gertrude's brush turned the blue candy into pale brown feathers.

"What do you suppose Sir Reginald and his family have found?" William mused, cutting out another leaf.

"Whatever it is, it cannot be as fine as this," Allison said, adding the finishing touches to the bark. "I hope."

"Certainly it won't!" Kitty said stoutly. "They could never have such a lovely partridge. Gertrude is making it look quite real."

Gertrude gave a shy smile.

"And no one could be better turtledoves than Bertie and Susan," Jane said. "You must just remember to hold hands and coo."

Bertie grinned. "Oh, we can do that! Can't we, Sue?"

Susan giggled, waving the newly pasted branch perilously close to the fire.

Allison silently prayed that all *would* go well with the presentation. It was far too late to search out new partridges and turtledoves now.

"All right, everyone!" Lady Kirkwood announced in the drawing room after supper, banging her cane on the floor to bring everyone closer to her chair. "It is time for you to show me what you have found on your hunt. Reginald, you will go first."

Sir Reginald and his family obviously had not had as successful a day as Allison and William. His dome of a forehead glistened as he nervously dabbed at it with a handkerchief. Letitia, sumptuously attired in cranberry-colored velvet, sat on a settee with her arms folded, not looking at her husband. The tall red plumes in her hair quivered.

Their son Edward was nodding over a glass of port, also not looking at his father. Miss Bates was totally absorbed in a box of candy.

Allison felt a new hope for their makeshift offerings. She looked up at William, who gave her an encouraging smile.

Reginald walked over to where a small, covered object sat in the corner. "After traveling far and wide, Aunt Harriet, we have found the finest partridge in a pear tree," he announced, obviously trying very hard to sound portentous and important.

Letitia sniffed loudly.

Reginald ignored his wife, and pulled off the cloth with a flourish.

Inside a small gilt cage was a bright yellow parakeet, perched precariously on a pile of evergreen boughs that was obviously meant to be a tree. It looked out at them with bewildered little eyes, and gave a tentative peep.

There was a moment of stunned silence in the room, then Gertrude burst out, "That is not a partridge! That is a parakeet!"

She turned as cherry-red as her satin sash, and clapped her hand over her mouth.

"You are quite right, Miss Bradford," Lady Kirkwood said, her own cheeks wrinkling even further into a smile. "I believe that *is* a parakeet, Reginald. Not the same thing as a partridge at all."

"I *told* you so, Reginald," Letitia hissed.

Kitty watched the bird in the cage indignantly. "He obviously hates it in there," she muttered. Before anyone realized what she was about, she ran across the room and flung open the door to the cage.

The parakeet, delighted at this new development, spread his small yellow wings and took off across the drawing room. He swooped across the fireplace mantel, sending a vase crashing to the floor, before plucking at Letitia's plumes. One came free, and he flew around triumphantly with it in his beak.

Letitia shrieked and screamed, clutching at her ruined coiffure while her son snickered into his port and her husband tried in vain to comfort her. Miss Bates hastily stuffed three pieces of candy into her mouth, as if she feared the bird would eat them.

Finally, William went and opened the drawing room door, and the bird flew off into the foyer, the plume still in its mouth.

Allison was too surprised to do anything but stand there. She ought to scold Kitty, she knew, for setting the bird free, but somehow all she wanted to do was laugh.

Just as Lady Kirkwood was doing. The old lady leaned back in her chair, laughing and gasping, her cane flailing in the air. "Oh, my! Well, after *that* little performance, I am most eager to see what you have to display, Miss Gordon and Mr. Bradford. I hope it is not quite as—active."

Their display! Allison closed her eyes in dismay. She had forgotten all about it in her excitement. Now everyone was looking at them in expectation, Reginald obviously hoping that whatever they had would surpass his in humiliation.

"Of course, Lady Kirkwood," William said. "We are most pleased to present our discoveries to you. But I fear we have gotten a bit ahead of ourselves. We have both a partridge in a pear tree and two turtledoves."

He gave Allison a reassuring smile, and beneath his calm charm she felt her pounding heart slow. Her hands ceased their trembling. Everything would be well, she thought.

Everything would always be well if William was there.

She nodded to Gertrude and the twins, who went into the foyer and then came back bearing the tray where their partridge in a pear tree was set up. They placed the tray on a table in front of Lady Kirkwood, and curtsied prettily.

The marzipan "partridge" gleamed in the firelight. Gertrude had done a superlative job, making each feather look soft and real. Even the hastily dried tree was intact.

The only thing amiss was that the little parakeet now nestled in the paper leaves along with the partridge, happily nibbling at one of the sugared pears.

"Er—a partridge *and* a parakeet in a pear tree," William said, his voice thick with laughter.

"I thought that went quite well," Allison said later as William escorted her up the stairs. The twins ran ahead, trailed by a still-shy Gertrude. "Lady Kirkwood seemed to like our partridge *and* our turtle-doves. Even though Sir Reginald said Bertie and Susan shouldn't count, since they are people and not doves." She was still rather disgruntled about that.

"But Lady Kirkwood accepted them, and that is all that matters," William said comfortingly. "Sir Reginald is just jealous because their parakeet in a pear tree was such a disaster."

Allison laughed at the memory of the bird swooping around with the red plume in its mouth. "Indeed! But we cannot count on him and his family being so—dare I say it?—bird-witted with all the objects. They have promised to present their turtledoves tomorrow morning, and they might come up with something quite clever."

"Do you really think so?"

"Anything is possible." She stopped in front of her chamber door. The twins were already inside; she could hear them running about and giggling. "This is my room," she said.

William looked down at her, his shadowed face serious in the flickering light of the wall sconces. "Miss Gordon—I . . ." His voice faded, and he glanced away from her, as if he longed to say something but could not quite find the words.

She wondered what it could be. "Perhaps you should call me Allison," she said. "When we are not in company. Miss Gordon sounds so very formal."

He gave her a small smile, and leaned closer. "And you should call me William. Since we are such old friends."

Allison scarcely dared to breathe. "Are we old friends?"

"Do you not remember the last party we attended here? We spent so much time together then."

"Time where you pulled my braid and called me

'Ginger,' " she said crossly, trying to distance herself
from the spell of his warmth. She had her family to
look after, a scavenger hunt to think about; she
couldn't afford to fall under William Bradford's attractive, distracting spell.

He laughed. "I only wanted to get your attention!
And I was too young to know better. I am sorry I
called you Ginger. Am I forgiven?"

"Perhaps," Allison murmured, leaning back against
the door. "Now, I should go in before the twins de-
stroy the room. I have French hens to think about."

"Oh, yes," William sighed. "The scavenger hunt. I
must think about that, too. And I should go check on
Bertie and Susan, see if they are happy where Lady
Kirkwood put them for the night."

"They seemed quite content with the cakes and ale
they were consuming with all the upper servants!" Allison said with a little laugh. "They were certainly having more fun than we were in the drawing room."

"So they were. Good night, then—Allison."

"Good night, William." Allison gave him one last
smile, then ducked into her chamber, closing the door
between them.

Kitty and Jane, already clad in their nightgowns,
were chasing each other around the room, swinging
pillows and laughing. They stopped to stare at Allison
when she came in.

"Allie!" Kitty cried. "You are blushing."

Allison pressed her hands to her cheeks, which did
indeed feel rather warm. "Don't be ridiculous, Kitty!"

"It is because she *likes* Mr. Bradford," Jane sang.
"She was talking to him out in the corridor for ever
so long."

"Allie likes Mr. Bradford!" they chorused, joining
hands and dancing about. "Allie likes Mr. Bradford!"

Allison forced down the urge to giggle, as if she were as young as they were. Instead, she went and took the girls by the hands, leading them briskly toward the connecting door to their own room. "What nonsense! You girls should employ your energies toward figuring out where we can find three French hens, not conjuring up romances for me."

William stood in the corridor for a long moment, staring at Allison's closed door. He could hear muffled laughter and chatter from within, and he longed to go inside and join in the merriment.

His life had been devoid of laughter for so long, and Allison and her sisters radiated it effortlessly. He was drawn to it like a fire on a cold day.

But he knew that he could not. He was in no position to take care of a wife properly. His estate was falling about his ears, and its gray halls were no place for Allison's merriment. He had his sad sister to take care of, and a scavenger hunt to win.

As if to confirm these thoughts, a small, cool hand slid into his. He looked down to see Gertrude had joined him, slipping up as silently as usual. She was still looking very solemn, but he thought her thin cheeks were pinker. The exercise of the day must have agreed with her.

"Hello, sparrow," he said. "I thought you would be asleep by now."

"I wanted to wait to say good night to you."

"Aren't you very tired?"

She shook her head.

"I was just off to check on Bertie and Susan in the upper servants' hall," he said. "Would you like to come along?"

Her eyes widened. "Won't there be—lots of people there?"

"Very probably. They were having some Christmas cakes. Perhaps they would give you one."

"Really? Cakes?" She considered this for a moment, then, much to William's surprise, nodded. "I would like that."

4

Three French Hens

"This is intolerable! Completely intolerable." Sir Reginald slapped his hand against his bedroom window, as he watched the Gordons and the Bradfords walk off down the drive in the pale morning sunlight. "I am meant to be the heir to everything. What good is this house without the money?"

Letitia did not even look away from her reflection in the dressing table mirror. She leaned forward and carefully applied rice powder to her thin cheeks. "You said if we came here we *would* be the heirs. I did not want to leave our comfortable house to travel in the middle of winter, but you said . . ."

"Yes, I know what I said!" he interrupted impatiently. "How was I to know she would make us play some silly game? Or that she would invite *them*."

"She seems to like them. More than she likes our dear Edward."

His eyes narrowed. "We shall soon see about that."

"We have looked everywhere, and no French hens!" Allison sat down at the last empty table in the village teashop, wearily reaching down to rub at her tired feet.

"No hens of any sort, I fear," William said, signaling to the serving maid for tea and cakes.

"We could go back to the confectioner's shop again, and see if they have any marzipan hens," Kitty suggested.

"We already did that!" Jane said, with a playful shove at her sister's shoulder. "We can't have candy birds again."

Kitty shoved back. "There is no rule that says that!"

The two of them giggled, while Gertrude looked on with wide eyes.

"Girls, please," Allison said. "You are not helping matters."

"I fear they may be right," William murmured, stirring cream into his tea. "We may have to repeat ourselves. We have no other ideas today."

Allison shook her head. "There must be *something*."

"Yes. Or the game will be over before it truly begins."

Gertrude bit her lip as she looked at her brother's tired, worried face. William *never* looked tired or worried, at least not in front of her. He usually maintained a merriment, a lightheartedness that could always reassure her in dark hours.

And in the last year, there had been many dark hours indeed.

She had hoped that this journey to Kirkwood Manor would help take away all that, help her forget. Last night, she *had* forgotten, caught up in the fun of making the pear tree and the excitement of the presentation. She had felt a part of a group again, not like an outsider always peering into life. It had felt like a true Christmas spirit, as she had felt when her mother was alive, and William would come home from school and all would be well.

Now she looked about the table, at her tired brother, at quiet, pretty Miss Gordon, and at the mischievous twins that she wished so desperately might like her. If there was only something she could do to help . . .

Then, as if in answer to her hopes, she heard voices from a nearby table. They seemed to float to her above all the other conversations in the room.

"As-tu vu le bonnet qu'elle portrait hier?" a woman's high, excited voice said.

Gertrude, who enjoyed her French lessons with her governess very much, translated in her mind, "Did you see the bonnet she was wearing yesterday?"

"Cinq annees demode!" another woman said.

A third chimed in. *"Je ne l'aurais pas cree!"*

"Des plumes oranges," the first woman clucked in disapproval.

"Tout a fait ridicule."

Gertrude wished she could have seen the unfashionable bonnet with the orange plumes; it sounded most interesting. She craned her neck to try to find the speakers.

The three women sat at a table not very far away. They seemed a matched set, almost like the twins except they were obviously of different ages. All three were short and plump, with glossy dark curls and stylish clothes. Each wore a pelisse and bonnet of the same style but different colors—violet for the oldest, yellow for the second, and bright blue for the youngest.

As she watched them, sipping their tea and disapproving the orange plumes, a wonderful idea took shape in Gertrude's mind. She slid off her chair and walked over to them, so caught up in this idea that she quite forgot her usual shyness.

She stopped beside the chair of the one in violet, and gave a little curtsy as the women ceased their conversation and looked at her in curiosity. *"Excusez-moi, mesdames,"* she said. *"Mais etes-vous peut-etre de la Bretagne?"*

The women laughed in delight, and clapped their plump white hands. *"Ah, quelle jeune fille intelligente!"* the one in yellow said.

Gertrude blushed at being called a clever girl, which sent them into more peals of merry laughter.

"Et si jolie, aussi!" the one in blue said. *"Tu es francais, ma petite?"*

"Non," Gertrude answered, then went on in English. "I am English, but I have studied French. I knew you were from Brittany because of your accents. I am Miss Gertrude Bradford."

"We are very pleased to meet such a pretty *petite anglais,"* the woman in violet said in heavily accented English. "I am Mademoiselle Sophie Millais, and these are my sisters, Mademoiselle Antoinette and Mademoiselle Margot."

"How do you do," Gertrude said.

"Won't you sit down for a moment, *cherie*?" said Antoinette. "And have a cake with us?"

Gertrude glanced back at her own table. The twins were watching her curiously, but William and Miss Gordon were speaking together quietly and did not seem to have noticed her absence yet. *"Merci, mesdames,"* she said, sitting down in the fourth chair at their table. "Have you been here very long in the village?"

Margot slid a very large cake onto Gertrude's plate,

and said, "Ah, not long at all. We have come with
Sophie to meet her, how do you say, *lettres-ami,* the
Reverend Mr. Johnstone, at his new church."

Sophie giggled at the mention of her "letter friend."
"We have never met before," she said. "Only have
written of our many mutual charities."

"But now they will meet, since this silly war is over,
and surely marry," Margot said.

Gertrude was fascinated by this romantic story. She
nibbled at her cake, and listened to them as they
talked on of the good reverend. She noticed that her
brother was now looking about for her; her time was
growing short.

"I wonder, *mesdames,*" she said, marveling at her
own boldness, "if I might ask you for a very great
favor. . . ."

5

Four Colly Birds

"That was marvelous, Gertrude!" Allison said as
they strolled along to escort Mademoiselle Sophie to
meet her Mr. Johnstone. William walked ahead with
the three sisters clustered about him like bright, chattering flowers. "Very clever of you to find our three
French hens."

Gertrude blushed, and ducked her chin into the fur
collar of her coat. "Thank you, Miss Gordon," she
murmured. "It was nothing at all."

"Nothing at all!" Jane exclaimed. "Why, you spoke
French like the veriest Parisian. I wish I had such a
lovely accent."

"Your accent would be a good deal more elegant if you would just do your lessons," Allison admonished.

"Pish!" said Kitty. "If we studied for ten years, we could not sound like Gertrude did. Perhaps you could teach us some of those words, Gertrude?"

Gertrude bit her lip, and glanced ahead to where her brother walked. Then she slowly nodded, and the three girls hurried off together.

Allison walked on by herself, watching William as he charmed the French sisters with his effortless smiles and little courtesies. They hung on his arms, giggling, enraptured by his attentions.

She very much feared that she herself looked like that whenever his attention turned her way. Silly and giggling.

She had felt nervous about seeing him again after all these years, remembering her schoolgirl crush. She had wondered if those feelings would come back upon her. And so they had. Only stronger. Much stronger.

When last they met, she had been practically a child, swooning over the first handsome young man she had ever seen, longing for his teasing, fleeting attentions. Now life had intervened in the passing years, life that was seldom easy. She was no longer the girl she had been; William was no longer that laughing boy. They were adults, and her feelings toward him were equally mature.

But she had no dowry to speak of, nothing to offer a husband even if he thought of her in that way, which she did not think he did. They had only a few more days of Christmas left. And then she would go back to the cottage, and her real life.

She watched William and the ladies turn into the churchyard gate, him gallantly holding it open while they fluttered past him. Well, then, even if they had only a few days left, she would make sure they were the very best days possible!

"Are you coming, Allison?" William called, still holding open the gate.

Allison hurried her steps toward him. "Oh, yes!" she called back.

The Reverend Mr. Johnstone turned out to be the perfect match for Mademoiselle Sophie, a round little man with pink cheeks and a merry countenance that belied his stark black clothes. He rubbed his plump hands together in glee when he saw the large party that had accompanied his "letter friend" to the church.

"Oh, my stars!" he cried, bowing right and left. "How very grand! You must all come into the vicarage and have some tea. My curate, Mr. Ellis, is here, as well as two old school friends of mine who are now settled in their own livings. My housekeeper has laid out far too much food for just the four of us, so it is blessed Providence that you have arrived."

"Oh, we could not possibly intrude . . ." Allison began.

"Nonsense!" Mr. Johnstone answered. "I will be most insulted if you do not come inside and join us. Is that not right, Mademoiselle Millais?"

Sophie beamed at him. *"Mais oui!"*

And so they gratefully accepted the invitation, except for the twins and Gertrude, who were engaged in a vigorous game of hide-and-seek amid the ancient headstones of the churchyard.

Later, happily sipping tea by the fire in the vicarage's cozy sitting room, Allison looked at the four vicars in their black clothes next to the bright, chat-

tering Frenchwomen. She thought, with a flash of
fancy, that they looked like a flock of blackbirds
among parrots. . . .

Blackbirds! Four colly birds.

Of course.

"Now, everyone. What do you have for me tonight?" Lady Kirkwood, seated once again on her
"throne," said, with a bang of her cane. "You may go
first, Reginald."

Allison had consumed two glasses of wine at supper,
far more than her usual amount, but she still felt quite
nervous. The three French hens and four colly birds
waited upstairs in her sitting room, excited to be part
of the game. She had no doubt that they would never
let them down; but what if Sir Reginald had come up
with something truly brilliant?

It seemed doubtful. Letitia looked as bored as ever,
languorously fanning herself by the fire. Edward and
his Miss Bates were sharing a bowl of sweetmeats over
in the corner. Only Sir Reginald looked as if he cared
at all about the outcome of the game as he wiped at
his brow with a lace-trimmed handkerchief.

"Of course, Aunt," he said, rising unsteadily to his
feet. He went to the drawing room doors, threw them
open, and called, "You may bring them in now."

A moment of deep, worrying silence followed. Then
the silence was broken by a great dissonance. A footman carried in a large cage, where three fat chickens
clucked and gobbled. He was followed by another footman, also bearing a cage, filled with four large blackbirds, cawing and flapping their great, glossy wings.

Feathers flew in large tufts from the cages, landing
on the satin chairs and valuable rugs. The birds had
used the bottoms of the cages as chamber pots, and a

rich barnyard smell filled the air, overpowering the scents of pine, wood smoke, and Letitia's perfume.

"Ugh!" Kitty groaned, burying her nose in the lace cuff of her dress.

Jane also groaned, but Gertrude was too polite. Her little nose just quivered and wrinkled in silence.

Allison passed her a handkerchief.

"What is *this,* Reginald?" Lady Kirkwood said, distrustfully eyeing the livestock.

"Three French hens and four colly birds, of course," Reginald answered, turning a rather appalling shade of crimson in his indignation. "What you asked for!"

"I never asked you to bring an entire farmyard into my drawing room. Heaven only knows where you got the poor creatures," Lady Kirkwood said.

"I sent all the way to France for hens," Reginald protested.

"Did you indeed? They look suspiciously like the ones Farmer Martin down the road raises." Lady Kirkwood gestured toward the footmen. "Take them away, please, before they ruin my furniture utterly."

As the footmen carried the cages away, Sir Reginald stamped his foot in anger. "Aunt, I must protest! I have played your ridiculous game according to your very own rules, and you just . . ."

Lady Kirkwood froze him with one sharp glance. He seemed to shrink back into himself, and went to sit quietly beside his wife.

"Fool!" Letitia hissed, turning her turbaned head away from him.

Lady Kirkwood looked at Allison and William. "Well? And what do *you* have for me? Nothing quite so odorous, I hope."

"No, indeed, Lady Kirkwood," William said, nodding at Gertrude to go and fetch their "offerings."

The French hens and colly birds entered the room with as much noise as the real birds had, but with a considerably better fragrance. The mademoiselles had changed into bright silk evening gowns, and fluttered with exclamations over the lovely furnishings and festive holiday decorations. They were followed by the four clerics, more subdued but obviously quite excited to be at Kirkwood Manor. Their best black coats stood out beautifully against the ladies' brilliant gowns.

"Well," Lady Kirkwood said with a satisfied smile. "*This* is more like it. How do you do, everyone?"

Sir Reginald glared. But Allison did not see that at all, because William's hand sought hers out in the concealing folds of her skirt, and squeezed it warmly.

6

Five Gold Rings

"Rose, I think what Kirkwood Manor needs now is a ball," Lady Kirkwood announced to her maid.

Rose paused in brushing Lady Kirkwood's hair for the night. "A *ball*, my lady? But there hasn't been a ball here in ever so long!"

"Four years. That was the last one, right before my husband died. I have not felt like dancing since then." She touched one wrinkled finger tenderly to the miniature portrait propped on her dressing table.

"What has changed your mind, my lady?"

"Watching the young people, of course. It has been a very long time since young people have been at

Kirkwood Manor! They are so energetic, so enthusiastic about everything. They make me laugh; they make me want to dance again. So we shall have a great Christmas ball! Fetch me my lap desk, Rose."

While the maid scrambled to find the desk, Lady Kirkwood took a small key from her jewel case and bent down to unlock the bottom drawer of her dressing table. She withdrew an exquisitely made music box.

A gilt goose made up the main portion, a glittering creature with emerald eyes surrounded by five other, smaller geese. When she turned a knob, the geese rotated in a circle to the tinny strains of "The Twelve Days of Christmas." The largest one then laid one perfect emerald egg.

"Oh, my lady!" Rose cried, coming back into the room with the desk. "It's beautiful."

"It is, isn't it?" Lady Kirkwood murmured. "It was a gift from my late husband on our last Christmas together. I want you to do something for me, Rose."

"What is it, my lady?"

"Take this to Miss Gordon's room and leave it for her. But do not tell her it is from me." Lady Kirkwood's gaze turned shrewd as she watched the golden geese float around. "I have grown awfully fond of the girl, and of her beau Mr. Bradford. And I have a feeling they will soon be needing this far more than I."

Allison's small sitting room was very crowded indeed for after-dinner tea. None of their "twelve days" had gone home yet, and they all sat about on chairs, settees, and footstools, drinking tea, chatting, and playing cards. Mademoiselle Sophie flirted with her vicar, while the other French hens sketched some Parisian fashions for Gertrude and the twins, who were in turn munching on leftover marzipan pears. The turtle-doves, Bertie and Susan, cooed about their wedding plans in the window seat. The colly birds played a wild game of whist beside the fire.

Allison sat in a relatively quiet corner next to William, a piece of embroidery held in her hands but quite forgotten. She watched the people crowded into the room, listened to the cacophony of all the voices blended together. Bertie and Susan's whispers, the sisters' French exclamations, the clergymen's chuckles as they slapped cards down on the table, the giggles of the twins.

It had been a very long time since she was in company with so many people. Usually it was just her, her mother, and the girls, with an occasional visit from the vicar's wife and sister. So much noise and energy was almost intoxicating.

She was so very engrossed by the scene before her that she did not even notice when a ball of thread fell from her lap onto the floor, until William scooped it up and handed it to her.

His hand brushed hers as he placed the pink ball on her palm, causing delicious shivers to go down her spine.

She felt her cheeks grow warm, as they always did around him, and she quickly looked down to tuck the thread into her basket. "Thank you," she murmured.

William grinned at her, and leaned closer, propping his elbow on the arm of her chair. "It is quite a lively crowd we have gathered, is it not?"

"Indeed it is!" Allison seized on the excuse to look away from his too-wise blue eyes and examine the company again. "But I fear that now they are ensconced here at Kirkwood Manor, they will never leave."

William shrugged, his dark coat rippling nicely over his shoulders. "Who can blame them? Good food, comfortable feather beds, servants everywhere. Why, I am tempted to stay here myself!"

Allison had begun to think the same thing, though she would never have said it aloud. The food and feather beds were seductive indeed, but she had her mother and the cottage to look after. "We may *have* to stay here forever," she said, trying to sound light and uncaring, as if she did not long for things she could not have. "We have only found four of the twelve days, and Christmas is rushing upon us. Sir Reginald and his family must be so very far ahead."

William laughed. "We beat old Reggie most handily last night! Did you see how Lady Kirkwood pinched her nose shut when he brought in all those smelly birds?"

Allison also had to laugh at the memory. "It *was* rather smelly! But he gave me such a smug look as we were leaving the drawing room. As if he had some trick up his sleeve."

"All Sir Reginald has up his sleeve are his skinny arms. We are much more clever than he is, and besides . . ." His voice faded, and he looked away from her.

"Besides what?" Allison asked curiously.

He still did not look at her, but plucked his fingers at the brocade of her chair arm. "Besides, would it be the end of the world if we did not win this game?"

Allison looked straight at him then in surprise. "Do you not want to win?"

"Of course I do. It would mean so much to have Lady Kirkwood like us, to have her help, especially for Gertrude."

Allison thought of their shabby cottage, of the

dresses and shoes the girls seemed to outgrow within a week, and her mother's medicines. "And for Kitty and Jane, and Mama," she murmured.

"But there are so many more important things, I am finding," he went on. "Things such as . . ."

"Things such as what?" she asked, a strange, deep hope growing reluctantly in her heart. Could he possibly be feeling the same way she was? Feeling that, if one had love, it would never matter how small the cottage was.

But then he laughed lightly, and sat back in his own chair, the intense light in his eyes gone. Allison felt silly for even imagining such things. She reached again for her embroidery, and began energetically plying the needle through the snowy cloth. She did not even notice what a puckered mess she was making of it.

"There are some things I would like to talk to you about, Allison," William said. "But this hardly seems the right time or place."

A small hope rose up again, but it did not have time to take root. Mr. Johnstone came up to them, Mademoiselle Sophie on his arm and all the other colly birds trailing behind them.

"My dear new friends!" he said jovially. "We have all had such a grand time here, we wanted to find a way to repay you for your kind hospitality."

"But you provided us with our four colly birds!" Allison protested. "That is more than ample."

Mr. Johnstone shook his head. "No, it does not seem enough. So, my friends and my dear Mademoiselle Sophie and her sisters have all decided to help you find your next day of Christmas."

"Five golden rings?" William said eagerly.

"Exactement!" Sophie cried. "It is the wedding rings, no? So romantic."

"And Mr. Smith here is conducting a wedding tomorrow morning!" Mr. Johnstone said. "I am sure the wedding couple could represent your five rings."

"And I pronounce you husband and wife. Amen."

William watched as the couple bowed their heads for the blessing, the veil of the bride's bonnet fluttering. He was all-too-aware of Allison, standing close to him in the shadows at the back of the church. Her black velvet hat brushed against his shoulder as she bowed her own head, and the scent of her rose soap seemed to wrap around him in the half gloom.

Before he had come to Kirkwood Manor and seen Allison again, he had thought of marriage as a sort of necessary evil, something one had to do to beget children and satisfy society. Now he was beginning to see it in a very different light indeed.

He only wished he could be worthy of her. Could offer her a grand mansion, fine gowns, jewels, and carriages. She deserved all that, and more.

Instead, all he had was his unworthy self, a ramshackle house, and a pile of his father's debts.

She would probably laugh him out of the room if he tried to propose.

Then he felt a tugging at his sleeve, and looked down to see Allison frowning up at him in puzzlement.

"The ceremony is over now," she said. "We can leave."

William looked about with surprise. The church was quite deserted. The happy couple had exited right past them in a shower of dried flower petals, and he had not even noticed. "I'm sorry," he said. "I was woolgathering."

"I could see that." Allison took his arm, and they made their way out into the winter sunshine in the wake of the bridal party. "What were you thinking of so deeply?"

"Of gold rings, of course," he answered. He looked down at her gloved hand on his sleeve. It would take a very small gold ring indeed to fit on that slender finger.

"I was thinking of that, as well. I only hope Lady Kirkwood will accept this couple, and their one gold ring."

"What about you, Allison? Would you accept one gold ring?" William blurted before he could stop himself.

Allison became very still. She stopped walking, and looked up at him. "Whatever do you mean?"

He glanced about them to find that they stood alone in the churchyard, with the bridal party waiting for them out beside the carriage.

"I—well," he said, not certain what to do. He wanted to pour all his heart out to her, to tell her what he was feeling.

But, once again, this hardly seemed to be the best time. And what if she did not feel the same way?

"What is it, William?" she said.

"I don't mean anything at all!" he said with a laugh. "All the candle smoke in the church must have addled my senses. Shall we go?"

"Yes, of course. We are supposed to meet Mr. Johnstone's friends back at Kirkwood Manor before luncheon, so that the bridal couple can go back to their wedding breakfast after meeting Lady Kirkwood."

"Well, I *did* enjoy that," Lady Kirkwood said, sitting back with a happy sigh to survey the remains of tea and cake on the table before her. The bridal couple had departed, full of the delicious refreshments and flushed with pleasure at their cordial reception by Lady Kirkwood.

Not even Sir Reginald's sour glances had spoiled the lovely afternoon.

"I am very glad you approve of our offering, Lady Kirkwood," Allison said, keeping a close eye on the twins and Gertrude, where they were plonking at the keyboard of the pianoforte.

"We could not find four other couples to round out the five rings," William added. "We feared we would be disqualified." Especially after Sir Reginald took the challenge literally and presented five *real* rings, he added silently.

"Not at all," said Lady Kirkwood. "It has been a long time since Kirkwood Manor saw a happy young couple, just starting out in life together. It was most delightful. And," she added, "*four* couples would have made the drawing room too crowded for me to enjoy it properly. As for Sir Reginald, the poor boy has no imagination, I fear. None at all."

"A wedding couple they brought here!" Sir Reginald fumed, pacing the length of his chamber. "How could anyone do better than that bit of cleverness? The old lady was delighted even though there was only one wedding ring! She even invited the happy newlyweds to tea, and ordered the chef to bake a wedding cake."

Letitia lowered the hand mirror she was looking into. "It is not your fault, Reginald," she said, in a rare show of support. "Those rings you bought at the goldsmith are lovely." She admired the one that now resided on her finger.

"They also set me back a pretty tuppence. And she scarcely even looked at them."

Letitia smoothed her hair back into its elaborate upsweep and said, "Do not worry, Reginald. You are the heir to the Manor, no matter what those silly people come up with. And Edward after you."

"But what good is this old house without the funds to run it? And she holds all the purse strings to *that,* thanks to my besotted old uncle."

"Exactly so." Letitia laid the mirror down with a loud chatter. "So kindly do not make a mess of things again."

7

Six Geese A-Laying

Allison held the music box in her hands, watching the tiny, perfect geese swim around and the emerald egg come down. "Who left it, though?" she asked the twins, deeply puzzled.

It was exactly right for the sixth day of Christmas.

But where had it come from? Jane had just found the package outside the bedroom door.

"I don't know," Jane said innocently, shrugging her shoulders. "The note just says it is for you."

"Maybe it is a love token from Mr. Bradford," Kitty said, and the two girls dissolved into giggles.

"Don't be so silly," Allison said, mock-stern. "Mr. Bradford would not be sending me tokens of any sort." Would he?

The only logical choice was Lady Kirkwood herself, but why would she be sending Allison a music box? It was all very odd.

She carefully wrapped up the delicate contraption again, intending to show it to William before supper and see what he might make of it. "Go and change your dresses, girls. We haven't much time before supper."

The twins traipsed off to their own room, still giggling. Allison turned to the mirror to make sure her own attire was in order.

Her red hair was unruly, as usual, curls escaping every which way from the coronet her braids made. There was little she could do about that, aside from cutting the whole mess off, but she did wish she had a new gown. She had already worn the pale green muslin once, for their first supper at Kirkwood Manor, and even though her mother had added some white bows and ribbons to it, it was obviously years out of fashion.

If only she had a proper gown, maybe one of deep blue silk or dark green velvet. One that swirled and shimmered. How would William look at her then? With admiration? With—love?

Allison laughed aloud at her own folly. Even if she had a hundred such gowns, William would not look at her any differently. She would still have wild red hair, and he would still be a golden Apollo. He might enjoy flirting with her a bit, since she was the only eligible lady in the house party, but that was surely all there was to it.

If only *she* could feel the same frivolous way.

"You are looking most pretty tonight, sparrow," William said, watching his sister as she practically skipped ahead of him down the corridor. In only the few days they had been at Kirkwood Manor, Gertrude had gone from a pale little ghost who hid in the shadows to an almost-normal young girl. Her blond hair shimmered, and her cheeks were pink with exercise and excitement.

She even seemed to have gained a little weight, and she smiled and laughed frequently. She still did not talk very much, and liked to stay close to his side, but she was much more the old Gertrude he remembered, a girl who would speak to strange Frenchwomen in tea shops.

He suspected the change was much due to the boisterous company of the Gordons and the distraction of Lady Kirkwood's game.

"I like it here," Gertrude said, twirling to a stop. "It's much more jolly than at our house. I wish we never had to go back there."

William nodded, thinking of the empty, echoing halls of their home.

Gertrude came back to his side, and stretched up on tiptoes to kiss his cheek. "This is the best Christmas I ever had," she whispered.

"Me, too," William whispered back.

Allison and her sisters appeared in the corridor then, and Gertrude hurried over to greet Kitty and Jane. Allison stayed behind to walk with William down the staircase.

"I received the most extraordinary gift today," she said.

"Really? What was it? A box of candy from our *dear* Sir Reginald, perhaps?" William teased.

Allison laughed. "Not at all! It is this." She unlooped the drawstrings of her overstuffed reticule and drew out a small, elaborately worked music box.

"Six geese a-laying," William said in wonder.

"Exactly. The next step in our game, the one we were having such trouble with."

"But where did you get it?"

"Jane found it in the corridor The note says it is a gift from Nobody."

"Nobody, eh? Don't you suppose it is from Lady Kirkwood herself?"

"Of course that's what I thought, but why would she be giving me gifts?"

William leaned closer, and whispered, "Perhaps she favors us to win her game. And wouldn't *you* favor us, too, if the alternative was Cousin Reggie and his family?"

Allison giggled, and just started to reply when the drawing room doors opened and a great rush of noise emerged. There was a rising chorus of shrieks, squeals, and screams.

Kitty, Jane, and Gertrude, who had gone into the drawing room ahead of them, came rushing out holding their noses.

"Oh, Allie!" Kitty cried. "You must come at once and see this. It is worse than the chickens and blackbirds. Sir Reginald has brought six geese into the house!"

"Six geese," Allison said, not sure she had heard them correctly. "Six real, live geese?"

"Very alive," said Jane. "One is eating Letitia's headdress, and the other is chewing Lady Kirkwood's carpet!"

"And one has been sick all over Miss Bates," Gertrude added.

"This I *must* see," Allison said, hurrying into the room.

William was right behind her.

8

Seven Swans A-Swimming

"Well, our music box was a great success," Allison said. "Especially after Sir Reginald's geese destroyed the drawing room so completely. But wherever will we find seven swans?"

They were once again walking the familiar road into the village, Gertrude and the twins gathering fresh greenery to add to the decorations at Kirkwood Manor. William offered his hand to help Allison over a puddle, then kept hold of it as they continued walking.

Allison found she did not mind a bit.

"Maybe we could find some on that pond where we saw the skaters?" Kitty suggested.

"Swans would not swim on a frozen pond, silly," Jane scoffed.

"*You* are the silly one!" Kitty cried, giving her sister a small shove.

"Girls, do not quarrel," Allison admonished distractedly. "We haven't time for that."

"Perhaps there are no swans there now," said William, "but maybe we could go skating this afternoon? I think we need a distraction from the game."

"Oh, yes!" Jane and Kitty chorused, their incipient quarrel quite forgotten. "Can we, please, Allie?"

Allison ached to go skating as much as they did, but, as usual, she had to be the sensible one. "We do not even know whose pond it is. They might not want us skating on it."

"It is a simple enough thing to find out. We can ask permission." William grinned. "Surely, in the holiday spirit, they would not refuse us."

"We saw a gate the other day," said Kitty eagerly. "I am sure it must lead to the owner's house."

"Very well," Allison answered. "If the owner says we may, and if we can find some skates to borrow, we will go skating."

It was quite obvious that no one had lived in the house next to the pond for some time. It was a very pretty place, of faded red brick with round corner towers, but many of the windows were shuttered, and ivy grew wild up the walls.

"It looks just like the Sleeping Beauty's castle," Jane said quietly. "Like in that story Mama read us when we were children."

"Maybe we'll find a whole family asleep in there," Kitty answered.

"Don't be silly, girls," Allison murmured, nudging a chunk of fallen brick with the toe of her half boot. "It is just a house."

But it *was* rather nice, quiet and echoing and sweet in the cold morning air. Almost like it really was out of a fairy story, she reflected, looking up at the white stone portico.

Then she saw it. Above the double front doors was a stone frieze, depicting six beautifully carved swans and one tiny cygnet, trailing after them.

"Oh!" she breathed, in awe at the lifelike beauty of them. "Oh," she said louder, recognizing the significance of them.

She tugged at William's sleeve. "Look," she said, pointing one gloved finger at the frieze. "Swans a-swimming."

The twins and Gertrude, who had gone off to try to peer in some of the unshuttered windows, came running back to join William and Allison in staring up at the swans.

"Perfect," William said.

"They are beautiful," said Jane.

"Our seven swans a-swimming!" Kitty cried happily. "They are just right."

"Unless you think we should find some real birds, like Sir Reginald seems to have a penchant for doing," William teased.

"Ugh!" Gertrude wrinkled her nose.

Allison climbed the front steps to get a closer look at the carving. "I think it is just what we need. The only problem will be getting it down from there. It seems quite solidly attached to the wall. Perhaps we could do a rubbing of some sort, like people do on medieval monuments. . . ."

The rest of her words were drowned out by the sound of a gunshot echoing across the overgrown courtyard.

The twins and Gertrude shrieked, and ducked behind a tangled bush. William dove across the front steps and caught Allison about the waist, pulling her down onto the cold marble and throwing himself over her.

Ordinarily, Allison would scarcely have complained. His hands were warm through the layers of his gloves and her pelisse, and he smelled utterly delicious. But the steps were quite cold indeed, and some sharp edge was jabbing her in the back.

It also somewhat lessened the romance of the moment that they had just been shot at.

"Are we under attack?" she said, her voice muffled against his wool greatcoat.

"Ye're trespassin'," a stentorian voice rang out,

along with the ominous click of a gun being reloaded. "I hates trespassers."

Allison peeked past William's shoulder to see a large, burly man in sturdy country tweeds and tall boots. His small eyes and cold-reddened nose were almost hidden behind bushy brows and a wild beard.

Did the Sleeping Beauty's castle have a guardian troll in it? Allison could not remember.

"Stay behind me," William whispered. He rose to his feet, pulling Allison up with him. "Forgive us, sir, but we never meant to trespass. Are you perchance the owner of this house?"

The man lowered his gun a fraction. "Nay. I be the caretaker, John Harper."

"Well, Mr. Harper, we only wished to ask permission of the owner to skate on the pond. We were struck by the beauty of this carving, and came over to examine it closer."

John's brows softened a bit. "Oh, aye. It's a pretty piece, that. But you can't ask the owner anything."

"Is he away?" Allison decided to ask, standing on tiptoe to peek over William's shoulder.

"Has been these last two years. He lost all his money, y'see, and went to America. I looks after it until a new owner can be found."

"You mean no one has yet bought such a splendid house?" Allison was incredulous. Why, if *she* had a chance to live in such a lovely place . . .

John Harper relented completely then, and lowered the gun to the ground. "It *is* a right pretty place, miss. But some folks thinks it's too far from London."

The girls had cautiously ventured out from behind the bush, and now stood crowded close to Allison and William.

"What is the house called?" Gertrude bravely asked.

"Swan's Court," John answered. "In the summer there's swans what lives on the pond. But in the winter everyone skates on it. So I suppose you could, too."

"Lovely!" the twins crowed, casting longing looks at the pond.

William stepped forward slowly to offer his hand for John Harper to shake. "I wonder, good sir, if we might ask you another great favor."

"Allie! Allie, watch me!" Kitty darted out onto the ice, and executed a small spin.

"Do be careful, Kitty," Allison called, reaching down to tighten the fastenings of her skates, that were borrowed from Swan Court's storeroom, before she joined the girls. "I do not want you to fall and break anything."

"Of course I won't," Kitty scoffed. She slid off to join Jane and Gertrude, who were circling the perimeter of the pond.

Allison looked back across the field at the house. She could just barely see where William and John Harper were standing on ladders to take a rubbing of the swan frieze.

Now that they were free of the threat of Mr. Harper's gun, she could think more clearly of the delicious sensations of having William practically atop her.

It had been truly most interesting, she mused, watching as William shed his coat to work on the frieze. And perhaps, if they had not been under attack for trespassing, he might have kissed her. . . .

She wondered what *that* would have been like.

"Allie!" Jane called. "Aren't you going to skate?"

Startled out of her daydreams, she looked up to find that the girls had stopped quite close, and were watching her expectantly.

"Oh, yes," she said. "Of course."

As she pushed out onto the ice and joined them in circling the pond, Kitty said teasingly, "You certainly had a dreamy look on your face, Allie."

"She was probably wondering what it would be like to live here," Jane answered with a giggle. "With a certain person, and a nursery full of babies."

"Girls," Allison said warningly, looking at Gertrude to see if she knew that the twins were talking about her brother. But Gertrude was looking back at Swan Court.

"*I* wouldn't mind living here," she said. "It would probably be lovely."

"Don't you like where you live, Gertrude?" Kitty asked, doing another little spin.

"It is very big and empty," Gertrude answered in a small voice. "Not cozy and pretty like here."

"Well, if it is cozy you want, you should come and see our cottage," said Jane. "It is so cozy, there is scarce room to walk!"

"We are always tripping over the dogs and Mama's sewing," added Kitty.

"It sounds wonderful," said Gertrude. "There is nothing to trip over at all in my house!"

"Not like here on the ice!" Kitty cried. "Come on, I'll race you all to the end of the pond!"

The three girls dashed off amid a tangle of cloaks and laughter, but Allison paused to wait for William, who was coming along the field with his skates in his hand.

As she watched him move closer, his golden hair tousled in the wind, she thought about Gertrude's words. It made her heart ache to think of William and Gertrude living in a cold, empty house, a house that must echo with sad memories of their father's death. At least in their cottage, as small as it was, there was always love and laughter.

Suddenly, their quiet life did not seem so bad after all. Allison missed her mother with a sharp pang.

"Why, Allison!" William said, coming upon her just as she felt a tear on her cheek. "What is the matter?"

She attempted a rather watery-feeling smile. "Nothing at all! How could anything be wrong on such a lovely day?"

"Nonsense. You were about to start crying." He dug out a handkerchief and pressed it into her hand. "Now, tell me what it is."

"I was just thinking about my family," she said, wiping carefully at her cheeks. The linen held William's own wonderful scent. "And I was missing my mother."

"Why did she not come with you to Kirkwood Manor?"

"She is not very well, and thought she had best not undertake the journey. But she would have loved this holiday so much."

William nodded thoughtfully, and sat down to strap on his skates. "Well, come skating with me now. The exercise will do you good."

"Yes," Allison said with a smile, tucking the handkerchief into her sleeve to launder later. "Quite right."

"And you will be glad to know we managed to take a fine rubbing of the frieze," he said, and took her arm to lead her back onto the ice. "Mr. Harper is just gone to find a box to transport it to Kirkwood Manor in."

9

"Are you going to go to the village dance, then, Miss Gordon?" asked Lady Kirkwood's maid, Rose, as she helped Allison dress her hair for the day.

"The village dance?" Allison said, enjoying the unaccustomed luxury of having someone else fix her hair. The curls actually looked smooth and glossy under Rose's hands.

"Oh, yes. It's a tradition, held every year on Christmas Eve on the village green."

"An outdoor party in December? Doesn't it get rather cold?"

"No, miss, not at all! There are bonfires, and the dancing keeps you warm." She giggled. "Not to mention the rum punch!"

Allison was intrigued. In the village back home, there was always a little Christmas party at the vicarage, with a claret cup and the vicar's sister playing carols on the pianoforte. It was the height of the social season there. But bonfires and dancing sounded ever so much more fun.

And there was always the chance that William might ask her to dance. That would indeed be a memory to cherish once she was back home again.

As if to echo her thoughts, Rose said, "Mr. Bradford, your young gentleman, looks as if he'd be a fine one in a jig."

"He isn't *my* young man," Allison protested weakly.

"Isn't he?" Rose peered at her closely. "Well, I'm sure he very soon will be. Especially if you come to the dance."

"Can children come to this dance, too?" Allison asked, already having visions of twirling around bonfires in William's arms. "I do not think it a very wise idea to leave my sisters alone at Kirkwood Manor."

"Oh, yes! Everyone comes."

"Then I am sure we will *all* see you there."

Indeed it seemed that everyone *was* there on the village green that night, gathered about the roaring bonfires and the refreshment tables soon after the sun went down. Kitty and Jane, pulling Gertrude in their wake, immediately joined a group of other young people, leaving Allison and William standing at the edge of the crowd.

Allison surveyed the scene with wide eyes. It was utterly marvelous. Several musicians were tuning up on a makeshift platform, while couples formed and milled about on a cleared space for dancing. The flames of the bonfires crackled and danced, mixing with the sounds of laughter and chatter and music in a glorious medley.

Allison shrugged deeper into her black wool cloak, and smiled with quiet pleasure.

"This is marvelous, Allison," William said, reaching for her hand and giving it a warm squeeze.

"Yes, it is."

"If we had to find all twelve days of Christmas, I would wager we could find all of them right here."

"Days of Christmas?"

"There are pipers piping, drummers drumming, ladies dancing . . ."

Allison laughed. "William!"

"What is it?"

"Let us not even think about the scavenger hunt tonight. It is over. Let us just dance and eat and have fun."

"Fun?" he said rather doubtfully, as if it was an unknown concept.

"Yes," she answered firmly, clutching his hand and leading him onto the dancing space. "There will be no more talk of days of Christmas tonight."

Four dances later, they were out of breath and exhilarated. Allison fell against William's shoulder, laughing, as the musicians struck up yet another lively tune.

"Shall we dance again?" William asked, holding her against him.

"I don't think I could. Not just yet. I can scarce catch my breath."

"Then let's go get something to drink, and sit down for a while."

"That sounds heavenly."

They obtained glasses of punch, and found a quiet, dimly lit nook from which to watch the festivities.

Allison smiled as she saw the twins playing blindman's buff with the other young people, their cheeks pink with merriment. The music rang out in the cold air. It had been a truly splendid evening, one she would never forget.

If only it could go on and on . . .

"Allison," William said, his suddenly serious tone at odd contrast with the holiday scene before them.

Allison turned to look up at him in concern. "William? What is it? Is something amiss?"

"No, of course not. It is just that I must talk to you about something. I was going to wait, to be patient, but seeing you tonight—I have to say it."

An odd mix of dread and excitement caused Allison's hand to shake. What could possibly be making

William, usually so calm and teasingly merry, be so pale and serious?

It had to be something either horrible or wonderful.

She carefully placed her glass on the ground before she could spill the punch, and steeled herself to face him.

"Yes, William?" she said quietly.

"Allison, I love you," he answered quickly, then looked as if he had swallowed a frog.

She felt her jaw drop as she stared at him like a lackwit. Were her ears deceiving her? Did he just say . . . "You love me?"

He nodded. "I do. I think I fell in love with you when we first met four years ago, but I was too young and foolish to realize it. But now I know. I love you, Allison Gordon. I love your red hair, and your smile, and your cleverness, and—everything." His shoulders dropped. "I'm saying this very badly, aren't I? I'm being terribly clumsy."

"Oh, William," she said, a silly grin twitching at her lips. "I love you, too."

His eyes widened, and he grinned a very silly grin of his own. "You do?"

"I do."

He swooped down and kissed her, the softest, sweetest, dearest kiss ever. Allison grasped his great-coat in her gloved hands and leaned into him, absorbing his strength and his warmth into herself.

When at last they parted, she leaned her cheek against his shoulder and sighed happily.

"I have no money," he said softly. "Nothing to offer you."

"I have no money, either!" she answered blithely, still floating about on love's pink cloud, where such mundane considerations as money had no place as of yet. "And you have one very valuable thing indeed to offer me."

"Do I? What is that?"

She looked up at him, and kissed his chin. "Yourself, of course."

He smiled, but still looked quite concerned. "I want to marry you, Allison, more than I have ever wanted anything. But I don't want you to regret being my wife."

"I never could. I know it will not be easy, but we can all live at my family's cottage if we have to. There is room for you and Gertrude." She rested her cheek back on his shoulder. "It will all be fine. You'll see."

His arms tightened around her.

They did not even see the dark-cloaked woman who stood hidden behind a nearby hedge. But Lady Kirkwood's faithful maid Rose saw—and heard—them. With a little smile, she slipped away and headed back down the lane to Kirkwood Manor.

10

Christmas Day

"Allie! Allie, wake up!"

"It's Christmas, slugabed! You are sleeping all the day away."

Allison groaned, and opened her eyes to find the too-energetic-by-far twins climbing onto her bed. They had opened the draperies, and pale yellow sunlight streamed into the room.

She pulled the bedclothes back over her head. It felt as if she had just fallen asleep. "What time is it?"

"Nearly nine o'clock! And we are meant to go to

church with Lady Kirkwood, remember?" Jane said, with a little bounce on the mattress.

"Even newly betrothed ladies can't stay abed all day," Kitty added, pulling the blankets down.

Allison and William had told the girls, in strictest confidence, about their intention to wed, and they had been able to speak of nothing but their plans to be bridesmaids all the way home from the dance.

Allison laughed, and sat up against the pillows. "You are quite right, my dears. Christmas is not a day for lying about."

"We brought you some tea," Jane said, producing a half-full cup from behind her back.

"And gifts!" Kitty in turn brought out two brightly wrapped packages.

Allison clapped her hands in delight. "Gifts! You two are the best sisters ever." She kissed their cheeks, almost upsetting the tea in the process. "And I think that if you look in the wardrobe, you will see something with your names on it."

With shouts of glee, the twins ran to the wardrobe, tripping over their nightgown hems, to pull two more parcels out.

Soon the whole bed was covered with colored paper and ribbons. Kitty and Jane put on their new satin slippers and silk stockings, bought from the egg money Allison had saved so carefully over the months, and paraded around the room. Allison wrapped the clumsily knit, but beautifully made, red scarf around her neck, and pulled the matching mittens over her hands.

"I will be the warmest person in church today," she said. "But I can't believe you made these yourselves, and I did not even know!"

Kitty came and snuggled against her side. "We've worked on them ever since the summer."

Jane sat down on her other side. "We made a blue scarf for Mama, but we will have to give it to her when we go home next week, since we forgot to leave it. Do you think she will like it?"

"I think she will love it."

There was a knock at the door then, and the twins tumbled off the bed to go answer it.

Lady Kirkwood's maid stood there, two large boxes in her arms. "Good morning, Miss Gordon," Rose said. "And Miss Kitty and Miss Jane. Happy Christmas!"

"Happy Christmas!" the twins chorused, eyeing the boxes.

"These are for you, from Lady Kirkwood. And she also sends a message for you, Miss Gordon." Rose handed the boxes over to the eager girls. "She wants to know if you and Mr. Bradford will join her in the library directly after church."

Then she smiled, bobbed a curtsy, and left, shutting the door behind her.

Allison was so puzzled by this odd invitation that she did not notice her sisters opening the boxes until she heard their shrieks of pleasure.

"Oh, Allie, just look!" Jane cried. "Ball gowns."

"And they match our new slippers perfectly," Kitty said, holding a gown of green velvet trimmed in cream-colored satin ribbons up to herself.

Jane clutched a gown of matching style, but made of rose-pink. "It is the loveliest gown I ever saw."

"Come and see yours, Allie."

Allison felt quite as excited as they were. She had never owned a ball gown; there was never a need for it at the cottage.

She lifted the lid on the box, and gasped when she saw the gown folded there.

It was of sapphire-blue silk, trimmed with rich frills of white lace and soft white ribbons at the neckline, the sleeves, and the hem, sumptuously cut and shimmering like a winter's night.

Allison spread the glory of it over her lap, and stroked the soft cloth with a gentle hand. She could hardly wait until William saw her in it.

"So we are finally alone," William said, cornering Allison for a quick kiss outside the library door.

"Was sharing a hymnal in church not enough for you?" she teased.

"Not at all!" He kissed her again, swiftly but tenderly. "What do you think Lady Kirkwood wants to talk to us about?"

"Maybe she wants to tell us we won her scavenger hunt? Or maybe she wants to know what your intentions are toward me." Allison's voice was light, but deep inside she was a bit worried herself. She had had very little private conversation with Lady Kirkwood, and to now be summoned to see her in the library seemed a bit odd. "But we will never know if we do not go in."

"Oh, very well," William sighed. "If we must, we must. But I would rather stay alone out here with you." He offered her his arm, and escorted her into the library.

Lady Kirkwood was seated by the fire, but she was not alone. In the chair next to her sat a slim figure, still bundled in a traveling cloak and bonnet, and sipping a cup of tea.

"Mama!" Allison cried. She ran across the room, and knelt down beside the chair to throw herself into her mother's open arms. "Oh, Mama! We have missed you so much."

"And I have missed my girls," Josephine Gordon said, pressing her cool cheek against her daughter's hair. "Lady Kirkwood very kindly sent her own carriage, and her own physician, to fetch me, so we could be together on Christmas."

Allison looked over at Lady Kirkwood, who was beaming at them. "Thank you so much, Lady Kirkwood," she said thickly, afraid she might burst into tears at the happiness of it all. "You have been kindness itself."

"Oh, my dear," Lady Kirkwood said, "don't you think you could start calling me Aunt Harriet?" Then she turned a stern glance onto William. "Now, Mr. Bradford. Isn't there something you would like to talk to Mrs. Gordon about?"

Kirkwood Manor had never looked grander. Its windows blazed with light to greet the carriages that streamed along the drive to the front doors. The ballroom, closed up for many years, gleamed now, festive in its trappings of greenery and red and gold bows. An orchestra struck up a lively tune for the well-dressed and bejeweled crowd.

It seemed that everyone in the county was there to celebrate Christmas.

Lady Kirkwood surveyed it all from her chair, placed high on a dais. It *had* been a delightful holiday, one her husband would have so enjoyed. And it was soon to get even better.

She smiled to see Sir Reginald and his family huddled together near the doorway, watching the merrymakers with sour faces.

Then she turned her head to watch as Allison and William skipped down the line of dancers, laughing and twirling around. How they reminded her of herself and her husband, once upon a time! How young they looked, how happy and in love.

"Lady Kirkwood," she heard a small voice say, and looked down to see Gertrude Bradford standing on the steps of the dais, a plate of delicacies in her hands. "I thought you might be hungry, up here all by yourself."

"How very thoughtful of you, my dear," Lady Kirkwood said with a smile, marveling at the change in the girl. When Gertrude had arrived at Kirkwood Manor, she had been a pale, sad little thing; now she positively glowed in her holly-green gown. "Why don't you sit here and help me eat them? And perhaps you could then help me make a small announcement. . . ."

"I want to thank all of you for coming to Kirkwood Manor tonight," Lady Kirkwood announced. "As all of you know, this is the first time I have entertained since my dear husband passed away, so this is a very special night for me indeed. And, as most of you also know, my houseguests have performed a great task for me in the last few days. Some of you may even have assisted them."

A ripple of laughter sounded across the ballroom.

Allison stood there, her hand in William's, and her mother and sisters standing beside her. This was the moment they had worked for, had traipsed all over the countryside gathering seven impossible "objects" for. And somehow that did not concern her one whit. No matter what Lady Kirkwood decided, or who she made her heir, Allison did not care.

She had everything she had ever wanted.

She only hoped that, if Lady Kirkwood chose Sir Reginald and his family, they would take care of her. Allison had grown awfully fond of the lady.

"And now," Lady Kirkwood continued, "I have a few very important announcements to make. First of all, I had my attorney come to call on me today, and he left this with me." She held out her ringed hand, and Gertrude stepped forward to hand her a piece of parchment. "It is a copy of my new will, in which I leave my entire personal fortune to Mr. William Bradford and his future bride, Miss Allison Gordon."

A murmur of excitement rose from the assembly, as it was well-known that Lady Kirkwood's personal fortune was very vast indeed.

"Oh, I say . . ." Sir Reginald began loudly, only to subside at a sharp glance from Lady Kirkwood. His face turned purple beneath a fierce hail of whispers from his wife.

"Of course, Sir Reginald Kirkwood will inherit Kirkwood Manor when I am gone, along with a small annuity to run it," Lady Kirkwood went on, with a gracious nod to him. "And I am very happy to say that the owner of Swan Court has agreed to sell me the estate, which I present to Mr. Bradford and Miss Gordon as a wedding present. I am looking forward to having them as my neighbors for many years to come." She turned to where William and Allison stood, and gave them a radiant smile. "My best wishes to you both, and thank you for all the amusement you have given me in these last few days. My dear husband would have loved it."

Applause broke out in the ballroom, and the musicians began a lively rendition of "The Twelve Days of Christmas."

Allison looked about at everyone, at her elated

mother and her laughing sisters, and felt utterly stunned. How very much had changed in the last few minutes; her entire world was different.

Her head was spinning.

Then she felt William's arm come around her shoulders, and he pressed a warm kiss to her cheek.

She looked up at him, and found his dear smile shining on her.

And suddenly the world steadied, and she knew she would never feel lost again.

"Do you want to cry off on our betrothal, now that you are a great heiress?" he said.

Allison laughed. "Never! Never, never. Do *you* want to cry off, now that you are a great heir?"

"And miss out on life at Swan Court with you, Gertrude, the twins, and Lady Kirkwood as a neighbor?" He caught her around the waist, and twirled her about, lifting her off of her feet in the very midst of the crowded ballroom. "Never!"

The Solid Silver Chess Set
by Sandra Heath

All elves wear stars in their hats at Christmas. It is a tradition that stretches back to the Nativity itself, when—although it is not widely known—there were actually four wise men. The fourth was an elf king, who had been guided to Bethlehem by a small star of his own. His gift to Jesus was silver, which is regarded by elves as the most precious metal of all. Every Christmas since then, they have given presents of silver to their friends and loved ones; and every Christmas since then, tiny stars have tumbled from the night sky and become fixed to their pointed red hats. One star for each hat.

This is a story about a young elf called Bramble Bumblekin, who one snowy Christmas had the task of delivering a particularly costly gift—a solid silver chess set.

1

It was two days before Christmas, 1819, and the elves of the Malvern Hills had been summoned to witness the trial and sentencing of one of their number. There was no need for torches in the underground cavern deep beneath the famous hills, because every hat boasted a seasonal star, and the light was dazzling. Silence reigned as the elf lord, seated on a dais, gave his judgment. "Very well, young Bumblekin, because you are the last of your line, I will give you one final chance."

Bramble's yellow eyes closed with relief, and surprised whispers rippled around the gathering.

"But be warned," the elf lord continued, eyeing the miscreant on the punishment stool in front of the dais, "this is most certainly your final opportunity to redeem yourself."

"Yes, master," Bramble whispered, hanging his head. He was twelve inches high, as were all elves, but today he felt so small and wretched that he might as well have only measured three inches!

"No more misdeeds, is that clear?" The elf lord's voice echoed through the cavern.

"Yes, master." But behind Bramble's acquiescence there lurked considerable indignation. Misdeeds? Why wouldn't anyone believe they had all been *accidents*? He hadn't deliberately set the washing lines on fire, or put too much salt in the bread. Nor had he purposely let all the water out of the fishpond, or left open the garden gates in the western cave, so moles were able to get in for the first time in two hundred years. How was he to know moles could be so sly and devious as to *lure* him into such an error? And how could anyone believe he, Bramble Bumblekin, would willfully deliver the mail to all the wrong people? It wasn't *his* fault that the elf lord's sister had a lover to whom she wrote indiscreet letters. The fact that the lover's wife received one such telltale letter was due to naughty goings-on and illegible handwriting, not the failings of the mail elf!

Bramble blinked back tears of frustration. His clothes were the same as those worn by all elves, a jaunty green doublet and hose, red shoes, and bright red hat, but he was a forlorn figure, his elongated ears drooping and crestfallen, his button nose scarlet with embarrassment. This was all so unfair. He had simply made mistakes. It might have happened to anyone. Except it happened to him . . . all the time! He must be the unluckiest elf that ever lived!

The elf lord pronounced his sentence. "It is my decision that you will be given a Very Important Task."

There were gasps, for if Bramble failed with a Very Important Task he would be banished . . . forever!

With a click of his fingers, the elf lord summoned two elderly serving elves, both bearded and bent. One carried a pair of thigh-length rabbit-skin boots and a warm cloak made of weasel fur; the other had a sack over his shoulder. They shuffled to the dais and put the things down in front of the punishment stool. The sack contained something that chinked metallically, and something flat and square, like a small tabletop the corners of which jutted sharply through the sacking.

The elf lord sat forward. "Young Bumblekin, you are to take this Christmas gift to my good friend the elf lord of the Forest of Dean."

"Yes, master." Well, that didn't sound too difficult, Bramble thought, for it was only fifteen miles or so to the forest. Elves could run without ever becoming out of breath, so he could easily be there and back in time for Christmas Day with those of his friends who would still speak to him.

"The gift is the solid silver chess set studded with rubies," the elf lord said then.

Fresh gasps spread through the cavern. Everyone knew the chess set, and few thought the elf lord at all wise to entrust such an object to a scatterbrained butterfingers like the last of the Bumblekins.

"Deliver it safely, or face the consequences," the elf lord warned.

"Yes, master."

"Well, get on with it."

Bramble climbed hastily down from the stool, and pulled the rabbit-skin boots over his red shoes, then put the weasel fur cloak around his shoulders. As he picked up the sack and swung it over his right shoulder, the silver chessmen clinked together. It was a horridly expensive sound.

"Go then." The elf lord waved him on his way.

"Yes, master."

Bramble turned, and everyone parted before him. His boots clumped on the floor of the cave, and it seemed to him that it took an awfully long time to reach the solid face of rock at the far end, where the magic entrance to the human's world was to be found, but at last he was there. He didn't glance back, but whispered the secret words.

There was a flash of vivid crimson light, then suddenly all was cold and dark, and he was outside on the bleak summit of the southernmost of the hills. To his horror it was snowing heavily, almost obscuring the lights of the human world far below. The hills were an eight-mile-long sequence of humpbacks that reared along the floor of the wide Severn valley, where the three counties of Herefordshire, Worcestershire, and Gloucestershire came together. It was in the latter county that the ancient Forest of Dean was to be found, fifteen longer-than-expected miles away because of the snow.

In daylight the hills formed a landmark that was visible for many miles from all points of the compass, but tonight they were barely discernible silhouettes against the lowering skies. The winter afternoon had

faded into night, countless snowflakes fluttered
through the air, and the cold was intense, so he was
glad of the cloak and boots, which would keep him
warm on his journey. He prayed all would go well
with this Very Important Task, so he could be home
for Christmas. Surely nothing could go wrong this
time . . . could it?

Taking a huge breath, he began to trot down the
steep slope. There was a winding road at the bottom,
and he could see the lamps of a carriage moving
slowly east. . . .

Sir Anthony Talbot, his wife, and his daughter had
been to the city of Hereford to stay with friends and
enjoy a little leisurely Christmas shopping. They were
now on their way home to Wentwood, their estate by
the River Severn near Tewkesbury, and having set out
just after breakfast, ought to have been at journey's
end before nightfall. However, there had been such
heavy snow for the past few hours that the progress
of their carriage was very slow.

The road led like a white ribbon through the darkness, few other travelers were to be seen, and Wentwood was still ten miles away when darkness
descended. Sir Anthony had to face the fact that
reaching his home that night was now out of the question, and muttering under his breath, he lowered the
window and leaned out into the night to call to the
coachman. "Harris? As I recall, there's an inn somewhere along here, isn't there?"

"Yes, sir. The Wellspring, at the crossroad about a
mile ahead," the man called back.

"Stop there. We can't go on in these conditions."

"Very well, sir."

Sir Anthony raised the window again and resumed

his seat. He was a plump, bewigged gentleman, with round cheeks and watery blue eyes, and was bundled up against the cold in a greatcoat, cloak, traveling rug, and shawl. His mood had been tetchy all day because of his gout; now it was worse because he loathed staying at inns. It was at this unfortunate point that his gaze fell upon his daughter Julia, seated opposite. She hadn't said anything to aggravate him, rather she had been guilty of saying little at all, and he knew the reason only too well.

"Now, see here, miss, you have now chosen once and for all to accept Lord Richfield, and this time there is no going back! It is—and always was—an excellent match, and you should be smiling, not sulking like a cat denied the cream!"

Julia was piqued. "I cannot sit here smiling all the time, Papa. People will think I have escaped from a bedlam," she answered, and immediately earned a warning prod of her mother's toe.

"Impudence will avail you of nothing!" Sir Anthony snapped, having long since lost patience with his only offspring. "To have two failed betrothals to your name is bad enough, acquire a third—even if it *is* to the same gentleman of the first betrothal—and it will be thought that the fault must lie with you."

Lady Talbot, elegant in a hooded emerald green cloak over an apricot velvet gown, turned reproachful brown eyes upon both of them. "That was not well said by either of you," she murmured. Her auburn hair was not an indication of a fiery disposition; indeed, she was of a very tranquil nature, and of late had been sorely tried by her husband's hasty temper and the problems occasioned by her daughter's embattled heart.

Sir Anthony remained irritable. "Plague take it,

Elizabeth, I refuse to have society chew upon the Talbot name *again!* Would to God we had stayed in Yorkshire, for then we would never have acquired the confounded Earl of Allensmore as a neighbor! I had the measure of him that day his gamekeepers fired upon me because I strayed onto his land! Any man who allows his men to shoot first and ask questions afterward is a blackguard! Besides, the fellow is a Whig, and so what can any respectable Tory family expect?"

"Stuff and nonsense," his wife observed, knowing full well that politics had nothing whatsoever to do with it.

He scowled at her, then shifted in his seat. "Well, whatever, I now believe it all to have been put up anyway."

His wife was bewildered. "Believe all what was put up!"

"That business with Allensmore's gamekeepers."

"Oh, hardly so, my dear, for Philip—er, Lord Allensmore—could not have been more apologetic."

"The gamekeeper was instructed to shoot at me— and to miss, of course—so that Allensmore had an excuse to call. Julia's seduction was his ultimate aim, and he eventually lost interest when he failed to lure her to his bed."

"Anthony!" His wife was shocked that he should say such things in front of Julia.

"Well, looking back, it's obvious," her husband replied unrepentantly.

"If that were so, and mere seduction was his purpose, I cannot imagine that he would go so far as to propose marriage. He is, after all, a great catch."

"So is Julia. My fortune is well worth chasing, even by the likes of Allensmore. Besides, who knows how the fellow's mind turns? If he were a clock, I fancy he would strike thirteen!" Sir Anthony's breath was clearly visible in the freezing cold. "It is his fault that Julia has been at the center of so much unsavory gossip. First she took up with him and broke things off with Lord Richfield, then the engagement to Allensmore was ended after the sorry mess of Bath, now she is betrothed to Lord Richfield again. The *monde* has had a field day with it, and I have had enough. This time she will *stay* betrothed to Richfield. No more gossip fare. Do I make myself plain?"

"Perfectly," his wife replied. She knew his gout was plaguing him, and that such particularly sharp words were not his usual way, but she did wish he would be a little more thoughtful. Julia was upset enough without having to deal with his bad temper as well. The poor girl had loved Philip to distraction, and did not need to be reminded how shabbily he had conducted himself in Bath. If, indeed, it had all really happened as had been reported. Somehow Lady Talbot was not so sure, even though both Julia and her father had witnessed his philandering.

Julia lowered brown eyes that were very like her mother's. She shouldn't have accepted Edwin—Lord Richfield—the first time, let alone repeated the mistake because Philip had broken her heart. The second acceptance had been a spur-of-the moment decision she had regretted ever since, but her father was right, she couldn't change her mind again. She had been like a pendulum, swinging from Edwin to Philip, and now back to Edwin again. All in all, she had to concede that her father's patience and understanding had been considerable.

If only Edwin was a little more romantic and thoughtful; a little more . . . like Philip. She was angry because of her own weakness. If Philip hadn't come into her life, she would have been content enough with the original arranged match with Edwin, whose late father had been her father's greatest friend. It had always been understood that the Richfield title should marry the Talbot fortune, and when they lived in Yorkshire she had no objection to that state of affairs.

Not that she had ever felt love for Edwin, who was far too devoted to gambling and sport to inspire passion in her heart. He squandered huge sums on his pleasures, but he had never given his prospective bride so much as a ring to seal the betrothal. It never occurred to him to pay court to her in any way, and he could not have made it more obvious that her fortune was his goal in entering into the match. Oh, he had written to her, but his letters were filled with dogs, guns, horses, and fishing rods. Any inquiry about her health or their forthcoming marriage had most certainly been an afterthought. Then, a year ago, came the move to Wentwood, and everything changed. Only a year? Had it really been so short a time since she first set eyes upon their new neighbor, Philip Charles Henry St. Keyne, fourth Earl of Allensmore?

Sir Anthony observed his daughter's continuing thoughtfulness. "Now, see here, Julia, if you imagine that moping will cause the facts to change, you may think again. Marriage to that unprincipled philanderer became out of the question the moment we discovered what he was up to in Bath! He may possess one of the most respected earldoms in the land, but his behavior proves he is not good enough for *my* daughter!"

Julia's brown eyes filled with tears at the renewed mention of Bath, a resort she had vowed never visit again. Ever! She had believed Philip when he said he had to go to London to attend to certain legal matters, and if her father's gout had not flared up again, she might never have discovered it was all lies. But the gout worsened, requiring the Bath cure. She had almost stayed behind at Wentwood, but at the last moment decided to accompany her parents. Thus Philip's clandestine dalliance with his former love, Lady Pamela Billington, had come to light.

Julia knew she would never forget that rainy dusk in Milsom Street, when she and her father had emerged from the circulating library and seen the fond embrace beneath the black umbrella on the pavement opposite. The light had been poor, but there had been no mistaking it was Philip, who claimed to have gone to London on legal business, yet was in Bath on business of a very different kind! Julia had always feared he still loved beautiful Lady Pamela, and those few seconds proved her fear to be justified. She had felt her heart splinter into a thousand fragments, each one jagged with pain. And every time it rained now, that tender scene in Milsom Street seemed to hover before her.

Neither she nor her father had crossed the street to confront the guilty pair, for she had been far too upset to cope with actually speaking there and then to Philip about what he had done. Instead they hastened back to her mother at their lodgings, and shortly afterward they all returned to Wentwood. As the days passed, the thought of speaking to Philip became more and more heartrending, and in the end Julia had taken the coward's way out, and simply refused to countenance any communication whatsoever. So her father had written to Allensmore Castle ending the betrothal. He gave no explanation, but simply informed Philip that the match was at an end. The letter instructed Philip on no account to come to Wentwood or attempt to contact her.

There had been a great deal of chitter-chatter when word leaked out in society that Miss Julia Talbot's second betrothal had foundered like its predecessor, but Edwin, Lord Richfield, had been equal to the moment. Ever with an eye to the main chance—in this case her considerable expectations—he offered for her again, and she, seeing a loveless marriage as a haven from heartbreak, had recklessly accepted. Her parents had been shocked, but the deed had been done, and Edwin wasted no time in announcing it to the world. He had duns to stave off, and the resumption of his hopes of the Talbot fortune was a certain way to do it. There was another great stir, of course, and her name again rang through fashionable drawing rooms in a less than flattering way, which incensed her father. She could not blame him, so even though she knew almost immediately what a terrible mistake she had made by accepting Edwin a second time, she determined to stand by her decision. That was how things now stood.

The carriage swayed on along the snowy road, and as the silence began to hang, Sir Anthony at last realized how harsh he had been to Julia. He moderated his tone. "My dear, earl or not, Allensmore is a scoundrel of the first water, and you are well rid of him. Richfield may not be as handsome, dashing, or romantic, and he may have debts, but he will be a faithful husband."

Lady Talbot pursed her lips. "That is certain, for no other woman would be foolish enough to have him," she declared.

Sir Anthony frowned. "That is enough, Elizabeth. He is the son of my dear friend, and—"

"That doesn't make him worthy."

Her husband stared at her. "Is that what you think?"

"Yes. I was delighted when the first betrothal was ended, for I thought we had seen the back of the fellow."

"Well, we haven't, and we have Julia herself to thank for that," Sir Anthony observed.

Silence resumed, and Julia plunged her hands further into her muff as she pondered her situation. Was there something wrong with her? Had she failed to let Philip know how much she adored him? Was she too rustic? Too plain? Too unsophisticated? Whatever the reason, the only man she had ever truly loved had thought nothing of betraying her with another man's wife. Granted that wife was Lady Pamela, who was not only gloriously beautiful, but had from the outset cast a shadow over everything.

Julia looked at her reflection in the window glass. Her auburn hair, darker and more curling than her mother's, was swept up in a knot beneath a white fur hat that exactly matched her muff, and beneath her warm crimson cloak she wore a high-throated, long-sleeved merino gown that was the color of holly leaves. She couldn't lay claim to being a beauty like Lady Pamela, but her oval face was—she believed—pleasant enough, with wide-set eyes, a straight little nose, and the sort of generous mouth that had always been ready to smile. At least, it had before the debacle in Bath.

Again her father's voice intruded upon her thoughts. "Julia, you may count yourself fortunate, for you have had a lucky escape."

"Anthony, will you *please* leave the matter alone?" Lady Talbot begged, foreseeing with dismay that he might continue in the same vein when they reached the Wellspring. Heaven forfend that he should harp on throughout dinner, and maybe all the way home tomorrow as well! If they could travel tomorrow, she thought, observing the snow again.

Julia's father glowered at his wife. "Leave the matter alone? I do that at my peril, for the foolish minx will probably give Richfield his congé a second time, and take up with some other ne'er-do-well! They will be taking wagers at White's before long, and our daughter's name will figure so frequently in the betting book that she will be notorious."

"Don't be ridiculous." Lady Talbot leaned across to tuck the traveling blanket more warmly around his knees. "You are upsetting yourself unnecessarily, my dear, and you know it is bad for your health. Your physician said—"

"To Hades with that fool of a nostrum-monger!"

His wife sat back with a sigh. "I am beginning to dread you, Anthony, for if you are not complaining about your aches and pains, or taking poor Julia constantly to task, you are falling out with your new cronies."

He was immediately on his dignity. "The Duke of Ledbury and the Bishop of Hereford are hardly to be termed cronies."

"No? Well, you certainly fooled me into thinking they were," Lady Talbot retorted. "Ever since we left Yorkshire, you have been thick with both of them. You have joined all the same societies and clubs, visited them at every opportunity, and so on and so on. The three of you were the scourge of the three counties, a veritable cabal, until you quarreled with them."

"I didn't quarrel with them, they quarreled with me."

"There is a difference?"

He was incensed. "Certes, there is a difference! Good heavens, woman, if you don't know that by now, I despair of you."

Not as much as I despair of you, she thought, then said, "You have never explained what happened between you and them. Am I never to know?"

He shifted uncomfortably, and sniffed. "They had the audacity to accuse me of carelessness with a gun. Me! I have never been careless with a gun in my entire life!"

"I agree, my dear."

"It wasn't even my gun, it was a damned thing belonging to the bishop. I *told* them it was faulty, but they insisted I had not been taking due care. The implication was that I might have killed either of them. Well, I wasn't having *that*! Oh, indeed not. So I left."

"In high dudgeon."

"Of course. I had been wronged, and that was that."

Lady Talbot patted his arm. "For what it is worth, I believe your side of it. Whatever else you may be, you are *not* careless with guns."

"What do you mean, whatever else I may be?" he demanded.

"Well, you can be a little difficult these days. Did you know that you are now referred to as Old Gout?"

"Which rather makes you Old Gout's wife," he replied.

"I fear it does. Oh, Anthony, what happened to the dashing young man I married?"

"He acquired a nagging wife, and a daughter who

changes beaux as often as other women change
shoes!" was the reply.

"He also acquired a bad temper. If you do not take
care, I fear you will die of apoplexy," she warned.

"Don't talk rubbish, woman."

"It isn't rubbish, sir, it's fact, and in the absence of
any indication that you are going to help yourself, I
will do it for you. In future the cook will be instructed
to serve you less red meat, and I shall see to it that
your consumption of port is greatly reduced as well!"

He glowered at her. "You will do no such thing!"

"Then conduct yourself with more decorum, my
dear."

"*I* am not the one without decorum!" he growled,
then winced as his foot gave him another savage
twinge.

His wife and daughter said no more, and an uneasy
silence fell over the swaying carriage. Large flakes fell
endlessly past the beams of the lamps, and there was
little sound from the wheels or the horses' hooves, just
the jingle of harness and the occasional squeak of a
spring. Suddenly they all heard the sound of caroling
from somewhere on the road ahead. A man and
woman were singing "The Holly and the Ivy." The
voices were clear and sweet; trained almost, Julia
thought, getting up to lower the window glass once
more in order to look out.

Snowflakes brushed her face as she saw jolting lanterns farther along the road, and the silhouettes of
three vehicles trundling in the same direction as the
carriage. There was a canvas-topped wagon laden with
people, a pony trap that was piled with baggage and
other property, and what appeared to be a handcart
being pushed along by two boys. The singing came

from a young man and woman on the pony trap. They had fine voices, and the ancient carol could seldom have sounded more hauntingly beautiful, Julia thought.

As the carriage caught up with the little procession, she heard the tinkle of bells, and saw brightly colored flags and streamers. There was a hobbyhorse leading the way, its eyes illuminated by a lighted candle inside the head. The man inside clacked the horse's jaw expertly, and capered and twirled so that the bells on the reins jingled prettily, and his sequined apron of red and gold flashed in the beam of the lantern on the pony trap. Then Julia saw that the handcart was carrying mumming costumes, including Father Christmas, St. George, the Old Woman, and a stag's head. It was a troupe of traveling players.

Julia's mother touched her elbow. "What can you see, my dear?"

"Traveling actors . . . well, mummers, actually, I think. There's a wonderful hobbyhorse!"

A boy dressed as a fox ran back toward the carriage, waving an upturned hat, and calling out, "Christmas is coming, the goose is getting fat! Please put a penny in the old man's hat!" He had a wreath of holly around his head, and a cheeky grin that was impossible to resist.

"Oh, do give him some coins," Lady Talbot urged, searching in her reticule and then pressing some pennies into Julia's hand.

Julia stretched down to drop the money into the hat, and the boy gave her another broad beaming smile. "Bless you, lady! May you have a very merry Christmas!"

"And you," she replied, then drew back into the

carriage and closed the glass. Thanks to Philip, a merry Christmas was the very last thing she would have this year.

The carriage drove on, leaving the ambling procession behind, and after a while Julia wiped a circle on the glass to look out at the shadowy countryside that lay to the north of the road. The hills were just visible, rising starkly against the snowy heavens. There were no candlelit windows to be seen on the lower slopes, for on a night like this even the remote farmhouses seemed to have curled up and drawn the snow blanket over themselves.

Suddenly she saw a tiny light bobbing down the hillside a little distance ahead, perhaps just above the Wellspring Inn, the position of which she vaguely recalled. The light was so small that for a moment she wasn't sure she could actually see anything through the heavily falling snow. Philip had told her about the mysterious lights that appeared hereabouts just before Christmas. The local people swore they were to do with the elves that were supposed to live in the hills. As she looked, the light vanished as suddenly as it had appeared. Which was, she thought wryly, more or less what could be said of her happiness with Philip.

She blinked tears away. One of the few good things about this Christmas was that he had gone to stay with an old friend in the county of Glamorgan, South Wales. No doubt the old friend was Lady Pamela, but that was the concern of Lady Pamela's deceived husband, not of Miss Julia Talbot, who was only too thankful that for the time being at least, there was no chance of accidentally encountering the master of Allensmore Castle.

*   *   *

But Julia's confidence as to Philip's whereabouts was again misplaced, for at that very moment he was urging his tired horse through the snow toward the same Wellspring Inn that was the Talbot carriage's destination. His Christmas plans had come to naught because his Welsh friend had been urgently called away to a dangerously ill relative, so a return to Allensmore Castle had become necessary. He had decided to ride home quickly rather than use his carriage, which was following at a leisurely pace, but right now, in the midst of such snow and raw cold, he knew he would have been better off in the carriage.

He was a tall rider, and beneath his navy blue greatcoat wore fine London clothes. His top hat was tugged low onto his thick dark hair, and his handsome face was taut from the freezing temperature. A veil of disillusionment shaded his clear gray eyes, which had once been so lively with charm and humor, and a twist of bitterness marred his finely wrought lips, banishing the quick sensitivity that had always been the mark of his smiles. He was twenty-nine years old, going on fifty, or so it felt of late. And all because he had been fool enough to entrust his heart to a woman who had clearly never felt anything for him.

Miss Julia Talbot. He could hardly bear to even think of her name. Why, oh why, had she had to come to Wentwood, the boundary of which marched with his own property? But for that singular event, he would have been spared the constant pain that now engulfed his existence. The warning signs had been there from the outset, but he, ever the fool where she was concerned, had ignored them. He had honestly believed that the misunderstandings that had spoiled their initial acquaintance had been settled to the satisfaction of all concerned. How could he have suspected otherwise when her father—Old Gout himself—had consented to let her end her betrothal to Richfield and become the future Countess of Allensmore instead? How wrong was it possible to be? Old Gout had clearly never forgiven or forgotten the unfortunate matter of the gamekeeper, and had more than been avenged when he terminated his daughter's match without seeing fit to offer a reason to the rejected bridegroom.

As for Julia herself . . . Philip's anger burned deep within. She behaved as if they had never met, never shared a kiss or caress, never whispered their eternal love. But they had done all those things, and *still* it was over without the courtesy of a reason. And in favor of that idiot Richfield, who knew more about salmon, dabchicks, and greyhounds than he ever would about women. Well, if that was the way Julia and Old Gout wanted it, that was the way they could have it.

Snowflakes touched his face with icy little fingers, and the winter darkness seemed to have seeped through to his very marrow as he did his best to keep the flagging horse at a good trot. He could no longer feel his hands and feet, and if ever the thought of mulled wine and a roaring fire had lingered tantalizingly in his mind, it was now! He damned himself for an idiot for deciding to travel this way, for the weather was always treacherous this time of year, especially in the vicinity of the hills. Allensmore Castle was beyond reach in such conditions, and he thanked heaven for the Wellspring, which offered good food and comfortable accommodation.

At that moment something startled the horse. It tossed its head uneasily, and lurched toward the verge, obliging Philip to rein in swiftly. "Steady boy," he said soothingly, patting the animal's neck and looking around for any hint of what had unnerved it. All was quiet, except for the gurgling of an ice-fringed stream beyond the hedge. Then, just as he was about to ride on again, he saw the tiny light descending the hillside.

A faint smile played upon his lips, for he remembered the old Christmas tales of the Malvern elves. As a child he had believed the stories, but now he was a little old for such things. A little too old, a little too bitter, and a little too jaded to believe in little folk, at Christmas or any other time of the year!

The light disappeared suddenly, and Philip thought no more of it as he urged the horse on toward the Wellspring.

2

The light seen by both Julia and Philip was, of course, the star on Bramble's hat. The scatterbrained elf scampered recklessly down a steep badger path, the precious sack bouncing over his shoulder. Remaining surefooted wasn't on his mind, instead he was wondering how best to remain undetected by humans when he reached the bottom of the hill.

Elves and their possessions are invisible to humans, which means they are safe from detection almost the entire year-round. But at Christmas the stars in their hats give them away, and the only way to remain completely unseen is to turn the hats inside out. However, this is only permitted as a last resort, because all elf lords regard the concealment of a star with great disapproval.

The problem took up Bramble's thoughts so completely that he didn't see the rabbit hole. Over he went, landing with a thud on his posterior, and before he knew what was happening, he and the sack were skidding down the hillside at speed, sending up a cloud of powdery snow. He squealed out as he hurtled toward the Wellspring, where the dogs set up a clamor as they heard him coming.

Clinging to the vital sack with all his might, Bramble closed his eyes and waited for the sickening crash, when he struck the wall of the inn's kitchen garden at the bottom. This was the end of him! He knew it! The lighted windows were spinning, as were his senses, and then suddenly he was launched into the air. He sailed over the wall, bumped painfully across the privy roof, and landed with a crunch on the snowman the innkeeper's children had built earlier in the day.

Bruised and winded, with the snowman's carrot nose prodding in a very delicate place, Bramble lay there with the sack, trying to collect his wits and his breath. The inn dogs, secured for the night in an outhouse, raised such a racket that the elf knew someone was bound to come out to see what was wrong. His hat lay nearby, its star thankfully hidden beneath bits of the snowman, so there was nothing to see as at last the kitchen door opened, and the burly landlord emerged with a lantern in one hand and a poker in the other.

Terrified, Bramble lay as still and quiet as a mouse.

Meanwhile, Sir Anthony's carriage still had three-quarters of a mile to go before reaching the inn. As Bramble's star disappeared, Julia sighed and leaned her head back against the green leather upholstery. How on earth had her life gone so very wrong? It seemed that one minute she had been joyfully walking on the air itself, looking forward to a lifetime with a handsome earl she adored with all her heart; the next she had been plunged into wretchedness because that same handsome earl had been cruelly false.

Her glance slid back to the window. The brief glimpse of the little light on the hillside now stirred memories of the first kiss she had shared with Philip— the first kiss she had shared with anyone. . . . It had been on the day after her father's unfortunate encounter with Philip's gamekeeper. There was snow lying as she rode out into the park to look for mistletoe, which her new maid had told her grew on a wild pear tree close to the boundary with Allensmore Castle. She did not know the park at all well, for it was not long after the move from Yorkshire, so the pear tree's promised crop of mistletoe remained to be seen.

She and Philip had already met formally on several times, and she knew how greatly she was attracted to him. From the very first moment she had wondered what it would be like to be kissed by him. Such feelings were to be denied, of course, for not only was she betrothed to Edwin, but Philip was expected to marry Lady Pamela Billington. But Julia was acutely conscious of an undertow of rich yearning that weakened the foundations of her match with Edwin. She experienced it every time she saw Philip, and once or twice she had been sure he felt the same toward her.

Oh, he was more practiced in the ways of the world, more able to conceal his emotions, but nevertheless she was certain that he was by no means immune to her. It was there in the warmth of his glance, the hesitancy of his smile, and the way he lingered longer than he should have done when taking her hand.

So as she set out that afternoon, she had no thought at all of even seeing Philip that day, let alone allowing things to progress to a kiss that was anything but innocent and accidental. It might not have happened at all if someone had not already denuded the pear tree of mistletoe before she arrived. The stump of the plant was all that remained among the branches, so she rode back across the snowy park, taking a different route in the hope of finding some elsewhere.

She succeeded, discovering another wild pear tree in a little holly copse, but the mistletoe was too high to reach. Instead of sensibly riding back to the house and sending men out to gather it the next day, she decided to climb the tree. She had gathered a few sprays when suddenly a branch snapped under her foot, and she fell awkwardly on her ankle. The pain had been so intense that for a while she lost consciousness, lying there in the snow with the mistletoe scattered all around. When she came around, she had the wit to frighten her horse into galloping off. She knew it would return to the stables, and that searchers would come out and follow the horse's tracks in the snow. But to her dismay it began to snow again, and she could only watch as the hoofprints began to fill in.

Not long after she originally set out on her ride, Philip came to Wentwood to apologize to her father for the gamekeeper's action the previous day. His charm and civility had won the day, and the visit had been very agreeable, or so she was told afterward. The pleasantries had ended abruptly when the return of her riderless horse set everything in uproar. By then the afternoon was beginning to draw in, and her mother was convinced she was freezing to death in some ditch, so every able-bodied man, including Philip, had set out to search with lanterns.

Darkness descended, the snow continued to fall, and Julia remembered growing more and more cold, more and more frightened. Then she had seen a light in the distance, and thought she heard a voice calling. She tried to call back, but her voice seemed as frozen as the rest of her. The light came slowly nearer, and gradually she became aware of a man's voice calling her first name. At last she managed to make a small responding cry, and to her joy the light grew steadily brighter as whoever it was rode toward her.

"Julia?"

"Here. I'm here . . ."

He urged his horse through the holly branches, and as he reined in a few feet away from her, she felt the powdery snow scatter over her face. The lantern swayed as he dismounted, and she caught a glimpse of his face. It was Philip. Even now, a year later, she could still feel the way her heart seemed to turn over. He removed his top hat and crouched beside her, then rammed the lantern upright in the snow and put a gloved hand gently to her cold cheek.

"Are you injured?" he asked.

"My ankle . . ."

"Let me see."

He turned slightly to draw aside the hem of her riding habit skirt, and only as his fingers touched the laces of her riding boot was she conscious of the impropriety of the situation. He knew what she was thinking, and smiled as he tested her ankle. "I am sure we do not break any rules, for I must touch you if I am to establish how badly you are hurt. Or is it perhaps that you feel I have played fast and loose with your first name? If so, let me assure you it was due to a desire to find you as quickly as possible. I felt that if you were lying close to unconsciousness, you would more readily respond to Julia than to Miss Talbot. However, I promise to be more correct and formal from now on."

She sought something to say. "If . . . if you have found me, my lord, does it mean that I, too, have strayed onto your land?"

"No, Miss Talbot, this time *I* am on *yours*," he said a little wryly.

"Then you are safe, sir, for no one here will fire willy-nilly upon you."

He was not in the least offended. "It is on account of my irresponsible employee that I called here at Wentwood. I believe I have made my peace with your father, Miss Talbot, but it seems I need to do the same with you."

"You are my gallant rescuer, sir, so I will not be churlish about anything."

He smiled again, and then retied her laces. "I don't think your ankle is broken, maybe just twisted. Allow me to help you to your feet." He took her by the hands, and drew her gently up from the snow. Then he brushed his hand over her clothes, and took off his greatcoat to place it warmly around her shoulders. "What happened?" he asked. "Did your horse throw you?"

She colored a little. "No. I . . . I was climbing the tree."

He was taken aback. "Climbing the tree? Whatever for?"

"Mistletoe." She indicated the sprays lying around, already buried slightly in the fresh fall of snow.

He gave a quick laugh. "One is only supposed to kiss beneath the mistletoe, Miss Talbot."

The atmosphere between them changed. Maybe it was the word kiss, or even just the presence of the mistletoe; whatever it was, they were both suddenly much more aware of each other. "I'm sure you're right, sir," she managed to reply, "but the smaller tree I was originally directed to had been pillaged by someone else."

"Ah." He grinned sheepishly. "Would you by any chance be referring to the pear tree on the boundary with my land?"

"Yes."

"Ah," he said again, then gave her a sheepish look. "I fear I am the culprit, Miss Talbot."

"You?"

"Well, mistletoe is as welcome a seasonal sight at Allensmore Castle as it is at Wentwood."

She was a little indignant. "But that tree is ours!"

"I know."

"Your keeper fired at my father for merely wandering onto your land, yet you had the audacity to not only *enter* our land, but to steal our mistletoe as well?"

He was rueful. "A heinous crime, I concede," he murmured.

"A capital offense, sir."

"But I plead mitigating circumstances."

"Oh?" She looked archly at him.

He spread his hands in a gesture of innocence. "How else am I, a lonely fellow who rattles like a solitary pea in his great colander of a castle, to win Christmas kisses if not with mistletoe?" He bent to retrieve the nearest spray of mistletoe, and shook it free of snow.

She looked at him, aware of the atmosphere moving around her like an enchantment. "Lord Allensmore, I think you will never have difficulty acquiring kisses, at Christmas or any other time of the year."

He held her eyes in the light from the lantern. "I will take that as a compliment, Miss Talbot. But, of course, it requires a compliment in return, for I am equally sure that you have no need of mistletoe in order to acquire kisses.''

They barely knew each other, yet their conversation turned upon such an intimate subject! Impropriety tapped her smartly on the shoulder, and hastily she endeavored to place things on a more correct footing. "I am not in the habit of seeking such favors, sir," she said, knowing she sounded almost prim.

"No? Not even from your betrothed?"

Her eyes flew back to him. "Not even from my betrothed."

He searched her face in the snow-speckled light. "May I ask you a very impertinent question, Miss Talbot?"

"Certainly not."

"Then I am obliged to ask it without permission. Tell me, are you in love with Lord Richfield?"

"That is none of your business!" She was a little shocked by his directness.

"It is my business, Miss Talbot, especially now that Lady Pamela and I are no longer together."

"You . . . aren't?" She couldn't hide the glad light that entered her eyes.

"We parted because we were no longer in love, and she is now to marry someone else, so I am free to kiss whom I please. So if you truly love Richfield, which I find impossible to believe, it would be a little wrong of me to impose my festive kisses upon you. But if you don't love him, which I think highly likely, my kisses seem positively necessary if I am to make the headway I desire."

The air seemed to hang, and her heart raced more foolishly and wildly than ever before in her life.

"You are very quiet, Miss Talbot," he said softly.

She was so bothered by her thoughts and feelings that she still couldn't speak.

"May I be direct . . . Julia?"

"I imagine that you will be so, sir, whether or not I wish it."

"As I understand it, your contract with Richfield was arranged because your fathers were friends who wished their children to marry. Love would not seem to have entered into anything. That makes you fair game in this hopeful hunter's sights, so I came to Wentwood today as much to further my dealings with you as to apologize to your father."

"You shouldn't say such things . . ."

"I know, but I may never be alone with you again like this. Tell me you love Richfield, and I will never transgress again."

She couldn't say the words, because the simple truth was that she didn't love Edwin at all. She hardly knew him enough to even like him.

"What if I were indeed to be so bold and unprincipled as to steal a kiss right now?" he asked softly, twirling the mistletoe between his fingers.

She didn't move, not even to turn her head away, because she wanted him to kiss her. She wanted it more than anything else in the world.

He reached out and tilted her chin, raising her lips to meet his. The kiss was gentle and tentative, then grew more warm and rich. The mistletoe fell from his hand as he caught her close and moved his lips yearningly over hers. Every sense she had tumbled into a wild confusion through which a passionate desire shone that seemed to catch her up in its palm and carry her away to the wilder edges of sweet oblivion.

Her fate was sealed, and the betrothal to Edwin
doomed. She had tasted the kiss of true love, and from
that moment on nothing less would do.

Then the lanterns of other searchers shone nearby,
lights like the one she had seen a moment since
through the carriage window. She recalled he laugh-
ingly suggested that the other searchers might be elves
who had wandered down from the Malvern Hills. . . .

As Julia thought of events of a year ago, Bramble
was still lying quite motionless amid the remains of
the snowman, peering with one eye as the Wellspring's
landlord advanced with his lantern a few yards into
the snow, still brandishing the poker in a most fearsome manner. He was a very large man, with immense
shoulders and a nose even bigger than the Duke of
Wellington's, and seemed very menacing indeed to a
helplessly sprawled elf who was only twelve invisible
inches from top to toe. The dogs continued their noise
as the man looked cautiously around. All he saw was
the deserted garden, and the fact that some miserable
wretch without an ounce of Christmas spirit had apparently destroyed the snowman.

Disgusted that anyone could do such a heartless
thing, he turned to shout at the dogs to be quiet. They
knew better than to disobey, and immediately stopped
their noise. As peace returned, he glanced up at the
torrent of snowflakes falling from the inky skies, then
he shivered and went back inside, where a pretty maid
was just taking hot mince pies from the oven. He gave
her a smart thwack on the behind, and she straightened indignantly, almost dropping the baking tray.

Outside, Bramble slowly sat up. He felt very sorry
for himself, for he was now battered, sore, cold, and
miserable. If only he didn't have a Very Important

Task to carry out; if only he were at home, curled up in his swansdown bed!

He winced as the snowman's carrot nose again made its presence felt, so he felt around underneath him and tossed it away. Then he glanced around. The kitchen garden was like any other at this time of year, with winter vegetables all but covered in snow and a washing line on which hung a few towels that were stiff with ice. A Yule log had been dragged close to the back door, ready to be taken inside on Christmas Eve. The inn was already fully decorated with seasonal greenery, the discarded remains of which lay beside the log. There was a higher wall to one side of the garden, with an open gate that led through into the yard of the inn, where there was noise and bustle because the weather had forced so many travelers to halt.

The landlord had left the kitchens to play host to his many guests, and the maid began to sing "Deck the halls with boughs of holly" as she placed a second tray of piping-hot mince pies on a rack on the table. Other Christmas delights were already there: saffron cakes, a number of round Christmas puddings wrapped in muslin, and an enormous fruitcake that was about to receive its coating of marzipan. When the landlord had first opened the back door, the delicious seasonal smells had drifted out into the cold night, especially the hot mince pies.

Bramble's mouth had soon begun to water. Oh, he *loved* mince pies! He hauled himself to his feet, shook the snow from his boots, and brushed as much as he could from his clothes and weasel fur cloak. Then he collected his hat and, feeling sure that the circumstances warranted it, turned it carefully inside out to keep the star hidden. When that was done, he tugged it onto his head again, being careful to tuck his long pointed ears beneath it, for they too were now very cold.

Only then did he bend to retrieve the sack. To his horror he saw that the drawstring around the neck had been loosened during his calamitous descent of the hillside. What if the chessboard had been damaged? Or one of the chessmen lost? Horrified by such a possibility, he peered inside. To his relief the board seemed intact, and the box containing the pieces was still tightly closed, so he carefully pulled the drawstring tight again and lifted the sack gingerly over his shoulder.

His intention was to seek an hour or so of shelter in the barn he could see in the adjacent yard, but before he went to the gate in the high wall, he could not resist peering in through the kitchen window. He saw a long, low-beamed room, with a stone-tiled floor and whitewashed walls that were lined with dressers. Copper pans gleamed on shelves, and blue-and-white crockery sparkled cheerfully. There was a traditional Christmas "bush" hanging from a corner of the ceiling. It was a ball made of twisted hawthorn twigs, with a dried-up sprig of last year's mistletoe inside. On New Year's Day, it would be ceremoniously burned, and a new one hung in its place, to bring good luck for the coming twelve months.

The maid had slipped out for a moment, and the festive delights were displayed on the table in as open an invitation as any Bramble had ever seen. There was even what looked like a steaming jar of mulled cider or ale keeping warm in the hearth! The elf felt suddenly very hungry and thirsty. Amazingly, the landlord hadn't quite closed the door on the latch, so that even a push from someone only twelve inches tall caused it to open.

In a trice Bramble was inside, leaving the sack on the threshold to prevent the door from swinging to. He hauled himself up to the top of the jug, and bent over the lip to guzzle as much of the hot cider as he could. Then he clambered up a wooden chair to the tabletop, where he began cramming mince pies into his mouth. To his dismay he heard the maid returning. There was no time to think. He grabbed as many of the mince pies as he could, and climbed down from the table, then ran to the door and shoved them into the sack. With the sack over his shoulder again, he dashed into the dark garden just as the maid entered.

The elf hurried toward the open gate in the high wall, and paused there to look through into the yard beyond. The Wellspring was a rambling building, gabled, half-timbered, and picturesque. It huddled on the crossroad, sheltered by the lee of the hills, and was well-known for its hospitality. The yard was consequently quite filled up with vehicles. There was a stagecoach, a London carrier's wagon, a curricle, three traps, a cart, and two private carriages. Bramble recognized the coats-of-arms on the doors of the latter, for it was part of all Malvern elves' education to know about the important humans living in the vicinity of the hills. The dashing maroon chaise belonged to the Duke of Ledbury, and the elderly navy blue traveling chariot to the equally elderly Bishop of Hereford.

Among various outbuildings, there was an immense barn, and it was upon this that the elf's gaze fixed next. He really felt too battered from his fall to continue his journey tonight. After a good sleep in a cozy hayloft, he would be much stronger in the morning.

With the sack over his shoulder once more, he threaded his way through the vehicles toward the barn.

He squeezed through a gap between the doors to find the interior quite deserted, except for two post chaises the landlord kept for hire. The barn was mostly used for storage, and for hay, mounds of which lay to one side. Bramble was glad to see a ladder leading up to the loft, where he could see more hay. It took quite an effort to haul the sack up, but at last he was there. He found a comfortable spot in the angle between the roof and the wall, turned his hat right side out once more, and by the light of his star opened the sack to enjoy the mince pies. Of course, it might have been wise to consider the dreadful mess hot sticky mince pies would make, especially when the box containing the chessmen had somehow opened after all, so that the individual pieces were jiggling around loose.

Horrified, Bramble stared into the sack, the interior of which was illuminated only too clearly by his star. He couldn't possibly take the chess set to the elf lord of the Forest of Dean in *this* state!

3

Bramble knew that he dared not deliver the chess set when it was in such a less-than-perfect condition, so he quickly gobbled the pies, licked his fingers, and then emptied the contents of the sack onto the hay.

First he tried wiping the chessboard, especially the ruby-studded border, where the crumbs and syrupy mincemeat seemed to cling almost willfully, but no matter how hard he worked at it with his handkerchief and sleeve, unsightly smears remained. And, as if this were not bad enough, there wasn't a chessman that had not come to similar grief. Nothing he did seemed to clean anything properly.

Knowing his efforts so far simply would not do, Bramble cast around for inspiration. His glance fell upon a horse trough near the bottom of the ladder. There was nothing for it but to wash everything, including the sack! Close to tears, he carried it all down the ladder again, and rinsed each item over and over in the ice-cold water, then with freezing fingers carried it up to the loft again. When he had wrung the sack as hard as he could, and draped it over a rafter to dry as much as possible, he set about drying and polishing the board and chessmen with the corner of his weasel fur cloak. Only when everything was gleaming and pristine again did he relax. Now he needed a little sleep, and by first light he'd be as right as nine pence for the rest of his journey.

He turned his hat inside out again, and snuggled into the hay, hoping to doze off quickly, but at that very moment Sir Anthony's carriage arrived in the yard below, although of course Bramble did not yet know whose vehicle it was. A small knothole in the wall gave the elf a clear view as the carriage lamps swung in a bright arc through the tumbling snowflakes, then swayed to a standstill. Ostlers ran to attend it, and Bramble watched as a middle-aged lady and gentleman alighted, the latter taking infinite care because of a gouty foot. They paused on seeing the two other private carriages in the yard, and Bramble sensed they had mixed feelings on realizing that the Duke of Ledbury and the Bishop of Hereford were at the inn.

Then a young woman began to alight as well, and

the elf saw her become rigid with dismay, but not on
account of the duke or the bishop. Following her gaze,
he saw a horseman in greatcoat and top hat riding
into the yard, his face momentarily illuminated as he
passed a lantern on the inn wall. There was no doubt
in Bramble's mind that the young woman knew the
rider, who reined in sharply as he observed her. They
stared at each other as if at ghosts.

Elves are very sensitive to human emotions, and
Bramble could almost feel the heady blend of shock,
anger, unwilling excitement, and denied desire that
swirled in the snow-filled air of the yard. But he was
warm in the hay, and too full of mince pies and hot
spiced cider to be bothered with humans and their
problems. With a yawn he closed his eyes, and sleep
soon tiptoed over him.

Julia was thunderstruck to see Philip. He had no
business being here, he was supposed to be in Glamorgan! Her glance fled uneasily toward her parents,
for the last thing she wanted was a scene of any kind,
but they were intent upon the apparent presence of
the Duke of Ledbury and the Bishop of Hereford. She
looked at Philip again, and felt her heartbeats quicken
in that way they always did when he was near. In spite
of all that he had done to hurt her, she was no nearer
to being over him than she had been that awful moment in Milsom Street. Perhaps she would never be
over him. Was that the way of first love? Clearly it
was the way as far as *his* first love was concerned, for
Lady Pamela had returned to his arms once more.

This last thought stiffened Julia's faltering resolve,
and she raised her chin in an instinctively defiant way.
It was bravado, of course, intended to conceal the hurt
within; but the truth lay like a shadow across the

depths of her brown eyes. The pain was still too fresh
and raw, and she had to look away again.

Had she but known it, Philip's reaction was scarcely
less wounded. He maneuvered his horse toward the
stables, and dismounted as the doors were opened and
a groom hurried out to attend him. Coins changed
hands, assurances of the very best care were given,
then Philip unstrapped his leather valise from the sad-
dle, and the horse was led inside. The door creaked
as it swung to once more, and suddenly he was standing there alone, the snow falling thickly and silently
out of the night.

He observed Sir Anthony and Lady Talbot as they
discussed the two private carriages already at the inn.
Philip recognized the vehicles, and knowing of the
quarrel between their owners and Sir Anthony, he
could imagine the quandary in which the latter now
found himself. Serves Old Gout right, for it was no
more than he deserved.

Then Philip observed Julia as she waited for her
parents. Lantern light seemed to fall upon her from
all sides, picking out the gentle folds of her cloak, the
softness of her white fur hat, the way a stray auburn
curl clung to her cheek. She had seldom been out of
his thoughts, and now, without warning, she was here.
Everything about her struck through him like the
sweetest of chimes, and he was reminded anew of how
very much he had lost. It had to be faced that she
had willingly returned to Richfield and his profligate
obsession with sporting and gambling, and the only
conclusion to be reached was that she loved the odious
fellow after all.

Philip drew a deep breath, and turned his face up
toward the snowflakes. All seemed lost forever, and
yet . . . New determination suddenly rushed over him.

It was Christmas, and fate had brought him to this inn at the same time as Julia. He had to use this opportunity. Somehow he had to speak to her, and get to the truth of what had happened. If she loved Richfield, then so be it.

Sir Anthony's exasperated tones rang out. "Oh, don't fuss, woman! I am quite capable of walking by myself!"

"Maybe so, sir," Lady Talbot replied, "but I wish to be inside before I freeze to death out here! And when we are there, sir, no matter what your differences with them, you are to be civil to the duke and the bishop."

"I would as soon be civil to Beelzebub!"

"Not quite the analogy I would have chosen. A little common Christmas courtesy to fellow human beings will suffice," her ladyship responded, and began to usher him firmly toward the inn door.

Julia's head turned, and briefly her eyes and Philip's met once more, then she began to follow her parents. As the snow blurred the scene, Philip was suddenly galvanized into action. He had to speak to her now, this instant, and *demand* an explanation for what had happened. It was his right to know! He ran across the snowy yard, and managed to catch her by the shoulder without Sir Anthony or Lady Talbot realizing. Julia whirled about with a silent gasp, and her parents walked out of sight beyond the bishop's traveling chariot, then into the inn.

"I must speak with you, Julia!" Philip said urgently.

"There is nothing to say, sir."

"Sir? Are we so far apart now that you cannot even bring yourself to use my first name?"

"Yes, sir, we are indeed that far apart," she replied,

her guilty glance following her parents, who were almost at the inn door. "I . . . I must go . . ."

"We have to speak about this, Julia. There is far too much left unresolved."

"I cannot . . ."

"Yes, you can." He nodded toward the barn. "I will await you in there."

"I am not able to simply leave my parents and—"

"I see no chains shackling you, madam." He spoke abruptly, but all the time he longed to drag her into his arms and cover her adored face with kisses. "All I am asking is a few minutes of your time. Surely there is at least sufficient between us for you to manage that?"

She hesitated, then shook her head. "No, it is better that things are left as they are."

"Come to me directly, Julia, or I swear I will approach you in front of your parents, the duke, and every damned bishop in the land!"

She recoiled a little. "This isn't fair."

"Fair? Since when has the thought of fairness entered into these proceedings? There was nothing *fair* about the ending of our betrothal."

She bit back the angry retort that blistered to her lips. After all the lies and subterfuge of Bath, who was he to lecture about fairness? But she couldn't risk him carrying out his threat, so she nodded. "Very well. I will come to the barn as soon as I can."

He waited as she hurried into the Wellspring, then turned on his heel to go to the barn.

Julia found her father discussing accommodation with the landlord, who was quite overwhelmed to find more titled guests gracing his establishment. He assured Sir Anthony that dinner tonight was the very

best roast beef to be had in the three counties, and
as an added attraction, if they cared for such things,
there were mummers expected at any moment. *St.
George and the Dragon* was to be played for all in the
dining room.

Sir Anthony's throbbing foot almost prompted him
to tell the landlord what the mummers could do with
their play, stags' heads, antlers and all, but then he
looked through the open door of the dining room and
saw the duke and the bishop seated amicably together
at a corner table.

Lady Talbot turned as Julia joined them. "Ah, there
you are, my dear."

"Mama, I am still a little stiff after sitting in the
carriage so long. If you do not mind, I would like to
stroll in the yard for a few minutes more."

Her mother was taken aback. "But it's *freezing* out
there, and snowing as heavily as I've ever known."

"I know, but nevertheless . . ."

"Oh, as you wish, my dear. Just do not be long, or
you will surely be ill over Christmas."

"I promise not to do such an inconvenient thing,"
Julia replied, and before her mother could say anything more, she hurried out once again. It was with
considerable trepidation that she crossed the yard to
the barn, and when she reached it, she had to pause
to compose herself before going in. The coming con-
frontation could not help but be difficult, the pain of
heartbreak still being so very fresh, but somehow she
had to conduct herself with dignity. She was the injured party, the one who had been betrayed, and for
her own pride's sake she had to hold her head high.
Nothing would permit her to let him know how
much—and how completely—his infidelity with Lady

Pamela had hurt her. With a trembling hand, she opened the barn door and went in.

Philip had lighted a lantern that hung on a wooden pillar, and was waiting by a ladder that led up to the hayloft. He had removed his cloak and top hat, and placed them over an empty barrel that lay against the wall nearby, and in the light of the lantern she saw that he wore a pine-green riding coat and close-fitting breeches. A diamond pin sparkled in his neckcloth, and a golden watch chain gleamed at his fob.

She advanced halfway across the barn, then halted. "What is it you wish to say?" she asked, her voice sounding inordinately loud in the silent barn.

Up in the hayloft Bramble stirred a little, his sleep having already been disturbed by the lighting of the lantern. He sighed, and turned over in the hay.

"Are you going to stand over there to talk to me?" Philip inquired.

"I think it best."

"Why? What on earth do you imagine I am going to do?"

She flushed. "Nothing, it's just that I . . ." She couldn't finish.

"That you what?" Philip pressed.

That I don't want to come closer for fear of giving myself away, she thought, but then decided such weak sentiments must be overcome, so she went closer. "Do you intend to spend tonight here at the inn?" she asked him.

"Yes."

"Please don't."

Bramble yawned and stretched, the voices now penetrating his slumber to the point of wakefulness.

"Would you prefer me to conveniently freeze to

death at the roadside? This is the only hostelry for
several miles, and the snow is too heavy for anyone
to sensibly continue," he answered coolly. "If you fear
I will make myself obvious to your parents, please
think again. I may have threatened to confront you in
front of them, but the last thing I really wish to do is
speak to your father."

"Or he with you," she replied.

"That I can well believe."

She looked away. "Will you at least promise not to
eat in the dining room? You could ask for your meal
to be brought to your room . . ."

"You have astonishing effrontery, madam."

She flushed. "I . . . just wish to avoid unpleasantness."

"So that is how you see me now—unpleasantness
to be avoided?"

Her flush intensified, and she didn't answer.

"Well, as it happens, I have yet to acquire a room,
let alone decide where to take my meal."

Silence fell for a few moments, then she spoke
again. "What is it you wish to say to me?"

By now Bramble was thoroughly awake. With a
frown he peered over the edge of the loft to see who
was talking. He forgot his hat, which slid forward over
his nose, and inside out or not, revealed a brief twinkle of his hidden star.

The light caught Julia's attention. "What's that?"
she gasped.

Bramble drew hastily back out of sight, and tugged
his hat firmly into place. Then he leaned cautiously
forward again, and stared invisibly down at them.

"What's what?" Philip replied, craning his neck to
look up where she pointed.

"There was a light, but it's gone now," Julia said.

"I saw nothing."

"Maybe it was one of the Malvern elves you told me of," she said, the words slipping out before she realized they were there.

Memories of their first kiss tingled over them both, and as their eyes met, each knew what the other was thinking.

Bramble's senses tingled in response to the suppressed emotion that enveloped the two people below him. He was alert to everything about them, and aware that both felt equally wounded. They each longed to go to the other, but were both determined not to make a move that might be perceived as weak. How foolish, the elf thought, wondering why humans behaved this way. If an elf loved another elf, he or she made the fact very plain indeed, without any of this painful beating around the bush. Or however the scene below could be described.

Philip glanced away first. "What made you think of elves?"

"I . . . saw a light a little earlier, from the carriage window, and I remembered what you told me. No doubt it was just someone on the hillside with a lantern, but it was pleasing to think of Malvern elves." She glanced up at the loft again. "All I know is that there was a light up there, then it disappeared."

Irony colored his reply. "A little like our betrothal, it would seem. There one moment, gone the next."

She drew back angrily. "If our engagement is over, sir, you only have yourself to blame."

"And how, pray, do you arrive at that conclusion, when *you* are the one at fault?" Philip demanded.

"Me?" She was incredulous. How could he, the miscreant of Milsom Street, possibly accuse *her* of wrongdoing? Her eyes flashed bitterly. "That is the sort of

base thing I should expect from one as shabby and deceitful as you!"

The inn dogs began to bark again, and there were sudden sounds of horses, wheels, voices . . . and jingling bells. Recognizing the latter sound as belonging to the hobbyhorse, Julia realized the mummers had arrived.

Bramble turned to put an eye to the hole in the barn wall to gaze down at the scene below, but then Philip's voice drew him back to the edge of the hayloft once more.

"It astonishes me that you, of all people, should accuse me of being shabby and deceitful! Let me remind you that the curt letter ending our betrothal without explanation came from your father. And you—ever the obedient daughter—meekly went along with it!"

"You are despicable," she breathed.

"So are you, madam," he snapped. "I was a fool to ever think you loved me, for it is clear now that you preferred Richfield all along."

Bramble winced as the painful emotions pricked at his senses.

Julia gave Philip a haughty look. "Your misconduct served to make Lord Richfield infinitely more agreeable to me," she said acidly.

"*My* misconduct? I assure you I have done nothing for which I need feel a moment of guilt."

She was transfixed by such breathtaking hypocrisy. He had lied to her about where he was going, and he had resumed his liaison—or whatever it was—with Lady Pamela, and now he claimed not to require a moment of guilt? It beggared belief!

Nothing more was said, however, because suddenly

the barn doors burst open and the traveling players and their vehicles entered in a swirl of snowflakes. They were a noisy, colorful, and boisterous crew, with the spangled hobbyhorse still cavorting and jingling, his glittering skirt brilliant in the light of their lanterns. They dropped their belongings, costumes, and property all around, and began to attend to their horses, chattering all the while about the performance they were about to give in the inn.

Julia turned and left the barn, and Philip did nothing to prevent her. Bramble again put an eye to the knothole, and saw her pause outside in the snow to wipe tears from her eyes. Then she composed herself once more, and hurried to rejoin her parents. The elf sat back in the hay. The agonizing emotions that had emanated from the divided lovers had been so intense that they had quite disturbed him. Here were two people who were obviously still hopelessly in love, yet were intent upon hurting each other because of . . . what? Misunderstanding? Pride? Obstinacy? Maybe all three? Yes, the more he considered it, the more he felt sure that it was a mixture of all three, for humans were capable of immense folly. It didn't occur to him to remember that elves were equally capable of folly, which was why he was here in the barn with the silver chess set, instead of at home with his friends.

The noise down below was now considerable, and he peered over the edge again, in time to see Philip departing to see if the inn still had an available room. The actors were already beginning to dress for their performance of *St. George and the Dragon,* although the man in the hobbyhorse had temporarily removed his costume in order to sew some ribbons more firmly into place. He was directly beneath the elf, and knew nothing of the little yellow eyes peering down at him from the loft, although once or twice he clearly felt something, for he glanced around.

At last the mummers were ready, and to the sound of tambour, drum, and fiddle, they left the barn to cross the yard to the inn, the weather having assured them of many benighted travelers to make their trouble worthwhile. At last some semblance of peace was restored to the barn, and Bramble made himself comfortable once more. He didn't notice that at some point he'd jolted the sack so that the box of chessmen had slipped out. Nor did he realize that it was open, and one of the chessmen was no longer with its fellows.

His tired eyes closed, and soon he was asleep again.

4

Before taking her seat in the dining room, Julia had discovered—by sinking to questioning an inn maid—that Philip had acquired a room right next to her own. Such knowledge did not assist her equilibrium, so she picked and poked at the inn's excellent food, and paid little attention to the mummers, who declaimed noisily throughout the pea soup, sirloin of beef, and orange pudding.

She still wore her holly-green merino gown, and had brightened it with a scarlet-and-gold shawl, but although she tried hard to put on a brave face, she failed abysmally. All around her the Christmas atmosphere was joyous. Garlands of greenery were festooned everywhere: holly, mistletoe, ivy, and pine, and there was even a kissing bunch suspended from the center beam in the dining room. It turned slowly in the heat, its red ribbons fluttering prettily, as if inviting all to join in kisses. But kisses made her think of Philip; and thinking of Philip made her more unhappy and crushed than ever.

Long before the dessert was placed on the table, Lady Talbot had become quite concerned about her. Sir Anthony, for one, did not notice anything amiss with his daughter's manner, being far more concerned about the duke and bishop, who confounded him with courteous greetings as he entered the room. Hope caught him up in its grip. Had they undergone a change of heart? Was he to be readmitted into their hallowed circle? Oh, he did pray so, for he had sorely missed their company, especially the little shooting and fishing expeditions. Encouraged, he set about his dinner with gusto; and he noticed that his gouty feet suddenly seemed less painful.

The players had been profusely applauded and rewarded when their performance ended, and immediately retreated to the barn with purses that jingled as pleasingly as the bells on the hobbyhorse's reins. But the clever intricacies of the traditional Christmas play had completely passed Julia by, as had the dexterity of the juggler and the two acrobats. The fearsome dragon did not make her flinch, nor had she wanted to cheer when it was slain by St. George. She found it impossible to join in the general merriment when the hobbyhorse clacked its jaws right in her face, or when the Old Woman's besom brushed busily against her hem. In short, she simply did not feel like laughing. How could she even smile when all she really wanted to do was cry her eyes out? She tried to tell herself that Philip was a maggot of the first water; but knowing it and being sensible about it were apparently two very different things.

As the party from Wentwood rose from their table
at the end of the evening, the duke and the bishop
made their decision to forgive and forget quite plain
by cordially inviting a delighted Sir Anthony to join
them for port and a little conversation. The silly falling
out was evidently at an end, and Lady Talbot and
Julia went upstairs hoping that a restoration of Sir
Anthony's good humor would now follow.

But if Julia thought she would be allowed to go
quietly to bed with her private miseries, she was soon
put right, for Lady Talbot accompanied her into her
firelit room, which lay at the rear of the inn, overlook-
ing the yard. It was a plainly furnished chamber, but
clean, with beams as low as those on the ground floor.
A floral coverlet brightened the bed, and there were
faded blue curtains at the windows. Several rugs were
scattered on the uneven wooden floor. In an alcove,
hidden behind a screen, there was a washstand, with
towels as white as the snowflakes outside.

Lady Talbot closed the door, then leaned back
against it, her plum velvet gown burnished softly by
the firelight. "Now, young lady, I want you to tell me
what is wrong. No, don't attempt to fob me off, for I
know that something has happened, and I do not intend to leave until you tell me what it is."

A little earlier, an argument out in the yard had
awoken Bramble with a start. The mummers had been
returning to the barn after their performance when
they had an altercation with two of the inn's ostlers.
The exasperated elf looked through the knothole
again, but instead of observing the disturbance in the
yard, his gaze was drawn to two upper windows at the
inn. In one he saw Philip seated at a lonely dinner, in
the other he saw Julia and her mother talking. The

elf's attention moved away from the windows again as the mummers came back into the barn, their difference with the ostlers settled amicably. Talking and laughing, they lit lanterns again, and relaxed before settling in for the night. Bramble frowned over the edge of the hayloft. Why couldn't humans make less noise? How was an elf supposed to have sufficient sleep to continue a journey to the Forest of Dean at first light?

Thinking of his destination reminded him of the Very Important Task, and he turned to check that the sack was still safe. He immediately noticed that the box of chessmen had not only fallen out, but had spilled its contents in the hay. Appalled, he hastily gathered the chessmen and counted them. Oh, no! One was missing! His yellow eyes grew huge with dismay, and beneath his hat his long ears stood on end. Panic set in, and he rummaged frantically in the hay for the lost piece. It was rather dark without his star, but there was sufficient light from the players' lanterns for him to see there was no sign of what he was looking for.

He took a huge breath, striving to calm himself down a little. He must think. All the pieces were there when he cleaned them, so it *had* to be here somewhere. Slowly his gaze moved to the edge of the hayloft. The missing chessman had dropped over the side! There was no other explanation. He peered over, just as he had when Julia and Philip were there. The mummers were lying and sitting where the mood took them, talking amicably together and discussing the performance they hoped to give in Tewkesbury the next night, Christmas Eve.

They did not sense Bramble's anxious gaze darting around, hoping to see a tiny silver, ruby-studded chessman. By now his little heart was pounding wildly, and he felt quite ill with anxiety. He hastened invisibly down the ladder, and searched diligently, but he found nothing. Where had the chessman gone? Then his eyes lit up a little. It must have fallen into the clothes of one or other of the lovers! The young lady had been wearing a cloak, with the hood unraised and therefore forming a perfect place into which a chess piece might fall. And the young gentleman had left his greatcoat and top hat over that barrel, which was also within reach of anything descending from the loft.

Bramble knew he would have to find them both, and conduct a thorough search of their garments! He took a huge breath to steady his nerves, then marched out of the barn into the yard. Fresh dismay immediately halted him, for the snow now reached almost to his waist! How on earth could he reach the Forest of Dean in this? But at least it wasn't falling quite so relentlessly; in fact, he was sure he could see one or two stars peeping through the hitherto endless clouds. Well, whatever the conditions, he still had to deliver the chess set safely, or face the consequences. Tugging his hat down over his ears, the unfortunate elf picked his way across the yard, making use of the players' footprints to reach the door into the inn.

Lady Talbot watched as Julia lighted the candle on the mantel. "Come now, my dear, it is as plain as a pikestaff that something has upset you since we arrived here tonight. Please tell me what it is."

Before Julia could answer, the door suddenly swung open, apparently of its own volition, for neither woman could see Bramble slipping into the room. A cold draft swept in from the passage before Julia closed the door again, this time making sure the latch was properly caught, which it hadn't been before. Bramble was having Christmas luck with the Wellspring's doors, first the kitchen and now again upstairs. But there was no time to reflect upon such things, for he had a chessman to find! He hurried across the room to examine Julia's cloak, which she had draped over a chair in front of the fire. He scrambled busily up the chair leg, and both women heard, but thought they were imagining it.

Julia returned to her mother. "Yes, something *has* happened." She drew a deep breath. "Philip is staying here."

The words shook Lady Talbot. "I . . . beg your pardon? Did you say *Philip* is staying here?"

"Yes. He arrived at the same time as us, and right now is in the very next room."

Her mother stared at the wall as if it would open up suddenly and she would see the gentleman in question. Then she looked intently at her daughter. "How did you feel when you saw him?" she asked.

"Feel?"

"Yes."

Julia's lips parted, then closed again.

Her mother's eyes cleared. "Silence is sometimes the most eloquent answer of all, and in this case proves that he is still everything to you. Did you speak to him?"

"Yes, that was why I went back outside. He wanted to talk to me."

"And?" Lady Talbot raised an inquisitive eyebrow.

"And nothing. I asked him not to come to the dining room, and it seems he complied with my request."

Bramble could not help eavesdropping as he began to delve through the fur-lined folds of the cloak.

"I trust you challenged him about Bath?" Lady Talbot demanded.

"No," Julia confessed.

Her mother was appalled. "*No?* Oh, Julia!"

"We were interrupted as we talked in the barn, because the mummers came in."

"Julia, has seeing him again made any difference?"

Julia shook her head. "I wish nothing more to do with him, Mama. He pretends that he has done nothing; indeed he plays the innocent so well I could almost believe him."

"I see."

"Don't look at me like that," Julia protested, and fidgeted a little with the cuff of her gown.

"My dear Julia, you were never a very good liar. If Bath had not happened, you would still be as happy as a pig in clover. Do not deny it, please."

Bramble balanced on the chair, and stretched around the back to reach the hood of the cloak. He leaned a little too far, and fell off the chair, landing with an audible thud.

"What was that?" Julia gasped, whirling toward the sound. "That's the second time I've heard something over by that chair!"

"I think it must be coming from the floor below," her mother replied.

"But it seemed to be right in here with us."

"It can't have been. Now, don't attempt to change the subject, my dear, for we were discussing you and Philip."

Julia summoned a wry smile. "Well, it is of no consequence whether I want him or not, for the simple fact is that I am now betrothed to Edwin."

"So if Philip were to walk in here right now and beg you to spurn Edwin again, you would tell him to go to perdition?"

"Yes."

"Hmm."

Bramble got up from the floor, dusted himself, then looked approvingly at Lady Talbot. His elfin senses had told him much about Philip, enough to know that he was probably innocent of the misdeeds of which he was accused. Now it would seem that Julia's mother not only knew Julia better than that young lady knew herself, but also was not convinced of Philip's guilt. Bramble twitched his lips. If it were not that he had his Very Important Task to consider, he might be inclined to assist these humans with their problems. As it was, the missing chessman had to come first. He clambered up onto the chair again, the sounds he made disguised this time because the fire shifted in the hearth. He resumed his minute inspection of the cloak, but was already beginning to realize that the chessman was not there.

Julia was indignant with her mother. "Don't say 'hmm' like that. Of *course* I would spurn Philip!" she insisted stoutly.

"Even though you wish with all your heart that you had declined Edwin's second proposal?" Lady Talbot looked wisely at her daughter.

Julia glanced away, avoiding her eyes. "What point is there in discussing it? I have accepted, and that is all there is to it. Papa is right to say I cannot possibly change my mind again."

"My dear, if you are standing by your word now simply on account of what your father says . . ."

"It is as good a reason as any," Julia murmured.

"Which itself is no reason to proceed," Lady Talbot said gently. "Tell me, my dear, is there an element in this of wishing to snap your fingers in Philip's face to show him you do not care?"

Julia bit her lip. Yes, of course there was that, too.

Lady Talbot read her child's face like a printed page. "My advice is that you tell the truth and shame the devil. Admit that you have made a mistake, and withdraw from this match. Wait for true happiness to come along again. As it will, sooner or later."

"Maybe it will not come at all."

"Oh, my darling girl, what a mess this is! I can see that you are going to be monumentally miserable as Lady Richfield."

"At least my heart will not be hurt anymore. If I had become Countess of Allensmore, can you even *begin* to imagine how utterly distraught I would soon have become, discovering Philip's faithlessness?"

"He has only been faithless if what you and your father saw in Bath was what it appeared to be."

Julia was caught off guard. "What do you mean? Of *course* it was what it appeared to be! A passionate kiss is a passionate kiss."

"With all due respect, my dear, I cannot imagine Philip being foolish enough to publicly indulge in a passionate kiss with another man's wife. Milsom Street always has eyes, you may count upon that, and from all accounts, Lady Pamela's husband is a jealous hothead."

Bramble nodded. That was true. Philip was a discreet gentleman, not a fool.

"I know what Papa and I saw," Julia whispered.

Lady Talbot went to her, and took her firmly by the arms. "My dear, it is Christmas, and you and Philip are both stranded here at this inn. I know that you still love him, and I know, too, that it is possible there has been a misunderstanding about Bath. Oh, yes, my dear, such a thing *is* possible, and unless you get to the truth, you will regret it for the rest of your life."

Bramble sighed. Oh, he *did* like this lady. She reminded him of his own mother. He wiped a tear away.

"Be sensible now, Julia, for you *know* that true happiness is worth fighting for," Lady Talbot went on. "Maybe he did betray you, and maybe he never loved you at all, but until you ask him to his face, you will never know. Fate has given you a chance, and I cannot urge you enough to seize it. You say he is just beyond that wall, which means that half a dozen steps or so will take you to him. Think on it now. I will not say more, but when I see you tomorrow morning at breakfast, young lady, I expect to be told what you said to each other."

"Mother—"

"Enough." Lady Talbot put a finger to her daughter's lips. "Good night, my dear, and pray do not sleep too tight, for you have things to sort out." She kissed Julia's cheek, then left the room.

Bramble slipped out, too, and was safely out in the passage again when Julia's door was closed. He glanced along to Philip's room. Did he dare to hope that a third latch would open at his touch? There was nothing for it but to try. This time, however, the door did not budge. The elf huffed and puffed, pushed, and shoved, but it remained sturdily closed. Infuriated, Bramble kicked it, stubbing his toe in the process. The door did not miraculously yield, but the kick had just been audible to Philip, who turned curiously to look at the door. What was that? Getting up, he went to look out. Bramble could hardly believe his luck, and dove into the room with an inch to spare as the door was closed once more.

Philip went to the window, and looked out at the snowflakes, fewer now, that still wended their way past the pane. He could see his own reflection in the glass,

and—so it seemed—Julia at his side. Her image was
faint, but she was there. He reached out to touch her.
"Oh, Julia, my beloved, do you even care that I still
love you with every ounce of my being?" he
whispered.

Bramble, already busily prying through Philip's
cloak and top hat, paused to look at him. Oh, if only
this foolish fellow knew how desperately in love with
him Julia still was. And if only *she* knew how Philip
was feeling. Shaking his head at the foolishness of
humans, the elf continued his search. But as he again
drew a blank, despondency set in like the blackest,
most dismal rain cloud that ever hung over the Malverns. He was doomed. Blinking back tears, he went
to sit dolefully on the rug in front of the fire. What
could he do now? He simply couldn't think where the
missing chess piece had gone. He'd searched everywhere in the barn, and now he'd thoroughly examined
the clothes as well. There simply wasn't anywhere else.

Philip's thoughts were scarcely less gloomy. Suddenly something came over him, and before he knew
it he was striding toward the door. He had to speak
to her one last time! There was nothing else for it,
otherwise he would go mad of the torment. But as he
snatched the door open, he came to a sharp halt, for
there, hand raised to knock, was Julia herself.

5

Philip stared at Julia, for she was almost the last
person he would have expected to see at his door.

She stepped back guiltily, her cheeks flushing in the
light from the candle she held. "Oh, I—I . . ." Her

tongue seemed suddenly tied in a knot, but then she managed to find some words. "I . . . think you were right earlier, we *do* need to talk. . . ."

"I feel the same, and was just coming to you." He gazed at her, beguiled as ever by the spell she had cast over him from the first moment he ever saw her.

"You were?"

"Yes, I—" He broke off as someone was heard coming along the passage. "Come in, it won't do for you to be seen like this." He drew her quickly inside, and closed the door. A moment later footsteps passed by outside, but whoever it was had not seen anything. As the steps died away again, Julia and Philip looked awkwardly at each other. They were both afraid to start the conversation; both afraid of what they might hear.

Philip remembered his manners. "Er, please sit down." He began to usher her toward the chair at the table, but she drew away.

"No. Thank you, I would rather stand."

Ill at ease, they looked at each other again, still unable to commence what had to be said. The moment was so filled with all those unspoken words that down on the hearth rug, Bramble forgot his own miseries and turned to look. He willed Julia and Philip to settle their differences and be happy again. It was Christmas, and everyone should be happy. Even stupid elves that made a mess of everything they touched! Turning to look at the fire again, he gave a long, heartfelt sigh. Fresh tears stung his little yellow eyes, and beneath his inside-out hat, his already drooping ears drooped even more. To make matters worse, snow had found its way inside his tall boots, where it had melted and made his legs and feet feel dreadfully cold and wet.

Oh, was there ever a more wretched elf? His lips began to quiver, the hot tears welled down his cheeks, and he began to cry silently.

Julia fidgeted with her shawl, then at last met Philip's eyes squarely. "I have to tell you that I know all about Bath."

"Bath?"

"Yes. Oh, *please* don't play the innocent again, for it simply will not do. My father and I saw you in Milsom Street with Lady Pamela."

He gazed at her as if she were quite mad. "When was this?" he demanded.

"When you were supposed to be in London. Philip, *please* stop pretending, for it only makes things worse."

"I really have no idea what you are talking about. When I told you I went to London, I *did* go there!"

She turned away exasperatedly. "Oh, I knew this would do no good," she breathed, and began to go toward the door.

He stopped her, and forced her to face him again. "Julia, I swear upon my mother's honor that I have never in my life been in Milsom Street with Pamela."

"My father and I *saw* you," she repeated.

"Not me. I do not doubt that you saw her with someone, but it could not have been me because I was in London."

"Are you claiming that I would not recognize you across a street?" she inquired hotly.

He bridled as well. "I suppose I must be, because it simply cannot have been me. I haven't been anywhere near Bath. I can't abide the place. Nor, these days, can I abide Pamela."

"If it wasn't you, who was it?" she demanded. The

words were a scornful challenge that rang with disbelief.

"How do I know who it was? One thing you can be sure of, Pamela likes fellows of my height and coloring. Her husband is not unlike me, and the lover she took after me was similar as well."

Julia began to turn away, her expression registering only contempt for such a paltry explanation, but he forced her to look at him again. "No, don't you dare reject this out of hand! Damn it, you've accused me unjustly, and the least you can do is hear my defense. Tell me, was your view of this mysterious man quite clear and uninterrupted?"

"You were directly across the street from us!"

"That isn't an answer to my question."

She drew back slightly. "Well, it was dusk and raining heavily, and there was a lot of traffic, but you were close enough for Papa and I to see you."

"Ah. So neither of you had a really good look after all; you simply put two and two together, made five, and allowed your naturally mistrustful inclinations to do the rest."

Her eyes flashed. "How typical of you to pretend that my father and I have defective eyesight and overly suspicious natures! You would say anything rather than admit that you have been caught out in your lies!"

"Why would I lie? What possible reason could I have? If I had resumed my . . . er, liaison with Pamela, it would be because I loved her, and if *that* were the case, I certainly wouldn't attempt to clear my name with you. So listen to what I'm saying, Julia. I have never been with Pamela in Milsom Street."

She fell silent. It *had* been him, she was certain. But

his vehemence was such that doubt began to creep in. Oh, surely she and Papa couldn't *both* have been mistaken? Could they? It had indeed been a terribly rainy evening, and the rattle and clatter of wheels and hooves on cobbles had been tremendous. The umbrella had concealed so much, only moving aside a couple of times to reveal the two people it sheltered. She paused, for a new memory suddenly slid into her mind. It *had* been Philip, for she had recognized his coat! "It *was* you, Philip. You were wearing that coat I loathe, brick-colored with a dark green collar and brass buttons."

He stared at her, and then to her surprise and indignation he laughed. "I've suddenly realized who you must have seen! My cousin, Daniel Heyworth."

Julia's lips parted. "I have never heard of him."

"That is not surprising. He was abroad until a few months ago. At school we were often taken for twins. I happen to know that he has indeed been to Bath since his return, and I can also tell you that he admired that coat so much that he had one made exactly like it. So if he wore it that day in Milsom Street, I can well believe you would mistake him for me, especially if he was embracing Pamela. He has pursued her relentlessly since his return, and from what you say, it would seem he has succeeded."

Oh, how plausible it sounded, but did she dare trust him? She was in a quandary, so wanting to believe, but afraid to put her heart in jeopardy again.

He watched the nuances on her face, saw how they alternated, and his resentment took hold once more. "It is the truth, Julia, and if that single instance of mistaken identity is all it took for you to allow your father to sever our match . . ." Now he was the one to show scorn. "I am innocent, and have been treated abominably by you and your family. And as if that were not bad enough, I have to face your forthcoming nuptials with Richfield. The ease with which you returned to his arms is further proof of your shallowness. I never meant anything to you, did I?"

"If that is what you wish to think, then think it!" she cried, stung beyond endurance. She couldn't cope with this anymore, it was simply too much to know that she and her father had probably made a horrible mistake in Bath.

A tiny voice suddenly piped up. "Oh, *do* stop arguing! You're both being very silly, you know, and your problems are very small indeed compared with mine!"

Startled, Julia and Philip whirled about, for there had been no mistaking what they heard, except there was no one else in the room with them. Was there? Who on earth would have such a high-pitched, squeaky voice? They glanced all around, but there seemed nothing there.

Bramble was past caring. "You think you are the only ones in trouble, but I am the unluckiest elf that ever lived and breathed!"

Elf? Julia's breath caught, and she reached instinctively for Philip's hand. His fingers closed reassuringly over hers, but he was less easily persuaded that the tiny voice was genuine. "This is a joke, I perceive," he breathed. "Come on, show yourself, whoever you are!"

Bramble was vexed. "I only wish it were a joke, for then I would not be in as much trouble as I am!"

Julia squeezed Philip's fingers. "I believe it, Philip. There really is an elf in the room with us."

"Thank you, Julia," Bramble said in his little high voice.

Philip gave an incredulous laugh. "Oh, come now, Julia, you can't possibly believe that there is a—"

"Why not?" She interrupted. "Philip, you were the one that told me about the elves on the Malverns."

"Yes, but they're only a story!"

Bramble felt insulted. "No, we're not, we're real, and we live in the hills."

Philip hesitated, then shook his head again. "No, I refuse to be taken in. This is someone's notion of a jape!"

But Julia was sure the opposite was the case. "I don't think so. After all, there isn't anywhere in here for someone to hide, and the voice certainly appears to be disembodied."

Bramble was confused. "Disembodied? I'm not disembodied! I have a head, two arms, and two legs just like you!"

Julia found herself smiling at the voice's squeaky indignation. "Who are you? Do you have a name?"

"Of *course* I have a name!" Bramble got to his feet, and swept a polite bow. "I am Bramble Bumblekin."

"I am pleased to meet you," Julia replied, and even went so far as to incline her head, although she did so in the wrong direction, having decided the voice came from the far side of the fireplace, not by the hearth.

"I'm here, not over there," Bramble said.

"Where?"

"Here. Oh, let me show you . . ." The elf snatched off his hat, and turned it right side out again. His Christmas star immediately shone brightly in front of the fire.

Julia realized it was the light she had seen in the barn. "You were in the hayloft!"

"Yes."

"Can we see you properly? I mean, not just your light?"

"Do you really want to?"

She nodded. "Yes, of course."

"Oh, all right. If I can remember how to do it . . ." Bramble concentrated hard, closed his eyes tight, and said the words he hoped were the correct ones. Gradually he became visible, beginning from the bottom of his boots and ending with the tip of his red hat.

Philip stared at the little being. "Good God," he muttered. "So there really are elves in the Malverns?"

"Yes, I keep telling you. We've been around longer than you humans."

Julia was enchanted. There was something so appealing about the little manikin, that she gathered her skirts and went to kneel by him. She held out the forefinger of her right hand. "I am honored to meet you, Mr. Bumblekin."

Bramble hesitated, then shook the finger with both his little hands. "Just Bramble will do."

"I am Julia, and this is Philip."

The elf nodded, then gave them a stern look. "You are both being very silly you know. We elves are very sensitive indeed to the emotions of humans, and I have seen enough of you two to know that you are still in love with each other. Julia, I heard everything you said to your mother, so I know you do not love this Edwin, whoever he is. Philip is the one you want. And, Philip, I know that you are still in love with Julia. I also know, because elves can tell such things, that you are telling the truth about Bath. It wasn't you in Milsom Street, it was most likely this Daniel Heyworth fellow. So, *please,* won't you both make up? Why should all three of us be miserable?"

Julia's heart seemed to turn over. Oh, what an idiot

she had been. Why hadn't she crossed Milsom Street and confronted the pair beneath the umbrella? If she had done that, instead of drawing back wounded into her shell . . . Slowly she turned to look up at him with eyes that shimmered with tears. "Oh, my darling, can you ever forgive me?" she whispered. "I should have *known* you would not lie to me."

"And I should have known that you meant it when you said you loved me," Philip replied. "I should have realized that you could never feel anything for a non-entity like Richfield." He covered the few feet that separated them, fell to his knees in front of her, and gathered her into his arms to kiss her passionately on the lips.

They clung together, their hearts beating close. A tumult of joy swept them both up in its grasp, and they were laughing and crying as they kissed, so wonderfully happy again that they could barely credit how silly they had both been. This time they knew they would never lose faith in each other again.

At last Philip brought the kisses to an end for a while, and cupped her face in his hands to gaze adoringly into her brown eyes, so dark with love for him. "You cannot marry Richfield, my darling, for you belong to me."

"I know."

"Nor does Richfield warrant any pity, for his sole reason for entering into the match has always been to get your fortune. You do know that, don't you?"

She nodded. "Yes, I know it."

"He only has himself to blame for his financial situation. If he squandered less on sports and gaming, he would still be a rich man. And if he laid hands upon your fortune, he would fritter it away in exactly the same way. He cannot help himself. It's his nature."

"I know that, too."

He kissed the tip of her nose. "Oh, I cannot bear to think of your unhappiness if you had become Lady Richfield." He paused. "Which brings me to an important point. What will your father have to say about this? I know he does not like me."

"Philip, it isn't that he does not like you. He only has my happiness and well-being at heart. He thought the original match with Edwin was a good thing, because Edwin's father was still alive then and the Richfield fortune was intact. Then Edwin inherited, and I confess my father had something of a shock to realize he was such a spendthrift. But it ceased to matter because I met you, and everything changed." She lowered her eyes. "I know my father should have spoken to you in person about the ending of our betrothal, but he saw how distressed I was after Milsom Street. He really believed that you were the man with Lady Pamela, so in his view, you did not warrant any consideration at all."

"And what now? Will he accept another change?"

Julia looked toward the window, where only a few snowflakes now wended their way past the dark glass. "Yes, I think he will. Mama has never entirely believed ill of you; in fact, tonight she insisted that I must come to sort it all out with you once and for all. She will support us."

Philip smiled. "I have always approved of your mother."

"You will approve of my father, too, I'm sure. Poor Papa, as well as falling out with the duke and bishop, and having to endure truly dreadful gout, he had my miseries to contend with, too. But tonight I think he, the duke, and the bishop are good friends again, and that he will be in mellow spirits when I—we—tell him what has happened."

"I trust so, for I do not relish an arguing match with Old Gout."

"Perhaps it would be wiser not to call him that, in case you forget yourself one day and do it to his face."

Philip was philosophical. "I'll warrant it is quite mild compared to some of the things he's called me of late."

"That is true, but nevertheless . . ."

"The point is taken."

She linked her arms around his neck, and gazed lovingly up into his eyes. "I adore you, Lord Allensmore."

"And I adore you, Miss Talbot," he whispered, bending his head to kiss her on the lips again.

Bramble had been quite forgotten for the moment, but the elf had watched approvingly as the disagreeable past was consigned to oblivion. Then he heaved a huge sigh, and turned away to sit forlornly in front of the fire again. His shoulders slumped, his ears flopped, and he stared into the flames. If only *his* troubles could be so easily resolved, but there was no one at hand to conveniently tell him where the missing chessman could be found.

Gradually Julia became conscious of the elf's overwhelming unhappiness. She and Philip looked at each other, and then went to sit on either side of the poor little fellow. "What's wrong, Bramble?" she asked, reaching out gently to touch his small arm.

"I've lost something very important indeed."

"Please tell us, for perhaps we can help you as you helped us."

He gave another enormous sigh. "Oh, it would be wonderful if you could, but that would be hoping for too much. I've searched your things, and it isn't there, so I can't begin to imagine where it is."

"What isn't where? Begin at the beginning, Bramble," Julia said soothingly.

6

Bramble stared glumly at the fire. "Do you *really* want to hear my problems?"

"Of course we do. Don't we Philip?" Julia replied.

"Yes," Philip confirmed. "Look, Bramble, you have helped us, so the least we can do is try to help you. And you know what they say, a trouble shared is a trouble halved."

"Elves say that, too."

"Then tell us," Philip urged.

Bramble swallowed, and began his tale. He told them all about his dreadful year, and all the things that had gone wrong. Then he spoke of the Very Important Task, and how he had ended up in the hayloft. And how the silver chessman had disappeared. "I've searched *everywhere*," he finished. "There just isn't any sign of it. And even if I do find it, how on earth am I going to reach the Forest of Dean in snow this deep? It comes up to my waist, and it was all I could do to cross the yard from the barn to the inn! I had to use people's footprints."

Philip smiled. "Well, the last is easily resolved. We will find the chessman, and in the morning I will take you to the forest on my horse."

Bramble brightened a little. "You will?"

"Of course. I am in your debt, Bramble, and will

gladly take you wherever you wish. We can deliver
the chess set, and then I will bring you back here. I
will even take you up the hillside to wherever it is
you have to go."

Bramble beamed at him, but then his smile wobbled
as cold reality returned. "That's all very well, but I
have no idea where to look for the missing piece. I've
thought and thought, but it's no good."

"Well, it has to be in the barn somewhere," Philip
decided, and Julia nodded.

"Yes, it does," she agreed. "It will not be easy to
find, but if we all three conduct a search . . ."

Philip sat up suddenly. "I have had a thought!
Bramble, Julia and I were not the only ones to be
directly below you in the hayloft. As I recall, when I
left, the hobbyhorse took my place!"

Bramble's breath caught, and he stared. "You're
right, it did! Oh, I must go back right now to look!"
He leapt to his feet, intent upon rushing to the door,
but Philip reached out to stop him.

"Hold there, little fellow. It's far easier if I take you
there. You can sit on my shoulder."

Bramble thought that an excellent idea. "Can I
really?"

"Yes, provided you are invisible, of course. It won't
do to have all the merry cider-filled souls at the inn
imagining they are seeing things! And when we reach
the barn, I'll enlist the assistance of the hobbyhorse
man." Philip got up, and went to put on his greatcoat.

Julia scrambled to her feet as well. "I'm coming,
too," she said.

"There is no need—" Philip began, but broke off
at the steely glint in her eyes. "Oh, very well, I know
better than to argue this particular point," he
conceded.

"I'll go for my cloak. Don't you *dare* go without me!" She dashed from the room.

Philip lifted Bramble onto his shoulder, and the elf made himself invisible again and turned his hat inside out, then held on tightly to the greatcoat's astrakhan collar. "By the way," Philip said as he donned his gloves, "how big is this missing chess piece?"

"Oh, the usual elf size. So big . . ." Bramble indicated with his thumb and forefinger.

"How big?" Philip could not see anything.

A tiny hand materialized for a moment, thumb and forefinger held just so, then disappeared again.

"Ah, so it's really very small."

The elf was a little puzzled. "You surely didn't think it was the same size as a chess set *you* would use, did you? I mean, if it was I wouldn't be able to carry it fifteen miles."

"I don't know what I thought," Philip replied honestly. "I confess I didn't even know that elves played chess."

Now Bramble was offended. "Didn't know we played it?" he repeated. "We *invented* it! Humans aren't always first with everything! You weren't even the first to take a gift to the stable in Bethlehem. An elf king arrived with his gift of silver long before your three wise men with their gold, frankincense, and myrrh. That's why we always wear stars and give silver at Christmas."

"Forgive me, I had no idea."

"Well, you're a human, so I suppose you can't help it. You're all rather silly."

"That is a little rich coming from you, Bramble Bumblekin. After all the things you've made a mess of this last year, I rather think you would be wiser not to criticize anyone else."

Bramble sighed. "Hmm, maybe you're right," he conceded.

"There's no maybe about it, I *am* right," Philip replied.

Julia returned promptly, and they hurried down through the inn, passing the dining room where Sir Anthony, the duke, and the bishop were now in a truly rosy Christmas glow. One glance told Julia that in the morning there would be three very thick heads, but at least their former companionship had been fully restored.

She followed Philip out into the yard. The snow clouds had all but dispersed now, and the sky was a lofty canopy of stars. There was a full moon, and its pale light shone on a world of white, giving everything a strange, almost unearthly luminescence. It was the sort of night that greater painters of the past had depicted for the Nativity, and therefore seemed quite perfect.

The crisp snow crunched beneath Julia and Philip's feet as they crossed to the barn, where fortunately the mummers were still awake, the innkeeper having sent them a tray of saffron cakes and several jugs of the mulled cider. The horses and ponies were resting peacefully near the inn's post chaises, and the children were asleep in hay beds. The adults, their faces shining in the light of a single lantern, were seated in a circle, enjoying the innkeeper's Christmas largesse. They all looked around in surprise as Philip and Julia entered, and the hobbyhorse man gave a grin. "Slipped away for another secret tryst, eh? Well, I fear you'll have witnesses this time." His friends laughed.

Philip went up to him. "This is not tryst, sir; indeed we are glad to find you here, for we have a boon to beg."

"A boon, eh? Well, it being the season of goodwill, I suppose I would be churlish to refuse." The man smiled. He was small and swarthy, with bushy eyebrows and a hollow face with high cheekbones. He looked, Julia decided, more suited to riding a blood racehorse than operating a hobbyhorse. He scrambled to his feet, and bowed to them both. "Johnno Bakewell, your servant, sir, miss."

Philip inclined his head. "I am pleased to meet you, Johnno. I am Lord Allensmore."

Johnno's jaw dropped. "The *Earl* of Allensmore? Master of Allensmore Castle?"

"The very same."

"Then I am honored to make your acquaintance, my lord." Johnno bowed deeply. "My friends and I halted at the castle a day or so ago, and were offered every hospitality. So I reckon I owe you your boon, whatever it is."

Philip smiled. "A friend of ours may have lost something rather valuable in your hobbyhorse costume, and with your leave we would like to search for it."

"By all means, sir, by all means. It's over here." Johnno picked up the lantern and led them to the barrel where earlier Philip had draped his greatcoat. Now the hobbyhorse had been carefully arranged over it. "Search as you will, my lord."

Philip and Julia went through the costume inch by inch, with Bramble hanging anxiously over Philip's shoulder, watching everything they did. Suddenly Julia's careful fingers found what they were seeking. She was feeling around where the horse's head joined its neck. There were many creases in the sequined material, and the tiny chessman was wedged between them. With a glad cry she held it out, but of course, it was invisible.

Johnno stared at her empty palm. "I can't see anything," he muttered.

She immediately closed her hand. "Oh, it's very, very small," she said.

"What is it?"

"A diamond," Philip said quickly.

Bramble was so joyful he almost fell off Philip's shoulder. "Oh, I'm saved, I'm saved!" he cried, his squeaky voice only too audible.

Johnno stepped back in alarm. "What on earth was that?" he cried.

His friends, who hadn't heard, looked curiously at him. "What was what?" one of them asked.

"I heard a shrill little voice!"

His companions laughed. "Too much cider again, eh, Johnno? Next you'll be saying you're seeing fairies again!"

"I heard it, I tell you!" Johnno said, then looked at Philip and Julia. "You heard it, too, didn't you?"

Philip looked blandly back at him. "Me? No, I didn't hear anything," he murmured.

"Nor did I," Julia added.

The other players chuckled, and one of them raised his tankard and shook his head. "Oh, Johnno, the Wellspring's brew must be a little stronger than you thought!"

"I heard a voice, I tell you," the hobbyhorse man insisted, giving Philip and Julia a slightly reproachful look, for he *knew* he couldn't be alone in hearing things.

Feeling a little guilty, Philip pressed several coins upon him—ample recompense for teasing the man was now bound to endure. Mollified, Johnno returned to show his spoils to his envious friends. While the players were thus diverted, Philip quickly sent Bramble up the ladder to bring the sack and the rest of the chess set down from the loft. Then, with the happy elf on his shoulder once more, he and Julia left the barn to go back to the inn, where the chessman was restored to its place in the box, and the damp sack was hung from the mantel to dry.

Bramble was overwhelmed by the change in his fortunes. Now he was not only assured of a warm night on a cushion in front of the fire in Philip's room, but had been promised his favorite porridge breakfast in the morning, and would be transported to and from the Forest of Dean on Philip's horse. Oh, it was going to be a good Christmas after all. His troubles were over, he'd be restored to favor with his friends, and he could look forward to a wonderful New Year. All was certainly well in his little world.

As the contented elf curled up on the plump cushion, Philip conducted Julia back to her own room, where behind the secrecy of the closed door, they indulged in enough kisses to more than make up for those they had missed since the awful misunderstanding over Bath. There was, of course, the matter of her second betrothal to Edwin still to be dealt with, to say nothing of how she was going to explain to her father, but true love—and Bramble Bumblekin—would conquer all.

Christmas Eve morning dawned bright and clear, with the countryside sparkling white beneath blue skies and winter sun. The Malverns sailed against the heavens, and the seasonal atmosphere seemed somehow more joyous and tangible than ever before. Julia and Philip, both feeling happy and transformed enough to face Sir Anthony a thousand times over, went hand in hand downstairs to the dining room to say what had to be said.

They approached the table a little apprehensively, hoping against hope that their news would be well received. Their hopes were granted, for headache or not, Sir Anthony was in amiable spirits. His gout appeared to have undergone a miraculous cure now that all was well with the duke and the bishop. It seemed they no longer held him to blame for what had happened at Michaelmas, for it turned out that the gun, not he, was faulty. And to seal his readmittance to the friendship, he had been invited to a day's shooting on the hillside above the inn, the innkeeper having promised to take them to where there was excellent sport to be had.

Julia was amazed at her father's placidness as she and Philip came to the table. He did not seem in the least surprised to see them together, or to hear what they said. "Well, if that is what you want, you may have it," he said, reaching for another slice of toast. "Just don't let it happen again, or I may have to leave my entire fortune to someone else."

Julia stared at him. "Is that all you are going to say?"

"It is, unless you wish me to be difficult?" Sir Anthony's gaze moved to Philip. "You had better look after her, sir, because earl or not, I'll wear your intestines for garters if you give her a single minute of unhappiness."

"I will cherish her for the rest of our lives, sir," Philip replied.

"See that you do. Of course, I am now left with the embarrassing business of Richfield, but then again, I am forced to admit that he is not the sort of man I wish to see married to my daughter. I may have grumbled a great deal, and said all manner of things about my wrath should she change her mind again, but, to be frank, I am relieved things have gone the way they have. Julia, I'm delighted that you will make a love match after all, as your dear mother and I did all those years ago. Now, off with the pair of you, for I have little doubt that breakfast is the last thing you feel like."

Julia ran to him and hugged him tightly. "Thank you, Papa! I do adore you!"

"Hmm," he replied, his thoughts turning to food as a maid placed a plate of eggs and bacon in front of him. "Ah, just the thing for the morning after the night before," he muttered.

Julia turned to her mother, who smiled sagely. "My dear, you do not simply have the duke and the bishop to thank for his mild temper, for I made sure he knew how things were with you."

Julia smiled. "Oh, Mama . . ."

"I'm so glad that you and Philip have settled your silly differences. Tell me, do you think it was Daniel Heyworth you and your father saw in Bath?"

Julia was startled. "Yes. But how did you . . . ?"

"Well, I saw Mr. Heyworth in the Pump Room, and it occurred to me how *very* like Philip he was. Even to that brick-colored coat. Why, I even thought it was the selfsame garment!"

Julia's face became wreathed in smiles, and she began to laugh.

After breakfast, Philip set off on his horse with Bramble and the sack, leaving Julia to wait impatiently for their safe return. Her father went out with the duke, bishop, and landlord, and all day the sounds of their guns could be heard on the hills. Although as it turned out, they did not actually bag anything at all.

But that did not seem to matter, for it was the day's sport they sought.

Philip and Bramble returned in the afternoon, the chess set having been safely delivered, and the elf lord of the forest having given Bramble not only a reward for his diligence, but custody of a gift for the elf lord of the hills. So the sack was once again full and heavy, this time with a solid silver teapot and coffeepot, which clanked together to the motion of the horse. Bramble sang all the way, and was eager to go home to his friends.

Once again, Philip and Julia came to the elf's rescue, for the snow on the hillside was far too deep for a twelve-inch manikin to manage. So he sat on Philip's shoulder again as the sun started to set, and they began to climb the hill behind the inn. Bramble sat snug against the astrakhan collar, the sack's contents still clanking together. The climb was steep and difficult, and the temperature was plummeting again, but the sunset was one of the most spectacular Julia had ever seen, a glory of crimson and gold that seemed to grow more beautiful by the moment. The stars began to come out, twinkling as if thousands of elves were up there, their hats alight with the season's joy.

At last they reached the summit, and Bramble directed them to the spot where lay the secret way back to his world inside the hills. He promised he would come back to see them from time to time, and said they could always leave a message here on the hill. Just address a note to Bramble Bumblekin, Esquire, and it would find him.

It seemed that he had gone before they had time to say good-bye properly. One moment he was standing there in the snow, his cheeky little face smiling brightly; the next he was nowhere to be seen. But they knew they would encounter him again.

Philip turned Julia toward him. "We will come up here this time next year," he promised, "and by then you will be my countess."

"I . . . can hardly believe we are together again . . ."

He put his fingertips to her chin, and made her look up into his eyes. "Believe it, my darling, for it is true. And we have an elf and a solid silver chess set to thank."

"We will not dare tell anyone such a story."

"Except maybe our children."

She smiled. "Yes, except them."

He bent his head to kiss her softly on the lips. It was a long, long kiss. A perfect Christmas kiss. Quite perfect.

No Room at the Inn
by Carla Kelly

"Mama, are we there yet?"

Mary McIntyre smiled, and added another entry to her growing list of what was going to make the single life so comfortable.

"I told you less than fifteen minutes ago that the snow is slowing our progress."

Mary glanced at Agatha Shepard, her seat companion, who was doing her best not to glare at her offspring. I understand totally, Mary thought. I am no more inclined than a child to enjoy creeping along at a snail's pace, through a rapidly developing storm.

She had left Coventry two days earlier, joining the travel of Thomas and Agatha Shepard and their two children from London, who were to spend Christmas in York with Agatha's parents. The elder Shepards—he was a solicitor with Halley and Tighe—already appeared somewhat tight around the lips when they stopped at her parents' estate. In a whispered aside, Agatha said that Thomas had not made the trip any easier with his deep sighs each time the children insisted upon acting their age.

Mary understood perfectly; she had known Thomas for years. What was that his younger brother Joe told her once? "If people could select their relatives, Thomas would be an orphan."

As much as she liked Agatha, Mary never would

have chosen the Shepards's company for anything of greater length than an afternoon's tour of Coventry's wonderful cathedral. The fates had intervened, and dictated that she be on her way to Yorkshire. Two weeks ago, her station in life had changed drastically enough to amuse even the most hardened Greek god devoted to the workings of fate.

She wished she could pace around the confining carriage and contemplate the folly of an impulsive gesture, but such exercise would have to wait. Tommy and Clarice quarreled with each other, their invective having reached the dreary stages of "Did not! Did, too!" My head aches, she thought.

They should have stopped for the night in Leeds, even though they had scarcely passed the noon hour. Agatha's timid "Thomas, dear, don't you think . . ." had been quelled by a fierce glance from her lord and master.

"My dear Agatha, I pay our coachman an outrageous sum to be highly proficient," he said. He glared around the carriage, his eyes resting finally on his squabbling olive branches. "Agatha, can you not do something about *your* children?" he asked, before returning to the legal brief in his lap.

We could dangle *you* outside the carriage until you turn blue, Mary thought. "Thomas, don't you think it odd that we have not observed a single wheeled vehicle coming from the other direction in quite some time?" It's worth a try, she thought. Let us see if I have any credit left with the family solicitor.

She discovered, to her chagrin, that she did not. Not even bothering to reply, the family solicitor stared at her. She sat back in embarrassment.

I suppose it is good to know where one stands in the greater scheme of events, she told herself later,

when she felt like philosophizing. There was a time,
Thomas Shepard, when you would have been nodding
and bobbing at my least pronouncement, she thought.
You would have at least considered my request to
stop, and there would have been no withering looks.
I think I liked you better when you were obsequious.
And *that* is a sad reflection upon me, she decided.

She thought about Colonel Sir Harold Fox, Chief
of Commissary Supply, currently serving occupation
duty in Belgium. His last letter to her had indicated
a season of celebration, now that the Monster was on
his way to a seaside location somewhere apart from
shipping lanes in the South Atlantic. "My dear, you
dance divinely," he had written. "I wish you were
here, as we endure no end of balls and routs."

I doubt you wish that now, she told herself. When
her father—no, Lord Davy—broke the news to her,
she had calmly retreated upstairs and wrote to Sir
Harry. He had made her no declaration, but in his last
letter, he had hinted broadly that he would be asking
her a significant question during his visit home at
Christmas. It seemed only fair to alert him that he
might not wish to make her an offer.

She sighed, then hoped that Agatha was engaged
with her children, and not paying attention. Should I
be angry at life's unfairness? she asked herself, then
shook her head. Here she sat, fur-lined cloak around
her, in a comfortable coach, going to spend Christmas
with . . . She faltered. With a grandmother I do not
even know, who lives on a *farm*, God help me.

They continued another two hours beyond Leeds,
with the coachman stopping again and again for no
reason that Mary could discern beyond trying to see
if he was still on the highway. She knew Agatha was

alarmed; even the children were silent, sitting close together now.

Another stop, and then a knock on the carriage door. Thomas pulled his overcoat up around his ears and left the vehicle to stand on the roadway with the coachman, their backs to the carriage. Young Tommy looked at Mary. "I have a pocketful of raisins, and Clarice has a muffin she didn't eat from breakfast this morning," he told her seriously.

Mary reached over to touch his cheek. "I think you are wonderful children," she told him. "How relieved I am to know that because of your providence, we won't starve." He smiled back, at ease now.

Thomas the elder climbed back in the carriage a few minutes later, bringing with him a gust of snow. He took a deep breath. "The coachman advises me that we must seek shelter," he said. "Thank God we are near Edgerly. If the inn there is already full, we will be forced to throw ourselves on my brother's mercy."

Tommy clapped his hands. "Clarice, did you hear that? Uncle Joe!"

"I didn't know Joe lived around here," Mary said.

A long silence followed. When Thomas finally spoke, there was an added formality to his careful choosing of words. "He purchased what I can only, with charity, describe as a real bargain, Miss McIntyre. I tried to make him reconsider, but Joe has ever been stubborn and inconsiderate of the needs of others."

And *you* are not? she thought.

The discussion animated Agatha. "Oh, my dear, it is a wreck!" she confided. "A monstrosity! He bought it for practically pence from a really vulgar mill owner who thought to retire there." She giggled, their plight momentarily forgotten. "I believe the man died of apoplexy after taking possession of the place. Thomas thinks the shock carried him away. The place was too much, even for him!"

A smile played around Thomas's lips. "I told him he'd regret the purchase." He shrugged. "That was four years ago. We haven't heard much from Joe since."

She tried to remember Joseph Shepard, the second son of her father's—no, Lord Davy's—estate steward, which wasn't difficult. She couldn't help smiling at the memory of a tall, handsome man who spent a lot of time in the fields, who was cheerful to a fault, and who seemed not to mind when both she and her little sister Sara fell in love with him. Edgar followed him everywhere, and there was never a cross word. Of course, he was a family servant, she reminded herself. He must be nearly thirty-three or so now, she thought.

The inn at Edgerly proved to be suffering from the same problem experienced many Christmases ago. The innkeeper came out to their carriage to say that he had no room for anyone more. "Of course, you could sit in the taproom," he suggested.

"We would never do that," Thomas snapped.

I wish your father could hear you now, Mary thought, and felt no regret at her own small-mindedness. Funny, but if my choice was for my family to freeze in a carriage, or sit among less renowned folk in a taproom, I would choose the taproom. She smiled. Perhaps I *am* better suited to the common life.

"Well, then," said the innkeeper. "I won't keep you from . . . uh . . . whatever it is you think you can do now."

"One thing more," Thomas said. Mary felt her toes

curl at his imperious tone. "Are you acquainted with Joseph Shepard?"

"We all know Joe! Are you a friend of his?"

"I am his brother."

"Who would have thought it?" the keep said. "Planning to drop in on him now?"

Thomas glared at him. "My arrangements are my business. Give me directions."

The innkeeper looked inside the carriage, and Mary realized exactly what he was thinking. She had no doubt that if Tom had been unaccompanied, he would have been given directions that would ultimately have landed him somewhere north of St. Petersburg. Mary couldn't resist a smile at the keep, and was rewarded with a wink.

Practically feeling his way like a blind man, the coachman finally stopped before a large house, just as the winter night settled in. The carriage shifted slightly as the coachman left his box and walked around to the door. Thomas stepped down after the coachman dropped the steps. "Agatha, I predict that Joe will open the door. He has probably sent his servants home during the Christmas season. Providing he has any to send home!"

The Shepards chuckled as Mary watched thoughtfully. "I suppose you have retained your regular household in London this week, even though you are not there?" she asked, hoping that the question sounded innocent.

"Of course!" Agatha exclaimed. "The housekeeper will release them for a half day on Christmas. Only think what an excellent time this is for them to clean and scrub."

"Of course," Mary murmured. "Whatever was I thinking?"

The house was close to the gate. Peering through the darkness, Mary could discern no vulgar gargoyles or statues. It appeared to be of ordinary brick, with a magnificent cornice over the door, which even now was opening.

"It *is* Joe himself," Agatha said. "There is probably not a servant on the place."

The carriage door opened, and Joseph Shepard looked around at them, his eyes bright with merriment. "Can it be? Lord bless me, do I see Tommy the Stalwart, and Clarice the Candid? Welcome to Edgerly, my dears."

It felt like a rescue, especially when he held out his arms and his niece and nephew practically leaped into them. Agatha's feeble effort at control—"Children, have you no manners?"—dissolved quickly when he beamed at her, too. "Oh, Joe, thank goodness you're here! I do not know what we would have done."

He only smiled, and then looked at her. "Lady Mary? What a pleasure."

His arms were full of children so he could not help her down. Instead of retreating to the house with his burden, he stood by the carriage while Thomas helped Agatha and then Mary from the vehicle. He brushed off Agatha's apologies with a shake of his head, then led the group of them to his house. Mary still stood by the carriage as the others started up the narrow walk. The coachman closed the carriage door. "Things are always a little better when Joe is around," he said, more to himself than to her.

She started up the walk after the others, when Joe came toward her. He had deposited the children inside, and he hurried down the steps to assist her. She did not think she had seen him in at least eight years, when she was fifteen or so, but she would have recog-

nized him anywhere. He bore a great resemblance to
his brother; both were taller than average, but not
towering, with dark hair and light eyes. There was one
thing about him that she remembered quite well. She
peered closer, hoping she was not being too obvious,
to see if that great quality remained. To her delight,
it did, and she smiled at him and spoke without thinking. "I was hoping you had not lost that trick of smiling with your eyes," she said, and held out her hand.

"It's no trick, Lady Mary," he replied, and he shook
her hand. "It just happens miraculously, especially
when I see a lovely lady. Welcome to my house."

He ushered her in and took her cloak. She looked
around in appreciation, and not a little curiosity. He
must have noticed the look, because he glanced at
Thomas and his family toward the other end of the
spacious hallway. "Did Thomas tell you I was living
in a vulgar barn I bought for ten pence to the pound
from a bankrupt mill owner?"

She nodded, shy then.

"All true," he told her. "I wonder why it is he
seems faintly disappointed that the scandalous statues
and the red wallpaper are gone?" He touched her
arm. "Perhaps he will be less disappointed if I tell him
that the restoration is only half complete, and he will
be quite inconvenienced in the unfinished bedcham-
bers. Do you think he will prefer the jade green wallpaper, or the room where Joshua and I have already
stripped the paper?"

She laughed, in spite of herself. "Joshua?" she
asked.

"My son. I believe he is belowstairs helping our
scullery maid, Abby, cook the sausages." Joe looked
at his brother. "Thomas, I trust you have not eaten
yet?"

"And where would that have happened?" Thomas asked in irritation. "Even the most miserable inn from Leeds on is full of travelers! Surely you have something less plebian than sausages, brother," Tom continued.

"We were going to cook eggs, too," Joe offered, with no evident apology.

"And toast," Thomas said with sarcasm. Her face red, Agatha tugged at his arm.

"Certainly. What else?"

"Brother, did you dismiss your staff?"

"I did, for a fact," Joe stated. "My housekeeper has a sister in Waverly, and she enjoys her company around the holiday. Ditto for my cook, of course. The two maids—they are sisters—informed me that their older brother is home from the war. I couldn't turn them down."

"I call it amazingly thoughtless of you!"

Mary stared at Thomas and curled her hand into a fist. Surprised at herself, she looked down, then hoped that no one had noticed. She was almost afraid to look at the brothers. The angry words seemed to hang in the air between them. "Thomas, I am certain your brother had no any idea that we were all going to descend on him," she said.

Thomas turned to glare at her. "*Miss* McIntyre, this is a matter between me and my brother," he snapped. "I'll thank you to stay out of it."

Joseph Shepard spoke quickly. "Thomas, have some charity. It's Christmas." He smiled at Mary. "Lady Mary, if you don't mind what I am certain amounts to delving deeper into low company than you ever intended, you might want to help Joshua belowstairs. I know that you are a game goer, and we need more sausages." He gestured down the hall. "It's through that door. I'll sort out some sleeping arrangements."

"Certainly," she said, grateful to flee the scene.

The servants' hall was empty, so she followed her nose into the kitchen, where two children stood by a modern Rumford stove. The little boy with the apron about his middle who poked at sausages sizzling in the pan was obviously Joshua. The young girl who cracked eggs into a bowl must be Abby. She felt their scrutiny, but also felt it was unencumbered by the tension that was so heavy upstairs.

"Hello, my dears," she said. "My name is Mary McIntyre. I think I'm going to be a Christmas guest. Joshua, your uncle Thomas and his family are upstairs. Your father says there will be a few more people for dinner."

"Good," he replied. "We like company." He smiled at her. It was Joe Shepard's slow smile, but without any other resemblance to the originator of it. As the boy put more sausages in the pan, she wished his uncle Thomas could have appeared belowstairs to witness real courtesy.

Mary rolled up her sleeves and placed herself at the service of the scullery maid, who shyly asked for more eggs, and showed her how to crack them. When she admired the way Abby whisked the eggs around in the bowl and told her so, the child blushed and ducked her head. "She's a little shy, Miss McIntyre," Joshua said.

Joe Shepard came downstairs when the next batch of sausages was cooking. He helped Abby pour the eggs into a pan. "You see what good hands I am in, Miss McIntyre," he said, "even if my own brother thinks I am a barbarian without redemption." He leaned against the table. "I think I offended Agatha's maid."

"Never a difficult task," Mary murmured. "Did you dare suggest that if she wanted a can of hot water that she come belowstairs to get it?"

"How did you know?" he asked. "She insists that the 'tween stairs maid bring it up to her." He looked at his son. "Josh, do we need a 'tween stairs maid?"

"I could take her a can," he suggested.

"No, no. Let's see if she comes for one. Some tea, Miss McIntyre?"

"Delighted." She accepted the cup from him. "It appears that your brother has told you of my fall from grace, since you are no longer calling me Lady Mary."

He nodded, and took a sip from his own cup. "I don't understand it, though." He glanced at the children. "Lord and Lady Davy took you in when you were a baby, and only decided just before Christmas to tell you that it was all a *mistake*? My Lord, that's gruesome." He took another sip. "I could almost think it cruel."

He was saying exactly what she felt, and until that moment, had refused to acknowledge. He must have noticed the tears in her eyes, because he gave her his handkerchief. "I didn't mean to make you do that," he told her. "Just another example of my barbarism, I suppose. Forgive me, Miss McIntyre. You can explain this a little later, if you wish. I don't want to pry, but I'm used to thinking of you as Lady Mary."

"I'm used to hearing it," she said. She had to change the subject. "Is Joshua's mother away?"

"Farther than any of us like. She died three years ago," he said. "I don't know if you even knew I had married, but she was a fine woman, a widow with a little boy."

"Josh?"

"Yes." She could see nothing but pride in his eyes as he regarded the boy at the Rumford. "Isn't he a fine one? I'm a lucky man, despite it all."

She looked at Joshua, and back at Joe Shepard. I think I have stumbled onto quite a family, she thought. "He's certainly good with sausages." It wasn't what she wanted to say, but it seemed the right thing, particularly since Agatha's maid was stomping down the stairs now. Joe got up to help her.

As the maid, her back rigid, snatched the can from Joe and started for the door, he called after her, "Miss, could you tell the others that dinner will be ready soon?"

She turned around, her expression awful. "I do not announce meals!"

"Good Lord, what was I thinking?" Joe said.

"Papa, why is she so unpleasant?" Joshua asked when the maid slammed the door.

"Happen someone forgot to tell her it was Christmas," he replied. He bowed elaborately to Abby. "My dear Miss Abigail, if you and Miss McIntyre will go upstairs and lay the table, we will bring up dinner. Do I ask too much?"

Abby laughed out loud. As Mary got up to follow her, she noticed the look that Joe and Joshua exchanged.

"She came to us from a workhouse in September," Joe explained. "I do believe this is the first time she has laughed, isn't it, Josh?"

The boy nodded. "Maybe she finds the maid amusing."

"I know I do," Joe said.

"Come, miss," Abby called from the top of the stairs.

"Right away, my dear!" She turned to Joe. "Did she stay here with you this Christmas because she has nowhere else to go?"

"Precisely."

I have nowhere to go, either, Mary thought as she went upstairs. And then surprisingly, may I stay here, too?

The thought persisted through dinner, even as she carried on a perfectly amiable conversation with Agatha, and everyone tried to ignore Thomas's elaborate, rude silence. His eye on his father, Tommy began a cautious conversation with Joshua, which quickly flourished into a real discussion about the merits of good English marbles over the multicolored ones from Poland.

Joe had placed Abby next to him. He kept his arm along the back of her chair in a protective gesture that Mary found gratifying. Joe carried on a light conversation about the changes underway in his house, but offered no apologies for the inconvenience.

"Did you construct that beautiful cornice over the front door?" Mary asked.

"I designed it, but I hired a stonemason for the work." He beamed at her in the way that she remembered. "Familiar to you, Miss McIntyre?"

"Indeed, yes," she replied. "I seem to recall a similar cornice over the door that leads onto the terrace at Denton."

"I always liked it," he said. He looked at his brother. "Tom, d'ye remember when we weeded the flower beds below the terrace?"

Thomas turned red in the face. "I see no point in remembering those days."

"Pity, considering what an enjoyable childhood we

had," Joseph said. He turned his attention to Mary. "I remember a time you and Lady Sara got in trouble for coming to help us weed. How is she, by the way? And Lord Milthorpe?"

"Really, Joseph," Thomas said in a low voice. "I already told you that Miss McIntyre has had a change in her circumstances."

"True, brother. What I know of Miss McIntyre, unless she has changed drastically, is that she couldn't possibly forget the people she was raised with, unlike some," Joseph replied, his voice calm, but full of steel. "I trust they are well?"

Oh, bravo, Mary thought. "Lady Sara has got herself engaged to a marquess from Kent. Our . . . her parents have gone there this Christmas to renew their acquaintance with the family. Edgar—Lord Milthorpe—is desperately disappointed that the wars are over and he cannot pester Papa . . . Lord Davy . . . to purchase a commission."

"Do give Lady Sara my congratulations when next you see her," Joseph said as his brother rose. "Thomas, I have no brandy, so I can offer you no inducement to stay at table. Agatha, I do not even have a whist table."

"That's all right," she replied. "I believe I will see the children to bed now."

"Oh, Mama!" Tommy protested. "I would very much like to see Joshua's marbles. Oh, please, Papa. It is nearly Christmas!"

Thomas opened his mouth and closed it again. He sighed and went to the door of the breakfast room.

Joseph looked at his brother. "Is that someone at the door? Could it be Father Christmas, or is someone else lost? Tom, could you answer the door?"

"I do not answer doors in strange establishments,"

Tom snapped. In another moment they heard him on the stairs.

"I doubt he would carry hot water, either," Abby said. She gasped, and stared at Agatha Shepard. "Begging your pardon, ma'am."

Agatha rose to the occasion, to Mary's relief. "I believe you are right, child."

Mary followed Joseph into the main hall and stood watching as he opened the door on a couple considerably shorter than he was, and older by several decades.

"Frank! We are saved!" cried the woman.

Mary turned away so no one would hear her laugh.

They were Frank and Myrtle King of Sheffield, and the driver of their hired post chaise, with a tale to tell of crowded inns, surly keeps, full houses along the route, and snow with no end in sight. "I can pay you for yer hospitality, sir," Mr. King declared as Joe tried to help him with his overcoat. "Nothing cheap about me! I'm assistant manager at the Butler Ironworks in Sheffield."

His eyes bright, Joseph turned to Mary. "Miss McIntyre, meet the Kings. I do believe we are all going to spend Christmas together."

The Kings had no objections to going belowstairs; Mary could see how uncomfortable they seemed, just standing in the hallway of Joe's magnificent bargain house. Frank repeated his earnest desire to pay for their accommodations, and Myrtle just looked worried and chewed on her lip.

While Mary stirred the eggs this time, and Joseph cooked more sausage, the coachman led his team around behind the house to unhitch them, and came inside again to report that he was going to be fine in the stables with the Shepards' coachman. He tucked away the first order of sausage and eggs, and assured them that they would both come inside for breakfast, come morning.

Provided there is anything left to eat, Mary thought as she poured more eggs into the pan on the Rumford. To her amusement, Joe nudged her shoulder. "We have a full pantry, Miss McIntyre," he told her. "Too bad there is not a cook among us."

"There is, sir," Myrtle declared. "There's nothing I can't cook."

"Then you are an angel sent from heaven, Mrs. King," Joseph declared.

She giggled. "It appears to me that you and your missus shouldn't have dismissed your entire staff for the holiday. Were you planning to go away, too, but for the snow?"

"I did dismiss my staff, Mrs. King," Joseph said. "As for going away, no. Miss McIntyre is an old acquaintance, and she and my brother and his family were stranded by the weather, too." He turned back to the stove long enough to fork the sausages around and allow his own high color to diminish, to Mary's glee.

"Orphans in the storm, eh?" Mrs. King said.

"Precisely. We will be in your debt, madam, if you would cook for the duration of this unpleasant weather. I have a scullery maid, and Mary here is a willing accomplice." He laughed. "Did I say accomplice? Did I mean apprentice?"

"I think you meant accomplice, Joe," Mary said, without a qualm that their relationship seemed to have changed with the use of her first name. "Mrs. King, I do hope you like your eggs scrambled. It is my sole accomplishment. Mr. King?"

She made no objection to Joe's suggestion, an hour

later, that they adjourn to the bookroom upstairs with a bottle between them. The Kings were safely tucked in belowstairs in the housekeeper's room. Abby had retired to the room that she shared belowstairs with the maids, and Mary promised to join her there later.

"Of course, more properly you should be upstairs, but the only room left unoccupied has two sawhorses and everything else draped in Holland covers. Joshua thinks it is spooky, and so do I."

"I am certain I will be quite comfortable in the maids' room. Is that brandy? Didn't you tell your brother you had none?"

"Hold your glass steady, Mary," he said as he tipped in a generous amount. "It is smuggler's brandy and my last remaining bottle. I doubt that I will drink it anymore now that the sea lanes are open and the challenge is gone." He took an appreciative swallow of his own glass. "Chateau du Monde, 1790. Would *you* waste that year on a prig?"

She propped her feet up on the hassock between the chairs. "Never!"

Joe took another sip, and leaned back. "I'll tell you my troubles, but you first, Mary, unless it makes you desperately unhappy. I want to know what happened to you. It's not every day that an earl's daughter turns into plain Mary McIntyre."

She settled herself comfortably into the chair, wondering if the late Mrs. Shepard had used the chair before her. If that was the case, Joe's wife must have been about her size, because it suited her own frame. "I don't suppose it is, Joe," she agreed. "My mother— oh, I know she is Lady Davy, but please, you won't mind if I call her my mother, will you? She still feels amazingly like my mother."

Joe was silent. She looked at him, startled to see

tears in his eyes. She touched his arm. "Joe, don't feel sorry for me."

"Call me a fool, then."

"Never," she declared. "Mama never let me read those ladies' novels. You know, the ones where the scullery maid turns out to be an earl's daughter? Isn't that what happens in those dreadful books? Who can believe such nonsense?"

"I can assure you that *my* scullery maid isn't an earl's daughter. Where do authors get those stupid notions?" He took another drink.

She held out her glass for more. "My case is the precise opposite of a bad novel. Papa and Mama had been married for several years, with no issue in sight, apparently."

"It happens." He held up his own glass to the fire-light. "I know."

"Mama had a modiste who called herself Clare La Salle, and claimed to be a French émigré."

"That's glamorous enough for a bad novel," Joseph said. "I take it that Clare was not her real name."

"No, indeed. Apparently Clare found herself in an interesting condition."

"Any idea who the father was?"

Mary giggled. "I think I am drunking . . . drinking . . . this too fast."

"You can't be too careful with smuggler's brandy, my dear," Joseph said.

"I don't think he was a marquess or a viscount," she said. "Clare came to Mama in desperation, and she and my parents hatched a scheme. You can imagine the rest."

"What happened to Clare?"

"She was so obliging as to die when I was born, apparently. Mama had retired to Denton, so no one knew I wasn't really hers," Mary said. "What could interfere now? Mama found herself in an interesting condition later, and Sara was born. And then Edgar." She tipped back the glass and drained it.

"You're not supposed to drink it so fast. A sip here, a sip there." Joe set the bottle on the floor between them. He settled lower in his chair. "So Lady Mary, daughter of the Earl of Denton, spent a blissful childhood of privilege, completely ignorant of her actual origins." He looked at her. "Do you think it was just two weeks ago that they had second thoughts about their philanthropy?"

She shook her head. "As I reflect on it now, I think not."

"You never had a come-out, did you?"

My stars, she thought, you were mindful of such a thing? "No, I never did. I am surprised that you were ever aware if it, though."

He took another sip. "Don't think me presumptuous when I say this, but your family was a choice topic of conversation in our cottage." He shrugged. "I expect this is true of any large estate."

She digested what he said, and could not deny the probable truth of it. The reverse gave her some pause; at no point in her life had she ever been interested in those belowstairs. "We never spoke of you, sir," she said honestly.

"A candid statement," he said. "I appreciate your honesty." He took another sip. "I wager that you do not remember the first time I could have come to your attention."

"You would lose, sir. I remember it quite well."

"What?"

"Let me tell you here that Sara and I both fell in

love with you when we were little. We decided you were quite the nicest person on the whole estate."

"My blushes."

"You rescued me from an apple tree when I was five," she said, enjoying the embarrassment on his face. "As I recall, Thomas put me there on a dare from the goose girl."

"That was it," he said, and took a deep drink. "I trust you and Lady Sara survived your infatuation?"

"I think we did. But you know, I never thanked you for rescuing me."

"You weren't supposed to."

"Then I thank you now."

They were both quiet. Mary smiled and looked into the flames. "Now that I think of it, by the time for my come-out, my parents were likely coming to realize the deception they were practicing on those of their rank regarding my . . . my unsuitability."

"I say, sod'um all, Mary."

She gasped. "Joe, your language!"

He leaned across the space between them, his eyes merry. "Sod them, I say. You always were the most interesting of the lot, Mary McIntyre."

"Joe, you're mizzled."

"No, I'm stinking. I do this often enough to know." He winked at her. "Did you want a come-out?"

"No. I like to dance, but I have no patience for fashion—can you imagine how my real mother is spinning in her grave? Idle chat bores me." She rested her chin on her hand. "Joe, I'm going to miss Denton." The tears slid down her face then. She had never drunk herself into this state before, and she decided to blame the brandy.

Joe seemed not to mind. He didn't harrumph and

walk around in great agitation, as Lord Davy had
when she cried after his terrible news to her. He regarded her for a moment. "What finally brought the
matter to a head? Who connected the McIntyres with
Clare La Salle?"

She took another drink. "It was a Bow Street Run-
ner, of all things. Mrs. McIntyre—she would be my
real grandmother—had long mourned that wayward
daughter. After some years, she contacted the Bow
Street Runners. After considerable time and much
perseverance, they connected her missing daughter to
Clare La Salle through one of London's houses of
fashion. They found me less than a month ago," she
concluded simply.

She took a deep breath. "Mama couldn't face me.
Papa told me the whole story. He offered me an annuity that Halley and Tighe drew up. I . . . I signed it
and left the room Mary McIntyre."

"Damn them all, Mary."

"No," she said quickly, startled at his vehemence.
"I have an income that most of England would envy,
and all my faculties. It could have been much worse."

The silence from the other chair told her quite elo-
quently that Joseph Shepard did not agree. She folded
her hands in her lap and felt greatly tired. "I will miss
them all. Lord Davy thinks it best that I quietly fade
from the scene. No family needs scandal. I have . . .
had a suitor, Colonel Sir Harold Fox. Perhaps you
remember him?"

"Yes, indeed. A tall fellow who rides his horses
too hard."

"Does he? I have written him a letter laying the
whole matter before him. We shall see what he
chooses to do. Rides his horses too hard, eh?"

Joe laughed. "Sod him, too, Mary."

She joined in his laughter, feeling immeasurably better. "Your turn, Joe," she said when she quit laughing. "Why are you and Tom so out of sorts?"

She thought he was disinclined to reply at all, considering the lengthy silence. Or it may have been only a few moments. The brandy had enveloped her in a cocoon that either shut out time, or let it through in odd spurts.

"I hope this won't offend you," he began finally.

"No one else has been concerned about offending me lately," she reminded him.

"Your father—well, Lord Davy—is a misguided philanthropist, I do believe."

Two weeks ago she would have disputed with him, but not now. "My father was his estate steward, as you know," he went on. "One day he told my father that he wanted to educate Tom and me. You know, send us to university, give us a leg up. Lord Davy paid Tom's charges at the University of London, and he became a solicitor."

"But not a barrister? Does that bother him?"

He looked at her with some appreciation. "Bravo, Mary! Poor Tom. No matter how fine his patronage, no one would ever call Tom, the son of a steward, to the bar."

She thought a minute. "I really don't recall seeing Thomas much at Denton, after he went to university."

"Try never. We weren't good enough," he said, and took another drink. "He never came around. Think of it, Mary: He was too good to visit the steward's cottage, and will never be good enough for an invitation to Denton Hall. Poor man, poor man."

She mulled it over. "There is a certain irony to this

conversation, Joe," she said after some thought. "Tom goes up in society, but never quite high enough. I go down . . ."

". . . but you will always be a lady, no matter what your former relatives do to you. He may just resent you, too, Mary." He was starting to mumble now from the brandy. "You're in good company, because he resents me, too."

"Because you didn't go to university? Obviously you turned down the same offer from Lord Davy."

"Oh, but I did go to university. I did well, even though it bored me beyond belief. It is . . . It is worse than that."

She stared at him, feeling definitely muddled from all that brandy. She closed her eyes, and after a moment, the matter became quite clear. She laughed.

Joe watched her appreciatively. "Figure it out?"

"Joe, you'll have to tell me what you do for a living, I suppose," she said.

"I am a lowly grain broker, but by damn, I am a hell of a businessman." He smiled. "Despite my lofty education!" He started to laugh again, which made him look suspiciously at the glass in his hand. He set it on the floor. "I decided to do what I like. Every spring I visit farms and estates in Yorkshire, make predictions, and give them an offer on their crops. It is called dealing in futures, and I am good."

She clapped her hands, delighted at his good fortune. "I can hardly imagine more lowly commerce."

"Thank you! I have considered developing a side line in the bone and hide business, just to spite Thomas." He grinned. "Imagine how I would stink! If I were to turn up at his London house, Thomas would probably fall on his knife."

She watched him, not flinching at his scrutiny, even

as she felt her whole body grow warm. Sir Harry never looked at me like that, she thought. I should go to bed. There was one more matter; the brandy fogging her brain reminded her. "Let us see how this tallies: Thomas is unhappy because he will never scale the heights he feels he deserves, and he resents your success. I have seen my hopes of a lifetime dashed. What about you? You said earlier that you spend too much time doing just this."

It sounded so blunt that she wished she had not spoken, especially when he avoided her gaze. "I miss my wife," he said, just as bluntly. "She was a grand woman, although I daresay Tom would have thought her common, had he ever met her."

"Would *I* have liked her?" Mary asked.

"You would have loved her," he replied promptly. "You remind me of her a little: same dark hair, eyes almost black, quiet, capable. Tall, for a woman. I like looking women in the eye." He reached out to touch her leg, then pulled his hand back. She held her breath, not moving, not wanting to break whatever spell he was under. He took one deep breath and then another, and she could tell the Chateau du Monde had worked on him. "Maybe I was even thinking of you when I met her, Lady Mary. Or maybe I am thinking of her now when I see you. Or maybe I am drunk beyond redemption tonight." He shook his head. "I will be sober in the morning and regret this conversation."

"I do hope not, Joe," she said quietly. She was silent then, as spent as he was. After a moment, she moved her legs away from the hassock, then gathered herself together enough to stand. Her head seemed miles away from her feet. "I am relieved that is your last bottle of Chateau Whatever-it-is."

He chuckled, and struggled to his feet. "Let me help you down those stairs, Mary McIntyre. I would feel wretched if you landed in a heap in the servants' hall."

She could think of no objection as he put his arm around her waist and pulled her arm around his. By hanging onto the wall, then clutching the banister, he got her to the door of the maids' room.

"Are you all right now?" he whispered. He turned his head. "Lord, can Frank King ever snore. Unless that is Myrtle."

They laughed softly together, his head close to hers. He leaned on her, and she thought for a moment that he was asleep. For no discernible reason—considering that her brain was starting to hum—she thought of Christmas. "Joe," she whispered. "Do you and Joshua not really celebrate the season?"

"I never quite know what to do," he replied.

"Have you any holiday decorations?"

"Melissa had quite a few, but I do not know that either of us are up to those yet."

"Any others?" He was leaning on her quite heavily now.

"There may be a box belonging to the defunct owner of this palace," he said. "Probably vulgar and destined to set off Thomas. Oh, do find them!" He laughed.

She put her hand over his mouth to silence him, and he kissed her palm, his eyes closed, then it was her wrist. His head was so close that she couldn't think of a reason not to kiss his cheek. "I think I will see what Mrs. King and I can do about Christmas," she murmured, "considering that we are snowbound."

He pulled her very close then, giving her brandy-soaked brain the opportunity to consider the feel of him in some explicit detail. They were about the same height. When she turned her face to look at him—so close he was out of focus—kissing him seemed the only thing to do that made any sense.

He must have been of similar mind. He kissed her back, one hand tugging insistently at her hair, the other caressing her back in a way that made her sigh through his kiss.

Mr. King stopped snoring. Joe released his grip on her hair when she pulled away, and regarded her sleepily, but with no apology.

"Do you think we woke him up?" Joe asked quietly, his voice a little strange.

"I don't know," she whispered back. "Lord, I hope not."

Joe touched his forehead to hers. "Good night, Mary," he said. "In future, have a care who you drink with. Yorkshire is full of scoundrels and skirt raisers."

She went quietly into the maids' room, closed the door, and leaned against it. She laughed when she heard him stumble on the steps, then held her breath, hoping he would not plunge to the bottom. Scoundrels and skirt raisers? she asked herself. Hmm.

She woke to the sound of someone screaming in her ear. Someone well schooled in torture must have placed weights on her eyes, because they refused to respond. She managed to open one eye.

Mrs. King, her eyes kindly, stood beside her bed. She held a tall glass.

"Someone was screaming," Mary gasped.

"Oh, no, dearie," she said. "I just said good morning." She lowered her voice when Mary winced. "Abby was concerned about you, but I told her you just didn't get enough sleep last night, Miss McIntyre."

And caroused well beyond my limit, Mary thought. "Thank you for that, Mrs. King," she whispered. "I believe I will never drink brandy with Mr. Shepard again."

The older woman put her hand to her mouth. "He said exactly the same thing this morning, my dear, when he prepared this little concoction for you."

"Do sit down, Mrs. King," she said, and pressed both hands to her head. "If I told you that I generally drink only lemonade, and take nothing stronger than sherry, upon occasion, you would probably call me a prevaricator."

Mrs. King did laugh then. "Of course I would not! My dear, I rather think that we shall lay the blame at Mr. Shepard's door. He *is* a persuasive gentleman, isn't he?" She leaned forward and held out the glass. "Do you wish this, my dear?"

Mary eyed the glass with disfavor. "It's so . . . black," she said. "What is in it?"

"He made me promise not to look, but he left the treacle can on the table."

"Oh, Lord, I am being punished for all my sins," Mary said with a sigh and reached for the glass. Her stomach heaved at the first tentative sip. Here I am, only a few days from my old life at Denton, and I have already yielded to dissipation, she thought. She took a deep breath and drank the brew, then slowly slid back into the mattress.

"He said I was to wait a half hour and then bring you porridge, well sugared."

"I will be dead before then!"

To her amazement, she was not. She lay as still as she could, wondering at the sounds around her. After a moment, she understood why everything sounded strange: she had never heard a house at work from the ground up. In the world she had just left, servants were silent and invisible, the kitchen far away. She listened to Mr. King talking, and heard Joe Shepard laugh at something he said. Chairs scraped against the floor, pans rattled. Mrs. King must have opened the oven door, because the fragrance of cinnamon drifted right under the door.

She looked around. The maids' room was tidy and attractive, with lace curtains, a substantial bureau, and a smaller bed for Abby. The furniture was old and shabby. She knew it must have come belowstairs after its usefulness ended abovestairs, but it was polished and clean. I wonder if servants' quarters are this nice at Denton, she mused.

She thought then about her own establishment. Lord Davy had promised to provide her with a house anywhere she chose to live. Although he had not stated the obvious, she knew he would be more comfortable if she were far away. "After a while, people will forget," he had told her. To her enduring sorrow, he had not even flinched as he threw away her entire life. *And your questionable background will not be an embarrassment* was unspoken but real.

I wonder if Canada would be far enough for Papa, she thought, or even the United States. I am an educated lady of comfortable means, but what am I to *do* with myself? I need never work. If Sir Harry does not choose to pursue his interest in me, I am unlikely to marry within that sphere I thought I was born to inhabit. And who of another class would have me? Joe Shepard, you are right: Lord Davy was a misguided philanthropist.

When the snow stopped, they would continue their journey, and she would be deposited at the home of her real grandmother, the woman who had begun the search that ruined her life. "A farm in Yorkshire," she said out loud. Joe, you may be at home on the farms, but I am not, she concluded. I have nothing in common with anyone on a farm.

She got out of bed slowly. Dressing taxed her sorely. Her own lady's maid had left her employ a week ago when the gory news of her mistress's changed social status filtered down to the servants at Denton. When Genevieve had approached her, eyes downcast, and said that she had found a position on a neighboring estate, she learned another bitter lesson: Servants cared about social niceties. Genevieve knew that working for the illegitimate daughter of a modiste was not a stepping-stone to advancement.

She took only a few minutes with her hair. Brushing it made her wince, but it was an easy matter to twist it into a knot and know she did not have to worry overmuch that it was tidy. In a rare burst of candor— he was a reticent man—Sir Harry had told her once that he liked her hair *en deshabille*. Well, you should see me today, Harry, she thought.

What she saw in the mirror surprised her. Her cheeks were rosy, and her eyes even seemed to smile back at her, despite the late night and the brandy. Suspecting that her lot today was to scrabble among boxes for holiday decorations, she had put on her simplest dress, a dark green wool with nothing to recommend it beyond the elegant way it hung. At least I won't frighten small children, she told herself as she left the room.

She had hoped that Joe would not be belowstairs, but there he still sat, chopping nut meats on a cutting board. Please don't apologize to me for last night, she thought suddenly, and felt the color rise to her face. Let me think that you enjoyed the kiss as much as I did, and that you wanted to tell me your story, as you wanted to hear mine.

She held her breath as he tipped the knife at her. "Good morning, Mary McIntyre," he said. "Did the magic potion work?"

"I am ambulatory," she said, "That, of itself, is a prodigious feat."

He nodded and returned to the work at hand. "I believe Mrs. King has some porridge for you. Do take these nut meats to her, and then come back, will you? I have all manner of schemes, and you have agreed to be an accomplice, as I recall." He funneled the chopped nuts into a bowl and handed it to her. "If she has any cinnamon buns left, could you bring me another one?"

She smiled at him and went into the kitchen, where Mrs. King presided at the table, rolling out dough while Abby stood by with a cookie cutter and a look of deep concentration on her face. Clarice hovered close by the bowls of sugar colored green, red, and yellow. "We are making stars, Miss McIntyre," she announced. "And then ivy leaves?" she asked, looking at Mrs. King, who nodded.

"Mrs. King, I believe you are a gift from heaven," Mary said. She set down the bowl of nut meats. "I believe I am to find a bowl of porridge, and there is a request for another cinnamon bun, if such a thing is available."

Mrs. King took the porridge from the warming shelf. "It already has plenty of sugar, and here is the cream, dearie." She touched Mary's cheek. "You look fit enough."

"I feel delicate," Mary said with a laugh. "Only think: I already know what my New Year's resolution will be!"

Mrs. King leaned toward her, and looked at the little girls before she spoke in a conspiratorial whisper.

"You have to beware of even the best men, Miss Mc-
Intyre." She straightened up. "Not but what your own
mother has not already told you that."

No, she did not, Mary thought. If someone had
given my mother that warning, or at least, if she had
heeded it, perhaps I would not be here at all. Then
she thought of Lady Davy, and her cautions about
fortune hunters, which was hardly a concern now.
"She warned me, Mrs. King," Mary said. "I intend to
be extremely prudent in the new year!"

She handed Joe his cinnamon bun, sat down at the
table, and stared at the porridge for a long enough
moment to feel Joe's eyes on her.

"It goes down smoother than you think, Mary,"
he said.

She picked up the spoon, frowned at it, then took
a bite. He is right, she thought as she swallowed a
spoonful, and another. "Who would have thought porridge is an antidote to brandy?" she murmured. "The
things I am learning."

She felt nearly human by the time she finished. She
pushed back the bowl, and looked at Mr. King, who
had been watching her with a twinkle in his eye. I am
in excellent company, she thought suddenly, and the
feeling was as warm as last night's brandy. "Mr. King,
I know that Joe and I are both feeling some remorse
at chaining your sweet wife to the Rumford, and here
you are, orphans of the storm."

She stopped, embarrassed with herself, wondering
why she had impulsively included herself with Joe
Shepard so brashly, as though they had conferred on
the matter, as though they were closer than mere acquaintances. She looked down in confusion, and up
into Joe's eyes.

"That is precisely what I have been saying to Frank," he said. "We should be ashamed of ourselves for kidnapping the Kings, and setting you at hard labor in the kitchen." He looked at his half-finished cinnamon bun. "Yet I must temper my remorse with vast appreciation of your wife's culinary abilities." He picked up the bun. "You have fallen among thieves, but we are benevolent thieves, eh, Mary?"

And there he was, continuing her own odd fiction. Do we want to belong together? she asked herself. Is there something about this season that demands that we gather our dear ones close, even if we must invent them? She knew without any question that she wanted to continue the deception, if that was what it was; more than that, she *needed* to.

"I agree completely, Joe," she said quietly. "Mr. King, we are in your debt."

To her complete and utter astonishment—and to Joe's, too, apparently, because his stare was as astounded as hers—Mr. King began to cry. As she sat paralyzed, unsure of what to do, tears rolled down the little man's face.

"I'm sure we did not wish to . . ." Joe began, and stopped, obviously at a loss.

Mr. King fumbled in his waistcoat for a handkerchief and blew his nose into it vigorously, even as the tears continued to course down his cheeks. "What you must think of me . . ." he said, but could not continue.

Mary sat in stupefied silence for a moment, then reached across the table to Mr. King. "Sir, please tell us what we have done! We would not for the world upset you."

Her words seemed to gather him together. He looked at the kitchen door. "It's not you two," he managed to say finally. "I have to tell you. You have to know." He gestured toward the door that led to the stairs. "Myrtle mustn't see me like this."

Without a word, they rose to follow him across the room, moving quietly because he was on tiptoe. As she looked at Joe, her eyes filled with questions; he took her hand, then tucked her close to him.

With the door shut, the three of them sat on the stairs leading to the main floor. It was a narrow space. Mr. King filled one of the lower steps, and she and Joe sat close together above him, their legs touching. Joe put his arm around her to give himself room.

Mr. King wiped his eyes again. "I'm an old fool," he said apologetically. "I want you to know that in ten years, this is my happiest Christmas."

"But, sir . . ." Mary said. "We don't understand."

He kept his voice low. "Fifteen years ago, our only child ran away. Myrtle had many plans for him, but they quarreled, and he left home at Christmastime." He tucked his handkerchief in his waistcoat. "We looked everywhere, sent out the Runners, even, put advertisements in every broadside and newspaper in England. Nothing." He shrugged. "We thought maybe he shipped out on an East India merchant vessel, or took the king's shilling." He looked away. "We followed every possible lead to its source."

"Nothing?" Joe asked. "You never heard of him again?"

Mr. King shook his head. "Not a line, not a visit. I thought Myrtle would run mad from it all, and truth to tell, she did for a while."

"Poor woman," Mary said, and felt her own tears prickle her eyelids. Joe tightened his arm around her, and she gradually relaxed into his embrace.

"Those were hard years," Mr. King said. "After five

or six years, Myrtle seemed to come back to herself again." He sighed, as though the memory still carried too much weight. "Except for this: Every year near Christmas, she looks at me and says, 'Frank, it's time to seek David.'" He spread out his hands. "And we do. For nearly ten years we've done just that. We set out from Sheffield with a post chaise and driver."

"What . . . what do you do?" Mary asked.

"We pick a route and drive from place to place, spend the night in various inns, ask if anyone has seen David King. Myrtle has a miniature, but it is fifteen years old now. One inn after another, until finally she looks at me and says, 'Frank, take me home.'" He shook his head. "He would be thirty-five now, but I don't even know what he looks like anymore, or even if he is alive."

Mary felt her throat constrict. What a fool I am for imagining that I have been given the cruelest load to carry, she thought. "Where were you going this year?"

"Myrtle got it in her head that we should go to Scarborough and drive along the coast up to the Tyne. 'Maybe he's on one of them coal lighters what ships from Newcastle,' she's thinking, and who am I to tell her 'No, dear woman'?"

"You're a good man, Mr. King," Joe said, his voice soft.

"I love Myrtle," he replied simply. "We're all we have."

Mary took a deep breath. "You're stranded here now, and this is better?"

She was relieved to see the pleasure come into his eyes again. Mr. King pocketed his handkerchief this time. "It is, by a long chalk, miss! You see how busy she is. She's going to make Christmas biscuits and buns with the little girls. There will be a whacking great roast going in the oven as soon as I get back in the kitchen to help her lift it. Wait until you taste her Yorkshire pudding!" He reached up to take Joe's hand. "Thank'ee, sir, for giving us a room when there was no room anywhere else."

It was Joe's turn to be silent. Mary leaned forward. "Oh, Mr. King, he's pleased to do it. I think Joe is a great host." She laughed. "Didn't he let me drink up all his smugglers' brandy last night? I think we have *all* stumbled onto a good pasture."

She had struck the right note. Mr. King laughed softly, his hand to his mouth. "I have to tell you, Mr. Shepard, Myrtle was nearly in a rare state, thinking that you and little Josh were doomed to eat sausage and eggs all through the holidays. 'It's not fitting, Mr. King,' she told me, 'especially since his cook left this full larder. Thank God we have come to the rescue.' " He held out his hand. "Do you understand my debt now?"

"I do," Joe said. "And you understand mine, as well." He smiled. "Mr. King, you had better help your charming wife with that roast. I like to eat at six o'clock. Does she stir in all those little bits of burned meat and fat into her gravy?"

"She does, indeed!" Mr. King declared. He stood up. "I do not know when she will tell me it's time to go home, but I know you will keep her busy until then."

"You can depend upon it, sir."

With a nod in her direction, Mr. King left the stairs and went into the servants' hall again, closing the door quietly behind him. Joe stayed where he was, his arm around Mary. He tightened his grip on her. When he spoke, she could tell how carefully he was choosing his words. "Do you know, sometimes I feel sorry for myself."

"You, too?"

They looked at each other. "Did you ever see two more certifiable idiots?" he asked her.

"Not to my knowledge, Joe," she replied, and let him pull her to her feet on the narrow stairs. She dusted off her skirts. "Did you find me some garish decorations?"

"I did, indeed." He started up the stairs. "They proved to be a major disappointment in one respect."

"Oh?"

"They are not nearly as vulgar as I had hoped. I do not think they will cause my dear brother any distress at all."

"That *is* a disappointment. By the way, where is your brother?"

Joe sighed. "He asked me where the mail coach stops, and walked there to see if the road is open. He says he is expecting correspondence from his firm." He shook his head. "Too bad that a man cannot just enjoy a hiatus from work. I always do."

He took her down the hall to what was eventually going to become the library, when the plastering on the ceiling was finished. When she stopped, he looked up at the ceiling with her. "The former owner had several well-bosomed nymphs doing scurrilous things around that central curlicue," Joe said, pointing up to the bare spot. "I didn't want questions from Joshua, so I am replacing them with more acceptable fruit and leaves."

"Coward," she teased.

"Wait until you are the parent of an inquisitive eight-year-old, my dear," he said.

"That is unlikely in the extreme," she told him as she opened up one of the boxes and pulled out a red silk garland.

"Oh? Your children are going to go from age seven to nine, and skip eight altogether?" he asked, pulling out another garland.

She laughed. "Joe, you don't seriously think any men of my acquaintance are going to queue up to marry a woman of such questionable background. Even one with two thousand a year?"

He surprised her by touching her cheek. "I will tell you what I think, Mary McIntyre. I think you need to enlarge your circle of friends."

"You are probably right." What had seemed just right last night seemed too close this morning, but she made no move to back away from him. You would think you wanted him to kiss you again, she scolded herself.

She wasn't sure if she was relieved or chagrined when he patted her cheek and went to the door. "I'm off to find my son and nephew and go hunt for the wild greenery. Can you decorate a wreath or two? I'll ask Mr. King to put a discreet nail over the mantel in the sitting room and another on the front door." He stood in the doorway a moment. "It may be time for Joe and his boy to consider Christmas again."

"A capital notion, sir," she told him. A few moments later, she heard him calling the boys. Why is it that more than one boy sounds like a *herd*, she thought. There was laughter, and then a door slammed. A few minutes later, Agatha Shepard stood in the library doorway, smiling at her. "Could you use some help, Mary?"

More than you know, she thought. Please take my mind off the molehills I am rapidly turning into moun-

tains. "I am under orders from your brother-in-law to
create some Christmas." She knew her face was rosy,
so she looked into the box of decorations. "What a
relief to know this is not a forlorn hope, my dear. I
do believe our late mill owner had some notions of a
proper Christmas. Look at this beautiful garland."

By the time the boys returned, red-cheeked and
shedding snow, Agatha was positioning the last star
burst on the window while Mary observed its hanging
from the arm of the sofa. "Mama!" Tommy shouted.
"Look! Joe says we are holly experts!"

The boys carried a holly wreath between them. "Father tied it for us, but we arranged the holly," Josh
said. He looked at Mary. "He said you were to be the
final arbiter, whatever that is."

Mary helped the boys carry the wreath to the box
of decorations. "It's marvelous, Joshua. If we tie this
red bow to the top, it will answer perfectly here over
the fireplace."

"See there, Josh, I knew she would know just what
else it needed."

She hung the wreath, then turned around to smile
at Joe, who held a larger wreath shaped from pine
boughs. "And this for the front door?" she asked.

"Yes, indeed, after you and Agatha give it the
magic touch." He looked at the room. "Boys, I believe
the ladies were busy while we stalked the greenery."
He touched his son's shoulder. "Perhaps you and
Thomas can convince Mrs. King that you are in the
final stages of starvation. She seems like a humane
woman." He looked at Agatha, and must have noticed
something in her expression. "Do let Tommy have
lunch belowstairs. I would not feel right in asking Mrs.
King to serve us upstairs. She is my guest, too."

"Mama, please!" Tommy begged. "I know Clarice

has been belowstairs making Christmas treats. We could smell them the moment we opened the front door!"

"You may go belowstairs, Tommy," Agatha said quietly. "These are special circumstances." She turned to her brother-in-law. "Thank you for asking, Joe."

He hugged her, and waved the boys off. "My dear sister, loan your shawl to Mary. I need someone to make certain I do not hang this wreath cockeyed."

Mary stopped him long enough to twine a gilt cord through the boughs, and tie it in a bow at the bottom. Agatha secured some smaller star bursts scavenged from the bits and pieces remaining in the box, then threw her shawl around Mary's shoulders. "I will go belowstairs and see what wonders Mrs. King has created."

He was still chuckling when he hung the wreath on the front door. "Mary, you must feel sorry for Thomas. He thought he was marrying a proper lady, only to find that she enjoys putting up her own decorations and will probably be rolling out dough when we go belowstairs. He will accuse me of ruining his efforts to be what he is not. Too bad there was no room for *him* at the inn. All right, Mary, what do you think?"

I think that sometimes philanthropy is sadly misdirected, she told herself as she walked backward toward the front gate, her eyes on the wreath. "Move the wreath a little to the left. A little more. There. Excellent."

To her gratification, Joe walked down the path toward her, then turned around for his own look. "You didn't trust me?" she teased.

"I trust you completely," he replied. "I am just wondering what you would think if we painted the trim white. Would that look right against the brick?"

She glanced sideways at him, but his attention was on the facade of his house. You are doing it again, she thought. You are including me in your decisions, as though I were in residence at this place. Dear, lonely man, are you even aware of it? "Yes, by all means," she said firmly. "And if you can arrange for a cat to nap in one of those windows this summer, that would be the final touch. Oh, flower boxes, too."

"Consider it done, madam. Pansies or roses?"

"Joe, you don't put roses in flower boxes!"

"Pansies, then."

She looked around her at all the snow. Mr. King had shoveled the walks earlier, but there was no getting away from winter's cold and stark trees and branches, with only the idle leaf still clinging. Not a bird flew overhead. "Joe, you speak of pansies and cats in windows," she said softly, "and here we are in December."

He took her arm through his. "I told you last night that I deal in futures, Mary. And excuse me, but you're the one who mentioned the cat. Do you deal in futures, too?"

"Perhaps it's time I did," she replied, her voice soft. How do I do it? I wish I were not afraid, she thought. She wanted to ask Joe about the courage to carry on when things didn't turn out as planned, but there was Thomas walking up the middle of the road, which had been cleared by a crew from the workhouse.

"Tom, the roads are still open behind us, I gather," he said. "Is that a newspaper?"

Tom held it out to him. "There will be a road crew through here by nightfall. Apparently the road to York will be cleared by tomorrow afternoon, or sooner."

"Any mail for you?"

Tom shook his head, but handed a letter to Mary. "It appears that Colonel Sir Harry Fox is in the country. Let us hope this is good news."

She took the letter, which had been addressed several times, as it went from Denton, then to Haverford, Kent, where Lord and Lady Davy had gone for Christmas, to her as-yet unknown grandmother's farm. "I assured the coach driver that I was your solicitor, and would see that you got your letter," Tom said. "I thought I would need to give a blood oath. What a suspicious man!"

"Just doing his job, brother," Joe said serenely. "Perhaps you and I can go to the house and wrangle over whether you must have luncheon upstairs or downstairs, and leave Mary to her correspondence. You are welcome to use my bookroom."

She watched them walk away, already in lively conversation. Poor Joe! Here he had thought to spend a quiet holiday with his son, eating eggs and sausage, and savoring the last of his smugglers' brandy. The only guests with any merit at all are the Kings, she thought. I drank up his brandy and cried, and his own brother is too proud to eat belowstairs. Thank the Lord that we can at least choose our friends.

Sir Harry had posted the letter from London, probably from the family town residence, a particularly magnificent row house in the best square. She had been there on several occasions, the last during a celebration of Wellington's victory in Belgium, when he had danced more than three dances with her, and, face red enough to match his uniform, had declared that she was the finest lady present. After asking Lord Davy's permission, he had corresponded with her through the fall, telling her nothing of interest, because she did not find troop movements or glum Frenchmen to her taste.

In the bookroom, she opened the letter, took a deep breath, and starting reading. When she was finished, she was too astounded to do anything but stare into the fire, ashamed that she had ever written Sir Harry Fox.

She looked up. Someone knocked on the door, but she made no motion to speak or rise to open the door.

"Dearie, don't you want something to eat?"

It was Mrs. King. She got up quickly and opened the door. "Mrs. King, you did not need to do this," she protested as the woman came into the bookroom with a tray.

"That's precisely what Joe said, but I told him I wanted to, and was he going to stop an old woman?"

Mary made herself smile.

"Now, sit back down there and I will set this tray beside you. There, now. May I pour you some tea?"

She started to cry, unable to help herself, helpless to do anything except hold out the letter. Mrs. King's face filled with concern. She closed the door, poured a cup of tea, and sat down, then handed Mary her handkerchief. "You cry until you feel better, dearie, and then you will drink this," she ordered.

Mary sobbed into the handkerchief. Mrs. King settled herself on the arm of the chair and rested her hand on Mary's back. Mary wiped her eyes, blew her nose, and leaned against the other woman, grateful for the comfort, but missing Lady Davy—the woman she would always think of as her mother—with every fiber of her heart.

"Joe told me about your difficulties, dearie," Mrs. King said.

"I think the entire world must know of them, Mrs. King," she said. "I am glad he told you. I would not have you think I am a habitual watering pot."

"I think you're rather a charming lady, and I know that Joe agrees with me," Mrs. King said firmly. "But this is bad news, isn't it? Mr. Shepard—Thomas—is even downstairs walking up and down, hoping that you have good news."

Mary looked down at the letter that she still held. "I suppose he would call this good news, then. Sir Harry has agreed to pay his addresses to me." She thought of Mrs. King's own trials, and tried to hide the bitterness in her words, even as she knew she failed. "He claims that he will not reproach me with my ignominious birth, should we decide to form an alliance." She held out the letter again. "Mrs. King, he has asked all his relatives what they think, and they are united in their opposition to me!" She leaned back and closed her eyes as shame washed over her. "There are probably men taking wagers at White's on what will be the outcome of this sorry tale!"

"And still Sir Harry persists?" Mrs. King asked.

"I suppose he does," Mary said quietly. "Mrs. King, I do not love him. I never have." She turned in her chair for a better look at the woman. "I have come with the Shepards this Christmas because they are to leave me with a grandmother I have never met . . . on a farm! Sir Harry is my last chance to remain in the social circle in which I was raised." She rested her cheek against Mrs. King's comforting bulk. "Am I too proud?"

Mrs. King's answer was not slow in coming. "P'raps a little, my dear, but if you do not love this fellow, marrying him would be a worse folly than pride." She laughed softly. "I think there are worse fates than farms. Didn't Joe say you had enough income to do what you want, should the farm prove unsatisfactory?"

"It's true," she agreed. She folded the letter, then looked at Mrs. King, who was regarding her with warmth and surprising affection, considering the shortness of their acquaintance. She took her hand. "It's hard to change, isn't it? I mean, I could have gone along all my life as the daughter of Lord Davy, but now the matter is different, and I must change, whether I wish it or not. Mrs. King, I do not know if I am brave enough."

She stopped then, noting the faraway look in the woman's eyes, and the sorrow she saw there. "Here I am complaining about what must seem to be a small matter to you," she said. "Do forgive me."

Mrs. King gave her a little shake. "It is not a small matter! It is your life."

She considered that, and in another moment took a sip of tea. "This will upset Thomas more than you can imagine. He places such emphasis on class and quality." She stood up. "You say everyone is belowstairs?"

Mrs. King nodded. "Thomas is there on sufferance, but Mrs. Shepard seems content to decorate Abby's batch of Christmas stars."

"And Joe?"

"He and Mr. King are playing backgammon."

"Are we a strange gathering, Mrs. King?" she asked. "I suppose that other than Joe and Joshua, none of us are where we really want to be."

Mrs. King rose. "I am not so certain about that, my dear. Are you?"

She could think of no reply that would not involve a blush.

The two of them went down the stairs. Mrs. King

gave her a little push when she reached the bottom
and stood there, the letter in her hand. Thomas's eyes
lighted up. "Do you have good news, Mary?" he
asked.

"That may depend on what you consider good
news," she replied, and handed him the letter. "Here.
I wish you and Joe would read it."

With a nod to Mr. King, Joe got up from the game-
board and sat beside his brother, who had spread out
the letter on the table. She watched them both as
they read, Thomas becoming more animated by the
paragraph, and Joseph more subdued. How different
they are, she thought, but how different they had always been.

When he finished reading, Thomas looked at her in
triumph. "There you are, Mary!" He smiled at his
wife, who was dusting the last of the cookie dough
with sugar. "She need not leave her sphere, Agatha."
He shrugged. "It may take a year or two before you
are received in the best houses again, Mary, but what
is that? People forget."

Mary looked at Joe, who finished reading and sat
back, his face a perfect blank. He stared at the letter,
then picked it up. "' . . . no matter how disgusting
the whole affair is to sensible people, the sort I wish
to associate with, I will never reproach you with your
ignominious birth,'" he read out loud. "Mary, he is
irresistible."

Ignoring his brother, Thomas took her hand. "Mary,
you are most fortunate. The road is clear south of us.
Any letter you write will reach Sir Harry in a mere
day or two."

Joe grabbed the letter. Without a word he crumbled
it into a tight ball. "Thomas, I am not sure I even
know you anymore," he said, his voice filled with emo-

tion. "You would have Mary McIntyre, this little lady we watched grow up at Denton, pawn her dignity for a crumb or two? I am surprised at you."

Thomas stared at him and his face grew red. Mouths open, Tommy and Joshua had stopped their game of jackstraws. Abby held the rolling pin suspended over another wad of dough. Agatha dabbled her fingers nervously in the sugar. On the other hand, Frank King appeared to be enjoying the drama before him. His eyes were bright as he looked from one to another.

"Joseph, Mary is no lady anymore," Thomas said. "But you are no gentleman."

Oh, God, Mary thought, and felt her face grow white. The brothers glared at each other. Clarice was already in tears, her face pressed against her mother. What has happened here, Mary thought in the silence that seemed to grow more huge by the second. If ever there were unwanted guests, we have met and exceeded the criteria. She knew that she could not please both men. No matter what she said, it would be wrong to someone, and she would offend people she never wished ill.

Her footsteps seemed so loud as she walked the length of the room and stood between the brothers. "You are probably right, Tom. I will write Sir Harry immediately."

"Thank God," Thomas said, his relief nearly palpable.

"I will assure him that even though I am grateful for the honor I *think* he is doing me, I chose not to further the alliance," she concluded.

"My God, Mary, do you *know* what you are saying?" Thomas gasped. "Do you seriously believe you will ever get another offer as good as Sir Harry?"

For the first time that day, or maybe even since

Lord Davy had ruined her hopes two weeks ago, she felt curiously free. "Thomas, Sir Harry is a boring windbag. You can't honestly think he would ever let me forget my origin."

"But he is so magnanimous!" Thomas exclaimed.

"To trample my feelings?" she asked. "I think not. Honestly, Thomas, I believe I would rather . . . rather . . . slop hogs and . . . and . . . oh, heavens . . . milk cows at Muncie Farm than endure life with a man who thought I was common!" She gave him a little push. "How unkind you are to call me common! A woman is only common when the people around her tell her that she is. And I am not."

Mary looked around her, noting the expressions of wounded reproach on Agatha's and Tom's faces. Mr. King winked at her, and she smiled back. To her confusion, Joseph was regarding her with what appeared to be amusement. *I should be grateful someone considers this imbroglio humorous,* she thought with some asperity. *In fairness, he is entitled to think what he chooses. Imagine how glad he will be when the road is open.*

"Joe, may I use your bookroom again to write that letter?" she asked.

"Of course." His expression had not changed. "Did you say Muncie Farm?"

"I did."

"But your name is McIntyre."

"Yes. From what I gather, the modiste's mother was widowed not long after her daughter ran away and later remarried. I gather I am still a McIntyre, though. You have heard of Muncie Farm?"

"I have. In fact, Thomas, rather than be any hindrance to you when you are able to bolt my vulgar establishment, I can transport Mary to Muncie Farm.

I could give you directions, but I can easily take her there." He bowed to them all. "And now, I have some work to do in my shop. Josh? You may come, and Tommy, too. Use my bookroom as long as you need it, Mary." He bowed again. "Mrs. King, I look forward to dinner at six o'clock."

Mary returned to the bookroom with an appetite. Mrs. King's meal, though cold now, took the edge off her hunger quite nicely. She thought she would have to use up reams of paper to find the right words of regret for Sir Harry, but one draft sufficed. After all, Lady Davy had taught her to regard brevity as the best antidote for unreturned love, and quite the safest route. Poor Sir Harry, she thought. You will miss me for a while, perhaps, but I suspect that your paramount emotion will resolve itself into vast relief. Humming to herself, she sealed the letter and set it aside for a brisk walk tomorrow to the inn to mail it. -

"Silly," she said out loud. "Tomorrow is Christmas. It can wait for the day after."

After a little more thought, and a long time gazing out the window, she took out another sheet of paper and wrote a letter to Lady Davy. It proved more difficult to write, because she found herself flooded with wonderful memories of her childhood. She knew down to her stockings that she would miss Denton, and her brother and sister, and even more, the quiet, lovely woman who had chosen to take her in, keep her from an orphanage or workhouse, and raise her. If events had not fallen out as Mary desired, it was not a matter to cause great distress now. She chose to remember the best parts. She decided then that she would write Lady Davy at least once each year, whether Lord Davy wanted her to, or not. Perhaps a time would come when she would be invited home.

She did feel tears well in her eyes as she remembered how many of her mother's acquaintances had called her the very image of Lady Davy. *I suppose we see what we choose to see,* she thought, then rested her chin in her hand. *I hope Thomas can see that someday. Joe already seems to understand.*

By dinner, the workhouse road crew was shoveling in front of the house. Thomas and Agatha had decided to take dinner upstairs, to Mary's chagrin and Joe's irritation. Mrs. King only laughed and assured him that the entertainment the Shepards had provided far outweighed any inconvenience. "Abby and I will take them food. If it is cold, well, that's the price for being better than the rest of us." She put her arm around Mary. "If they want seconds, they can come downstairs. It is Christmas Eve, after all, and Mr. King and I are on holiday. Dearie, you lay the table here."

Mrs. King's roast beef was the perfect combination of exterior crust and interior pink tenderness. Abby glowed with pleasure when Mrs. King pointed out that the scullery maid had made the Yorkshire pudding. "I may have directed it, dearies, but I think the secret is in the touch, and not the telling. Mr. King, don't be hoarding the gravy at your end of the table!"

The coachmen joined them, coming into the servants hall snow-covered from helping the road crew. "We met a mail coach coming from York, so the highway is open now," the Shepards' coachman told them as he reached for the roast beef. He jostled the King's driver. "We can all be on our way."

Mary could not help noticing the worried look that Mr. King directed at his wife, who was helping Abby with the gravy. Her heart went out to him as she imagined what it must be like to wonder every Christmas when the melancholy would strike her, and how long she would struggle with it. She leaned toward Joe, and spoke softly. "I wonder, do you suppose a parent ever recovers from the loss of a child through an angry word, or a thoughtless statement?"

He shook his head, and rested his hand on Joshua's head. "It doesn't even have to be your own child, Mary, to fear such a disaster. I pray it never happens to me."

She sat there in the warm dining hall, surrounded by people talking, spoon clinking on dishes, wonderful kitchen smells, and fully realized what he was saying to her. I have a grandmother at a place called Muncie Farm, she thought with an emotion akin to wonder. She has been looking for me. Me! Not to shame me with my shaky background, but to *find* me, because I am all that remains of her daughter. I have been dreading this, when I should be welcoming the chance to put someone's mind at rest. It is a blessing ever to be denied the Kings, I fear, and I nearly passed it by. God forgive me.

"You know where Muncie Farm is?" she asked Joe.

He nodded and ruffled Joshua's hair. "We could take you there tomorrow."

"Then you may do it," she said, and took the bowl of gravy from the Kings' coachman, "*after* we have Christmas dinner here with the Kings."

Thomas and Agatha did not invite her to attend Christmas Eve services with them at St. Boniface, which troubled her not at all. There would have been nothing comfortable or even remotely rejuvenating in celebrating the birth of a Peacemaker with people who chose so deliberately to divide. When Joe told the Kings that indeed there was a Methodist establishment in town—although not the better part of town, and certainly not close to St. Boniface—she demurred again. She had heard much about Methodism and the enthusiastic choirs that it seemed to produce, but Abby was accompanying the Kings. She wanted that kindly couple to give the scullery maid their undivided attention.

"What do you generally do on Christmas Eve?" she asked Joe, while they were washing dishes. (Joe had insisted that Mrs. King did not need to do dishes, and Mrs. King had not objected too long.)

"What do we do, Josh?" he asked his son, who sat on a stool, drying plates.

"We read Luke Two, because it talks about shepherds, I think," Josh said. "Then we watch for the carolers." He looked at his father. "Will there be carolers this year?"

"I rather doubt it, son, considering the depth of the snow."

"Do you feed them sausage and eggs after they sing?" Mary teased.

"I will have you know, I make an excellent wassail," Joe replied. He laughed and flipped his son with the drying towel. "The secret to living here is to maintain low expectations."

When the other guests had left the house—the Shepards by carriage and the Kings on foot—Joe and Joshua made wassail. They carried it outside to the road crew, which was beginning work now on the side streets of the village, now that the main thoroughfare was open for travel. As she watched from the sitting room window, a steady flow of traffic worked its way in both directions, coaches full of travelers anxious to be home by Christmas, or failing that, Boxing Day.

She thought she would find the house lonely, but she did not. She took her copy of *Pamela* into the bookroom, made herself comfortable in the chair where she already fit, and began to read.

As she read, she gradually realized that she was waiting for the sound of Joe returning with Joshua, and then the Kings coming back, probably to sit belowstairs, drink tea, and chat. At peace with herself, she understood the gift of small pleasures. It warmed her heart as no other gift possibly could, during this season of anxiety for her. She smiled when she heard them finally, realizing with a quick intake of breath that she was as guilty as Joe of thinking and speaking as though she were part of the family. We have to belong to someone, don't we? she asked herself. If we don't, then life is just days on a calendar.

She closed the novel when they came into the bookroom, bringing with them a rush of cold, and the fragrance of butter and spices. Joe carried a pitcher and a plate, and Josh dangled the cups by their handles. "We had a little wassail left, and Father purloined the cookies from belowstairs," Josh said as he sat down beside her on the hassock. He held out a cup while Joseph poured, and handed it to her. "Father says I am to read Luke Two all by myself this year, but if I get stopped on a word or two, he will help me."

Joe handed him the Bible and opened it to the Book of St. Luke before he sat down with a sigh and stretched his long legs toward the fire. He closed his eyes while Joshua read about governors, and taxes, and travelers, and no room. Mary watched his handsome profile and felt some slight envy at the length of his eyelashes. This is a restful man, she thought, not someone tightly wound who is never satisfied. She wondered what he was like in spring and summer, when his life in the fields and among the grain brokers probably kept him in motion from early light until after dark. Did he become irritable then, restless like his brother? She decided no, that Joseph Shepard was too wise for that.

" 'And there were in the same country shepherds abiding in the field, keeping watch over their flock by night.' " Joshua had moved closer to the fire to see better, his finger pointing out the line. He leaned against his father's legs.

As she watched him, Joe opened his eyes and looked at her. He smiled and reached across the space between them to take her hand and hold it firmly, his fingers intertwined in hers. She almost had to remind herself to breathe. You keep watch over your own little flock, don't you, sir, she thought. You even care about your unexpected guests. It was a wild notion, but she even dared to think that he had been caring for her for years, in his own way. She tried to dismiss the notion as patently ridiculous, but as he continued to hold her hand, she found herself unable to believe otherwise.

He released her hand when Joshua finished, and took his dead wife's son on his lap, holding him close. "Well, Josh, we have almost rubbed through another year," he said, his voice low and soothing. "What do you say we go for another one?"

Joshua nodded. Mary had to smile as she realized this must be a tradition with them.

"What about you, Mary? Will you go for another one?" Joe asked her suddenly.

"I . . . I do believe I will," she said. Even if it means things do not turn out as we wish, some hopes are dashed, and the future looks a bit uncertain, she added to herself. "We are all dealing in futures, eh?" she asked.

He reached for her hand again. He held it until he heard the Kings returning, when he got up to become the perfect host, and carry his son to bed. When he returned to the bookroom, she was standing by the window, admiring the snow that the moonlight had turned into a crystal path. He stood beside her, not touching her in any way, but somehow filling her completely with his presence. When he spoke, it was not what she expected; it was more.

"I loved Melissa," he told her, his eyes on the snow. "I have to tell you that in some measure, I think I loved her because she reminded me of you." He glanced at her quickly, then looked outside again. "I'm not completely sure, but it is my suspicion. I . . . I've never admitted this to myself, so you are the first to hear it."

He took her hand, raised it to his lips, and kissed it. "I am quite sober tonight, Mary McIntyre, so I will say Happy Christmas to you, and let it go at that for now." He shook his head and laughed softly. "Oh, bother it, I would be a fool to waste such a celebratory occasion." He kissed her cheek, gave her a wink, and left the room. In a moment she heard him whistling in the hall.

The Shepards left as early as they could in the morning, Thomas just happy to be away, and Agatha shaking her head and apologizing for the rush, but wouldn't it be grand to be in York with grandparents before the day was entirely gone? Of the two, Mary had to admit that Thomas's attitude, though more overt, at least had the virtue of honesty. Joe must have felt the same way. As they stood in the driveway and saw the Shepards off, he turned to Mary. "My brother is honest, even when he says nothing."

Joe declared that his Christmas gift to the Kings was breakfast. "Mary and I will cook eggs and sausage for *you*, my dears." He winked at Mary. "And do I see some presents on the table? That will be the reward for eating my cooking."

By keeping back two presents she had ordained earlier for Thomas and Clarice, Mary had gifts for the children: a sewing basket with a small hoop and embroidery thread for Abby, and a book with blank pages for Joshua. "This is your journal for 1816," she told him. "And let us pray it is a more peaceful year than 1815."

"It usually is in Edgerly," he assured her, which made Joseph look away and cough into his napkin.

Mr. and Mrs. King presented both children with aprons, Abby's of pale pink muslin that had probably been cut down from one of Mrs. King's traveling dresses, and Josh's of canvas, which turned out to be a prelude for his present from his father of carpenter tools. "I saw what 'e was giving you yesterday, lad. Every man needs his own carpenter's apron," Mr. King said.

Nothing would do then but they must all troop out to Joseph's workshop to see the bench Joe had made for Joshua that did not require a box to reach, and the tidy row of tools with smooth grips right for an eight-year-old's hand. While they were there, Joe pointed to a hinged box held tight in a vice. "That is for you, Mary," he told her, and his face reddened a little when he glanced at the Kings. "I will have it done by Twelfth Night and bring it to you at Muncie Farm." He smiled at her. "Provided you are still there. I was thinking of painting it pale green, with a brass lock, unless you have a better idea."

She shook her head, unable to trust her voice. She

thought of the presents she had received from Lord and Lady Davy through the years, not one of which had been made by hand. "I . . . I . . . wish I had something for you," she stammered when she could talk.

Mrs. King was merciful enough to distract them all by throwing up her hands and admonishing Abby because she was faster on her feet to rush back to the kitchen and remove the sponge cake from the Rumford before it turned into char. Mary followed quickly enough herself, happy to leave the men in the workshop, comparing notes on the construction of a miter box.

When crisis, agony, and certain doom had been averted belowstairs, Mary went to the maids' room to pack, a simple task, considering that she had worn her plainest dresses of the entire Christmas season. The coachman had removed her luggage from the old carriage that traveled with the Shepards, and the sheer magnitude of it caused her to blink and wonder what her grandmother at Muncie Farm would think of such extravagance. *Does a woman really need all this?* she asked herself, wondering why she had ever thought it so important. *I should have left some of my hats at Denton with Sara.*

They ate Christmas dinner when the noon bells tolled in Edgerly, a charming tradition reserved for Christmas and Easter. Mr. King had been pleased to offer grace, and did his Methodist best with enough enthusiasm and longevity to make Joshua begin to squirm, and Mrs. King finally whisper to him that the food was getting cold, and what was worse than a shivering Christmas goose?

Mary knew she had never eaten a better meal anywhere. She was asking for Joe to pass the stuffing when Mrs. King suddenly set down her fork and stood up. "Mr. King, I think it is time for us to go," she announced, her face calm, but her eyes tormented. "Don't we have to look for David? Won't he wonder where we are?"

"I am certain of it, my dear," her husband said. He rose and gently pressed her back down to her seat. "We will finish this wonderful dinner that you have made, and then we will be on our way to Scarborough."

To Mary's amazement, Abby burst into loud sobs. She covered her face with her Christmas apron and cried into it. "I don't want you to go, Mrs. King," she cried, getting up from the table to run from the room.

Before she could leave, Mrs. King was on her feet and clutching the child to her ample belly. There was nothing vague in her eyes now, nothing tentative in her gesture. She hugged the sobbing girl, crooning something soft. Mr. King seemed to be transfixed by this unexpected turn of events. He looked at Joe; the glance that passed between them was as easy to read as headlines on a broadside.

"I just had a thought, Mrs. King," Joe began. "Tell me how you feel about it. Hush, now, Abby! You may want to hear this, too." He propped his elbows on the table and rested his chin in his hands. "Abby's a grand girl in the kitchen with the pots and pans, but did you see how she handled that rolling pin yesterday?" He shook his head. "I'm not entirely certain, but it is possible that when my cook returns tomorrow, she just might be jealous of Abby. Where will I be then?"

"These are weighty problems, Joe," Mr. King said, and there was no disguising the twinkle in his eyes. "You could find yourself without a cook, and forced to live on sausage and eggs."

". . . and wassail . . ." Josh interjected.

". . . for a long time." Mr. King cleared his throat. "Would you be willing to part with Abby?"

"Well, this is a consideration," Joe said.

Mary looked from Joe to Mrs. King, whose eyes were alert now.

"We would give her such a home, Mr. Shepard," the woman said. "I could certainly use the help, but more than that . . ." She stopped, unable to continue.

Joe didn't seem to trust his voice, either, because he waited a long moment to continue. When he did, his voice sounded altered. "We could ask Abby what she thinks. Abby? Would you be willing to go home with the Kings?"

"You wouldn't be angry with me, would you?" Abby asked.

"Not a bit! We would miss you, but I look on this as an opportunity for you." Joe smiled at her. "I think you should do it."

Mr. King looked at his wife. "Myrtle?"

"Oh, yes, let us do this," Mrs. King said, her voice breathless, as if someone were hugging her tight. Her eyes clouded over for a moment. "Mr. King, I think we should return to Sheffield now, and forget Scarborough this year. I hope this does not disappoint you, but Abby must come first."

"I agree, Mrs. K," he replied. There was no disguising the relief in his voice, or the optimism.

Joe stood up. "I do have one condition: The three of you must return here for Christmas next year. I think we should make a tradition of it. What do you think, Mary?"

There he was, including her again. "I think it is a capital notion," she said.

"Then we all agree," Joe said. "Abby, Happy Christmas."

*   *   *

The Kings and Abby left when the dishes were done, their driver smiling so broadly that Mary thought his face would surely split. Abby hugged Joe for a long moment then whispered, "Mr. Shepard, I think you should go to the workhouse and ask for Sally Bawn. She cried and cried when you picked me in September."

"Sally Bawn, it is," he said. "I will tell her she comes highly recommended." He kissed her cheek and gave her a pat in the direction of the Kings. "That may be the wisest thing anyone ever did," he said to no one in particular as the post chaise rolled south. "Mary, it's your turn. Joshua, shall we take her to Muncie Farm?"

She blushed over the amount of luggage she had, but Joe got what he could into the spring wagon and assured her he would bring the rest tomorrow. Joshua climbed into the back, and he gave her a hand up onto the high seat. "Not exactly posh transportation," he said in apology. "I could probably hire a post chaise, but I'd rather not trouble the innkeeper on Christmas."

"I wouldn't have wanted that, either," she said, while he arranged a carriage robe over both of them. She knew she should keep it light, even though the familiar dread was returning. "After all, I am destined for a farm, and this will, in all likelihood, be the mode of transportation, will it not?"

Joe only smiled and spoke to the horses. She looked back at Joshua. "Are you entirely warm enough, my dear?" she asked.

He nodded, his eyes bright.

"I think it is awfully nice of Joshua to come along, especially when I suspect he wants to get back in your workshop," she told Joe.

"He likes Muncie Farm," Joe replied. The road was open, but narrow still with snow, and he concentrated on his driving.

Likes Muncie Farm? she asked herself. "He has been there before?" she asked.

"A time or two."

He was grinning now, and she wanted to ask him more, to pelt him with questions, but he appeared to be more interested in staying on his side of the road than talking. I will keep my counsel, she thought. He has been so obliging to put up with a houseful of unwanted guests, and I should not pester him.

They had traveled on the road to York not more than an hour, when he turned the horses west onto a lane that had been shoveled quite efficiently. "Do the road crews come out here, too?" she asked, surprised to see the road cleared.

"No. Muncie Farm is rather well organized."

She touched his shoulder and made him look at her when he started to chuckle. "Joe, are you practicing some great deception on me?"

He laughed out loud. "Just a little one, Mary, just a little one." He pointed with his whip. "There. Take a look at your grandmother's home." He grinned at her. "And resist the urge to smite me, please."

She looked; more than that, she stared, her mouth open. Located at the end of what by summer would probably be a handsome arch of trees, the farmhouse was a sturdy, three-storied manor of the light gray stone common in the shire. The white shutters gleamed, and at each window she could see a flower box. The stone cornice over the double doors was even more imposing than the one Joe had commissioned for his house in Edgerly.

Barely able to contain himself, Joe pointed with his

whip again. "See? Flower boxes already." He dodged
when she made a motion to strike him with her reticule. "Be careful, Mary. I am the only parent Joshua
has!"

"You are a scoundrel," she said with feeling. "You
let me wallow in self-pity and . . . and . . . talk about
learning to slop hogs and milk cows!"

He ducked again. "Do you have rocks in that reticule, my dear? I am certain that if you wished to slop
the hogs, your grandmother would let you, although
she might wonder why. Ow! Joshua, you could quit
laughing and come to my defense!"

"You don't deserve any such consideration, sir!"
she said, then stopped when the door opened. "Oh,
my."

An older woman stood in the doorway. From her
lace cap, to the Norwich shawl about her shoulders,
to the cut of her dark dress, she was neat as a pin.
Her back was straight, and she did not look much
over sixty, if that. Mary looked closer, and then could
not stop the tears that welled in her eyes. "Oh, Joe,
I think I look a little like her," she whispered.

"You look a great deal like her," he whispered
back, "but do you know, I didn't really see it until
you mentioned Muncie Farm yesterday. Strange how
that is."

Joe stopped the wagon in the well-graveled drive in
front of the manor, leaped down, and held out his
arms for her, his eyes bright with amusement. She sat
there a moment more, watching as Joshua jumped
from the back of the wagon and ran up the front steps.
The woman hugged him, then kissed him and wished
him Happy Christmas. "Your present is inside in the
usual place, my dear," she told him, and stepped aside
as he hurried into the house.

"I really don't understand what is going on," Mary said, completely mystified.

"I think we can make this clearer, if you will let me help you down, Mary," he said. This time there was compassion in his eyes. "Don't be afraid."

She did as he said. If she stood for a moment longer than necessary in the circle of his arms, she did not think he minded. He offered her his arm then, and they started up the short walk. "Mrs. Muncie, Happy Christmas to you!" he called. "I told you last week I would bring Josh over after Christmas dinner, but I have another guest. She was stranded at my house in all that snow, imagine that!" He stopped with her at the bottom of the steps. "May I introduce your granddaughter, Mary McIntyre?"

As Mary watched through a fog of her own, the woman began to cry. Mary released her death grip on Joe and ran up the steps. When the woman held out her arms, she rushed into them with a cry of her own. Mrs. Muncie's grip was surprisingly strong. As Mary clung to her, she saw in her mind's eye Abby clutched close to Mrs. King. Her heart spilled over with the sheer delight of coming home.

In another moment, Joe had his arms around both of them. "Ladies, do take your sensibilities inside. You know that Mr. Muncie would be growling about warming up the Great Plain of York, if he were still here." He shepherded them inside. In another moment, a maid had Mary's cloak in hand. Her bonnet already dangled down her back, relegated there by the tumult of her grandmother's greeting. She stood still, sniffing back her tears as Joseph untied the ribbon from her neck and handed the bonnet to the maid, who curtsied and rushed off, probably to spread the news that something amazing was happening in the sitting room.

The sitting room was as elegant as her own favorite morning room at Denton. Mary looked around in great appreciation, and then at Joe, who continued to grin at her. She sat next to her grandmother on the sofa and reached for her hand again. "Mrs. Muncie, he let me believe that Muncie Farm was on the outer edges of barbarism. What a deceiver!"

"Yes, that is Joe," she agreed. She laughed, and then dabbed at her eyes with a lace handkerchief. "I tried to warn Melissa six years ago, but she thought he would do." She smiled at Joe, and blew him a kiss. "And he did."

Mary looked from one to the other. "I am beginning to suspect that an even greater deception has been practiced on me than I imagined! Will someone please tell me what is going on? Joshua, does your father run mad on a regular basis?"

From his spot on the floor where he had already opened his present—which looked like more tools— Joshua grinned at her. She felt her heart nearly stop as she took a closer look at him. "Oh, God," she whispered, and reached for Joe's hand, too. "Joe, don't tease me anymore. Is Josh . . . oh, my stars . . . is he my *nephew*?"

He squeezed her hand, then put his arm around her. "That he is, Mary. Melissa's first husband was Michael McIntyre, your mother's younger brother." He held up his free hand. "Don't look at me like that! I didn't know about the McIntyre name when I courted Melissa. It's common enough in these parts, and I didn't give it a thought when you were introduced to me as McIntyre." He touched her forehead with his own. "There were hard feelings about your mother running away, and Michael had told Melissa next to nothing." He looked at Mrs. Muncie. "He was younger, and he may not have known much. I never put your mother together with you until you mentioned Muncie Farm. And I can tell you don't believe me. Help me, Mrs. Muncie!"

The woman laughed and touched Mary's face. "Oh, my dear, he is a little innocent, or at least not as guilty as you would think. Yes, your name is McIntyre. I was married to Edward McIntyre, and had two children by him, Michael and Cynthia."

"Cynthia," Mary said. "In all this, no one ever told me her real name."

Mrs. Muncie closed her eyes for a moment. "Oh, my dear, all these years, all this sadness." She opened her eyes. "Cynthia was a lovely girl, and such a brilliant seamstress. I suppose there was something in her that none of us truly understood." She inclined her head toward Mary. "At any rate, when she was eighteen, and resisting a perfectly good marriage to a farmer, she and her father quarreled and she ran away." She held her handkerchief to her eyes again. "I cannot tell you how I grieved, but there was never a word from her."

"It is hard to take back harsh words," Mary murmured.

"It is," her grandmother agreed. "Edward McIntyre died two years after Cynthia . . . left us. I ran the farm by myself for a while, and two years later married a neighbor, Stephen Muncie, who owned this wonderful place. He absorbed the McIntyre farm, and adopted Michael, because he had no children of his own."

"I only came into this district nine years ago, Mary, and I never knew Michael as a McIntyre," Joe said. "He was killed in a farming accident, and after a few years, I married his widow." He smiled. "And acquired Joshua, Melissa's son. Lord, this is strange!

Mary, you have a grandmother and a nephew, which makes you Joshua's aunt, a closer relationship than I can claim with this lad I consider my own son." He shook his head. "We'll have to write the Kings and tell them about this."

And there you are, including me, Mary thought. I like it. Overwhelmed by the sheer pleasure of it all, she looked from Joe, to her grandmother, to Joshua, who had turned his attention back to his present. She released her grip on Joe and took Mrs. Muncie by the hand. "Grandmama, may I stay here with you?" she asked. "I do not think now that I would be happy anywhere else."

Mrs. Muncie embraced her. "This is your home." She held herself off from Mary to look at her. "In fact, it probably will belong to you and Joshua some day, considering that you are my heirs."

"I could even teach you how to milk," Joe teased. "Used to do a lot of that at Denton. Lord, wouldn't Thomas suffer palpitations if I actually mentioned that to anyone of his acquaintance!"

"What I expect you to do, dear sir, is find a way to come to terms with him," Mary said. She looked at Mrs. Muncie. "Let us here be your cautionary tale. Life is too short to foul it with petty discord."

"Your point is well taken," he admitted. He rose then, and motioned to Joshua. "Son, we had better go home before it gets too dark and the wolves start howling."

"Joe! Really!" Mrs. Muncie said. "Do you ever have a serious moment?"

"Plenty of them, madam," he replied, "but maybe not on Christmas. Mary, I promise to bring the rest of your numerous trunks tomorrow." He looked at

Mrs. Muncie. "Do you want Joshua here for a couple of days?"

"Any time is fine with me . . . with us . . ." Mrs. Muncie replied. She touched Mary's hand. "My dear, you will see much of Joshua in the spring, when his father makes the rounds of his clients in the shire. Josh always stays with me then."

As Mrs. Muncie summoned the housekeeper to make arrangements for Mary's room, Mary walked Joseph and Joshua to the door. "What can I say?" she asked as Joshua scrambled up into the high seat of the wagon.

Joseph hugged her. "Just forgive me for not spilling out my suspicions and realizations sooner, Mary."

"Sooner? Sooner?" she exclaimed. "You played that hand awfully close to your vest!"

He laughed and joined her nephew in the wagon. In another moment, they started down the lane. He looked back when they were near the end of the trees. On impulse, she blew him a kiss, then went up the steps and into the house again.

Mrs. Muncie was motioning to her on the stairs. She put her arm around her grandmother and walked up the steps with her, and into a room easily as beautiful as her old room at Denton.

Mrs. Muncie touched the bedspread. "I made this for your mother when she was five years old," she said softly. She patted the pillow, then leaned against the mattress as though all her strength had left her. "When I first contacted Bow Street and told them to search for Cynthia McIntyre, I put this back on the bed. Oh, Mary, welcome home."

Her heart full, Mary hugged her grandmother. "Happy Christmas, my dear," she whispered.

She didn't want the embrace to end, but her grandmother started to chuckle. "Oh, my dear," she said finally, "you should be looking out the window right now from my vantage point. Better still, I think you should hurry down the stairs."

Mary opened her eyes and turned around to see what was causing Mrs. Muncie so much amusement. "Why is he coming back?" she asked, and then she knew with all her heart just why. "Oh, excuse me," she said as she started for the door.

"Here. Take my shawl. It's December, remember, my dear?"

She snatched up her grandmother's shawl and swirled it around her shoulders as she hurried down the stairs. She flung open the door, then closed it quickly, remembering the late Mr. Muncie's admonition about heating all of Yorkshire. Joe was out of the wagon seat, and she was in his arms before she had time to clear the last step. With a shaky laugh, he took her down the last step and held her off from him for a moment.

"I'm perfectly sober, Mary McIntyre," he warned her. "I'm really going to mean it this time. Did you just blow me a kiss?"

"Only because you were too far away," she replied. It must have been the right answer, because he kissed her soundly, thoroughly, and completely at her grandmother's front door. He held her close then, and she wrapped Mrs. Muncie's shawl around both of them.

"Poor Mrs. Muncie," he murmured in her ear. "I mean, what kind of a common scoundrel and skirt raiser would take away her granddaughter so soon?"

"You would, my love," she whispered.